COLD CRUEL
KISS

COLD CRUEL
KISS

Toni Anderson

ALSO BY TONI ANDERSON

For everyone we lost in 2020.

CHAPTER ONE

K RISTEN SKIPPED ALONG with her arm linked through Gemma's, their shopping bags bouncing awkwardly against their sides. Gemma dragged them both to a stop, laughing so hard she had to fold over to catch her breath.

The crowd was thick at the popular artisan market near Recoleta's famous cemetery. Tomorrow was Christmas Day, and everyone was intent on finding last-minute gifts.

"Come on!" Kristen yelled over her shoulder at the third member of their little group.

Irene shot Kristen an amused glance and finished paying for the fused glass dish she'd picked out for her mother. Irene was the smart one, the sensible one. She'd come with a list of gifts to purchase and had now finished ticking them off.

Kristen was the boring one of the group. She'd bought and wrapped all her family's and friends' gifts weeks ago. She saw a stall with leather belts coiled up like snakes and bit her lip. Should she get something for Miguel? They hadn't actually met…but what if they did finally meet up over Christmas and he gave her a gift? Shouldn't she at least have something for him too, just in case?

She could always give it to her little brother for his next birthday. Or even her dad.

As she paid for the belt, someone bumped against her.

1

"Ooff."

The man was gone, hurrying through the bustling crowd and out onto the street without even bothering to check on who he'd jostled. She felt for her wallet, but everything seemed to be there.

Irene caught up to them.

"Who'd you buy the belt for?" Gemma asked Kristen with a sly smile.

Kristen shrugged but couldn't quite pull off nonchalance. "I might give it to my dad."

"Sure," said Gemma.

The other girls grinned. Kristen's skin prickled as she felt a blush heat her cheeks. She'd discovered long ago that, if she wanted to keep a secret, she couldn't afford to tell anyone. She lived in a place where she was checked for electronic listening devices before she entered her home, where her phone was tracked by a federal agency and her social media accounts were monitored by her parents and her mother's security team.

If they discovered she'd set up an anonymous account, they'd ground her for a month and delete everything.

She didn't want this deleted. She wanted this small degree of autonomy. She wanted to have some say in what she did, with whom, without having to clear it with security. She hadn't mentioned Miguel to a single soul—except her little brother who'd read a couple of texts over her shoulder a few days ago. She'd chased him and beaten him with a pillow in his bedroom until he'd sworn not to mention it to anyone. She had enough dirt on him to make the promise stick.

"Leave her alone," Irene admonished when Kristen's embarrassment started to show.

"It's fine." She forced herself to smile serenely. "Gemma

has an overactive imagination."

Her friend didn't mean any harm. She'd been poking at her for weeks, suspecting she was seeing someone, but Kristen really wasn't. She was only texting some guy who seemed nice. Too nice, actually. She was smart enough to know he was probably hoping to get her to send him some nude selfies or let him into her pants if they ever met in person—before he revealed he wasn't the beautiful poet whose image he cultivated.

Boys weren't that difficult to figure out, and yet…she still wanted to take a chance that the poet was real.

But her mother would kill her.

Her mother didn't need to know.

Kristen wouldn't do anything rash. She wouldn't meet him somewhere that wasn't safe or public. Maybe she'd ask a friend to come with her and watch from nearby.

Because *that* wouldn't be weird at all. She rolled her eyes at herself.

They stopped at *Starbucks* and grabbed iced lattes. It was hot out and the excitement from the lead up to Christmas was palpable.

They wandered down Avenue Alvear laughing and joking. Kristen blushed at the admiring glances some of the local men sent them. She averted her gaze and bowed her head, uncomfortable with the wolf whistles and avid interest in some of their eyes. She was tall and blonde like her father. Lots of curly hair that reached down to her waist. The other girls were prettier, but she always felt exposed because of her height. Irene didn't notice the attention. Gemma's smile grew.

Kristen came to a standstill when she saw a dress in a shop window. It was the most gorgeous creation she'd ever seen, all form-hugging but frothy and pale, pale pink.

Irene jogged her elbow. "That would look great on you tonight. Let's go try it on."

Kristen shook her head. "It's too expensive."

Irene shrugged. "Try it on and see."

"I will, if you don't," Gemma chimed in.

Kristen shot her a look. Gemma's parents were loaded and let her buy whatever she wanted. Kristen really wanted that dress and the idea of Gemma wearing it to the party they planned on sneaking out to later when they met up with the rest of their friends…

Her stomach clenched.

It didn't hurt to try it on, right? They were supposed to be having fun. "Okay. Let's do it."

Thirty minutes later, Kristen piled out the store with more shopping bags, laughing and euphoric, and also terrified by the amount of money she'd just spent. The dress was amazing and made her look skinny and sexy and *hot damn*.

Gemma had also bought a dress that cost even more than the one Kristen had fallen in love with. Gemma had added matching shoes to her purchases, but Kristen knew that spending any more money would get her into serious trouble if found out.

Serious trouble.

She owned a pair of heels that would work, and she could sneak her mother's diamond studs that looked good with everything. Kristen was already going to have to lie about what the dress cost and hoped she received enough cash for Christmas from her family to pay back the money she'd borrowed from her savings.

Those savings were supposed to be for college, but Kristen

didn't know what she wanted to study yet. Didn't even know if she preferred arts or sciences. She'd applied for a general first year at four different colleges back in the States, but she didn't want to leave her family yet, or Argentina. Which sounded lame so she hadn't mentioned it to anyone.

She wanted to meet Miguel. She wanted to fall in love. One thing she didn't want to do—and that was work for the Foreign Service. The most boring job in the world.

The girls linked arms and started skipping down the pedestrian street. Kristen had only been here a little over a year, but these girls would be her friends forever.

"I love you guys!" she shouted happily.

Fireworks exploded in the background. The Argentine people were big on fireworks, especially at Christmas. Her dog, Roo, would be hiding under her brother's bed all day and night.

She and her friends planned to sneak out to a club after midnight. Irene was going to drive them. Kristen's parents were booked solid with official Christmas parties until the early hours of the morning and were unlikely to miss her. Kristen would simply tell whoever was on duty at the embassy that she was going to hang out with her friends for a few hours. She wasn't a prisoner and was free to come and go as she pleased—to a degree. They would not be happy with her going to a club, but they didn't need to know about that.

She'd promised to always tell someone where she was going to be—so she'd leave a note on her dresser and carry her cell phone.

She would do that.

She wasn't stupid.

The idea of texting Miguel that she was going to be at the

club tonight was tempting. She shouldn't. She knew she shouldn't. But she might.

The girls danced in a circle and blew air kisses at one another. They needed to get home and grab some food and shower and get ready for the party.

"Tonight is gonna be wicked." Gemma giggled.

It was. It really was. Best night ever. They carried on walking until they hit the intersection for Rodríguez Peña, heading toward where Irene had parked her mom's car.

A white van screeched to a halt in front of them and the girls all backed up a step.

Whoa.

"Asshole," Gemma muttered under her breath.

Kristen went to walk around the van, but a man wearing a mask jumped out of the passenger door and grabbed her around the waist.

"Hey! What the hell?"

Another man followed him. He also wore a mask.

Fear sliced through her. Was this a joke?

Gemma started screaming. Kristen dropped her bags as she tried to pry her way loose from the steely arm encircling her.

He didn't let go.

Panic started to overtake her. "Get off me! Help! Help me!"

His hand clamped over her mouth. She tried to bite him, but he shifted his grip with his palm under her jaw, fingers digging hard into the skin on either side her nose. Her heart pounded violently, beating against her ribcage like a frantic bird trying to take flight. She heard the others shouting.

She tried to pull the man's hands off her face, but he was

too strong. She reached behind her head and raked her nails down his face, going for his mask. The side cargo door of the van was now open, and her assailant lifted her off the ground and stepped inside the dim confines of the vehicle. She latched onto the edge of the doorway, but he peeled her fingers off and yanked her away. He had to release her mouth to do it.

"Help me. Help me!"

He staggered inside the van and sat with her squeezed between his legs, restraining her arms and legs. She kicked at his ankles, but her sandals weren't built to inflict damage. Desperate to escape, she threw her head back and connected hard enough with his nose to make him cry out in pain. Even so, he didn't let go.

Another masked man in the van shoved a thick canvas hood over her head and pulled a drawstring tight. Her world went black.

What's happening?

She couldn't breathe, but she screamed until her lungs hurt. She was pushed forward, and her wrists were cuffed behind her back with metal bracelets.

She screamed again, and a blow to her head had light whirling through her brain as pain fused her teeth together. When the pain faded, she tasted blood. It shocked her into silence, more effective than the terse orders to shut up and be quiet.

Another yell pierced the cargo hold. Irene. She was shouting and screaming until she suddenly made an *oof* noise and went quiet.

Oh, god. They'd hit her too.

The doors banged shut, and the van squealed into traffic. Kristen fell sideways and only remained upright because of the grip her assailant had on her.

"What are you doing? Where are you taking us?" Her voice was muffled and feeble.

"Quiet." The voice was fast and agitated. He spoke in Spanish. "Or I'll gag you so you cannot make a sound."

His grip on her tightened. She whimpered.

It hurt to sit this way with her arms cuffed behind her back and pressed against this man's groin. Desperate tears dampened her eyes, and her throat hurt.

The hood was musty with old sweat and made her want to vomit. Who else had worn it? Where were they now? Alive? Or dead?

The driver was going fast.

Was someone giving chase? Surely someone had called the cops? Where was Gemma?

"What do you want? Where are you taking us? It's Christmas!" she cried.

"Quiet!" He shook her. "Don't cause trouble, and you might live to enjoy it. Fight us, and it will be unpleasant for you and your little friend. Understand?"

So, she was supposed to be a good girl so they could abduct her more easily? It was absurd and, yet, she didn't have a choice. Kristen jerked her head up and down. Yes, she understood. She understood they were terrible people.

Where was her cell? Her mom said she had to always keep her cell phone on her person so Diplomatic Security Service could use it to track her. Even as she thought about it, someone ripped away her small purse.

Was this real? Kristen kept expecting them to stop the car and start laughing. Rip off their hoods and say this was all a joke.

Ha ha.

So funny.

If this was a prank, she was going to punch everyone in the face the first chance she got and, oh, how she would laugh.

Her arms brushed bare skin where her captor's t-shirt had ridden up. She raised her arms, trying to avoid touching his privates, and the gems in her rings scraped his skin. Then she realized he'd made a big error in judgment. She was about to lunge for his penis and twist as hard as she could when he shifted her away from him and pushed her, face-first, against the floor of the van. Someone began wrapping rope around her ankles.

Oh, god.

As she lay with her chin jarring against the metal floor with every bump, she knew this wasn't a joke. She and Irene weren't going to any party this evening, and they might not be alive tomorrow. Her heart gave a panicked squeeze.

It seemed like forever, but eventually, the van slowed and started turning through windy streets.

Were they at their destination?

The van jerked to a stop, and the doors opened. She yelped as she was dragged over the grooved surface and hauled across someone's shoulder.

She heard doors opening on another vehicle. *Crap*! They were changing cars. No one would know how to find her. No one would know where they'd taken her.

She'd be gone. Disappeared.

Her mouth parched. She might never see her family again. Panic flooded her body, but she knew fighting wouldn't save her. She wasn't strong enough to physically defy these bastards.

She suddenly realized she needed to leave as many clues behind as possible. DNA. Fingerprints.

She eased off one of her rings and let it drop to the ground.

The man dumped her into the trunk of another vehicle, this one a lot smaller than the first. The pain was excruciating as she rolled onto her back. Something heavy was dropped on top of her, smacking her in the face. *Irene?*

The trunk slammed shut, and the darkness was all consuming. She shifted to ease the tension in her arms, relieved when Irene—she was pretty sure it was Irene—also wriggled.

The engine started, and the stench of exhaust fumes wafted into the tight compartment, making her feel nauseous.

The car shot off, and the two of them rolled helplessly around the small space. Her stomach roiled, and her equilibrium was unsteady like a cork in a stormy ocean. Kristen braced herself as best she could, closed her eyes, and prayed.

CHAPTER TWO

L UCY ASTON, FORMER cheerleader and sorority girl, who'd captained both the debate and softball teams in high school, stood unmoving and completely unnoticed against the back wall of a ballroom as a glittering array of glamorous men and women drank, ate, and generally celebrated the holiday.

Lucy was not one of those people.

She was working.

It was late afternoon, hot in Buenos Aires. Thankfully, the AC blasted away inside, and Lucy positioned herself beneath one of the vents, grateful for the cool draft.

Two sets of garden doors opened onto an incredible old-stone patio with a magnificent fountain as the main focus of attention. Brilliant jacaranda trees with their unique mauve blossoms provided a stunning backdrop.

Everyone who was anyone in this town was in attendance today, including the Argentine president. Christmas Eve was a massive party in this country, and fireworks had been going off all day.

Rather than pretty sparkles, Lucy was wearing a boring pant suit, the jacket two sizes too large. No one paid any attention to the mouse Lucy had transformed herself into over the past ten months. It wasn't simply the drabness of her dyed, mid-brown hair which hung frizzily around her face from an unflattering center part. Nor the insipid paleness of her skin, nor the thick-framed glasses that hid her eyes. No, it was her lackluster demeanor. Her obedient compliance. The body language that clearly stated she was part of the furniture, not part of the festivities.

It had been a huge adjustment for Lucy to not only be ignored, but to be completely *unseen*. She didn't mind the shadows anymore. In fact, she preferred them.

The ambassador's husband raised his face to the ceiling and gave a belly-laugh at something the French ambassador's wife said. The latter was wearing a sheer black and white polka dot number that was a lot more revealing than it appeared at first glance. The woman was witty and spoke with constantly moving hands. She was so animated, it was a wonder she didn't spill her champagne.

The ambassador looked over at her husband, and Lucy noticed a crinkle of the woman's brow. Catherine Dickerson didn't like *loud* but there was no way she'd chastise her husband. She didn't pull rank on the domestic front. Lucy liked that about the woman.

Lucy's direct superior and the ambassador's long time Personal Assistant, Miranda Foster, stood close to the ambassador, attentive to her boss's immediate needs. The senior agent from the US Diplomatic Security Service (DSS) flanked the other side of the doorway from Lucy, along with a few other security guys who were all hyper-focused on the officials they were tasked with protecting.

The ambassador was always adamant that she couldn't do her job with a bodyguard hovering over her shoulder. DSS didn't like it, but they'd learned if they wanted to keep the peace, they had to give Catherine Dickerson some space.

Chandeliers glittered in the bright afternoon sunshine. Guests sipped expensive bubbly and snacked on caviar. The noise level was growing exponentially with the level of alcohol consumption.

Lucy would rather eat a burger than fish eggs, but her stomach growled regardless. She'd covered for Miranda during the ambassador's luncheon with her British, French, German, and Spanish counterparts, and it had been a long time since breakfast.

Lucy pushed hunger out of her mind and instead admired the frescos on the far walls. This former palace now belonged to a Russian billionaire who'd made his fortune after the collapse of the former Soviet Union. Being here made her skin crawl.

A flurry of movement in the corner of her eye caused her to glance left. Sure enough, the seemingly friendly and effusive Boris Yahontov had finally arrived with his family at his own party and was keen to make an entrance. He greeted a couple of friends near the doorway and began making his way around her side of the room, probably toward the Argentine president who held court near a dessert table that was complete with a melted chocolate waterfall.

Lucy tried to sink into the wall as Yahontov drew closer, but his gaze fell on her as he neared her position. So much for blending. She bowed her head and stared at the gleaming hardwood floor, praying he walked on by.

Yahontov straightened a chair at a nearby table, and she flicked a glance in his direction. A mistake. It gave him an opening.

"You look familiar…" His accent had only a thin edge of Russian to it. He'd lived in the west for many years, assimilating. A smile was fixed on his lips as he stared at her. "Now where have I seen you before?"

She stared down at the carpet. "You must have mistaken me for someone else, sir."

The man stepped closer and leaned toward to her ear. Alcohol-saturated breath brushed her cheek, although he didn't appear drunk.

"You were prettier in the photographs."

Ice-cold dread washed through her, but she knew better than to show weakness to a predator. She looked at him blankly. "I'm sorry, sir. I really think you have me confused with someone else."

"Of course. My mistake." He laughed and threw up his hands in a jovial manner, but his eyes were appraising as they locked onto her for another long moment.

Her knees wanted to sag, but she didn't let them.

Yahontov finally passed on by, leaving only the smell of vodka behind him. His hulking bodyguard followed like a giant shadow in his wake.

Acid coated her throat, and Lucy swallowed repeatedly to get rid of the need to gag. Then she noticed her boss, Miranda, giving her a discreet wave of her hand indicating she needed her. Lucy thrust herself away from the wall.

Yahontov's glamorous wife, a former beauty queen and model, was greeting the ambassador. Lucy wondered what the woman knew, but her gaze didn't even flicker away from her guests as Lucy approached.

"How are the children?" Mrs. Yahontov gave the ambassador and Phillip, who'd joined his wife, air kisses on both cheeks. "You should have brought them with you. They could have played with ours."

Lucy subdued a frown. The Yahontovs' kids were several years younger than Catherine and Phillip Dickersons' two and had nothing in common with them.

"Our son is at the age where all he wants to do is play video games, and our daughter is in the city with her girl-friends doing some last-minute Christmas shopping," Phillip answered amiably.

The group carried on chatting, and Miranda pulled Lucy aside and whispered in her ear, "What did Yahontov say to you?"

Lucy looked at her vacantly. Of course, her boss had noticed their interaction. "Nothing," she whispered back. "He's been drinking and wished me a Merry Christmas."

"I hope he wasn't inappropriate." Miranda gave Lucy a worried look then let it drop. "The ambassador has a head-ache. Do you have any of her pills?"

"In the car, but not on me." Lucy kept a whole host of emergency supplies in the vehicle, but Miranda usually handled more pressing needs.

"Go and ask DSS if they have any. If they don't, please go and fetch something from the car." Miranda gave her arm a squeeze in silent thanks.

Lucy hurried away, ignoring the fact she was sure that bastard Yahontov was watching her. What did it mean?

Humiliation wanted to rip her to shreds, but she'd known this would happen one day. She still had a job to do.

Didn't make it any easier.

Lucy reached the Diplomatic Security Special Agent just as his phone buzzed, and he held up his hand in that authoritari-an way he had about him and moved to the side where he could have direct access to the ambassador and still answer the call.

Lucy sighed and stood to one side, hugging the wall while she waited for her opportunity to speak to him.

The DS agent's shoulders stiffened, and he covered one ear. "Repeat."

He was already moving toward the ambassador, and Lucy followed him, instinctively knowing whatever had happened was bad news. He pressed the communication button on his wrist. "Bring the car around. Now."

A second DS agent crossed from the other side of the room to meet them in the middle. Other bodyguards were taking note of the Americans' actions, probably trying to figure out if there was a threat to their principals or not. The whole room seemed to tense.

The agent reached the ambassador and leaned down to whisper in her ear. All color drained from Catherine Dickerson's face.

What the hell happened?

Catherine grabbed her husband's arm and spoke quietly into his ear. Phillip fumbled the champagne flute he was holding, and Mrs. Yahontov rescued it. Phillip gripped his wife's free hand. "Where?"

"Is everything all right?" Mrs. Yahontov asked with concern.

The ambassador's mouth opened, but no words came out. The usually calm and unflappable diplomat looked like she was about to faint.

"We need to leave. My apologies," Phillip offered.

"If there is anything we can assist you with..." Boris Yahontov offered. He'd come over when the bodyguards had started to move.

The ambassador was shaking her head, already backing away.

The DS agents had the ambassador between them and hustled her out of the ballroom. Lucy rushed after Miranda whose heels clicked noisily through the now almost silent room, into the ornate hallway and out onto the private driveway, straight into the bulletproof limo.

The driver, another DS agent, sped away from the palace as soon as everyone was onboard.

"What's going on?" Miranda asked breathlessly.

"Kristen has been abducted," the ambassador answered woodenly. Her eyes glassed over, but she didn't cry. Phillip blindly clasped his wife's hand, an unfocused look on his face.

Lucy had about a million questions but also knew the ambassador probably didn't have any answers yet. "Is Kevin okay?"

The ambassador shot a look at the DS agent who nodded. "Back at the embassy. No issues at the soccer match."

The ambassador straightened in her seat. "I want to know exactly what happened. And I want to know what the hell the local police are doing to get my daughter back."

As ONE OF the FBI's top negotiators, Supervisory Special Agent Max Hawthorne was used to being in the eye of the hurricane. At the center of the storm. He'd be lying if he said, most of the time, he didn't enjoy it.

No one noticed him step into the chaotic atmosphere of short-tempers and cardiac-arrest-inducing tension in the FBI's Legal Attaché's office on the second floor of the US Embassy in Buenos Aires. He let the mayhem roll over him and tried to gauge the players.

Ten people. Six men, four women. People who'd normally be home enjoying family time or unwrapping gifts from under the tree. Instead, they dashed from one side of the room to the other, grabbing pens, paper, intent on some invisible but urgent task. Others were speed-talking on phones, voices cracking with tension. One guy, clearly in charge judging by how many people avoided him, leaned over a desk, staring at a loop of surveillance footage. The guy's suit jacket was removed, tie long gone, shirtsleeves rolled up, cotton wrinkled and limp. He gestured sharply to the woman at his side and snatched the pen out of her hand when she didn't respond fast enough.

"Call CNU again. The sooner this asshole from Quantico shows up, the better. This situation is a freaking nightmare, especially with everything else going on right now."

"He's due any time. We were lucky they had a negotiator so close," the woman stated.

Lucky for them. Less so for him, considering he'd been visiting friends in Cartagena.

"Who the fuck vacations in Colombia?" the man muttered irritably.

Max had cut his holiday short as soon as he'd gotten the call from Eban Winters at the Crisis Negotiation Unit in Quantico and had traveled all night on his buddies' private jet to get here as fast as humanly possible. He let go of the door and let it slam shut behind him.

The man swung around. His red-rimmed eyes swept over Max's board shorts and faded green t-shirt featuring a character from his favorite video game.

"Who the hell are you?" the man demanded.

"I'm SSA Hawthorne. The asshole from Quantico? Most people call me Max." He held out his hand, a friendly smile pasted firmly on his face. "Sorry I'm late."

It took a fraction of a second longer than it should for the man to shake his hand. The agent didn't apologize for his earlier words. He was either too arrogant or too jaded to bother. Or too something else. Max decided to reserve judgment for now.

He lowered his duffle to the floor. "Who can bring me up to speed on recent developments?"

"I'm the Legat. Brian Powell."

Legat was Bu-speak for "Legal Attaché." The FBI's official representative abroad. In this South American posting, Powell was responsible for Argentina, Uruguay, and Paraguay. Max figured it was a cushy gig, the sort of posting he might go after on his way to retirement.

"Any contact from the kidnappers?"

"Nothing yet." Powell swiped a hand through his thinning blond hair. "I can't believe they haven't called yet with their list of demands."

Max looked around the room at the other people who had paused in their activities to listen to their conversation. "It's not unusual for hostage takers to wait a few hours, days, or weeks before they make contact. Leave the family frantic and desperate for information. Make sure they cover their tracks and get well away from the abduction zone to somewhere they feel safe and in control." Argentina was a massive country, and the kidnappers could also have crossed one of the many international borders. "You have an agent with the ambassador?"

Powell nodded. "We followed the instructions your boss at CNU sent us. One of the ALATs,"—Assistant Legal Attachés— "took some basic recording equip up to her rooms. He has some negotiation training."

"Great." Max didn't really consider Eban Winters his boss. They shared a place and were good friends. Eban was acting head of CNU though, so technically, Powell was correct.

"At this point, all the guy needs to do is answer the phone and *listen*. Tell whoever is on the other end that he will pass on the demands to the family." It was all listed in the basic instruction package the Crisis Negotiation Unit sent out following abductions and Eban would have emphasized the point over the phone. "I thought the US Ambassador to Argentina lived at Bosch Palace?"

The Legat nodded. "Usually, but the palace is under renovation. Has been for months."

Max wondered if that was relevant to the current situation but doubted it. Security would be tight at both locations. "What can you tell me about the actual abduction?"

"Take a look." Powell sat down in front of a large monitor, and the woman sitting in the adjacent chair jumped up and offered Max a seat.

"I can stand." He smiled reassuringly at her.

She shook her head almost shyly. "I need to stretch my legs. I've been sitting for hours." Her eyes turned quizzical. "How come they let a Brit into the FBI?"

Ah, the accent.

He flashed her a grin, not flirting, but he knew how much further his charm got him than his rank. "Apparently, the Bureau was desperate for someone who spoke proper English."

She giggled, and Powell shot her a derisive look. Her

cheeks reddened, and she murmured an excuse before escaping out of the room.

"How *did* you end up in the Bureau?" Powell asked.

Max sat in the chair and leaned forward to watch the screen. "Someone from headquarters requested that I apply. So I did."

Powell looked irked by Max's minimalistic and slightly egotistical response, but Max had just gotten off a plane after cutting short his Christmas vacation with three of his best friends whom he hadn't seen in years—without a single word of thanks or appreciation. And while it might not be necessary, it was good manners. And he'd been raised by a mother who believed in manners and courtesy as basic cornerstones of daily activity.

Powell hit play on the video, and Max concentrated on the black and white surveillance film. It showed pedestrians walking down a busy shopping street. Time stamp said 18:01 yesterday when Max had been happily flirting with an extremely attractive cocktail waitress at a seaside bar. It was still light down here in Bueno Aires at that time though. A white van stopped on a road that intersected with a pedestrian street, close to a small group of young women who were about to cross. Two men jumped out—not the driver. One man grabbed a young woman wearing jeans and a flowery shirt. He picked her bodily off the ground, and she kicked her legs, dropping her shopping bags as the two teenagers she was with scattered in fear.

The abductor climbed back into the van via the side door with her, and the second man went to slam the door shut, but one of the other girls found her courage and grabbed his arm. He wrapped her in a bear hug and tossed her in the back of the van too. Slammed the door, opened the passenger door, and climbed in. The van shot off. The whole thing had taken under twenty seconds.

The kidnappers all wore masks that disguised their features.

"Were they caught on any other cameras?" Max asked.

"We've asked local authorities' permission to gather as much information as possible but being the holidays..." Powell raised his hands in frustration. "Trust me, I've been pushing all my contacts at *Policia Federal de Argentina* and so have the State Department and the Diplomatic Security Service. One of the Argentine *comisarios* was here earlier and promised to do everything possible to catch these people."

"Kristen Dickerson wasn't assigned a bodyguard?"

Powell shook his head. "DSS didn't deem it necessary."

Max raised his brows but said nothing.

"She was to keep her phone with her at all times, and DSS has a tracking capability with it."

"But the kidnappers dumped the phone ASAP. Correct?"

Powell nodded, looking miserable.

"Any idea how the kidnappers knew where the girls would be at that specific time?"

Powell shook his head. "We interviewed the friend who was with her, but she was hysterical, and her parents were hovering and overprotective."

As parents should be under the circumstances. Max kept his thoughts to himself.

"We need to find any surveillance we can of the women during the day. See if we can spot anyone following them."

Powell nodded. "You think someone had eyes on them."

"Either that or one of the shopping party is involved with

the kidnappers, or they were being tracked in some other way."

"You don't think this was random?"

"Absolutely not. The kidnapper by-passed another potential target to get to Dickerson. The second girl was an afterthought. They had the manpower and the space in the van, and it was more expedient to take her with them than fight with her in the street."

Powell's mouth twisted. "That's what I think too. I'll put in another request with the local police to examine all available footage of the group from yesterday. They should be able to track them using the live facial recognition system they have in the city."

"Good. See if they can find out where the van went."

"They already found it. Dumped in the La Boca—a barrio in the south of the city. It was stolen the previous night from outside the city."

"We need forensics on that van."

"Being done by the locals."

Max frowned. "It's safe to assume they changed vehicles several times before they headed to their final destination. The city police might be able to track them for us or provide photographs of the kidnappers without their masks on."

"I discussed this with the *Comisario General*. The problem is, we don't know what they climbed into after the van." Powell looked more alert. The guy had probably been up all night working the case. He dragged his fingers through his hair, making it stand up on end. "These guys look like professionals."

That they did. They looked like they'd performed this sort of high visibility rendition many times. Kidnap and Ransom was endemic in certain parts of the world—a business, nothing personal, nothing political. Until it was.

"What do you think it means to abduct the US Ambassador's daughter?" Powell asked. "What do you think they want?"

War? Max pushed to his feet. "I'm not sure. But something tells me we're going to find out. I need to get changed before I meet the ambassador. Can you point me to a restroom?"

Powell finally seemed to defrost. "Use my office."

He led the way, down a corridor with a series of closed doors off to the right, then to a much larger room that was sparsely furnished with a big-ass, wooden desk and a couple of wingback chairs in front of an actual fireplace. Thankfully, the fire was unlit as the temperature was already sweltering. The room had an amazing view of the park across the street. Stars hung off a large green plant, but Christmas festivities had been largely abandoned following this incident. There was a large Chinese screen in one corner of the room.

Max glanced at the Legat's desk, which was strewn with paper files. Maybe this wasn't the quiet posting Max had envisioned. The man scooped up folders and placed them in a filing cabinet that he locked.

"Big case?" Max asked, intrigued.

Powell nodded. "Very." Which probably explained the Legat's frustration and why there were ten FBI agents working in the office. "And put on hold for twenty-four hours while we get this situation under control."

"Time sensitive?" Max asked.

Powell sighed. "I'm afraid even that much is classified." He was keeping it need-to-know which Max appreciated.

"Not a problem, but could your case have anything to do

with the ambassador's daughter being taken?" Max probed.

"I doubt it. The investigation is so tight only a few people in the States know it even exists. Not even the ambassador knows the details. That was her choice when she was assigned to Argentina. She told me that, unless there was a good reason for her to be informed, or a danger to herself or anyone associated with the mission, then she'd rather not know, and that way she wouldn't have to test her acting abilities at social events around the city." Powell scratched his head. "Unfortunately, the agents we have here working the case are highly specialized and need to get back to working on Operation Soapbox as soon as possible."

Max nodded. "Understood. Did you request extra agents to be assigned to this office to help out with the kidnap case?"

Powell slumped into his chair. "Yes. Immediately after I received word of the abduction. Let's hope the suits at headquarters agree. The Diplomatic Security Service has a robust and experienced group of people here, and there are a couple of people from NCIS, Homeland Security, DEA, and even our resident spook who can all lend a hand if necessary."

Max grimaced. He wasn't a fan of spooks, probably because, despite the way his country had shafted him after he'd left the British SAS, MI6 was still constantly trying to recruit him.

Max let rip a yawn and headed behind the screen to change. He hadn't slept on the flight, instead keeping his friends company in the cockpit. His buddies had decided to use the impromptu trip as an opportunity to head to Montevideo for some party time. If Kristen Dickerson was found quickly, then Max might be able to meet up with them and finish his Christmas vacation in style.

He wasn't holding his breath.

It took less than three minutes to transform from beach bum to professional law enforcement officer. He clipped his creds onto his belt, wishing he could wear his service weapon. His buddies had slipped him a SIG that was inside his suitcase currently being held by security at the main door. Right now, he didn't even know which hotel he was staying at.

He didn't rely on his handgun for protection—his training went well beyond that, but a weapon was a nice addition to basic security when away from the embassy.

Hopefully, the head of mission would sanction his wearing of a firearm for this temporary duty assignment.

His eyes caught on the stars suspended from the large rubber plant again, and he thought of his mother who'd begged him to come home for the holidays. She lived in the countryside north of Sheffield, a region that accounted for his slight accent that had smoothed out over the years. He thrust aside thoughts of his family back in England. It was what it was. He'd learned to live with it.

Time to start interviewing the ambassador's family and figuring out everything he could about the victim. Get the girl back in one piece and let this office go back to the important job of fighting crime.

CHAPTER THREE

As soon as Lucy closed the door on the Commissioner of the Argentine Federal Police and his entourage, the ambassador lost her composure and swore a blue streak under her breath. Dark circles beneath her eyes underscored her worry and exhaustion.

Miranda hovered over Catherine and gently placed a reassuring hand on the diplomat's shoulder. Phillip sat on her other side, holding his wife's hand. Iain Bartlett, the Senior Regional Security Officer (RSO) for the Diplomatic Security Service, looked pale and stricken as he walked over and slumped heavily into the armchair the commissioner had just vacated. Iain blamed himself for the abduction. Technically, he was correct.

A massive Christmas tree stood in the corner of the room, the still-wrapped presents beneath it a poignant reminder that something had gone terribly wrong with the celebrations this year.

Phillip's expression looked increasingly grim. "I don't trust the police commissioner, Catherine. He'll pull some macho bullshit and get Kristen killed."

The ambassador swallowed noisily and raised her chin. "I don't trust him either, but I can't exactly call in the Navy SEALs to swoop in and take over, no matter how desperately I want to. Kristen should be here with us right now, opening gifts. She should have been safe on that street at that time with a group of friends." A sob escaped, and she covered her mouth as if to physically stuff the sound back inside her mouth.

Iain Bartlett's fingers clenched the end of the arms of the chair. "I should have insisted on an agent shadowing her."

"That was our call. Kristen hates having bodyguards, and you can't be in four places at once." The ambassador picked up a tissue out of the box on the coffee table and wearily blew her nose. "I should have been spending Christmas Eve with my family, not sipping champagne with some Russian Oligarch who was trying to buy me and everyone else with his fancy hors d'oeuvres."

"I could have stayed with her." Phillip closed his eyes and shook his head. "You have an important job to do."

"Your job is important too. She wanted to go out with her friends." Her voice rose in anger. "This posting shouldn't be a prison for our children. She should have been *safe*." Catherine forced the last word out between gritted teeth. "It was the middle of the day on a crowded city street."

"We need to push the Argentines about why that wasn't so," Miranda agreed calmly.

Not that it made much difference now. Kristen was missing, and all the complaining and handwringing in the world wouldn't change that salient fact.

"Should I contact the president again and repeat the request for a personal audience?" Miranda asked.

Catherine narrowed her eyes at her assistant. "Yes. Keep pushing until I can meet with him in person. I will not let him evade responsibility simply because he wants to spend the holiday with his family. I want to spend the holiday with my family too." Catherine craned her neck to look over into the corner of the room. "Are you sure that telephone line is hooked up properly?"

Lucy glanced at the FBI agent. He'd set up at a desk in the farthest corner of the large formal suite the ambassador usually used to entertain dignitaries. Lucy had seen the guy around the embassy building but didn't know his name. Late thirties. Bald head that was red with a recent sunburn. He was trying to be as unobtrusive as possible, but he hadn't yet mastered the Lucy degree of invisibility. That took special training.

"Yes, ma'am." He looked away again.

Catherine grunted, unconvinced.

In fairness, the ambassador was overwrought and emotionally drained and probably not at her best from a diplomatic perspective. They'd all been up for more than thirty-six hours. The Dickersons' son was thankfully sleeping now.

Lucy's stomach twisted as she recalled Kevin Dickerson's heart-broken reaction to his sister's abduction last night. It had been emotionally wrenching enough to mist the eyes of even the most jaded embassy staff. This was not exactly the Christmas anyone had anticipated—except perhaps for the kidnappers.

Lucy's mouth went dry. *Is this my fault?*

She crossed her fingers behind her back and prayed they found Kristen and Irene unharmed. The Dickerson kids were funny and kind. Not the brats you might expect as the over-indulged children of one of the United States' top diplomats.

The ambassador inhaled audibly. "I keep imagining what these animals could be doing to my baby..." Catherine covered her mouth.

"Don't, love. Don't torture yourself with those thoughts. We have to concentrate on getting her back, not worry ourselves sick about the what-ifs and maybes of how she's being treated. We *will* get her back. Whatever they want, we'll find a way to get it for them. I've already spoken to the bank about what stocks we can liquidate. Or the DSS and Special Forces will rescue her. Our baby will be okay. She will be." Phillip rubbed his wife's back and kissed her hair. "Allow yourself to be a mother for a few hours rather than a diplomat. You should lie down. Get some rest."

Catherine closed her eyes. "I don't want to sleep. I don't want to miss anything."

"A drink then?" Phillip suggested.

"I'll get you some coffee," Lucy offered quickly.

"I was thinking something a little stronger." Phillip smiled tiredly. He had a thick crop of ash-blond hair, and the blue of his irises was striking against his pale face. He was a world-renowned engineer who followed his wife wherever her job dictated, which wasn't something many men would contemplate. He was both handsome and charming. The perfect spouse for a diplomat.

Lucy didn't trust him. She didn't trust anyone anymore.

"Coffee is fine." Ambassador Dickerson responded with a small wave. "The stronger the better. I need my wits when I talk to these people."

Lucy went to the coffeemaker on a side table in the suite and made five cups of expresso, exactly how the ambassador, her husband, and Miranda took it. She delivered each cup, including one for the RSO and another for the FBI agent sitting quietly in the corner.

There was a knock on the huge doors that led into the apartment, and the ambassador stood, clearly fearing whatever news was about to arrive. She gave Lucy a nod, and Lucy leapt forward to open the door, mentally rolling her eyes at herself for acting like a puppy eager to please its master.

Through the thin crack, she spied a white shirt and dark suit. She raised her gaze and met a pair of the darkest, prettiest eyes she'd ever seen on a grown man—save one.

"Supervisory Special Agent Max Hawthorne to see Ambassador Dickerson." His smooth voice was complete with a glorious British accent that slid over her skin like a sensory overload. "I'm the FBI negotiator," he added when she made no move to let him in.

Lucy averted her gaze and opened the door, using it as a shield between the intense heat of his gaze and her almost-forgotten role as a nobody.

"The negotiator is here," she said so quietly she wasn't sure the others heard her. Miranda was already striding across the thick carpet to shake the guy's hand. Lucy closed the door after Brian Powell, the FBI Legat and all-round asshat, stepped inside the room. He didn't spare her a glance as she took up her space against the wall.

Her eyes were drawn back to Max Hawthorne.

"Have you found her?" the ambassador demanded immediately after the introductions were finished.

The Legat answered. "Not yet, ma'am. We are currently concentrating every resource we have in the region on your daughter's abduction but also asking for additional agents to assist with other ongoing cases that cannot be delayed."

"Surely Kristen's kidnapping takes priority over any other matters?" Miranda spoke firmly. Lucy's boss was beautiful and compelling and rarely raised her voice.

Powell glanced at Miranda, clearly unimpressed. "I'm not at liberty to discuss active cases. We're working with local police agencies to gather as much information about the kidnapping as possible, and I'm sure DSS is pursuing every avenue they have looking for any connections to known terrorist groups."

Iain Bartlett nodded.

"Do you have any new leads?" Catherine's tone was sharp as a wasp's sting.

"Not yet," Powell admitted reluctantly.

"What can you tell me about your daughter's movements yesterday?" Max Hawthorne asked, stepping in and breaking the tension.

The ambassador switched her full attention to the negotiator. Catherine was a smart, dedicated professional who knew her way around politics in a male-dominated world. Lucy admired the woman greatly.

"Kristen had arranged to go Christmas shopping with some of her friends. They'd been planning it for weeks."

"Did many people know about this outing in advance?" Max Hawthorne asked.

Iain Bartlett opened his mouth to answer, but Catherine raised her hand in silent command.

The ambassador gave the Fed a look. "I have no idea how many people knew about it outside of the three girls who'd arranged to meet up. Their parents and boyfriends perhaps?"

"You didn't call them all and ask them?"

The ambassador's eyebrows shot up. Miranda, as always, took her lead from her boss and frowned at the newcomer. Lucy swallowed an amused laugh.

Kudos to the negotiator for figuring out the ambassador's bulldog personality after only being in the room with her for thirty seconds. Catherine had called everyone she could think of in the hours after she was notified her daughter had been taken, demanding answers and interrogating everyone—from tearful teens to sweating generals. Phillip had barely been able to keep his wife from scouring the streets and going house-to-house knocking on doors. Had the woman been anything except the US Ambassador, Lucy didn't think anyone would have been able to stop her taking things into her own hands.

The ambassador sipped her coffee, clearly gathering her thoughts and her temper. "I spoke to the parents of all Kristen's friends briefly, especially to offer my condolences to Irene's parents and to offer any help the US can provide. The British Embassy is presumably sending people to assist them. Everyone was shaken, naturally. Irene's family is as devastated as we are. Aside from members of their household, the remaining girl didn't recall telling anyone about their plans except two other girlfriends from school and her boyfriend."

"So quite a few people knew Kristen would be in downtown Buenos Aires yesterday." The negotiator held his hands loosely in front of him.

Lucy didn't think she'd ever seen a more beautifully put together man. Even his hands looked sexy, capable and strong. Light brown skin, hair close shaven. It was his eyes that gave him the added edge. Intelligent but with a calm humor lurking beneath the surface. And that *accent*…feeding every 007 fantasy she'd ever had—and she'd had a few.

Definitely someone to avoid when possible.

"Did the girls post their movements on social media?" asked Hawthorne.

"Kristen knew better than to post her whereabouts online." Iain Bartlett sounded pissed. He took his job seriously and didn't have much of a sense of humor even on a good day.

"I checked all the girls' social media feeds," Phillip assured Hawthorne, "and didn't see anything that could be used to pinpoint their location. They go to the International school and tend to be on guard regarding potential danger in the region. Irene Lomakin, the other girl who was kidnapped, posted a picture from a Starbucks, but there was no way anyone would know where in the world she was unless they have psychic abilities. Her father works for a big petrochemical company in the city." He paused then asked hopefully, "Is it possible Irene was the intended victim, and Kristen was caught up accidentally?"

"Did you watch the surveillance video?" Max Hawthorne asked.

The ambassador and her husband nodded before turning their gazes to the thick carpet on the floor.

"It looks as if the kidnappers targeted Kristen but scooped up Irene when she tried to intervene." Max's tone was calm and soothing. "I currently believe Kristen was the primary target of the abduction, but the FBI will be examining Irene's background also. Have either of your children mentioned anyone following them recently? Anyone asking questions that seemed inappropriate or probing?"

"Not that we are aware of. We questioned Kevin, our son, last night. And the people who usually drive them around town. No one noticed anything, correct Iain?"

The RSO nodded tiredly. "We would never have let her go outside the embassy walls if we'd suspected someone was surveilling her movements."

"Did Kristen have a driver yesterday?"

Iain Bartlett nodded. "He dropped her off at a downtown shopping mall, and Kristen was supposed to call when she needed to be picked up again, although she mentioned to him she might get a ride home with Irene instead. Again, she knew to call."

Catherine reached for and squeezed her husband's hand. It made Lucy's throat go tight. She couldn't imagine how hard this would be on a parent.

Phillip went back to talking about social media. "Kristen might upload an image of an establishment after she's left, but not while she was still there. And she was always cautious of giving away details of her connection to her mother online for this very reason."

The FBI negotiator eyed the Diplomatic Security agent. "Is it possible she was tracked in some way?"

Iain shifted in his seat. "We screen people, devices, and accommodations regularly for electronic bugs. It's an invasion of privacy, and we try to be respectful, but we don't let it slide. If Kristen was bugged, it was planted very recently and most likely after she left the embassy yesterday."

Which still suggested prior knowledge of the outing, or surveillance on the embassy itself. The latter would have to be professional and covert. It wasn't as if the Americans weren't actively checking for spying eyes and employing countersurveillance methods.

"Or they bugged one of the other girls if they knew they'd be together," Phillip suggested.

Lucy was impressed with his critical thinking skills under the circumstances.

"That would suggest someone close to one of the families

feeding information to the kidnappers. Could anyone track Kristen's phone, apart from the Diplomatic Security Service?" asked Hawthorne.

Iain Bartlett shook his head. "The signal has military-grade encryption. I'm not saying it's impossible, but its advanced and classified tech. Not something a low-level thug would have access to. And I taught her to watch out for anyone following her." His face was pale, mouth strained. "I can't believe this happened on my watch."

Kristen was a smart cookie, and Irene had shown great courage in trying to protect her friend. This whole situation sucked.

Lucy made two more coffees and placed the cups on the table, along with a sugar bowl.

Powell ignored her and picked up the cup without comment. Max Hawthorne followed her movements with a slight smile. "Thanks."

She fought against returning his smile. Kept her gaze averted and stepped back against the wall. He was observant. That made him even more dangerous.

Max's eyes wandered back to the group at the table, but she knew he had made a note of her. Probably as a potential suspect.

It was to be expected, especially as it might be true, however inadvertently.

The FBI would be checking everyone's bank accounts and background information. Despite her training, it was hard to not react to him. Maybe she should pop a Xanax.

"Does she have a boyfriend?" asked Max.

"No boyfriend." The ambassador spoke quickly.

Phillip smiled softly and sniffed. "She's a beautiful, seventeen-year-old girl. I'm sure there are plenty of young men out there who are interested. However, she wasn't going steady with anyone we know about. She was earlier in the year, but they broke up."

"It would be helpful to get a list of all her friends and contacts, here and abroad, including the ex. And information on the school she attends. I'd like to talk to some of the people who know her best outside of the family."

"Of course. Miranda will collate everything and send it to you," the ambassador said.

"Yes, ma'am." Miranda tapped a note on her cell. Lucy's pocket buzzed as Miranda put her cell back in her pocket. Lucy's instructions had arrived.

Max Hawthorne sent Lucy a smile, and she blinked. He'd noticed too.

No one ever noticed.

She wanted to fan her cheeks dramatically. The guy was hot, observant, and had an accent to die for. Exactly the type of man that had plunged her into this nightmare in the first place.

"Did anyone trace her cell yet?" the ambassador asked with a strained voice.

Lucy knew the ambassador was pinning her hopes on the kidnappers somehow missing the presence of the phone on Kristen's person and the authorities tracking it.

Not likely.

Powell cleared his throat. "Yes. The police found Kristen's cell inside the van the kidnappers used to grab her, which was abandoned in La Boca." He shifted uncomfortably. "They said they were sending it to their forensics department for analysis."

Catherine's hands clenched in her lap. "Fuentes was here and never said a word. I knew I couldn't trust him." She looked incensed. "I want that cellphone back. It belongs to my family and has private photographs and text messages on it. I want the FBI to examine it. Not the Argentine authorities."

"Technically, it is evidence." Powell squirmed.

Lucy figured he didn't want to get caught between two powerful figures.

The ambassador leaned forward and pointed her finger at the guy. "Technically, it is personal property of the US Ambassador to Argentina. Make the call and make sure they realize it is an official diplomatic request with all that that implies if they don't hand it over immediately."

Max Hawthorne straightened. "We have a team of people at Quantico who can unlock it and gain access to her texts and photographs with your permission—unless you already know her access code?"

"Kristen changed her passwords and codes every time DSS checked it for spyware," the ambassador said. "She knew they had to monitor it, but she wanted some privacy in-between times. Kevin might know her most recent codes though. They play a lot of online games together. The FBI can access everything, but whatever they find is not to appear online or be used in court without my permission."

"Our permission," Phillip corrected.

"*Our* permission. Sorry. Of course, that goes without saying." Catherine nodded then stood. "What else can *I* do except talk to the kidnappers when they call?"

Max Hawthorne stared at Catherine Dickerson, clearly deciding how to respond. "You are not going to talk to the kidnappers, ma'am."

The silence stretched out as everyone held their breath. The ambassador's expression hardened.

"Giving them direct access to the family—especially one who is a high-ranking diplomat for the United States—is not a good idea."

"I've spent years talking people into things they don't want to do. I've spent years finding compromise."

"Me too. Let's role-play it then," Max Hawthorne said easily. "Ambassador Dickerson, I have your daughter. Give me ten million dollars by tomorrow, otherwise, I'll slit her throat from ear to ear and post the video of her bleeding out on YouTube for America's enemies to savor."

Catherine Dickerson's expression froze for a moment, reflecting her horror. "That was harsh."

Hawthorne shook his head. "I went easy on you compared to what these people could do, and you know it."

Lucy's stomach clenched. Someone in a city of thirteen million people must know something about the kidnapped young women. Why hadn't anyone come forward?

"You'll be the point of contact, then?" Catherine's eyes brightened as her shoulders sagged, clearly torn between disappointment and relief.

Max Hawthorne canted his head to the side. "To begin with, I will talk to the kidnappers if they call, but we usually train a local to negotiate. A family friend or trusted employee. Someone who speaks the local language fluently, but who is not as emotionally vulnerable to threats the kidnappers make. This time, the stakes are slightly different. All the phone numbers that can be used to reach you are being changed so we control access to you, your husband, and your son. And also, your email will be vetted before you see it. Your assistant can do this if she's allowed to work independently. Otherwise, someone at State will handle it."

"You're shutting me out." The ambassador's voice held the bite of a northern winter.

"I'm taking away the ability of the hostage takers to directly influence the actions of a US Ambassador."

"You think they'll try to blackmail me into doing something contrary to the interests of the US?"

"It's a distinct possibility that they'll try. I know I wouldn't want to be put into the position of deciding whether or not to give away State secrets or my daughter dies. It wouldn't be fair to put anyone in that position."

The ambassador stared hard at Max Hawthorne. The woman could make things very difficult for the negotiator if she chose, and everyone in the room knew it. He didn't look away or flinch from her steely gaze. Lucy enjoyed watching them go toe-to-toe. She only wished it was for something less dramatic than the life of the ambassador's daughter.

"Do you want to take a leave of absence from your duties, Ambassador Dickerson, and let the Deputy Chief of Mission take over temporarily?"

No one said anything. The only sound was the noise of traffic along Avenue Colombia.

"I do not," Catherine declared firmly.

No way would Catherine Dickerson cede her power when she needed it most.

Hawthorne nodded as if he'd already known the answer. "Then I suggest we follow the Crisis Negotiation Unit's playbook for the time being. We cannot predict the outcome of any one case, but the Bureau has extensive experience dealing with hostage situations. I am going to need a trusted interpreter for a few days to speed things along."

Miranda looked at Lucy. *Damn.* "I can spare my assistant if she doesn't mind. She speaks fluent Spanish."

Lucy clenched her jaw. No matter the danger to Kristen, Lucy had important things to do that did not involve waiting by a phone with zero skills in negotiation. "I-I'm not sure I'm capable—"

Brian Powell spoke over her dismissively. "Your assistant doesn't have the backbone to negotiate with street vendors, let alone kidnappers."

Lucy blinked, even though he was theoretically correct. The Lucy he knew was spineless. One thing spineless Lucy had noticed was that the lower you were on the totem pole, the more assholish some people became.

Max Hawthorne shot her a concerned look. She bowed her head to hide the fact it was anger rather than humiliation pulsing through her.

After a brief pause, Lucy risked a glance back at the tableau who'd already dismissed her.

Hawthorne dipped his head toward the ambassador, and Lucy found herself watching him, intrigued, despite her training.

"Unfortunately, I can't guarantee I'll be here for the duration of the case. Long term—"

"What do you mean '*long term*'?" The ambassador spilled her coffee on the cup's way back down to the saucer.

Hawthorne's tone was steady. "It's not unusual for cases like this to take weeks if not months to resolve. You know this."

Lucy's fingers curled into her palm at the thought of Kristen and Irene in the hands of unscrupulous men for that amount of time. The chance of them getting out of this unscathed seemed to be becoming slimmer and slimmer.

"You expect me to let these monsters hurt my baby for weeks or months while we sit here drinking coffee and doing nothing?" The ambassador's voice cracked.

Powell flinched, but Max Hawthorne calmly held the powerful woman's gaze.

"None of this is going to be easy, Ambassador. I can't even imagine the pain and anguish you and your husband are going through right now or the fortitude required to withstand it. But you need to trust the experts at the Crisis Negotiation Unit on this. The very worst thing we can do for your daughter is rush the process or attempt an armed rescue mission until we have exhausted all other options and figured out what these people really want."

"If it's money they want, we can raise it," Phillip Dickerson put in angrily. "I've calculated we can raise about seven hundred thousand dollars in the next couple of days if we liquidate all our stocks or beg and borrow from friends using our property as collateral."

"Let me tell you something about kidnappers, Mr. Dickerson," Max Hawthorne said patiently. "They want to squeeze you dry for every last cent they think they can get. If they ask for six million today and you say 'okay, tell us where the drop-off location is', chances are that by tomorrow they'll raise the demand to twelve million. A trained negotiator lowers their expectations to reasonable levels, until they believe they really have every penny you can get your hands on."

"We will sell everything we own—"

"Phillip, the US government won't officially allow us to pay a ransom," Catherine said woodenly as if she was starting to understand exactly how difficult it was going to be to get

Kristen back unharmed.

"We might be able to get a nominal amount approved to *compensate* the kidnappers," Max said quietly. "Enough to start tempting them, especially after a few days of living on the edge, scared the local SWAT teams are lining them up in their crosshairs." He shifted his attention to Phillip. "The FBI will assist both remotely in the US and with local authorities to help figure out who took your daughter and if they have any criminal history regarding kidnap and ransom situations. See if we can discover any leverage or background that we might be able to use to get them to release the girls sooner and unharmed. I'd like to take a look at your daughter's room before I head down to the scene of the abduction, if I may."

Phillip nodded. He was clearly too emotional to speak.

Max's voice was low and soothing. "I am sorry you are going through this, and I will do my very best to get Kristen and Irene home as quickly and safely as possible, but it will require patience and restraint on your part. I'd like to request we keep the information we discuss here private amongst ourselves and not risk any leaks to the media that might undermine our position."

The Dickersons nodded.

Iain Bartlett stood. "That goes without saying for DSS."

"Thank you," Max Hawthorne said. "I realize this is not how you expected to spend Christmas Day."

With a jolt, Lucy realized it was exactly one year ago today since Sergio Raminsky had been shot dead in DC, shortly after he'd assassinated the Russian Ambassador on the steps of Capitol Hill. She found herself shivering suddenly in reaction. She'd hated him, but she'd loved him too. A sea of regret and grief washed over her. She knew he hadn't really loved her, but she had to wonder if he'd been forced to do what he did to her.

The way she'd been forced to make choices she wouldn't have even contemplated in the past.

Her throat ached with suppressed emotion. She hadn't expected to be hit this way by the anniversary. She thought she'd pushed the man and the feelings she'd had for him firmly out of her mind...

"Lucy." Miranda raised her voice to get her attention.

Lucy snapped up her chin and realized everyone was looking at her with an array of expressions that ranged from anger, to condescension, to almost pity. Max Hawthorne watched her with more intensity than her frumpy outfit warranted. So much for nobody noticing her.

She shook her head slightly. "Sorry, can you repeat that?"

"Are you okay?" Miranda asked with concern.

Lucy blinked. Was she okay? *Ha.* "Of course."

Miranda repeated what she'd said. "Can you show Agent Hawthorne to Kristen's room and then drive him wherever he might want to go in the city for the rest of the afternoon? Those other things can wait until later when you return."

Lucy froze, her eyes sliding to meet the dark, intelligent gaze of Supervisory Special Agent Max Hawthorne.

"If you don't mind?" he added gently.

She dragged her gaze away from his and clasped her hands in front of herself, bowing her head so he wouldn't read the truth in her eyes. Damn right she minded. "It's no problem at all."

That was also a lie. Max Hawthorne was definitely going to be a problem, and Lucy had better remember that her priorities did not involve FBI negotiators or getting lost in tragic memories of past indiscretions.

Her mission was here at the embassy. She didn't have time for diversions.

CHAPTER FOUR

A DOOR SLAMMED somewhere in the house, sending a jolt of fear through Kristen's veins. Her heart was set on a trip wire, and her pulse exploded whenever she heard a noise. She tried to calm herself. Whenever she panicked, she started to hyperventilate and then there wasn't enough air to breathe inside the thick hood she wore. It was a sickening cycle of terror that left her wrung out and exhausted. She held back a whimper and tried to inhale a slow, lungful of air, rather than shallow, frightened breaths.

She heard the echo of footsteps from somewhere in the building where she was being kept.

The *whoosh* of her pulse in her ears slowly eased. She didn't know what was worse—the smothering heat and cramped conditions, the thick, cloying cloth that suffocated her, or the fear that consumed her every thought.

She didn't know what they'd done with Irene, but her friend wasn't here with her. At one of the many vehicle swaps, Kristen had heard someone hitting Irene so hard that the other girl had stopped making any noise. Kristen had called out her name, but then had felt the prick of a needle, and she'd passed out.

She whimpered now and then stuffed the sound down into her lungs. She was alone in her small, cramped prison, some sort of locked, wooden cabinet that was as oppressive as an oven. Sweat soaked her hair and clothes.

The first time Kristen had woken, she'd rattled the doors and kicked the sides in desperation. To no effect. The wardrobe was thick wood, solid like a coffin. One of the kidnappers had eventually banged on the door and told her in thickly accented English that if she made another sound or tried to attract attention, he'd slice out her tongue. He'd informed her there would be no other warning. No second chance.

She believed him with every cell in her body.

His threats kept her secreted here, too scared to make a noise. Too scared to attempt an escape. Too chickenshit to even try to remove the hood that smothered her.

Thirst parched her throat with relentless precision while her cheeks burned feverishly. Her brain pounded with a dehydration headache making her mother's admonishments about drinking enough water rattle inside her mind like the desiccated segments of a rattlesnake's tail.

Mommy.

She squeezed her dry eyes shut; her body unable to spare the moisture to cry.

She wanted her mother. And her father. And her little brother. And her dog.

She wanted to go home.

She hugged her knees to her chest, knowing her mom would be tearing the world apart to get her back. God, she'd be furious.

What were her dad and little brother thinking? After the initial hit of disbelief, Kevin was probably immersed in whatever video game he was into. Kristen pressed her lips together and tried to swallow. He was only fifteen. She didn't want him traumatized. She loved him and knew he loved her.

God, she'd ruined Christmas.

She sniffed. To think yesterday she'd been worried about how much money she'd spent on a stupid dress. All on the remote chance she might see Miguel at the club. She didn't even know what had happened to the things she'd bought. Didn't care. Everything she'd agonized over in the stores yesterday forgotten in this nightmare she now found herself starring in.

A pain in her hip from when she'd landed hard in one of the vehicles wouldn't go away.

She shifted onto her side, even going up on her knees until her kneecaps burned from the burden of pressing against a hard surface too long. It wasn't easy to move around with her wrists bound tightly together—with rope now—but she was grateful that they were no longer tied behind her back.

She was covered in bruises.

She tried to gauge the time of day from the sounds of the world outside, but it was impossible inside this damn cabinet.

It was hot so the sun must be up.

She clenched her fingers into tight fists as she resisted the nearly overwhelming desire to scream.

She wanted to keep her tongue.

But she might die from heatstroke anyway so who cared? At least she'd go out fighting. She pulled in another slow, steady breath.

Don't go crazy. Not yet.

How long had it been? A day? Two? She wasn't sure. It was all so confusing. Her memories were broken and blurred. She'd woken terrified and disorientated. Scared they'd beat her. Rape her. Kill her.

They hadn't.

Yet.

At least she didn't think they had. Her jeans were still on. She wasn't sore.

Nausea rolled through her stomach.

She tried to swallow again and panicked a little when the lump in her throat didn't budge. She took more small gulps of air that managed to pierce the thickness of her throat. Forced herself to concentrate on something else as her esophagus slowly eased open.

Where was Irene...?

Did people think they were dead? Were they searching for them? She scraped her teeth over her dry lips. Did her mom and dad and Kevin know how much she loved them? When was the last time she'd given them the words?

It had been a while. Everyone had been so busy lately. She'd been distracted by thoughts of Miguel and the idea of sneaking out to a Christmas Eve party at a club. Her parents both worked hard. Kevin... Kevin was Kevin.

The quiet grind of a hinge hit her ears. The soft tread of a footstep.

Oh, god. She tensed, her heartbeat galloping. *Someone was coming.*

She sat up, feeling an odd mix of dread and desperation. Dread they'd hurt her. Desperation for water and the chance to stretch her cramped limbs.

The handle of the cabinet rattled and opened. She spilled onto the floor and rolled over onto her side.

"Water," she begged, ignoring the aches and pains that screamed through her body.

Cruel fingers bit into the soft flesh of her arm and dragged her to her feet. The man—she assumed it was a man—sat her on a rough wooden surface. A crate or a bench?

Slowly the bindings on her wrists were loosened a little, and he placed a cold bottle of water into her hand.

"Quédese quieto."

Stay still.

Her Spanish was good, but she didn't want him to know that.

He grabbed the front of her hood, and she felt him jab something into the fabric. She caught sight of a knife point piercing a hole in the thick material and let out a keening sound she couldn't control. She tried to lean away from the sharp blade without moving her head.

Fuck.

The knife disappeared, but she knew it was real now—not that she'd ever doubted it.

A sharp, keen-edged blade, silent and deadly. Such a basic weapon. Every kitchen had one.

Hysterical laughter bubbled inside her, but she pushed it down. She'd go crazy later when she didn't need to worry about survival, or maybe when she'd truly given up all hope.

He took her hands, forced them closer to her face. She felt him feeding something through the hole in the canvas. A straw.

"Drink." English this time. Thickly accented, but not the same guy who'd grabbed and hauled her into the van. This guy sounded older.

She captured the straw with her lips, sucking deeply on the contents. She'd downed more than half of the bottle before the chemical taste registered.

She paused.

"Finish it." Gruff and authoritarian.

She swallowed nervously. "I need to use the bathroom."

He grunted. "Drink first. Then I'll take you to the toilet."

Oh, god. Even though she was desperate to pee the idea of doing it in front of anyone else was *awful*.

She couldn't stand it any longer. "Why are you doing this to me?"

"Drink the water." The growing edge of anger was unmistakable, and Kristen shrank away from him.

She took another long suck. "Can I keep a little in the cabinet with me? Please? It's so hot in there I feel like I'm going to roast." She waved blindly toward where she assumed the wardrobe was.

She assumed they wanted her alive...for now.

Or not.

The quiet suddenly felt menacing. She quickly finished the water and meekly handed the bottle back. He took the empty bottle and grabbed her arm, marching her across the room. She almost tripped, he moved so fast.

He spun her around, and the back of her knees touched the cool edge of a porcelain toilet. She froze. He hadn't let go of her arm.

"T-thank you."

He stepped away, but she could feel him watching her.

"Tell me when you are finished." His voice was from a few feet away, but she sensed the door was wide open.

With shaking hands, she undid her pants and sat on the unseen toilet seat, shielding herself as much as she was able to from the onlooker's gaze. She refused to think of the hygiene factor. The smell alone made her want to gag.

Don't think about it. Think about surviving.

She finished. She felt around for paper and was ridiculously grateful to find some.

She stood and pulled up her pants. Jolted when someone brushed past her to flush.

"May I please wash my hands?"

Was that really her voice? That tiny, scared, pathetic squeak?

The man's breath washed over her as he expelled a weary sigh. He was clearly tired of this already. Tired of her *demands*. Was that good or bad? Was he the main kidnapper? Or was he an underling? Did he hold the power, or did he have a boss he answered to?

"I don't mean to be any trouble, señor." She needed to elicit as much compassion and basic human kindness as she could eke out of the people who had snatched her. She would be meek and mild and cooperative. And first chance she got, she'd find Irene and they'd run. They'd be gone.

She heard a faucet turn on. He guided her to the basin, and her fingers found an unsteady trickle of lukewarm water coming out of the tap. The water slid over her wrists, and she stole a few seconds to enjoy the coolness.

"Hurry."

She blindly turned off the tap and dried her hands on her jeans. Hopefully, she was leaving her fingerprints and DNA on every available surface. Although, it wouldn't help her if she was dead.

She was cooperative as he led her back to the cabinet. He tightened the rope on her wrists again. She was beginning to feel woozy.

Her stomach rebelled, and she thought she might throw

up when she was forced to step into the wooden box. She turned to face her captor.

"Please, could I take off the hood? Please? I mean I'm in a locked cabinet... I can't see anything. I can't breathe." She hated being so subservient. Begging. She heard the grind of the hinges and felt whatever drug he'd put in the water begin to kick in. "I promise I won't try to escape. I promise I'll be good." The last came out as a sob. Tears pricked her eyes.

He paused.

His voice rumbled. "You need to be patient. Behave, and you won't be harmed. You will go home as soon as your parents pay the ransom."

Ransom? This was about money? Of course, it was. She wanted to spit and snarl.

What sort of person did that? *Monsters*. Monsters did that. And desperate men.

He pushed her to the floor, and her legs seemed to collapse beneath her.

She inhaled raggedly, her bound arms clasped around her knees in an effort to contain the panic. What if he was lying? What if he drugged her to slit her throat, or forced himself upon her?

His fingers squeezed her arm as if he could read the terror in the stiffness of her body. Then he let her go.

She felt a hard tug at the back of her neck. Then wet condensation as he placed another chilled bottle of water into her bound hands.

She wanted to cry with gratitude.

He shut the door and said loudly enough for her to hear through the wood, "You can take off the hood, but you put it back on whenever anyone comes into this room or opens this door. If you see any of our faces, I'll poke your eyes out with the tip of my knife. Your parents won't care if you're blind, but you will. Your boyfriends will. Understand?"

Her stomach clenched. She didn't have a boyfriend, but that was the least of her issues with his threats.

"Yes. Yes. Of course. Thank you." *Thank you?* Fucking *thank you?*

He grunted.

Gratefully, she dragged the heavy canvas over her head, her hair a tangled mess which she pushed back behind her ears as best she could with bound hands. She cradled the cold bottle against her sweaty forehead. Her lids grew heavy, and her head started to nod.

Maybe being drugged wasn't so bad. And if he was going to kill her or rape her, she welcomed the oblivion if it meant she wouldn't feel pain or fear. If it meant she wouldn't behold the atrocities committed on her person. She held tight to that bottle of water and her slipping sanity as she drifted off, trying to dream about the Christmas her family had planned, not the terror she was enduring. Trying not to worry about where Irene was or whether she was alive or dead.

CHAPTER FIVE

M AX STOOD IN the middle of Kristen Dickerson's spacious bedroom. The family had been here since August last year, and the young woman had pinned a few art prints on the wall and arranged a string of Polaroid photos across one wall attached to fairy lights. There was a large silver-framed family portrait on the chest of drawers. They looked happy together, though looks could be deceptive.

Max was optimistic he could get the girls back for a reasonable price if this crime was motivated purely by dollars and cents. If it was political or ideological, then all bets were off. But experience had shown him that viewing the other person's position with empathy was often enough to get kidnappers to release their hostages unharmed.

An FBI team in the John Edgar Hoover building was working this case out of the Strategic Information & Operations Center (SIOC) trying to pin down the identities of the kidnappers by listening to electronic chatter and monitoring social media and dark web channels. The Diplomatic Security Service would be doing similar things out of their HQ.

Security had been beefed up around the world at US embassies and consulates, and personnel had been warned to take greater precautions. The last thing anyone wanted was for other groups to get similar ideas.

Too late for Kristen and her friend though.

A small pile of wrapped Christmas presents sat on an armchair in the room, a sad reminder that things weren't going to happen the way they were supposed to this year. He checked the labels. Mom. Dad. Kevin. Lucy.

Lucy, huh? The beleaguered assistant to the ambassador's PA. *Interesting.*

The woman herself wandered over to a small desk where a laptop sat.

"Should I fire this up?" she asked.

"Not yet."

Something about her triggered his sixth sense.

She seemed to be deliberately avoiding the spotlight, which immediately made him pay attention.

One of the most underrated techniques taught in the SAS was how to be the gray man—someone no one noticed, who faded so thoroughly into the background that people didn't even register they'd seen them.

Lucy tweaked his interest because it looked as if she didn't *want* to be noticed. She didn't want to look good. She seemed…muted somehow.

And that suit and her ugly shoes?

He hid a grimace. Max prided himself on not judging people purely by their looks but like, most people, he definitely appreciated physical attributes. Beauty came in many forms—it could be raw and untamed, sleek and sophisticated, natural and simplistic.

He wasn't a fashion guru, but even he knew that brick-brown was an unflattering color on anyone who didn't already look like a Brazilian supermodel.

Lucy Aston was definitely underplaying her assets. The

question was why? Was she simply shy? The Foreign Service didn't generally attract the shy type.

"Lucy." He hesitated. "Do you mind if I call you Lucy?"

Her eyes widened. "Not at all."

He picked up the framed family portrait. "What's your story, Lucy Aston?"

She gave a little snort of disbelief. "My story? I don't have a story."

"Everyone has a story. How come you ended up working in Argentina for the US Department of State?" He watched the wheels turn behind her purposely blank features.

She spent time straightening a pile of textbooks on Kristen's desk. "I wanted to travel after I left college. I had decent grades, and I speak three languages, so I applied to the Foreign Service. Seemed like a good fit."

Her smile was designed to kill interest. Self-deprecating. *Move along now, nothing to see here.*

"Three languages? That's impressive."

"Not really. It's pretty much all I'm good at." She relaxed a little. "My mom is originally from France, and I had a nanny who was Spanish, and she basically raised me from a young age as my parents were never home. They're both physicians."

"You have brothers or sisters?"

She frowned and shook her head. Folded her arms across her chest, her body language clearly stating further questions were not welcome.

Was she simply a private person, and he was prying too deep? Part of his job was building a rapport with others no matter how adverse the situation. Another thought struck him that had to do with her downplaying her looks. Had she experienced some trauma that made her want to eliminate her femininity? He'd met many victims of sexual assault, and people sometimes reacted by trying to make themselves unattractive to the opposite sex.

The thought had him reassessing his desire to get her to open up. First, he needed to prove he was worthy of earning her trust—at least as much trust as it took to establish a good working relationship.

He redirected his questions. "You know who these individuals are?" he asked, putting the family photo back and pointing at the wall of Polaroids.

She stepped towards the string of photographs and started identifying different faces. She paused on one. "This is Gemma, who was in the group that went shopping yesterday." Her finger hovered over another face in a separate photo. "This is the other girl who was taken, Irene."

Max would be lying if he said he wasn't even more worried about Irene than he was about Kristen. The kidnappers had plans for Kristen. Irene was excess baggage. Or a bonus. Depending on how they looked at it.

He moved closer to peer at the small images. Caught the subtle scent of jasmine in Lucy's hair.

"What's your impression of her other friends?" he asked.

"I don't know them that well, but they seem like nice enough kids. They all attend the same international school, and many of that group move around the world regularly with their ex-pat parents' jobs."

"Can't be easy."

"No worse than being in the military, I guess." Lucy tucked her hair behind her ear. Adjusted her glasses.

"Do you know Irene at all? What's she like?" He wanted to know as much about the victims as possible. How would they hold up under pressure? How would they deal with being confined for any length of time? How would they react to fear, pain, pressure?

"She's been here a few times." Lucy looked thoughtful. "She's a natural leader, although she's always quieter when other adults are around." Not surprising. "Decisive, but not pushy. I have the impression she knows how to read people and reacts accordingly."

"That's quite a lot of insight."

She pulled up the sleeve of her jacket, but it immediately fell back down. "I often drove Kristen and her friends around town when I arrived in the spring. Irene got her license a couple of months ago, so she's taken over a lot of that now."

Maybe that's what an assistant PA signed up for? Chauffeur duty. Sounded boring as hell to Max.

"What is Catherine and Phillip's marriage like?"

She frowned at him from behind the wide, black frames. "You think that is relevant?"

"Everything's relevant." Max's gaze was drawn to where her teeth sank into her lower lip. He looked away.

"They seem devoted to one another."

"Seem?" He swung back to face her.

Her shoulders bobbed, and she shoved the sleeves of her jacket back up her arms again. "They *are* devoted to one another. Well, they fight a little when they think no one else is watching, but no more than other couples. Phillip likes to flirt—"

"Does he flirt with you?" Was Phillip Dickerson the reason Lucy dressed like Max's grandmother on an Easter Sunday?

"No. He doesn't flirt with me." Her chin angled up, and her thick hair fell away from her face as she took offense. Up close, Max got a better look at the features she liked to hide.

Clear eyes that were more hazel than brown. Smooth, unblemished skin with the barest hint of a tan. Her nose was slightly upturned. Her mouth wide and lush.

The roots of her hair were pale gold, which was a surprise. Her hair was dyed a darker brown to match her brows.

Intriguing.

"Who does he flirt with?" Max asked.

Lucy let out a long-suffering sigh, obviously reluctant to say more. "People at social events."

"People at social events?" he mirrored.

"Generally, the wives of other diplomats."

Made sense. "How does the ambassador feel about that?"

She shot him a distrustful look. "Despite what you saw today they both generally use charm to get what they want. I've seen her roll her eyes at him sometimes and get a little snippy if he's had too much to drink."

"Too much to drink?"

"He likes a few drinks, but he's not a drunk." She peered at Max with one eye narrowed. "You don't think he kidnapped his own daughter, do you?"

"I doubt it, but we have no idea of motive yet, and it has been known." Max glanced over the makeup and jewelry strewn across the girl's vanity and then used the opportunity to watch Lucy in the mirror. "Anyone he likes to flirt with in particular?"

"No." Lucy took a step away from him. "I can't talk about them like this."

As much as he admired loyalty, he needed to know every relevant thing about the family that he could uncover. "You work for the federal government, Lucy, not the Dickersons."

"I am well aware of who I work for." Her voice snapped, and her eyes sparked. Her stance shifted to a much more confident one than she'd exhibited earlier.

He held her gaze. "Lucy, I'm not looking for gossip. I'm trying to get Kristen home in one piece. To do that, I need a crash course in the family dynamics, and that includes any dirty secrets that might otherwise bite me on the ass halfway through the case. Like when some unknown-to-me lover decides to get involved and starts negotiating on the ambassador's behalf with less than pure motives, or some political rival in the government here instigates an armed raid because he doesn't give a shit about the ambassador or her kid, only for the opportunity to look like a hero." And the FBI would be a convenient scapegoat if things went south.

A noise in the doorway had him turning.

A lanky youth stood there with a rough collie at his feet. The kid looked upset.

How much had he overheard?

"This is Kevin, Kristen's brother." Lucy introduced him.

Max nodded. "Hi, Kevin. I'm Max. I work for the FBI."

"Are you going to get my sister back?" The voice was deep and the attitude hovering somewhere between hostile and admiration.

"I'm going to do my best."

"Are you any good?" Kevin asked defiantly.

Max drew in a long breath. "Yeah. I'm pretty good."

Kevin's eyes shot to Lucy as if for confirmation. She nodded. "The FBI Crisis Negotiation Unit has some of the best people in the world working for them. They deal with kidnappings all the time."

The weight of responsibility on Max's shoulders started to

grow. Kristen was becoming more real to him. More human. With people who cared about her.

"Any chance you know the passwords or codes for her phone and computer?" he asked the kid.

Kevin scratched his arm. "She'll be mad if I tell you."

"It could be important, Kevin," Lucy encouraged. "Very important."

In a criminal case, law enforcement would have to obtain a warrant from a judge, then the computer would be bagged as evidence and sent to the lab for forensic digital analysis. They didn't need a warrant here, the family was fully cooperative, and Kristen was a minor. He'd clone the machine and send the laptop to the FBI's lab for thorough DNA, trace, and forensic analysis. See exactly who'd been on her machine, and inside it.

"The FBI can crack the codes, but the time it takes might be crucial in finding your sister." Max didn't say that it might be vital to her survival. The kid didn't need to know just how dicey a situation Kristen found herself in right now. Or the fact that, when she came home, she was unlikely to be the same girl who'd left the embassy yesterday.

"I'll tell Lucy. No one else," Kevin insisted.

Max looked at Lucy. The kid trusted her and yet the ambassador barely registered her existence except to make the coffee.

Lucy smiled at the kid, and her face transformed. It gave Max a bit of a jolt.

The kid walked over to the laptop and tapped some keys and showed Lucy how to get inside. Then he wrote down the cell phone code on a green sticky note.

The screen lit up, but there were no programs open.

"I really appreciate the help, Kevin." Max needed to establish his own relationship with the kid. Wanted Kevin to feel able to talk to him if he thought of anything relevant.

"You'll get her back, right?" Kevin stared hard at Max, a boy on the precipice of manhood.

"My colleagues and I will do everything in our power to bring your sister and her friend home safely." Max rarely made promises he couldn't keep. "If you can think of anything that might help then let us know, okay?" He gave the kid his card with his personal number written on the back. He wanted Kevin to be able to contact him any time.

Kevin pressed his lips together and frowned.

"What is it?" Max sensed there was something else on the kid's mind.

"It probably has nothing to do with her being taken." His eyes flickered nervously. "I know she was messaging with some guy she met online." Kevin looked worried, as if he was in trouble. "Mom and Dad don't know. They'll kill me if they find out I knew and didn't tell them. Kristen will kill me if they find out because of me."

Max nodded. "I can't make any promises, but I'll do my best to keep your sister's private life private. And you didn't have to tell us this, but I'm glad you did. We'll find the information on her cell and obtain all the records from the phone company too. She doesn't need to know it was you who told us, but it is useful to know what to look for."

Kevin nodded, his head slumped forward. "I want my sister back."

Max offered him a fist bump which the kid reluctantly responded to. "If there's anything else you think might help us, tell me or Lucy, okay? And don't give up hope. The Bureau has all its top people working on this."

Kevin left, his dog on his heels. Max went over to the desk with the laptop.

"Do you want to look at this now or later?" Lucy schooled her features into a blank mask of disinterest again.

She was a puzzle he wished he had time for.

"The laptop?" She pushed when he didn't immediately answer. "Do you want to look at this now or later?"

Max gave her a small smile. He knew what she meant. He was torn. He wanted to go through Kristen's technology, but he also wanted to see the street where she was abducted, and the area where the van was dumped, before it got dark. Teams back in Quantico and at headquarters were already going through the texts from the phone company. The Dickersons had provided a list of social media accounts their daughter used and all known passwords.

"Later, I think." Max pulled out a large evidence bag used specifically for this purpose and slid the computer inside. He'd create a backup to work on so he didn't destroy evidence.

He sent a message to Eban Winters at CNU and asked him to follow up with the tip about Kristen messaging some unknown guy online.

Max quickly went through the girl's bedside table and came away with two journals.

"Before we head to the abduction zone, I'm going to drop these with my stuff in the Legat's office and change back into street clothes that make me look less like I'm a government drone." His eyes swept her up and down. "I want to look around town without anyone pegging me as law enforcement. Do you have anything suitable to change into?"

Lucy picked at the limp cotton of her brown blouse. "I have another suit in my car."

"Like that one?"

She nodded.

Max pulled a face. "No jeans, t-shirt? Shorts or sundress? Anything that looks casual. We can go to your apartment first."

Lucy's nostrils flared. Obviously, that was not in her plans. However, there was no way an observer wouldn't peg her for a bureaucrat the instant they looked at her.

She studied him intensely with a narrowed gaze when she realized he wasn't backing down from the request. "Would workout gear be suitable?"

"That'll do. Meet me at the Legat's office in ten minutes."

CHAPTER SIX

"THE WHITE VAN was stolen from a small town southwest of the city yesterday around noon. I spoke to my contact in the Argentine Federal Police, and he says they are currently backtracking the van's progress through the city to see if they can figure out where the kidnappers kept it before the abduction. The thieves put false plates on it so, again, not so easy. But perhaps it'll lead us to a garage or to their homes if they're really dumb." The Legat Brian Powell's voice was muffled as Max unbuttoned his clothes behind the screen. "It's slow and painstaking work, and they are short-staffed due to the holidays."

Max shrugged off his shirt and folded it carefully into his go bag. Eban had packed him another suitcase full of business clothes and would send it with another negotiator who was heading to Argentina soon. Looked like Max was going to be here for a while.

"Worth the effort if we catch a break." Max pulled a clean t-shirt over the board shorts he'd worn earlier and repacked his go bag. He pulled on socks and laced up his sneakers because running in flip-flops never worked out well.

Kristen's laptop was being cloned by DSS and Iain Bartlett had arranged to have the original couriered to Quantico.

"Do you know if there have been any other kidnappings

with similar MOs in the city?" Max asked as he came out from behind the screen. "Perhaps of non-Americans so not immediately on our radar?"

Powell sucked in his upper lip. "Now you mention it, there was an incident with a Canadian last year. Low-level guy who worked in their embassy. They paid the ransom—although they denied it publicly, of course. He was released and, from what I understand, got on the first flight back to Ottawa. Probably hasn't left the frozen tundra since." Powell laughed.

Max didn't laugh. He knew how badly a kidnapping could mess someone up. How terrifying it was to be at another person's mercy. That lack of autonomy. Lack of control. The fear and frustration. Max had only experienced it during training exercises where he'd known he was actually free to walk away any time he wanted. It had still been one of the most harrowing experiences of his life. One he didn't ever want to repeat.

He needed to check out the Canadian case.

"And there was a series of kidnappings for ransom two years ago that were the work of a street gang with connections to Brazil." Powell ran his finger around his collar. "They killed the first two hostages whose families contacted the local police after the kidnappers instructed them not to. After that, families were too scared to call the cops. Unofficial reports suggest at least a dozen other people paid up, and those hostages were released unharmed."

"Were they caught, or did they stop?"

"Died in an armed shoot-out. The last victim's family had contacts who were friends with a local police officer. They contacted him privately, and he put together a high-level operation to take them down. The antiterrorist unit was sent in after the ransom was paid and the last hostage released. There were no survivors."

Max pressed his lips together. Although that outcome had at least not involved an innocent victim getting caught up in the crossfire, it underlined the fact he couldn't control the Argentine police. He had no jurisdiction here. If they located the kidnappers, it was possible they'd use the same tactics. Kristen and Irene might not survive the rescue attempt.

"Could you get me the name of the police officer involved?" Max asked Powell. "I'd like to talk to him to rule out any similarities between kidnappings."

"Hector Cabral. He was promoted to *Oficial Inspector* after that operation. He's one of *Comisario General* Fuentes' most-trusted sidekicks now." Powell tapped out a text to someone on his phone. He'd ripped his tie off since leaving the ambassador. His collar was askew. "My office manager will find his contact number for you." Powell eyed him from under his brows. "No guarantee any of the cops speak English though. What's your Spanish like?"

"Not good," Max acknowledged with a wry grin. He needed to find a translator he could rely on while he was here. His cell dinged with an incoming text. The administrator who ran the CNU office had booked his hotel room in the Hyatt downtown. His eyes widened when he looked at the image. It appeared extremely fancy. He'd requested something secure and central, close to the embassy—but not too close. She followed the link with a smiley face and a "Merry Christmas."

She knew his vacation plans had been ruined. Max had taken off last Christmas to visit his family back in the UK so it was technically his turn to work through if the need arose. Thanks to these kidnappers, the need had arisen.

A knock sounded on the Legat's door.

"Come in," Powell shouted impatiently.

Max hadn't quite got a handle on the Legat's personality yet. He placed his shoes into his duffle, zipped it, and then straightened.

The first thing Max noticed was Powell's bug-eyed expression.

The door swung wider, revealing Lucy Aston in skintight workout gear. Despite the top layer of a slouchy, off-the-shoulder t-shirt, the outfit did nothing to disguise the hot bod she'd been covering up.

Her hair was pulled back from her face in a low, no-nonsense pony, and she'd removed her glasses. Max had been right about the woman hiding her assets beneath an ugly brown suit.

Powell was more vocal about the transformation. He whistled. "Lucy, you should wear yoga pants more often."

Max frowned.

Lucy glared at the man. "That's Ms. Aston to you, Legat Powell, and what I wear is none of your business."

Damn straight. A smile tugged one side of Max's mouth. She wasn't as timid as she first appeared.

The man reared away, clearly taken aback by the animosity in her voice and annoyed by the fact he had zero authority to call her on her tone. Score one for Lucy Aston.

Considering how casually the guy had insulted her earlier, he deserved the slap down. But why was she so subservient in front of her boss?

Because she wanted to keep her job and diplomacy was the name of the game? Something about her tweaked his suspicions, and he intended to follow up on her background check.

"Ready?" She turned her attention to Max, clearly not happy with being forced out of her camouflage. He hadn't meant to make her feel uncomfortable. He simply wanted to blend in like a local or a tourist.

"Yes, ma'am. I need to pick up my case from security before we leave. I believe my hotel is close to the scene of the abduction so I can drop it off on the way. Assuming you don't mind?"

Lucy gave him a curt nod.

Max raised his hand to Powell before following the woman out of the room. Her back was ramrod straight. Spine as rigid as a soldier on parade. Jaw clenched. Chin set to challenge mode.

They went past the closed doors and into the main office. People watched them as they left.

"I take it these guys don't usually see you in casual gear?" Max was searching for a way to break the tension.

"They don't see me at all." She shot him a glance and strode away. Clearly not liking being without her armor.

"You don't work out here at the embassy?"

"No. There is a small gym in the basement here, but I use a place near my apartment. I go on my way home from work most nights. I prefer it."

Was that due to the equipment or the people?

"I take it you're not a fan of the Legat?" Max might be completely off-base with his observations but even mislabeling her emotions was a viable way of eliciting information. Label something incorrectly—or not—and wait for the response was a tactic they regularly used in negotiations.

"He ignores me most of the time." Lucy grunted. "And I

don't mind him ignoring me, but I resent him only deeming me worthy of notice when he realizes I have tits and an ass." Her gaze nailed his, and he dared not look anywhere except for her eyes.

"It's a problem a lot of guys have." He decided to use truthful humility to attempt to bridge the icy gap she'd constructed between them. She blamed him for having to reveal herself. He was simply trying to do his job.

Now Lucy Aston was closed off and pissed, and he felt a little guilty for causing friction in her life when she was obviously walked all over at work.

"What about you? Are you immune?" she asked angrily, striding through the empty corridors toward the entrance of the building.

To tits and ass?

Max held up his free hand in defense. "Never pretended to be immune, but I noticed you as soon as I walked into the ambassador's office, so I think I get a free pass on this one."

Her eyes acknowledged the truth in that statement, and a little of the starch went out of her form.

"As a student of human behavior, I do recognize when a woman does not want to be complimented on her appearance," Max added tactfully.

She snorted. "Score one for the Bureau."

"I didn't mean to make you uncomfortable when I asked you to accompany me in street clothes."

Max was easygoing until he had to arrest or kill someone. He didn't like the idea he'd upset this woman who seemed particularly vulnerable, although growing a pair never hurt anyone.

Lucy's hazel eyes were once again devoid of expression

when they met his. She'd gotten herself under control and was back behind the mask where she appeared to be happiest. Max was content to let her stay there. For now.

They arrived at security, picked up his luggage, and exited through the side door while he followed a silent Lucy Aston along the asphalt until they came to her car—a British racing green Mini Cooper S 5 Door with two white stripes down the bonnet.

Max fell in love on the spot.

She popped the boot, and he tossed his suitcase and bags inside.

"My first car was a Mini—the old kind, so cramped I had to drive with my knees up around the steering wheel and my head touching the roof, which was fine until I went over a pothole." He climbed in, moving the passenger seat as far back as it would go, thrilled he could stretch out his legs.

That earned him a warm glance. "I'm surprised you fitted in at all."

"You should have seen people's faces when five hulking soldiers climbed out of the thing." He smiled. A happy memory. He needed to remember more of those. Not the deaths that had followed. Or the spiraling sense of heartbreak, outrage, and betrayal.

She put the car into gear, and he was surprised to see a manual transmission, but he decided not to insult her by mentioning it.

"Where are you staying?" she asked, all business.

He gave her the address.

"So that's where my taxpayer dollars go."

"We usually stay in a Travel Lodge so the office adminis-trator must have found a coupon or been drunk on Christmas sherry—in which case, I'll be switching hotels in the next couple of days."

He watched as a smile twitched the corners of Lucy's lips, but she shut it down.

She drove through the quiet downtown traffic with competent ease. She wasn't a mouse behind the wheel, if anything, she drove aggressively. The Mini was nimble and maneuverable. A wave of nostalgia hit him. He was going to get himself one of these when he got back to the States. Forget that he was home less than fifty percent of the time. Life was short, and he needed a little fun to counterbalance the grim. He'd earned it.

Took them ten minutes to arrive at the hotel, and he stared up in shock. This was probably the nicest place he'd ever stayed. "Definitely too much sherry. I better enjoy it while I can."

He grabbed his stuff out of the boot, impressed despite himself. It was bloody palatial. He'd spent Christmas in much worse places. Iraq. Afghanistan, Mali. Countries most people hadn't even heard of. Life in the FBI was a cake-walk in comparison to his career as a soldier, but it was still demanding and required his brain as much as his body. He figured most special forces soldiers needed that when they left the military. They weren't good at boring routine. They weren't good at soul-destroying monotony. Sure, they could sit for hours in a pool of freezing mud waiting for the right moment to strike, but they didn't have the patience to stand in a long queue to buy groceries.

His brain shied away from some of the memories that wanted to intrude. He and his buddies in Colombia had raised a few pints to the men who hadn't made the successful transition back to the civilian life. Some were dead. Some were in prison. He'd tried to help them and failed. Former soldiers were still living homeless on the streets of Britain in ever increasing numbers. It had been another reason to leave a country he loved, not that the States was much better.

Right now, it was time to concentrate on the things he might be able to fix.

The hotel's uniformed valet tipped his hat, and Max gave him an appraising nod as Lucy handed over her keys. He wasn't here to enjoy himself, but a drink in the bar later was something he was determined to look forward to.

He checked in and went upstairs to dump his bags in his room, which was also a knockout. Lucy hung around the lobby.

He took the time to place Kristen's diaries in the safe. He contemplated wearing the SIG his buddies had loaned him but didn't want to take the time to change clothes yet again, and there weren't many places to conceal a handgun in a pair of board shorts. Plus, he wasn't sure how Lucy would view him carrying a weapon. Officially, he needed permission from head of mission to wear a firearm, and it hadn't felt like the right time to ask the ambassador today.

He couldn't pin down the type of personality Lucy was, and that bothered him. He was usually adept at rapid assessments of people. Maybe that's why he found himself so aware of her. He placed the gun in the safe along with his encrypted laptop. He locked the room, placing a Do Not Disturb notice on the outside. He didn't want housekeeping going inside for any reason. Nothing he'd brought with him was classified, but it paid to be careful.

He headed back downstairs with his wallet in a zippered pocket, sunglasses on top of his head, and work cell in his hand.

Lucy was sitting on a plush sofa in the most secluded spot of the opulent foyer, clearly avoiding attention. Of course, she was.

"Ready?"

She nodded and adjusted the crossbody bag she carried, and he tried not to notice how the strap slid between her breasts and emphasized her curves. He wanted to ask about the ugly suit she wore for work but insulting her clothes wasn't the way to a frictionless working relationship.

"It's only a short walk to the abduction site. I gave the valet your room number for any charges." Her eyes lit with a sparkle of mischief she quickly doused.

Why did she do that?

Something about Lucy Aston seemed slightly forlorn. Max didn't enjoy seeing people suffer. Maybe that's one of the reasons he'd gravitated to negotiation. Talking people into getting help when they needed it formed a big part of his job. Lucy looked like she could do with a friend.

It took less than twenty seconds to arrive at the junction where the abduction had occurred. He recognized the scene from the surveillance video.

Lucy stood in the shade of the building behind him, across the road where Kristen had been grabbed.

He went over and stood next to her. "Do me a favor, start scrolling through your cell phone as if you're looking for a restaurant or taking a call. Give me a chance to check out the area without looking conspicuous."

She nodded. Pulled out her cell and tapped the screen, putting the cell to her ear and turning away from him. It sounded exactly like she was calling her mother.

Max scanned the other pedestrians to see if anyone was paying them attention—they weren't—then he examined the local architecture, looking for surveillance cameras that might give them a better angle. The one that had recorded the footage he'd watched that morning was about ten feet above his head, aimed at the pedestrian crosswalk in front of them.

He put his hands on his hips as though he were waiting for Lucy to finish her call. He stretched out his neck and turned his attention to the flow of traffic and the types of shops in this part of town. The traffic was light, but last night it had been a lot busier.

Whoever lifted the ambassador's daughter had known exactly when the girls were going to reach this intersection. Someone had to have been tailing them. Or tracking them. And communicating with the men in the van. He snapped a photo of another camera along the street on the opposite side that might give them different footage. Maybe the van had parked up for a little while. The local police should have canvassed all the shops along this street for their CCTV footage, but he'd double check.

The stores around here were in the same league as the hotel—high-end and really fucking expensive.

Was this where these schoolgirls actually shopped? Or were they taking in the designer glamor? Max knew what those dollars could do in poorer parts of the world. Places not far from here where a person could live for a year on the cost of one of the dresses in the window.

Apparently, Lucy really was on the phone to her mother, or she was a consummate actress. Lucy was reassuring the woman that she was safe inside the embassy, and she sounded convincing as hell.

Lucy's mother seemed to be expressing concern for the ambassador's daughter. The fact news of the kidnapping had spread so far wasn't good. It was much easier to negotiate outside the media spotlight. Considering Kristen Dickerson had been lifted off a Bueno Aires street on Christmas Eve in broad daylight made it unsurprising that the press had caught wind of it. And, it wasn't just Kristen, it was also Irene who was a British national. He needed to visit her parents to discuss what the FBI would do to assist them and figure out what the Brits were up to.

He texted the Legat a photo of the second camera and asked Powell to request the footage from local business owners via the cops.

He glanced back at Lucy and noticed the smile on her face lit up her features. Her expression closed down the instant she caught him watching her.

He frowned.

"I have to go now. I love you, Mama. Tell Daddy the same. Happy Holidays."

"I'm requesting the surveillance footage from that other camera across the street," he told Lucy when she hung up. Not because she needed to know but because he wanted to include her in the process. She knew Kristen well enough to have been getting a present for Christmas and for Kristen's brother to trust her with their passwords, so she probably had more insight than most into Kristen's actions and how she might react in captivity.

"Do you know what happened to Kristen's shopping bags?" He remembered the scattered purchases lying on the pavement in the surveillance video.

Lucy's brow crinkled. "I imagine Gemma picked them

up."

"Any chance you could prioritize getting me a contact number for her when you get time tonight? I know you're busy, but I need to examine all of the things they were carrying."

Lucy frowned slowly. "You think Kristen might have had a tracking device on her?"

Max shrugged. "It's distinctly possible. I'd like to figure out that part of the story—how they knew her exact whereabouts. It might give us a clue into who did this."

Lucy chewed on her lip and then nodded. "I'll get you those numbers before I go home tonight. It's the details from the school that will prove difficult on the holiday."

"Just get me the name of the principal and any guidance counselors you may know of today. I'll get what I need from them. I probably won't get the chance to talk to them until tomorrow at the earliest anyway."

Her brows pinched.

"You look like you got as much rest last night as I did," he noted.

She huffed out a laugh. "Only if you got none."

She probably had a ton of work waiting for her back at the embassy.

"Look, Lucy, I know you're busy. I'll grab a cab to the dump site in La Boca—"

"Oh, no." She shook her head decisively. "I know my way around this city, and that part of town is dangerous once you stray away from the tourist area. The last thing I need is anything happening to you when I'm supposed to be chauffeuring you around."

Max allowed a small smile to crease his mouth. It was

amusing that she thought she needed to protect him. "I'll be fine."

"It's not about you. If anything happens to you, my life will be hell."

They started wandering back to pick up her car from his hotel.

"I don't want to put you in a difficult position."

Her laugh was unexpectedly bitter. "Trust me, it's not you making my life difficult."

She was starting to relax around him.

The valet brought the car around and they climbed in.

"We shouldn't spend too long when we get there. In and out for a quick look. Do you know exactly where the van was found?" she asked.

He gave her the location Brian Powell had given him.

Lucy programmed her Sat Nav which spoke in French.

A slight blush touched her cheeks as she changed the settings to English. "I find a good way to keep up my language skills is by putting all my electronics in whatever language I'm not currently using."

"Good idea." Max couldn't claim any language skills. It was right up there with his ability to sing.

She shot him a hesitant glance as if she expected more judgment.

He decided to keep quiet and hope she filled the silence. She didn't. Funny, because a lot of people found silence intimidating. Negotiators used it as a tactic all the time, but Lucy Aston wasn't falling for it.

He relented because he wanted to know more about her. Apparently, she was better at this game than he was. "You enjoy living down here?"

Her expression was that familiar blank slate. "I love the city, the country."

He wanted to shake something free. "But your boss treats you like the coffee girl."

Lucy turned to face him, and her mouth dropped open in shock. She quickly turned her attention back to the road. "The ambassador? She's not so bad usually."

"Reminds me of a sergeant I worked with in my first regiment long before I became an FBI agent. He used to make me and another lad run laps for any perceived infraction. I guess it worked out for us in the end. By the time I applied for Selection, I was probably the fittest man in the paras."

Which had been the baseline for men in the Special Air Service.

Instead of talking about her work colleagues, which was what he'd been aiming for, she turned the conversation back to him.

"British military, right?" She looked at him, but it wasn't really a question. It was a statement of fact. "What made you change sides?"

Anger flashed inside him, but he squashed it. "I never 'changed sides.' I was a dual citizen. My father was from Chicago. He and my mom split up when I was five. He took a job back home, and she refused to move with him. I stayed with her and my sisters back in England."

"Was that hard?"

Was that hard? He was the one who was supposed to be good at subtly digging into people's lives and yet she'd cut to his core in a few minutes.

"Yeah. That was hard."

Made worse somehow by his father dying not long after

Max joined the FBI, having had to renounce his British citizenship. He wasn't sorry for the choice he'd made, but he missed his mother and his sisters and the security of knowing he could go back and live near them anytime he wanted.

"What about you?" he asked as the traffic flew by. "Where's your mom live? I assume that was your mom you called earlier."

She nodded, eyes on the road ahead. "Yeah. You made me realize I'd forgotten to call her to wish her Happy Holidays. Both my parents still live in So-Cal."

That might explain the blonde hair roots but not why she dyed it a dull brown—although why not? People did the opposite all the time. No one questioned that.

"You miss your family?" he asked.

"I miss the idea of them more than the reality. I mean I *love* them." She adjusted the flow of air toward her face. "I'm sure you're not interested in pathetic stories of rich kids feeling sorry for themselves." Her laugh sounded brittle. "I mean, I had a great upbringing—my nanny was as close to me as my family. My parents paid her well and even gave her a place to stay on the estate when she retired."

Estate?

"I didn't always see eye-to-eye with my parents when I was growing up. They wanted me to go into medicine."

"You didn't fancy that?"

"Actually, I tried," she eyed him sideways, "I didn't have good enough grades in the sciences, but they were always pushing me to do better."

Max kept one eye on their surroundings even as he watched Lucy's face try to come to life despite that inner restraint.

"People tend to do better in the things they love."

"Which, for me, obviously wasn't physics, chemistry, or biology."

"Instead, you get to travel the world, and you don't need to pull on a uniform or a semi-automatic weapon to do so."

She snorted. "You don't sound like you enjoyed being a soldier."

"On the contrary. I *loved* being a soldier. I just hated going to war." *And losing my friends.* He put his sunglasses over his eyes because, once again, she'd cut to the core of him while he'd barely glanced off the surface.

They headed south through streets that grew increasingly narrow and neighborhoods that started to look a lot poorer than upscale Recoleta. Fewer mansions and designer stores. Small apartments. Modest homes. Then, after twenty minutes, two-story stucco houses with corrugated tin roofs. Garbage blew along the sidewalk. Stray dogs slept in the sun.

They drove along Drive del Valle Iberlucea and passed the blue and yellow La Bombonera football stadium.

Lucy eyed the landmark. "Wearing the wrong soccer shirt around here can get you killed."

Max jerked his brows. That was true for parts of the UK too.

Lucy drove down to the water and pulled up at the nearly empty harbor. She cut the engine. "The car should be safe enough here for an hour, even though most shops are shut today."

There were still some tourists milling around, photographing the brightly painted buildings of El Caminito. Lucy checked directions on her phone before applying a steering lock and climbing out of the Mini.

Max got out and looked around.

"The area was originally settled by Italian immigrants when Europeans flooded the region in the early nineteenth century. *Boca* means mouth because we're at the mouth of the river," Lucy told him. "The story is that the mismatched colors of the houses originate from using whatever was left over from painting the boats."

Max inclined his head.

A young boy with shiny black hair and eyes as dark as his own pretended not to stare at Lucy's car. Lucy spotted him too. She locked the Mini and walked over to the kid. She flashed a bill and spoke in a rapid stream of Spanish. She pointed at the car and at Max and then put the larger bill into her bag and waved it around before handing him a smaller one.

The kid said something, and Lucy started in on another long stream of Spanish. She sounded like a local and showed no fear.

Max thought about the woman who'd virtually hidden behind the door when he'd met the ambassador. That was not the same woman bribing and threatening this kid to make sure her car wasn't stolen or stripped while they were gone.

"What did you say to him?" Max asked when they started walking south of the main drag.

"I told him you were a cutthroat assassin who would find him and kill him in his bed if he let anyone so much as lay a finger on my car. I also promised him more cash if it looked exactly the same when we got back."

Carrot and a stick. He was the stick. "Is that the approved diplomatic approach?"

Lucy gave him the side eye. Her stride was loose and confident—as if she belonged here. Max added a certain swagger to his gait. It was important not to look like a victim in order not to become one. It was one of a million variables that influenced how predators picked their targets.

"The van was ditched a few blocks from here." She strode down a narrow lane and then south again into a dirtier, dingier part of the neighborhood. There were glimpses of decayed Spanish architecture amongst what amounted to a shanty town in places interspersed with the occasional palm tree. The scent of garbage wafted from a dumpster.

They walked onto another street that was cooler under the shade of some dark, leafy trees. She didn't pause to check her bearings or hesitate in any way. She went right and then left until they hit a small, deserted alley.

"Here." She pointed.

Max scanned the nearby houses. No cameras. Even if there had been, they wouldn't have lasted the night. The doors and windows were all shut up tight. It had an abandoned feel to the place.

He raised his gaze and saw a quick movement as someone immediately withdrew from a window. Max spotted an entryway in an adobe wall. He walked over, muscled open the gate before climbing the outside staircase and knocking on the door of a ramshackle apartment.

CHAPTER SEVEN

L UCY MUTTERED A curse as she followed the negotiator up the rickety staircase. "Where are you going?"

Max ignored her. Of course, he did.

Lucy glanced around nervously. This was not the sort of place where it was wise to go off the grid. This neighborhood could swallow someone whole and not even spit out the bones.

Max knocked loudly enough to attract attention inside the rundown apartment. The two of them were hidden from general view by the dense foliage that formed a canopy around the small veranda. There was only one apartment up here. The brief glimpse she'd seen of the person suggested an older woman lived here, but it didn't mean she lived alone.

Neither she nor Max Hawthorne were armed as far as she could tell, and the last thing she needed was a bullet-hole to deal with in either herself or the Federal Agent.

Max went to knock on the door again, but Lucy grabbed his hand to stop him. His skin was startlingly warm, and she released him immediately. "Wait. Let me try."

She leaned closer to the door and spoke softly in Spanish. "Hola? No queremos hacerte daño. ¿Puede ayudarnos, por favor?" *Hello? We mean you no harm. Can you help us please?*

Max stood close enough she could smell his scent.

The sound of shuffling inside had Lucy tensing. Were they

about to meet a gangbanger with a submachine gun, or a mother, or a scared child? She raised her brows at Max as they both moved to the side of the doorway in an effort to avoid gunfire should the worst-case scenario become a reality.

The door opened a crack. An older lady peered out at them, face wrinkled, faded brown eyes full of fear.

"Sorry to bother you on Christmas Day, señora." Lucy spoke in Spanish. "We are looking for information about an incident that occurred down in the alley yesterday evening."

"I'm sorry, I can't help you." The woman also replied in Spanish and tried to shut the door.

Max's running shoe was planted firmly in the gap and, while he didn't use his size to intimidate the woman, he was over six foot of solid male and probably scared the shit out of her.

"Ask if she saw a car parked in the alley for any length of time yesterday," Max insisted.

"She doesn't want to talk to us." Lucy didn't want to bully an old lady.

"Ask her."

Lucy blew an annoyed breath out of her nose and glared at him. She detested being ordered around and figured she didn't have to be quite as compliant and obedient as she usually was when she was outside the embassy and alone with Hawthorne. He wasn't a fixture in her life, and she was unlikely to be spending much time with him in the future. But, even though she wanted to tell him to take a hike, the stakes were too high. She couldn't afford for word of her actions to get back to the embassy. And then there was Kristen, a sweet and harmless young woman, and Irene, a feisty and strong individual who'd only been taken because she'd tried to defend her friend.

Lucy spoke in rapid-fire Spanish. "Please, they took two friends of ours. Two innocent young women. We are trying to get them home to their families to celebrate Christmas." She appealed to the woman's empathy and religion, hoping it might override her fear of strangers or reprisal. "Was there a car parked down there yesterday?" She pointed to the alleyway. "Or possibly a van?"

The woman's mouth turned down in defeat, and she seemed to deflate. "No one can see you here."

After another brief hesitation, she opened the door and ushered them inside.

Lucy glanced around the small living room. It had a massive, old-fashioned TV. Brightly colored throws and cushions covered the sofa. Faded prints of showy flowers covered the walls. A tiny kitchen with huge, antique-looking appliances was visible through a doorway that had a beaded curtain, then a small corridor led off the room, probably to a bedroom and bathroom.

There was no evidence of anyone else being in the apartment, although they could be hiding in one of the other rooms.

Lucy stood awkwardly inside the door. She glanced to the side and saw a stack of mail addressed to Señora Abigail Blanco.

Max sat on the opposite side of the couch to the woman. His hands were clasped, elbows resting on strong thighs. Making himself smaller, she realized, and less of a threat.

He certainly didn't look like a Fed in those board shorts or with those boyish good looks.

"We don't mean to cause you any distress," Max began.

Lucy interpreted in a gentle voice trying to mimic Max's

tone.

"We know a vehicle was parked in the alley below yesterday evening. Did you see it?"

Lucy repeated Max's words, but it was his soft baritone that cast a spell.

"I can't talk to the police. I don't trust the police." The old woman's fingers knotted with agitation. Her shoulders were hunched from a lifetime of hard labor. "They will find out it was me, and they will beat me and kill me."

Lucy interpreted for the woman and watched Max acknowledge the woman's fear of not only the criminals but also local law enforcement.

"We are not the Argentine police. We will not reveal our sources, ma'am. We won't betray any information you give us."

Lucy repeated the words, but she could tell the old woman was already hooked on Max's promises. She didn't even need to speak the same language to trust the man. Must be a negotiator's psychic mind trick as his voice was also lulling Lucy into a feeling of safety too. She needed to remember his specialties when dealing with him in the future.

"Did you see a white van at all yesterday? Probably around five thirty PM?" Max asked.

The old woman's lips compressed, and she ran her veiny hands over the long, orange skirt she wore.

"Si," she whispered. "I saw three or four men, and they were moving something from a van to the trunk of a car. I did not see what it was." Her hands moved faster over her skirt, gripping the material in agitation.

"Could it have been a young woman?" *Or two?*

She nodded then looked away.

"What kind of car?" Max asked. Lucy translated the question. Due to the intense nature of the interview and her part in it, Lucy found it hard to maintain her usual background position. Maybe it didn't matter here today, but she would need to find a way to extricate herself from being with this man and on the front lines of this investigation. This wasn't her job.

An image of Kristen rose in her mind, and she knew it wouldn't be so easy to abandon the two young women if there was any way she could help. But her work was important too, and she wasn't paid to be an interpreter.

The old woman shook her head. "I didn't see. I don't remember."

Conflicting statements but a reminder that getting involved could cost the woman her life, and they all knew it. The police weren't going to provide 24/7 protection to one old lady in the barrio. The police could be the problem. Corruption was rife. The old woman was on her own. No backup. No support.

She spoke quickly. "They left all the van doors open with the keys inside."

Almost inviting it to be stolen before the cops arrived. What better way to destroy evidence?

The woman wrung her hands. "I went downstairs as I needed to buy milk before the stores closed." She mashed her lips together.

Max and Lucy exchanged a glance and waited her out. The woman had definitely seen something.

The woman stood abruptly and went to her tiny kitchen and opened the door to her massive refrigerator that looked heavier than Lucy's Mini. The woman pulled something out of the icebox. Lucy's pulse gave a skip. It was a cell phone.

"I saw this on the ground. I knew if I left it, it would be stolen." The woman probably thought she could sell it for a little cash. She held it out to Max.

He didn't take it. "Ask if she has a plastic bag she can put it in."

The woman immediately turned around and did as he requested, suggesting her English was better than Lucy had appreciated. Abigail Blanco was trusting them—a pair of strangers—to not get her in trouble with either the police or the kidnappers. It was a humbling responsibility and one they might not be able to uphold.

"Did the police come here and question you last night?" Max asked when the old woman handed Lucy the plastic bag of evidence which she tucked into her small purse.

"If they did, I was not home. I went to Mass. You need to leave now." She spoke in English and ushered Lucy toward the door. "No one can see you here."

"One thing." Max took the woman's hand and pressed his business card into her palm. "Thank you. If we get these young women home, know that you helped us. We both thank you, as do their parents."

The woman closed her eyes and muttered a quick prayer. "The men got into an orange VW Passat. It stank of dirty exhaust fumes when they drove away."

Max squeezed her hand and slipped her some American dollars. He thanked her again.

Lucy opened the door, checking no one was around before slipping outside.

CHAPTER EIGHT

"**Y**OU THINK SHE was telling the truth?" Lucy asked.

Max headed down the outside stairs that were in desperate need of repair. He avoided a particularly dodgy-looking step and held his hand out to help Lucy around it too.

He immediately let go of her hand. "Hard to know for sure, but she seemed genuine. She probably saw a lot more than she let on." Max carefully checked the street. He held the ramshackle gate for Lucy. Manners might be sexist, but they were ingrained in him from birth.

The neighborhood was poor and quiet. It was Christmas Day in a predominantly Christian country.

"I wonder if a VW was also reported stolen yesterday." Max wrote a note to himself on his phone. "We might be able to get a license plate number from a street camera and trace it."

"It's probably burnt-out somewhere."

Max shrugged. "Or it belongs to one of the crew, and they reported it stolen to cover their tracks. With luck, they aren't as smart as we think they are."

"How do we inform the locals without revealing the woman's identity?"

Max had no intention of outing the woman to anyone outside his immediate circle at CNU. "We have to report finding the cell phone. We can say someone handed it to us in the alley and left without giving their name."

Shadows were starting to lengthen and thicken between the buildings. He took a few photos of the narrow street with his cell. The van would have filled it almost entirely. Garbage littered the alley, so he really had to wonder how thorough the evidence collection had been. Most of it would be worthless, but it was also possible the locals had missed something. He squatted and scanned the ground.

Lucy bounced on her tiptoes for a few moments and then stopped as if consciously suppressing the outward display of emotion.

"So they left the second getaway car here prior to the kidnapping. Presumably, they would do the same with any subsequent vehicles that were used yesterday? The van was stolen on Wednesday, correct?" she said.

He nodded.

"And all these cars had to be in place at least an hour before the kidnapping took place." Lucy's brows furrowed. "It suggests they knew Kristen planned to be out shopping without security at least twenty-four hours in advance of taking her."

He moved north a few feet, still crouched down as he searched the ground. "It was well organized and thought out. They left vehicles where they would attract minimal notice from the authorities. No cameras and few people. Also, Christmas Eve...it's a time when routines are broken up and people's guards are down." It should have been a time of celebration.

Lucy looked up. He followed her gaze. The sky was darkening to a dull mauve with vivid red clouds. "We should go."

"Yep." He went to rise when the glint of something golden near a dandelion caught his attention. He moved closer, took a photograph of the object in situ, tucked the phone back into his zippered pocket. Then he scooped the delicate metal band into a small paper evidence envelope he habitually carried folded in his wallet.

"What is it?" Lucy asked.

"A ring." He didn't know if it had anything to do with the case or not. He shoved it into his pocket. The hair on his nape began to vibrate with warning. Footsteps told him someone was coming.

He murmured, "Let's get out of here."

A noise from behind them had him glancing over his shoulder as a gang of five youths came into view.

"¡Hey, hombre!" One of the young men shouted. Then he said something Max's limited Spanish couldn't decipher, but it didn't sound like "Merry Christmas."

They'd lingered too long.

Lucy opened her mouth to say something, but Max shook his head. He didn't want her getting hurt. Time to move. "Let's go."

They began to hurry away and, immediately, shouts went up behind them as the men gave chase.

He and Lucy started running and shot out of the end of the alleyway and turned right. Lucy grabbed his wrist. "This way."

They raced down a one person-wide gap between buildings. He let Lucy lead. She seemed to know her way around, and it allowed him to cover her back.

The young men were keeping pace, and he heard shouts and excitement as others joined in the chase. Max pulled a piece of rusted, corrugated tin across their path behind them. Rats scuttled in the shadows.

A sliver of light up ahead showed their escape route. Lucy sprinted towards it, and Max kept pace with his much longer stride but, boy, she was fast. He wished he was carrying his weapon right now. The realization that he'd put this woman in danger did not sit well.

Just as they were about to exit the narrow gap up ahead, a silhouette appeared of a man carrying a knife. Someone shouted at them. Shit. They were trapped.

Lucy didn't slow. Neither did he. No way did he want to end up rotting in this cesspit of an alleyway with his carcass ripped apart by rats and feral dogs. No way would he let Lucy get hurt because she'd been forced to accompany him.

"Let me go first," Max shouted.

Lucy shook her head, breath coming hard, as she pumped her legs even faster.

Damn the woman was *quick*. His foot slipped on something unidentifiable which cost him a fraction of a second but, thankfully, he didn't go down.

Up ahead, Max watched Lucy use her momentum to launch herself at the man blocking their way. Despite being solidly built, the guy was unprepared for the flying dropkick that knocked him flat onto his back while Lucy rolled on the ground and came up into a low crouch ready to defend herself from another attack.

Another guy stood to one side, watching them open-mouthed. His hand rested on a pistol stuffed in his waist band. Max put him down with a single strike to the jaw and quickly disarmed him, taking the weapon so it couldn't be used against them. Both men cowered on the ground as their bravery evaporated.

"Come on." Max grabbed Lucy's hand, and they took off again, weaving between people who were milling around. They seemed unconnected to the thugs who were chasing them. People scattered when they saw Max holding a gun, probably fearing they were about to get caught in a firefight.

Which was fine with Max. The fewer innocent civilians on the street the better.

A shot whistled over their heads.

Lucy darted left again, dragging him along another cramped street. Max let her lead and hoped he didn't have to spend Christmas explaining to his superiors why doctors were digging bullets out of his ass.

Or worse.

"Are you okay?" he shouted.

"Yep."

They hit the end of that street and he recognized how close they were to the main tourist area, El Caminito.

"Car's along here." Lucy pointed right, chest heaving, eyes bright, cheeks flushed.

Despite her acrobatics, she seemed completely unfazed. Max was impressed. This was not the same woman who'd stood with her head bowed in the ambassador's apartment.

Adverse conditions brought out the best in some people. Maybe it was as simple as she needed her job, and her boss was a bit of an asshole. Whatever the cause for the difference, there was much more to Lucy Aston than first met the eye.

He liked it.

They didn't stop running, even though noise of pursuit had faded away. When they reached the harbor, Max was grateful to see the Mini intact. Lucy jumped behind the wheel and removed the steering lock while Max slid into the passenger seat. He considered throwing the gun he'd confiscated into the harbor. He had no desire to leave it lying around the streets to be picked up by children, nor did he want to deal with the local authorities and make a report. Instead, he tucked it under Lucy's passenger seat. It *was* evidence. It might connect the people who'd pursued them to the kidnap case, although that was unlikely.

They were probably a bunch of local thugs. They'd noticed his and Lucy's presence pretty damn quick and had probably been searching for them around the barrio. He bet whatever vehicle had been parked in that alley yesterday had been equally observed and catalogued. Maybe a local cop had a source they could leverage for more details—like a license plate.

Lucy reversed fast in a wide arc, and he braced his arm against the dash. Then she buzzed down her window and held out a bill for the kid who stood gaping at them with an angry expression on his face as though he expected them to leave without paying him.

"Muchas gracias." Lucy thanked him.

The kid vanished by the time Lucy buzzed up the window and pressed her foot on the accelerator. They shot forward.

The ringing of a phone interrupted the sounds of them both catching their breath.

"Want me to answer that for you?" asked Max.

Lucy frowned in confusion. "That's not my phone. I thought it was yours."

Max dug his cell out of his pocket. "Nope."

"Oh, crap." Lucy dragged her purse strap over her shoulders and handed him her bag, driving one-handed. "It's the phone Abigail Blanco gave us."

Max unzipped her purse and pulled out the device, still inside the baggie.

"Don't say anything." He pressed the answer button. Put the call on speaker. "Hello? You're speaking to Max. Who's this?"

He opened a voice recording application on his own cell phone to catch as much information as possible.

"I have the women." The man on the end of the phone spoke in English. The voice was electronically disguised, which matched the almost military-level sophistication of the initial abduction. But some voice encryption was easy for the experts to disentangle. "I want ten million US dollars for each hostage by noon tomorrow or they both die."

"How am I supposed to do that?" Max's tone was deferential not scathing. Genuinely requesting assistance, trying to get the kidnapper involved in solving his problems. "Of course, I want the girls back safely, but even if the families had that amount of money, how can I assemble that much cash—twenty million US dollars—overnight? Especially when all the banks are closed." He texted Eban what was going on.

Lucy's eyes were huge with shock at the fact he was arguing with the hostage taker. Always assuming it was the kidnapper, which Max would never take for granted.

He caught her gaze and gave her a smile to reassure her he knew what he was doing. This was a proven method of negotiation even though it probably appeared unsophisticated.

She blinked and turned her attention back to the road.

"I don't care how you do it, but if you want to see them alive…"

"I do want to see them alive. I will do everything within

my power to get you all the money we can raise, but you must understand that to find even a fraction of that amount will require the ambassador to sell her house in the US, which will take time, and it still won't be ten million dollars. What else can we do to reach a fast and peaceful settlement?"

"The US government will pay."

Max laughed, even though it wasn't funny. He was trying to diffuse the tension. "The US government will not pay a ransom. The US government will not even officially allow families to negotiate with kidnappers."

"You lie. They say that on the news but, in private, they pay."

"Not the US." Or the UK, for that matter. "The American government will not pay a ransom. It would put US personnel and their families all over the world at increased risk. The ambassador is willing to talk to you anyway. She wants her daughter back unharmed, as do Irene Lomakin's parents. But we need time to raise funds and we also need to know the girls are safe and unharmed." Which was now the kidnappers' problem.

Was the man on the phone in the place where he was holding the girls? He couldn't be that stupid and yet stranger things had happened.

Max could hope. He waited silently on the open line. The longer the call went on, the more likely the FBI or local authorities would be able to trace it back to at least one cell tower. However, he didn't want the guy to hang up.

After a few more seconds, Max decided to reengage. "The ambassador doesn't have ten million dollars, but I know she has ten thousand US dollars in cash available right now. *Today.*"

FBI headquarters had couriered that money to the embassy last night to use as a potential tracking method. The bag contained an electronic beacon, and the serial numbers of all the bills were logged into a system that allowed agents to track the distribution of the money. The money bag actually contained thirty thousand dollars, but Max was a negotiator and never started at his highest number. "I can bring that ten thousand US dollars to a drop-off point right now. Then you let the girls go, and we can all go home and enjoy the holidays."

Ten grand was a low anchor, but one that might be tempting enough for kidnappers already overwhelmed by the magnitude of what they'd done. Someone with regrets might say *fuck it*. Ten grand for grabbing a couple of girls off the street and holding them overnight was a good day's work, especially in a country where the US dollar had value, and poverty was rife.

"Ten thousand?" The man sounded pissed. "That is all they are worth to you?"

Lowering the man's expectations to something that might actually be reasonable was part of the process. Why kidnappers across the globe always demanded ten million as a starting point was a product of watching too many Hollywood movies and certain poorly implemented UN resolutions.

"Catherine Dickerson and her husband are not wealthy people, but they will do anything they can to get their daughter and her friend safely home. Before we can deliver any money, we'll need to know both girls are well and that I'm talking to the right person."

The man made an impatient sound. "I will call again tomorrow morning. Be ready to pay a lot more than ten thousand dollars or I will send them both back to their parents, piece by piece." The man rang off.

Max stared at the phone which had gone dead. Clicked off his recording app. Texted Eban that the call had ended.

"You think it was wise to argue with him?" Lucy asked, her eyes fixed on the road ahead. They were well out of La Boca now. On their way to the center of town.

"It's a case of wearing the kidnappers' mindset down to a more realistic number."

"You said the US government did not pay ransoms," she said pointedly.

"And yet here I am, negotiating the deal."

Lucy huffed out a quiet laugh.

Max called CNU and passed on the cell number and carrier information and uploaded the audio recording to the cloud where Eban could access it and make sure it was passed on to the right people for analysis. From now on, the FBI would be able to record calls and use this number to talk to the kidnappers, presuming the locals didn't have a problem with that.

So far, they seemed happy to pass the buck on the negotiation front, probably so they weren't blamed if anything bad happened to the girls. The political fallout from the kidnap and murder of the US Ambassador's daughter would be massive.

Max put those thoughts out of his mind. He would do everything in his power to rescue both girls and not just because Kristen's mom was a diplomat.

"Do you want to go back to your hotel or the embassy?" Lucy asked, speeding up Av 9 de Julio, obviously having taken the scenic route to La Boca and now the fastest route home.

He dug around in his pocket and pulled out the other evidence bag. He slid the ring out onto the lip of the envelope so Lucy could see. "Recognize this?"

She glanced at it, and her expression hardened. "It looks like one of Kristen's. She wears a stack of them on two different fingers, but I might be mistaken."

Max slid the thin ring back into the paper bag and put it into his pocket. "If you're heading to the embassy, drop me there, please. Otherwise, drop me somewhere I can grab a cab."

"I'm heading back to the office. I still have a lot to do."

And that was mainly thanks to him.

"I'm sorry for taking up so much of your time today, Lucy. I'll brief the ambassador and then clean up a bunch of loose ends." He held up the cell phone in the plastic bag. "This explains why they didn't call before now. The cell wasn't receiving a signal while in the old lady's freezer."

"You think she'll be all right?" Lucy's fingers clenched tightly around the leather steering wheel. "Abigail Blanco?"

"I hope so. The men who chased us might have not seen us enter her house." He couldn't get the woman protection without revealing her name, and he wouldn't break his promise to her.

"I'll get the kidnappers' cell number rerouted to a desk in the Legat's office so that the Dickersons are completely removed from the negotiation process. Last thing we need is the family going rogue. The FBI will be recording everything from now on. Then I need to courier the cell and the ring to the lab at Quantico overnight so they can run forensic tests."

"You're not going to hand them in to the local police?" Lucy's stare was divided between him and the road.

He noticed suddenly how pretty she was with her hair drawn back and small tendrils escaping to softly frame her face.

He shook his head. "Local police already processed the crime scene and...honestly? I don't want them shaking down the area and finding Abigail. There's nothing to be gained unless we have some reason to believe the old woman is involved."

"How do we know she's not?"

"We don't, but her DNA will probably be on that cell and also inside that Ziplock. I'll ask my colleagues at CNU to dig into her background without alerting Argentine authorities. Confirm her ID. See who she's related to and to keep an eye on her bank balance."

Lucy pressed her lips together as if saddened but resigned to the fact the woman could be involved in this plot and playing them for fools.

They arrived at the gates of the embassy. They both showed their passes to security, and she drove inside the embassy grounds and pulled up in a designated parking spot and cut the engine.

He opened the door.

"Don't forget the handgun under my seat," Lucy said wryly.

"I want to send that to Quantico too. See if the lab techs can pull anything off it, or if ballistics can link it to any known crimes in the area, but I doubt that's going to fly with Legat Powell."

"You don't think the local police can be trusted with that either?"

Max laughed softly. "I don't know. I hate to let go of evidence. I'll ask Powell if he has any trustworthy contacts in the police force here. I'm not keen to explain about our run-in or how I got the weapon. Are you?"

Her eyes widened as she seemed to recall the way she'd dropkicked that man with the knife. It had been pretty bad-ass, but it also didn't fit with the woman in the ugly, brown suit.

"Not really," she admitted softly. "How do you plan to get the gun through security?"

"I don't suppose you have any surgical gloves or large-sized FBI evidence bags on you, do you?"

"As it happens…" Lucy canted her head and fluttered her lashes, "no."

Max grinned at her. "Then I'll call Brian Powell to come down here with those supplies." He checked his watch. It was well after five. "Or whoever is left in the office."

Immediately, her demeanor changed from open smiles to blank features.

He remembered the man's scathing comment earlier and the way he'd leered at her when she'd turned up in spandex. Then he recalled the rather awesome self-defense moves Lucy had pulled in the alleyway. A sheet of icy calm settled over him.

If Lucy was the victim of a past sexual assault, it would explain so much.

"I know I asked you earlier, but do you have an actual issue with Powell?"

She raised her chin and held his gaze. "He's not my favorite person."

"Did he ever give you cause to worry about your personal safety?"

"Who? Brian?" Her snort was derisive. "No. He's an egotistical jerk who's an old-school sexist. But he's never given me reason to be worried that he might hurt me. Why?"

"No reason. Okay then." He fished the weapon carefully from under the seat. He'd already touched the grip, which was unfortunate but necessary under the circumstances.

She looked at him holding the weapon, then toward the side entrance where US Marines guarded the door.

"You can't stand in the parking lot clutching that thing."

"Because I'm Black?"

"Well, that definitely doesn't help, but they'd be suspicious of anyone. It's their job."

She had a point.

Her fingers ran around the leather steering wheel. "How about I leave you my car keys so you can wait here until one of your colleagues arrives. Hand the keys in to security when you're done, and I'll pick them up on my way out."

She dangled the keys in the air until he opened his palm. She dropped them.

"Thanks. Hey, I don't suppose you fancy a drink and some food when you're done…"

She gawked at him.

Max raised his hands. He didn't want her getting the wrong idea. "Purely platonic to celebrate the holiday." He wasn't looking to start anything down here. His life was complicated enough, plus Lucy might have a boyfriend or even a family in Buenos Aires. He knew nothing about her. Not to mention he wasn't interested in her except as a colleague, but he found himself hoping she'd say yes.

She held herself still as she watched him, searching his face for the true intentions behind the words. Then she said almost regretfully, "I'm sorry. I'm probably not going to be done for a few hours."

"Me neither."

She opened her mouth to probably say no, but he laughed and climbed out of his seat to stretch his legs. He turned and leaned down to look at her inside the car.

"It's no sweat, Lucy." He kept his voice level and calm, wondering why he'd even asked, except there was something about her that intrigued him. She was interesting. He enjoyed spending time with her. "I appreciate everything you've done for me today, especially that dropkick."

A look of surprise swept over her features, and then she choked on a laugh. "Well, it was a pretty awesome dropkick."

"Damn straight it was," Max agreed.

"Sorry," she sighed tiredly and leaned her head against the back rest. "It's been a long day, and I don't socialize much."

No mention of a husband or kids. No ring on her finger. He frowned. Why come on a foreign service posting if you didn't socialize much? He didn't ask. Patience and silence were two of his best friends.

She dug into her purse and placed her business card on the dash. "Call me when you finish up tonight. If I'm still around, I might take you up on that drink. Then again, I might not. It is Christmas, after all."

"No pressure either way. I can get a cab back to the hotel."

She got out of the car, walked away, then called over her shoulder. "Don't forget to lock up my baby, Hawthorne. I don't want to have to hurt you."

Max grinned and tried not to admire her figure as she headed into the embassy. He really was not interested in Lucy Aston for anything except work. Likelihood was, he'd need her help again soon, whether she liked it or not. Least he could do was buy her a drink.

CHAPTER NINE

I RENE COULD HEAR the men arguing about her again, though they'd been quiet for most of the day. They'd put a cloth bag over her head, but the ties had come loose, and she'd been able to lift it up and look around. They'd chained her to a massive cast-iron radiator in a bedroom that was empty except for a double bed with a bare, stained mattress that had stuffing falling out of it. Mouse droppings covered the floor.

She was careful not to jingle her chains too much as she had to assume they might hear her the same way she could hear them. She wanted them to forget about her existence if at all possible.

The floor was unforgiving hardwood which meant her butt hurt. This room was bigger than her bedroom at home. Ceilings were higher, the edges trimmed with crumbling plaster cornices. Walls were water stained, some lath and plaster showing where chunks had fallen off. The windows had wooden shutters pulled closed. Some of the slats were broken, and afternoon light seeped through. There was another wooden door on the other side of the room. She didn't know if it led to a closet or maybe a bathroom, which she desperately needed as she'd been holding it for hours.

Last night, they'd drugged her, and she was pretty sure the water they'd given her that morning had contained a sedative because she'd slept for most of the day.

Sounds of birds chirping pierced the quiet, along with the occasional distant drone of a car, suggesting the house was set back a ways from the road. Too far away for anyone to hear her scream, except for the men who'd taken her in the first place.

She hunched over, a shiver working over the bare skin of her arms and down her spine.

She wished she hadn't gone after the men yesterday and yet someone had had to try to stop them taking Kristen. Everyone around them had scattered like roaches. *Cowards.* If all of them had attacked the men and tried to free Kristen, they might have rescued her and run away.

Or they might have all been shot dead in the street.

Irene gnawed her lip. She didn't want to die.

Her parents would be freaking out.

Dammit.

She clenched her jaw together, trying to hold back tears, knowing how badly they'd be dealing with this. Her mother was always stressed out trying to raise three daughters when they had to relocate every five years because her dad's company was always moving him around. Her mom had stopped trying to make friends outside her dad's work. She struggled with depression. Sometimes she used the contents of a bottle to cope. Irene didn't blame her, but she wanted both her parents to recognize they had issues to deal with.

And now this.

It would tear them apart.

Irene was used to moving around, but she was ready to go to college and make her own decisions about where she lived from now on. She liked Argentina but wanted to go back to the UK to study. At least she had, until yesterday. Now…now she wasn't so sure. She simply wanted to go home to her family and let them keep her safe.

The sharp metal edge of handcuffs pressed against the thin skin of her wrists. The red marks somehow made this whole thing seem more real. Irene's throat went tight.

She didn't want to die.

But it was a distinct possibility.

Her life circumstances had done a complete one eighty. She'd gone from looking forward to Christmas to wondering if she was going to be raped and murdered overnight.

She closed her eyes. According to what she'd overheard, one man wanted to rape and then kill her and dump her body in a completely different part of the country to draw suspicion away from where they were holding Kristen—as Kristen was the one they'd actually wanted. Another man argued that led to another potential trail of evidence if someone spotted the vehicle or if the police discovered trace evidence on her body.

On. Her. Body.

She shuddered. They were arguing about her like she wasn't even human. One man said the police never needed to find her body. Another argued she could be worth something too.

She latched onto that. Her dad's company had kidnap insurance. She knew they'd paid ransoms in other countries in the past. It happened all the time.

The idea gave her a small sliver of hope. She had value—if only in the form of what they could get for her.

Slow, steady footsteps scraped along the hallway outside the door. She pulled the hood lower and threw the strings over her shoulder. The door opened, and she bowed her head.

Subservience might not come naturally to her, but she would learn it quick if it could keep her alive.

The footsteps came closer. A tap of a foot against her knee made her jolt.

"Aquí. Comida." *Here. Food.* Then the sound of something touching the floor. "¿Qué? ¿No habla español?"

He asked her if she spoke Spanish which she did, thanks to Ms. Mair at school. Irene had an affinity for it, unlike German which felt like trying to talk with a cactus stuck in her mouth. He didn't need to know that.

"I'm sorry. I don't understand what you are saying, señor."

Hands tugged at the ties behind her neck. The man seemed unconcerned by the fact they were already loose.

"I'll tell you what I told the other one." He spoke in English with a heavy accent and weary tone.

He didn't seem to like what he was doing to her. Maybe she could persuade him to let her go?

"You can remove your hood when you are alone. But if you see my face or any of my comrades' faces, I will poke out your eyes with the tip of my knife without hesitation. I will not risk being identified. I will not risk going to prison because some girl was defiant enough to disobey my instructions. You were not part of the plan. Your death will mean little to anyone here."

Blood drained from Irene's head, and she felt dizzy. The good news was that Kristen must still be alive and possibly somewhere close by. The bad news was a man had threatened to blind her and considered her nothing more than an inconvenience. She refrained from pointing out that she would have been happy not to have been kidnapped.

She shook her head. "Don't worry. I'll keep the hood on."

He grunted like he didn't believe her.

"My father's work has kidnap insurance on all its employees and their families. I bet they'll pay for me. They won't involve the authorities."

He laughed. His voice gruff though not unkind. "The Americans already know, and they're who concern me, not the British. Also, if a captive tells the kidnappers they have kidnap insurance, sometimes that breaks the rules and means the insurance is null and void, *mi hija*."

Irene flinched at the endearment. It was something her father called her on the rare occasions he was home.

"Best not to mention it to anyone else that you told me, si? Now, I expect you need to use the toilet?" he said as if that were something normal to discuss between a stranger and a teenage girl.

She cringed but nodded. Thank god she didn't have her period, but what happened when she did? Her mouth went dry, and her insides clenched. What if she was here for that long? She'd read stories of people being kept for months, years even. Some kept as hostages but also as sex slaves.

The idea made her gag. She put it out of her mind. She needed to take it one thing at a time. She needed the bathroom. She couldn't hold it any longer, and she did not want the added humiliation of peeing her pants. That's all she needed to think about right now.

He unlocked the padlock that secured the handcuffs to the thick, heavy chain. She rubbed her wrists even though they were still cuffed together. He helped her to her feet and walked her toward the second door in the room. He went inside, and she could smell the stale odor of an unused bathroom.

He walked her all the way to the toilet.

"I will stand outside the open door. I will not look unless I think you are going to try anything foolish."

"I won't do anything foolish." She heard him walk away.

"You already did."

The words stung.

"If you try to escape, I will take away all your clothes and let the men downstairs do what they want to you. After that, you'll be lucky if you can walk at all."

Irene took a huge, shuddering breath. "I won't try to escape. I promise."

"Do what you need to do. Do it quickly while my patience lasts."

She eased the hood away from her chest enough to look down at her feet and see the toilet seat. The toilet bowl was stained a rusty color with disuse. There was no cistern visible. If she had to guess, it would be above her head and there would be an old-fashioned pull chain off to one side, used to flush. Her grandparents had had a similar one in their old house. The memory made her chest ache. She pushed the thoughts away.

It seemed clean though. She quickly did what she needed to do and washed her hands and dried them on her jeans. She flailed around until she hit the pull chain and tugged on the ancient plumbing.

"Why did you do it?" the man asked from the other room. "Come after your friend that way?"

Irene swallowed. What would happen if she said the wrong thing? Did it matter? "She's my friend. She's a good person. No one deserves to be grabbed off the street that way." A sob caught at the back of her throat, but she pushed it down and made sure the hood fully covered her face as she walked gingerly toward the man with her cuffed hands outstretched in front of her. "Is she okay? Could we be kept together, do you think? Might be easier to look after us if we were together."

He didn't answer, and she knew better than to push.

"My father is the director of operations for South America. His company has offices all over the world. He's an important man." She might not be the daughter of an ambassador, but she was worth something, surely?

The man grabbed her elbow and led her back across the wooden floor and forced her to sit down beside the radiator where he reconnected the chain to the handcuffs, making sure the cuffs were tight around her wrists. So much for her dreams of slipping free of their metal grasp.

He held on to her hands. "Someone will take you to the bathroom again later this evening. They may even feed you."

Who? Who would take her if not this man? She shivered. What else would they do to her?

"Drink the water I brought you. Keep quiet. Don't make any trouble, and you might survive this. If you try to escape or disobey…" His pause was dramatic. "I won't be able to protect you anymore."

He let her go, and she immediately felt bereft. Was this sudden attachment to him Stockholm syndrome?

"What about Kristen?" she whispered fiercely. "Couldn't she be in here with me? Wouldn't it be easier to keep us together?"

The man walked away.

And Irene would have given everything she owned to have not tried to save Kristen yesterday. To have not been abducted with her friend. Hot tears welled up and rolled down her face.

It proved that, despite her pissy attitude, she was as big a coward as Gemma. Worse, she was also stupid. So stupid she'd been kidnapped even though she hadn't been the target. So stupid she was now chained to a radiator while strangers discussed how best to dispose of her body after they'd assaulted her so badly, she wouldn't be able to walk. Irene leaned back against the unbreakable radiator and let the tears fall.

She needed to figure out a way out of this mess but, right now, all she could do was despair.

———————————

LUCY WAS HOT, sweaty, and grouchy as she headed back to her desk. Her muscles ached from her rough and tumble in La Boca. Worse than that, spending time with Max Hawthorne had left her feeling exhilarated and had reminded her of the good old days. Of living life to the fullest and enjoying every minute.

God, she missed that life. She'd been so naive. So arrogant and untouchable.

She felt different today. Lighter. Confident. Free. Her hair was pulled off her face, along with it, a heavy weight. She wasn't wearing her fake reading glasses. She could feel the rigid steel infusing her spine and the way her shoulders were pulled back, and her chin lifted as she strode along.

Damn, this was all wrong.

This was not who she was anymore. Lucy had spent months being a mouse, and she wasn't about to waste all that effort and thankless humility simply because a good-looking guy had arrived on the scene and treated her like an equal.

Max Hawthorne wasn't even interested in her romantically. Even the offer of a drink was only a way of unwinding after a long day.

And that was *fine*.

Before this posting, she had vast amounts of experience dealing with people coming on to her. Today, even the brief notion had surprised the shit out of her. She no longer felt attractive. She no longer felt worthy of anyone's attention. She frowned into space because that was messed up and, yet, here she was, suppressing her sexuality and her innate desires and doing her best to imitate a female eunuch.

None of that mattered right now.

She sank into her cubicle chair and slumped forward on her desk, holding her face in her hands. Her desk was innocuous and impersonal. No family photographs. No pictures of pets. Not even a dying plant. The only splash of color was a blue ID tag from a conference she'd attended with the ambassador that hung off the edge of her computer monitor.

Her hand found the band holding up her hair, and she released the heavy mass, and it fell around her face with the weight of shackles. It smothered her features and made her look unkempt like Argentina Lucy usually was.

Not that anyone was around to care.

If only Kristen hadn't been kidnapped.

But there were a lot of things over the last fifteen months that she wished hadn't happened and wishing hadn't changed a damn thing.

She released a sigh and fished her glasses out of her bag, slipping them on. Her gaze caught on a sealed manilla envelope in her in-tray that hadn't been there earlier. She frowned, picked it up, and flipped it over. It had her name typed on the outside. She opened it and pulled out a large eight-by-eleven-inch photograph.

Blood drained from her head, and a wave of vertigo slammed into her so hard she swayed in her seat. Her fingers shook, and she tried to swallow the bile that crawled up her throat.

The image was black and white. A woman crawling over a man who lay naked on the bed, her fingers curled around his erection, her lips wrapped around the head. Her facial features were largely hidden by her long blonde hair.

The man was gorgeous. Every inch of his glorious, ripped body on show. And he'd known it.

Sergio Raminsky.

Fucker.

She laughed like a maniac and smothered the sound with her fist.

He was literally a fucker.

She hadn't known his identity when she'd bumped into him in a bookstore in DC. He'd claimed to be a tourist, and she'd foolishly believed him. Looking back, she'd been an easy mark. He'd charmed her, fucked her, and then dumped her, as soon as he had enough incriminating photographs to satisfy his Kremlin masters.

The photograph brought back a sea of unwanted memories. It was one thing to know the images were probably in existence and another to be confronted by the reality.

How many people had seen these? How many more images existed where she could be easily identified? Boris Yahontov's face swam into her mind. He'd definitely seen something recently, hence his comments at the party. How many others? Had he sent this? Why? And why now?

She really would need a drink later.

This was supposed to be a reminder that they owned her. That they knew about her disastrous liaison with Raminsky and intended to use that *krompromat* to control her every move. It wasn't the first time they'd contacted her. She'd given them everything they'd asked for so far, so why this new, overt threat?

There was no way anything she'd given them would have aided in Kristen's and Irene's kidnapping, but still, doubt found a way to creep in. She wouldn't breathe easy until the girls were both home safe.

Footsteps sounded off the parquet flooring in the corridor outside. Miranda. Lucy recognized the pin-hammer tap of the woman's gorgeous but impractical heels. Lucy slid the photograph into the envelope as Miranda came into the room.

"Oh, good. You're back." Her boss smiled at her. "Did you collate the information on Kristen's friends for the FBI negotiator like the ambassador requested?"

Lucy stretched her neck to the side to ease out a kink. "Not yet. I only just returned from ferrying him to La Boca."

"This is important," Miranda explained with excruciating patience. "The FBI wants to interview all Kristen's friends in case they have any clues in regard to the abduction."

Lucy almost snapped that she understood that. She wasn't an idiot. Then she jolted. The excitement of having outrun an armed gang followed by receiving the photograph had thrown her off her game, and she needed to regain her balance. "I'm so sorry, Miranda. I'll gather all the information we have on hand, and I'll get that to SSA Hawthorne in the next half hour. From what he said, I doubt he plans to talk to them tonight." She checked her watch, surprised to see it was already after eight. Where had the day gone?

Miranda came closer. "Are you okay?" Her blue eyes were wide with sympathy.

Lucy blinked. She must look worse than she felt. "I'm fine. Really. I forgot to eat today with everything going on."

"Well," the woman huffed out a quiet laugh, "it's not like both of us couldn't afford to lose a few pounds."

Hurt sliced through Lucy, but she was careful not to show it. Miranda was pencil-thin. No one in their right mind would ever accuse her of being overweight.

Her boss's gaze ran over Lucy's form. Miranda frowned. "Although you look as if you just worked out." Her voice revealed confusion.

"The negotiator asked me to change as he wanted to blend in with the tourists downtown and—"

"Oh, now I understand." Miranda laughed. "One of these days I'm going to take you shopping to some of my favorite boutiques. Men are going to fall at your feet."

Lucy had to look at the desk to hide her expression. Miranda didn't mean to be offensive or condescending, but she did consider herself far superior to Lucy when it came to style and fashion. Lucy's clothes were two sizes too big to hide her figure and avoid attention. And, while she might not be twig thin like Miranda, Lucy was fit and strong, and she liked her body.

She glanced at the envelope holding the black and white print of her giving a Russian operative a blowjob.

At least, she *had* liked her body until she'd realized how many people were likely to see it without her permission, and that realization still made her want to puke.

"Well." Miranda crinkled her nose. "Get those details to

the FBI agent and go home and get some food and sleep. Be back here early in the morning in case there's any new developments in the case. I plan to sleep in the spare room of the ambassador's suite until Kristen is recovered so I'll be here overnight if Catherine needs anything."

"Okay, thanks." Lucy forced away her earlier hurt. Miranda wasn't to know why Lucy behaved the way she did. Her boss had always been kind and helpful even if she was demanding. Lucy didn't mind demanding. She liked to be busy and involved and could do most of her assignments with one hand tied behind her back. "I'll do that. Call me if you need anything else."

Miranda touched her shoulder and gently squeezed her arm. "Good job today, Lucy."

"You too. Night." Lucy's fingers curled around the envelope. She couldn't imagine the reaction of the people she worked with if they ever saw these—or her parents, for that matter. Why had the Russians sent her the photograph now, though?

She pulled it out again, ignoring the image, and turned it over. A time and place were written on the back. They wanted a meet.

It wasn't even encrypted, but then she didn't have any of their cyphers so it would have been useless anyway.

They still didn't trust her.

In the past, she'd received instructions via a letter that appeared anonymously in her mailbox at home. This was bolder. They must want something from her. Something more substantial than on previous occasions. Had they organized Kristen's kidnapping? As a distraction? Or was it an unhappy coincidence that they intended to exploit for their needs?

Either was possible.

She slipped the envelope into her purse and went to work finding contact information for all Kristen's friends, adding any personal details she could remember. She collated the school info Max had requested and also emailed Gemma asking what happened to Kristen's belongings after the kidnapping. Then she sent all the data to Max Hawthorne's email address.

It was dark throughout most of the building by the time she headed to the bathroom to change into her office clothes again. She stared at her drab reflection in the mirror, suppressing the grim smile that wanted to spill over her lips. She looked like shit. That photograph had been a kick in the gut, and the proof was scrawled all over her strained features.

She drew in a deep breath. She could deal with this. This was what she'd trained for. This was what she'd sacrificed for. She couldn't waver from her path now.

Her cell rang.

It was Max. She hesitated before answering and then realized his invitation gave her the perfect excuse for going downtown again tonight.

"Lucy?"

"Yes?" she answered, ignoring the magic of his voice.

"I'm about to head to the hotel. Can I buy you that quick bite to eat before we both keel over from lack of food and exhaustion as a small thank you for all your help today or does your earlier refusal stand? No worries if you want to head home."

"Actually, I'm starving so that sounds great." Did he think she needed to lose a few pounds too? She didn't ask. "Meet me at the entrance in five minutes."

She hung up and gave her frumpy reflection one last look and then blew herself a kiss. This version of Lucy was as worthy as the confident blonde who attracted male interest so very easily. More so in fact. This Lucy was calculated and cunning whereas the other Lucy was gullible enough to fall for the oldest spy trick in the book. The honeytrap.

Old Lucy had thought she was smarter than everyone else in the room. New Lucy knew with certainty that she wasn't even close. At least she wasn't a trusting fool anymore.

The photograph in Lucy's bag was proof of her mistakes. Her mind shied away from the other images they probably had of Old Lucy. She didn't want to imagine how many of them had jerked off to photographs and videos of her making love to that rat bastard who'd died a year ago today.

Her throat tightened and not just with humiliation. With grief too. She'd fallen hard for Sergio Raminsky. Built fairytales around their future. Those dreams had turned out to be foolish fantasy that had shattered when faced with reality. Worse, they'd compromised her in the eyes of an enemy foreign government.

Raminsky and his Kremlin bosses had left a wake of victims behind them. Lucy wasn't only fighting for herself, she was fighting for all of them. For every other person duped by the man's beautiful dark eyes and that deep, sexy accent.

She saw clear parallels between Raminsky's masculine beauty and Max Hawthorne's. She had absolutely no intention of acting on her attraction to him—not that she imagined for a second he'd be interested in her dowdy self.

More fool him.

She applied some red-brown eye shadow that emphasized the hollows of her eye sockets in a bad way and dabbed a smokey gray under her eyes. She looked like death warmed up.

Perfect.

She snapped the small box shut with a degree of satisfaction and tossed it in her bag. Time to go to work.

CHAPTER TEN

MAX DROPPED HIS stuff back in his room while Lucy saved them a table in the bar.

He quickly changed into a pair of jeans and a t-shirt. The place was swanky, but they were only grabbing a quick bite to eat so he didn't need to wear his suit. Board shorts would be a tad too casual though. He was starving, and he definitely owed Lucy a drink after everything she'd helped him with today. He was glad she'd said yes to coming out. He hated eating alone, especially on Christmas.

He found her in the far corner of the Oak Bar ensconced in a black leather chair. She sat with her back to the wall. The room was wood paneled, and exposed wooden beams lined the ceiling. The place smelled of power and opulence, whiskey and oak. An old boys' club. He wondered if this was where the Nazis had hung out after the war. Probably best not to mention Hitler.

"Did you get served yet?" Max took his seat beside Lucy.

Her lips pinched in amusement as she jerked her chin toward the barman who was taking the order of three women at the bar. The women were all gorgeous, in their mid-twenties, wearing party clothes, with an air of celebration about them. They were all dark-haired, possibly sisters. One of them caught Max's eye and knocked the elbow of the woman beside her.

Max turned away and found Lucy staring at him with a small smile on her lips.

"I bet you're wishing you hadn't invited me now."

Max gave her a frown. "Why?"

"Oh, please. I've totally ruined any chance you might have had for a *very* Merry Christmas."

Jesus. Did he look like he chased after women at every opportunity? "What makes you think I don't have a wife or girlfriend back home?"

Her mouth opened a little in shock. "*Oh, man.* That would actually make perfect sense for a guy who looks like you do, but it doesn't always make a difference when that sort of opportunity presents itself." Her gaze landed on the three women who were all checking him out now.

The heat of a blush rose up in his cheeks. Damn. "As it happens, I'm not dating anyone right now, but if I were, I would never cheat on her. And I'm not looking to hook up during a case. And besides all that, why the hell would you put yourself down that way?"

"How do you mean?"

"By assuming I'd invite you for a drink and then dump you the moment someone else turned up?"

Lucy sobered. "You're right. I'm sorry. That was all way too personal."

"That's not what I said."

"I know, but it was." Her lips quirked to one side. "I guess I'm a little out of sorts after someone told me I could do with losing weight, which made me feel particularly grumpy. Aside from making me want to eat every cake in Buenos Aires, it made me angry and petty. My comments were inappropriate.

My apologies." She looked down at the table. If she'd had a drink, she would have been hiding her face in it.

"Whoever said that was rude as hell." Obviously, they hadn't seen Lucy in yoga pants because Lucy had a perfect body. Not that he could say that out loud without revealing that he'd noticed her perfect body, which wouldn't be a good idea.

He wanted to ask her why she downplayed her looks and why she let people walk all over her, but that wouldn't help either of them decompress after a hard day. "Forget them. It's Christmas, and I reckon we get to enjoy at least an hour of it."

"You don't feel guilty having a beer when Kristen and Irene are still in danger?"

There was curiosity rather than criticism in her tone and it was a valid question, so he answered her honestly.

"I have active cases three-hundred and sixty-five days of the year. I need to compartmentalize my job from my basic need for downtime now and then. It's a form of dissociation that means we law enforcement types don't burn out and all go crazy and quit." He glanced around for the waiter. He was starving. "It's not that I am not concerned about those girls. I am. If I thought I could go out and rescue or help them this minute, then I would be out there doing it. But when a case is in progress or I simply need food or sleep, I have to take it and forgive myself for being human. It allows me to be sharp and focused when I need to be."

The waiter finally came over as Lucy quietly digested what he'd said. Max rarely bothered to justify his existence but, much to his surprise, he liked Lucy. He wanted her to gain a little confidence. Although the woman dropkicking knife-wielding assailants in the barrio didn't need a crash course in confidence.

The character traits didn't quite mesh. He needed to check out her background but knew she'd have had to pass stringent background checks to get into the Foreign Service and regular assessments by the Diplomatic Security Service to stay there.

Maybe the ambassador was a bully behind closed doors and that made Lucy act so downtrodden at work. He didn't know and, frankly, was almost too tired to care. He ordered a beer and *tostado de jamón y queso con ensalada verde o papas fritas*. Pricey for what amounted to a cheese and ham toasty and fries, but he hadn't eaten all day. Lucy ordered a glass of wine and *Empanadas*.

He raised his glass. "Thanks for all your help today."

Lucy chinked her glass to his, but her expression was wry. The women on the other side of the room were giggling and staring over at them.

"Ha. They just heard the accent. You might not get out of here alive." She sipped her wine. "I might not get out of here alive."

He felt his cheeks grow warm again. Damn. He was not the type of guy to blush.

Then she asked him the question everyone asked. A question he never really truly answered. "Why the FBI?"

He shrugged. "Like I told you earlier, I was a dual national. After I left the SAS, I got a gig training FBI agents in close-quarter combat techniques with another Special Forces guy I know in Arizona. One of the agents I trained turned out to be a recruiter, and he wanted me for the Hostage Rescue Team. Unfortunately for him, I'd already decided my days of kicking down doors were finished."

He worked a kink out of his shoulder. He needed a hot

shower and a few hours' sleep. "I have another former-SAS friend who works the K&R circuit for an insurance company out of London. He'd been trying to persuade me to come work with him for years because he thought I'd be good at it. I guess that idea clicked inside me because I decided to pursue being a negotiator for the FBI."

"You're what? Mid-thirties? And already on your second illustrious career?"

"Depends on whether or not we're counting the modeling gigs I did to get myself through university?"

"Wait. What?" She guffawed and gazed up at the ceiling. "Of course, you were a model."

He laughed. "It's not as cool as it sounds. I was mortally embarrassed by the whole thing and never told anyone when I was a student. When I was accepted into the SAS, one of the instructors outed me by plastering my locker with pictures he'd somehow tracked down and torn out of magazines. I don't know how he found out or got the pictures. *That* was, without doubt, the most embarrassing day of my life."

It felt good to remember the fun times of being a soldier. The laughter. The camaraderie. Not the blood and despair.

"In that case, you're a very lucky man." Her lips twitched.

"Why? What's your most embarrassing story?"

The smile evaporated.

He'd said the wrong thing. Thankfully, their food arrived, and he was so hungry he was ready to gnaw on the table. They both ordered another drink and consumed their dinner like they were ravenous. Neither saying a word until their plates were clean.

Lucy dabbed her mouth with her napkin and grinned at him, and he was once again treated to her face lighting up in a smile. And he felt like he'd been let into a secret. For some reason, Lucy Aston generally hid her inner sparkle.

Max was a live-and-let-live kind of guy as long as no one was breaking the law. It wasn't his business why she'd made the choices she had, but he enjoyed the glimpses of something more interesting that snaked beneath the bland surface, glimpses the others appeared not to notice.

"Do you think she's still alive?" she asked suddenly. "They," she corrected herself quickly. "Do you think *they're* still alive?"

He pushed his empty plate away and pulled in a deep breath. "Yes, I do. The phone call put my mind at ease that this was a kidnap for ransom and not one for political reasons, which is what I most feared. If the hostage takers wanted the release of prisoners in the US or something else similarly impossible to deliver, then I'd be more worried."

"Do you think they'll harm them?" Lucy asked.

Max swallowed the last of his beer. Even though he'd like nothing better than to have another he didn't let himself. If he was called out in the middle of the night, he'd need his wits.

"It all depends on the type of men who took them and who's in charge. How the girls behave. The longer it goes on, the more opportunities the hostage takers have, so I want to keep the girls' welfare high in the talking points every time they make contact. I want to make the kidnappers actively care about the girls' health and wellbeing."

"How do you do this all the time? I get that you give yourself downtime to deal with the necessities, but how do you cope with the constant uncertainty? The fear that what you say and do might get a hostage killed."

He actually didn't think about it. Someone had to deal

with the kidnappers, and he and his colleagues were among the best negotiators in the world.

Maybe it was because he knew these abductions were happening around the world whether he was on the job or not. Had been going on since the dawn of human history. And life as a soldier had shown him how unstable the world was. Society clung to a thin veneer of civilization that could crumble at any time. He wanted to be someone who contributed to the stability of the democracy not someone who fed the chaos. That had evolved into a life of service and applying his intelligence and integrity to every case. Doing the best he was able to do. Saving those he could and helping prosecute the rest.

"We have some of the best people in the business working at the Crisis Negotiation Unit. We don't get everyone back and we don't always get them back unharmed"—he thought about Darby O'Roarke who they'd rescued from a volcanic island in Indonesia that summer—"but we know the most effective techniques to use, and we never stop trying to refine those techniques. We never stop trying to get people home—even when we're in a bar having a drink."

Lucy leaned toward him, clearly intrigued. "What do you mean?"

"Well, hopefully the things we've set up and the conversation we had with the kidnapper are already working in the hostages' favor."

Fairy lights twinkled, reflected in the crystal glasses on the table. Lucy was staring at him through those unflattering spectacles she wore as if she expected more.

"The Crisis Negotiation Unit is good at what it does. My colleagues are good at what they do. We have a lot more experience than most of the kidnappers we encounter, and we've seen almost every scenario before, but we also know to expect the unexpected." The black swans. "That experience, combined with the massive resources of the FBI, often allows us to bring people home if there's any reasonable chance of doing so."

Bargaining with the likes of ISIS had been rough, but kidnappings in that part of the world, at least in the early days, had also often been about money. And many of those kidnappers were now in custody. The Department of Justice had a long arm and an eidetic memory.

The ladies at the bar were flirting with the barman again. Max had definitely missed his chance there, but he wasn't bothered. He was enjoying spending time with Lucy.

"Do you think the police will attempt a rescue?" she asked.

"I hope not, but probably." Max noticed the widening of Lucy's eyes and explained, "The most dangerous time for any hostage is during the abduction itself or during a 'rescue' operation. Bullets are flying, and the hostages are as likely to be killed by friendly fire as by hostage takers. Negotiation takes longer and can be time consuming and frustrating, but we get consistently better results than armed intervention. I know it's hard to wait when someone is worried about a loved one."

"Kristen's a good kid. I'd hate to see her or Irene hurt by this." Lucy checked the time on her Fitbit. "Wow. I better get home. I have to be back at work by seven." She went to open her wallet, and he closed his fingers over hers.

He was unprepared for the sizzle of electricity that arced between them, but he was experienced enough not to show it. "My treat, remember?"

She nodded and quickly rose. "Thanks."

"Let me walk you to your car."

"I'm safe enough. I valet parked, and this is a good area."

"If that were true, I wouldn't be here." The reminder that two young women had been snatched a dozen yards from the front of this hotel in broad daylight hung in the air between them. Max still wanted to know how the kidnappers had tracked the women. He'd spoken to the ambassador earlier with a brief update. Confirmed the ring probably belonged to Kristen. He'd arranged for all the items to be securely couriered to Quantico. It had been too late to act on the other information Lucy had gathered for him.

Lucy's gaze was unflinching. "I can take care of myself."

He thought back to the flying kick she'd executed perfectly earlier that day and how it didn't fit with the woman from the embassy. "Where'd you learn to do that?"

She smiled. She knew what he was talking about. "I spent years in after-school martial arts programs, and I still train at a dojo."

"Then the guy who tried to grab you today was a brave man. He just didn't know it."

Lucy laughed and finished her water. "Don't let the ambassador find out about that. She can send me back any time she wants. I don't want to have to crawl home to my parents and admit I failed at my job."

That explained a lot. He knew all about letting parents down. His mother still hadn't forgiven him for immigrating to the States. He didn't think she ever would.

They stood.

The ladies at the bar turned to watch him and Lucy leave. Maybe if he hadn't been with Lucy, he'd have indulged in a little harmless flirtation, but he didn't have the time for even the most superficial of flings. And from the way they turned their attention back to the bar keep, Max figured the guy was in for a very big tip.

As a young and horny soldier, Max might have been game, but as Supervisory Special Agent Hawthorne, he had a professional reputation to maintain. After all, he wasn't in the Secret Service.

"I'll be fine," Lucy insisted once again in the lobby. "I live here, remember?"

She was right. They weren't on a date, but…

They stood in front of the massive Christmas tree that dominated the center of the entryway.

Perspiration dampened the hair around her face, and her makeup appeared smudged, even though she didn't really look as if she was wearing any. The suit jacket she wore was wrinkled, and the sleeves were obviously too long for her arms. Her blouse was the same brown his sisters had worn to their brownie troop.

"Why the ugly suit?"

Her eyes flared.

So much for his way with words, but the suit didn't fit. Anyone in the twenty-first century could find better clothes by walking into any department store. Lucy's clothes required effort.

Rather than being offended, she laughed and stuffed her hands in her pockets. "It's a perfectly good suit."

It was hideous and was also way too hot for this climate.

Then he got it because he'd already known the answer. It was a disguise, but why?

He kept his thoughts to himself. He was done sticking his foot in his mouth. That reminded him of all the notice boards he needed to set up first thing in the morning. "Build Empathy and Rapport." "Do not insult someone's choice of clothing."

"You're right. It's a perfectly good suit. Good night, Lucy Aston. Sorry your Christmas was ruined. Thank you for all your help today."

Her hazel eyes grew somber. She jerked her head in a nod and headed out the front of the hotel. He watched the doorman hold the door for her, then Max turned away, heading for his room and the stack of files and diaries and emails he needed to read before he could go to sleep.

CHAPTER ELEVEN

L UCY GRABBED THE keys from the valet and gave him a good tip to compensate for the fact the poor guy was also working on a holiday.

She pushed aside the feelings of happiness she'd been experiencing with Max Hawthorne. No doubt he was charming and fun to be around, but she needed to stop thinking of him as a friend. He wasn't her friend. She didn't have any friends. Not right now.

So what if she was attracted to him? He'd be gone soon, and her job was still here in Buenos Aires. She wasn't going to build fairytales around anyone ever again.

Plus, he'd despise her if he knew the truth.

She drove around the corner from the hotel and pulled over. She pushed her seat back, grabbed black leggings and a black, long-sleeved tee from her workout bag and quickly changed in the front seat. She switched her shoes for black sneakers. Took her Glock-19 from its hidden compartment under her seat and placed it in the custom holster sewn inside the back of her leggings. She dragged on a black hoodie and stuffed her ugly suit back into her bag. The fact Max had commented on it meant she might need to do a slight upgrade on her looks. Enough to avoid notice—although Max was the only person to confront her head-on about her style choices in the seven months she'd been here.

She adjusted her seat forward again and drove a few blocks east and parked in Parque Thays, a small public space that had once been an amusement park but now housed statues and a museum and provided green space for the city's inhabitants. Last night, the square would have been full of revelers watching a fireworks display. Tonight, it was almost empty.

The note on the back of her photograph told her to meet near the MARQ. Museo de Arquitectura y Diseno.

She opened the door and was immediately hit by the humid quiet. The traffic was almost nonexistent in this part of town this close to midnight. Apartment buildings to her rear were strewn with colorful lights and fake Christmas trees in the windows. On the ground, the shadows were thick with menace. A figure crossed the park heading toward the railway tracks. No one else was visible, but she had no doubt there were unseen eyes in the darkness. The scent of the ocean skimmed the breeze as she padded silently across the grass to the museum at the south end of the park.

Once she got there, she walked around the place and then stood at the black railings at the rear of the building. She was early. Garbage was scattered on the other side of the road near the fence that separated the railyard from the rest of the world. Dead trees and stunted palms rustled in the darkness.

Footsteps approached from the south, and a man wearing a light jacket and flat cap headed in her direction. The red glow of his cigarette flared every time he inhaled.

He crossed the street and kept strolling towards her. Was this her contact or simply a man walking home after visiting relatives or friends or having a drink in a fancy hotel bar?

He stopped a few feet from her, and she had her answer.

"It's a pleasure to meet you, Ms. Aston. My name is Felix."

Sure it was.

The accent was cultured with only a faint edge of Kremlin.

Lucy said nothing. Just waited.

"Did you have nice Christmas?" He had hollowed-out features with a sharp nose and what looked like a bald head although it was hard to tell with the tweed cap.

She grunted. "Certain events overtook the festivities. I'm wondering if you had anything to do with that?"

He didn't pretend to not know what she was talking about. "What would we want with two young women?"

Whatever expression was on her face made him snort out a laugh. "Ah yes, our insatiable appetite for sex slaves."

Lucy bristled. "You say that like it isn't a booming business for the Russian mafia."

His eyes narrowed. "I don't work for the Russian Mafia."

It was Lucy's turn to snort. "You keep telling yourself that."

The man's jaw hardened. He definitely did not like being challenged this way. But he knew her secrets—that she'd been working for the CIA when Raminsky had targeted her. That's *why* Raminsky had targeted her. Not because he was charmed by her beauty or personality. He'd been a weapon used on her heart and her pride and now this guy, Felix, was using the ammunition Raminsky had provided to wield the final blows.

She'd been blinded by love and lust, and it had been her ruin. Or so they thought.

"Do you know where the girls are?" she asked.

The man smiled, but his eyes remained lizard-like in their coolness. "I was about to ask you the same question."

Which wasn't a hard "no."

"If I did, they'd have already been released."

The Russian took a long drag of his cigarette. Blew the smoke in her face. She took a small step to avoid it, and he smirked as if he'd won a victory.

Asshole.

"They are lucky to have you on their side." He sounded as convincing as a second-hand car salesman desperate to make his quota for the month.

"Why am I here?" She let her confusion show.

A pigeon flew down to land near their feet, clearly hoping for food. Felix flicked out his foot, and it flew away to safety.

"I heard you were close to the investigation," he said finally.

"Heard?" She crossed her arms. His words confirmed her worst suspicion. Someone was watching her.

"A little bird told me."

A little bird? A spy? Was he actually confessing...? "Why don't you have this 'little bird' get you what you need and leave me the hell alone?"

His smile didn't reach his eyes. "Not everyone is capable of getting me the information I need, Lucy."

Really. "Probably because a US citizen feeding Russians classified information is considered treason."

He stepped closer so he was within touching distance. "What do you think the authorities will term what you've already done for us? Do you think they'll see a blackmail victim? Or a traitor?"

Lucy took a half step back.

His mouth pursed. Eyes narrowed. "How does that stack up with your perception of yourself, Lucy Aston?"

She closed her eyes. Showed defeat and despair. Felt it

down to her bones. That she had allowed herself to be compromised this way. This thoroughly. That she'd fallen for the Russians' ploy.

He made a clucking sound. "Take for example that information you fed us regarding the Dickersons' schedule. If that had fallen into the wrong hands, it might have made kidnapping the ambassador's daughter easier. Don't you think?"

The skin across her knuckles stretched tight as her fists clenched. The information she'd given them had not included anything on the children.

"Did you kidnap Kristen Dickerson and her friend?" she asked flat out.

Was he playing some kind of vicious game? It wouldn't surprise her. Did he want her to beg for their lives or perform sexual acts to prove exactly how humiliated and beaten she was?

Would she do it?

No. But she couldn't afford for him to test her. He couldn't suspect she wasn't completely cowed.

He tilted his head to the side. "How guilty would you feel if we did kidnap those girls?"

Lucy glared at him, gritting her teeth. "Very. Did you?"

He shocked her then, wrapping his hand around the base of her throat. Then he leaned forward and kissed her. He forced her jaws apart and stuck his tongue in her mouth, the taste of tobacco making her stomach recoil. Despite her revulsion, she didn't bite or fight him. She held perfectly still as he mashed his lips against hers.

After a few moments, he pulled back and whispered, "I bet you would like to hurt me now, wouldn't you, Lucy Aston?"

She held his gaze not bothering to hide the hate. "Yes."

The man's grip was an implicit threat. Lucy wished she'd worn her knife because her pistol was harder to reach. "Especially if you're responsible for hurting innocent, young women."

"Innocents have always been caught up in the power struggles between East and West."

"Does that make it okay?"

"It is what it is." He let her go and took a step back.

She rolled her eyes at his fatalistic bullshit.

His eyes narrowed. If he touched her again, she was going to shoot him. "What would you do if we *were* the ones who took the women? Would you be willing to confess your sins to your superiors? Would you be ready for the world to see those photographs of you fucking Sergio Raminsky?" He spat out the name.

Because Raminsky had betrayed Mother Russia and shot dead the Russian Ambassador on the steps of the US Congress. How they must hate him and everything he stood for. One of their golden boys had gone rogue. Maybe that's why it had taken them so long to contact her. To start blackmailing her. They hadn't wanted to use Raminsky's *kompromat*.

The spy game was full of smoke and mirrors. Truth was nothing but a moment of clarity.

She shook her head to answer his question. She didn't want anyone to see those photographs.

"We want to be kept informed of the progress of the FBI's investigation into the kidnapping."

"What? Why?" There was no way she could do that. "Surely you have other people you can blackmail who can give you that type of intel." She hoped for a reply, but he gave her nothing. "I'm a junior assistant to the ambassador and, with this crisis, I'll be needed in the office now more than ever. I won't be privy to details of the investigation."

"You underestimate yourself." He traced the neckline of her hoodie. "You were already spotted having dinner with the FBI negotiator. Why don't you use your 'charms' on him to find out what we want to know?"

She resisted sticking her gun in Felix's face and pulling the trigger. Barely. Her issues with suppressed rage would have to be dealt with eventually. But not today.

"We both know that, if you put a little effort into your appearance, you'll be able to seduce him the way you did Raminsky."

"Raminsky is the one who did all the seducing, and we all know why." Humiliation rose up and made her face flame. "I'm not sleeping with someone and setting them up for the same fall I took." Especially not Max Hawthorne who deserved better.

"Is that why you dress like a Siberian nun? So no man is tempted?" Felix barked out a laugh. "Does that mean you'll never spread your legs again, Lucy Aston?"

He stood so close, she wanted to back away. The cigarette smoke was pungent on his breath. His nicotine-stained thumb brushed her lower lip, but she kept her mouth firmly closed. "That would be a shame. After studying those photographs in great detail, that would definitely be a shame."

"You're a pig." Lucy drew in a shuddering breath as she shifted away from him. Conceding the battle if not the war.

"So my wife tells me."

She cleared her throat. She had no option but at least to appear to go along with his nefarious plan and they both knew it. "How do I contact you?"

The Russian exhaled a lungful of smoke, and Lucy scrunched up her nose and looked away, not pretending to be cool or unaffected. He handed her a business card. "Use this email address and inform us if there are any developments in the case. *Any* developments."

Lucy's fingers trembled when she slipped the card into the pocket of her hoodie. "If you didn't take the girls, will you help us get them back? You must have plenty of contacts on the street?"

The condescension in his gaze made Lucy's insides shrivel.

"This isn't a two-way street." He spoke with a sneer on his lips. "We *own* you. You work for us now." The threat in his voice had her leaning away from him. "I can destroy you in an instant. Don't forget that, little girl."

Then he walked past her into the darkness.

About twenty feet away, he threw his cigarette butt on the ground before crossing the street and disappearing into the park.

Lucy held her breath until her pulse slowed down to a reasonable beat. She drew in a shuddering breath. Vile man. She waited another five minutes and then headed in the same direction Felix had taken.

His cigarette butt glowed on the sidewalk. She waited for it to burn out. Then she bent down and gathered it into a small envelope she had in her pocket. Felix wasn't the only one who valued information.

THE NEXT TIME her prison door opened, Kristen found herself dragged out by her bound arms. Someone then kicked her in the thigh and hissed at her to stand up. Thankfully, she'd woken as he'd stomped into the bedroom, and she'd quickly pulled the canvas bag down over her face.

Kristen rolled onto her front and pushed herself onto all fours. Another kick in the stomach had her crying out in pain.

"¡Levántate!"

Even with the hood on, she could smell beer on his breath. She forced her cramped limbs to do what was asked of them. The drugs didn't help. They made her slow and clumsy. She tucked her face toward her chest away from the direction of the last blow, fearing another strike as she scrambled unsteadily to her feet. Then she stood in the darkness, swaying.

He grabbed her arm and dragged her along with him. He took her into the bathroom and barked at her to use the toilet.

"Can you leave me for a minute, please?" she asked in Spanish. Her voice shook. She was beyond trying to manipulate these people. She only wanted to survive, but she'd been surrounded by diplomats her entire life and, sometimes, the simple act of asking for something produced results.

She thought he'd hit her or jeer at her, but instead the words seemed to pull him up. Remind him he'd been ordered to treat her with a little respect? Perhaps the man in charge had warned him not to touch her, and this guy was trying to figure out exactly how far he could push it.

She didn't know. She was simply grateful he didn't hit her again.

He grunted out another impatient word. "Hurry."

Kristen felt like her dog, Roo. Taken to the bathroom twice a day so she didn't have an accident on the living room rug. Kristen wasn't being cared for out of love or consideration, instead, taking care of her basic needs caused her captors less inconvenience than the alternative.

At least it was dark.

She finished using the toilet and quickly washed up. She told herself he wasn't watching her every move and made sure to blindly touch as much of the sink as possible in case the police ever traced her to this place.

Impatiently, he came inside the bathroom, grabbed her hands, and tugged her by the rope back to the cabinet.

He roughly pushed her inside and then put pressure on her shoulders and forced her to her knees. Suddenly afraid of what else he might do, she shrank farther into the depths of the wardrobe.

He laughed nastily as if he knew why she'd reacted that way. Something about that laugh was calculating and mean. As though he was thinking about all the things she was terrified of and how he'd do them to her as soon as he'd figured out how to do so without getting into trouble with his fellow kidnappers.

"Take this." Again, in Spanish. Unlike the first man she'd encountered, this man's English wasn't very good. She held her hands out hesitantly. He placed a paper bag and another bottle of water in each hand. The water bottle crinkled loudly when she grasped it.

He closed the door, and Kristen shuddered with relief. He was her least favorite kidnapper so far.

She lifted the hood enough to draw in a lungful of air. She carefully placed the water bottle on the ground and opened the brown paper lunch bag. Inside she found what felt like an apple, a hunk of bread and small pack of butter, and a small block of cheese. Her mouth watered.

Her fingers brushed the blunt serrated edge of a small

plastic knife. She decided to eat the cheese first and save the bread and butter and apple for when she was hungry later.

She sliced a piece off and nibbled, savoring the taste of the *provoleta*. The flavor flooded her senses. It was the first thing they'd given her to eat since she'd been taken. At first, she hadn't felt hungry but, before long, her stomach had started to crave food.

Were they treating Irene the same way they were treating her? Was she scared? Irene was never scared. She was always so brave and smart. But it wasn't a normal situation. Even Irene would be terrified of what was happening to them now.

Guilt ate away at Kristen. She'd heard them shouting at Irene that it was her own fault she was here and that they hadn't wanted her. Except they'd taken her. They had kidnapped her and stuffed her in the back of a van. No one had forced them to do it.

What if they weren't taking care of her friend? What if they'd hurt her? What if they hadn't given her any food? Kristen would be happy to share her meager stash with Irene. If only she could get out of here...

Frustrated, she took the plastic knife and wedged it in the old-fashioned latch on the door. To her absolute astonishment and horror, the catch sprang open.

She knelt there with the knife in her hands, holding her breath, listening to see if anyone had heard. There was no sound. Nothing at all.

Slowly, she placed the knife beside the bag inside her wooden cage. The hood sat like a beanie on the top of her head. If she was discovered, she'd pull it over her eyes before she caught sight of their faces. She knew they'd hurt her if she tried to escape—but if she saw their faces they might blind or kill her regardless of ransoms or promises.

Freedom beckoned, even though she knew it was a massive risk. And even if she couldn't get out of the room, she couldn't ignore this opportunity to at least explore the margins of her prison. To look for signs of where they might be holding Irene. Maybe find her friend and the two of them escaping.

She looked around the room, scanning for cameras because it was entirely possible they'd set something up in order to watch over them. The room was completely bare except for the wardrobe and an old packing crate but showed remnants of past grandeur. Now the mansion smelled of rot and decay.

Her feet were bare and slid silently over old, polished wood. The large window had boards nailed over the outside shutters, and it was impossible to make out what might be beyond in the hushed predawn quiet.

Kristen crept carefully to the black, painted door and held her ear to it for a silent count of thirty. No sound came from anywhere within the house.

Saying a quick prayer, she grabbed the handle with her bound hands and eased the door open an inch. It didn't make a sound. She peered out into the gloomy shadows, again searching for security cameras, but there was nothing visible. Another inch and just the barest creak, which she tried to absorb with her body.

Finally, it was wide enough for her to slip through. The hallway was large with a grand staircase winding through the middle. She went to stare gingerly over the edge of the balustrade. She was two flights up with at least another floor above her. The bottom of the stairwell was shrouded in darkness.

Enough ambient light penetrated the windows for Kristen

to make out several paneled doors along this level. It would make sense to keep Irene nearby—assuming she was in this same building. Kristen crept across the hallway from her room and snuck a look inside. The room was empty. She tiptoed across to the window and stared outside. There was a crumbling stone window ledge. A tall tree overhung the property, obscuring whatever lay beyond.

She slid the catch free and tried to lift the window, but the wood rattled noisily. She stopped, not wanting to risk forcing it and making a noise until she found Irene.

She went back out into the hallway, carefully listening for sounds that might indicate someone was awake or nearby. The thought of being caught threatened to paralyze her. She did not want to get caught. She did not like pain.

Several doors were ajar, and Kristen quickly poked her head into each but didn't spend time searching them. It made more sense that they'd keep a hostage behind a closed door rather than an open one. She came to a room, four down from hers, near the back of the house. This place was huge. It must have twenty bedrooms.

If the kidnappers came up the stairs, she'd be trapped, unable to get back to her room without them seeing her. Her hands shook as she very slowly turned the handle and peeked inside. There was only a bed and no wardrobe. Kristen almost turned away, but the slight chink of metal had ice forming along her spine.

Was one of the kidnappers inside? Her eyes searched the darkness. Then she spotted a figure lying on the floor near a massive, old radiator. Irene.

Joy and horror swept through her. This was their reality. Chains and worse. She snuck over to her friend.

"Irene," she whispered.

The girl stiffened and then raised her head cautiously. "Kristen?"

Kristen grabbed her friend's hands. "Yes, it's me."

"Quiet," Irene murmured. "I can hear them talking in the kitchen sometimes. They can probably hear us."

Kristen lowered her voice even further. "I managed to free myself. Are you okay?"

She pushed the hood back so she could see her friend's face. Skin pale. Eyes a little wild.

"How did you escape the cuffs?" Irene asked, raising her hands. The chains jingled, and they both tensed and waited a few seconds. Irene nestled the chain carefully into her lap like a pet cobra.

"They tied me with rope," Kristen raised her bound hands to show her. "And kept me in a locked wardrobe, but I managed to open the latch." Kristen traced the metal on Irene's bracelets and realized they were too tight to slip off.

She knelt beside the radiator and felt cautiously along its length. The thick chain was secured with another large padlock. "Do you have anything we can use to pick the lock?"

"Not on me." Irene's attempt at humor failed. "You have to escape. You have to run and get help. Now."

"I'm not leaving you."

"You have to."

"I'm not leaving you," Kristen repeated.

"This might be our only chance to escape."

"No. They don't know I figured out how to get out of the wardrobe."

"What if they move you somewhere else, dummy? Or chain you to a radiator like me?"

Kristen ignored the sting of the insult. Irene was trying to push her away on purpose. She refused to go.

The pitch of Irene's voice dropped to barely audible. "If they catch you here like this, they will beat and rape us both, and probably kill me."

Shudders made Kristen's teeth chatter. "Even more reason to figure out a way to get you free."

Irene's expression turned desolate. "Kristen, there isn't a way. I know you're trying to save me but, if they catch you here like this, it is going to become a thousand times worse. You have to leave. Now, while you can. Before they catch you. Find help and send them back for me. Please, Kristen. Please. I beg you."

The pleas tore at Kristen. As desperate as she was to run, she would not leave her friend behind. Tears threatened to flood her vision, but she blinked them away. She would be here for her. She would find the same courage that Irene had shown.

"Listen to me. There's a room when you head out this door—turn right, straight ahead until you reach the end of the corridor and it's the last room on the left. There's a tree next to a window. If we can figure out a way out of those cuffs, we can both escape. Tomorrow, when it's dark, I'll come again. Before dawn. I'm across the hall from there. If you aren't free by then I'll go for help alone."

The sound of a door banging downstairs had both girls tensing.

"Go. Quickly, before they catch you," Irene whispered desperately.

Kristen nodded. She moved stealthily back to the door and closed it behind her even though she hated leaving her friend.

Then she scooted silently down the hallway until she came to her room. She shut her door quietly again and crept back into her wardrobe. She stepped inside and used her fingernail to hold back the latch until she could pull the door properly closed. The snick of the lock felt a lot less like a prison now and a lot more like a refuge. She curled up in the bottom and pulled out the bread and butter they'd given her—damn, she'd forgotten to take Irene any. Too late now. She spread the butter with the precious plastic knife which she then placed on a small ledge higher up in what was hopefully a safe spot.

Then she knelt in the bottom of her cramped, stuffy, wooden box and concentrated not on the fear that buzzed constantly through her, but on the pleasure of each tiny bite of bread and butter, and the thought of getting out of here.

CHAPTER TWELVE

*T*HINGS TO REMEMBER: *Active Listening Skills. Feeling Words.*

Max printed the headers on a large whiteboard he'd borrowed from a nearby hallway. He'd sent the Assistant Legal Attaché, a guy called Adam Quinn, who not only spoke Spanish but also had some basic negotiation training, home to grab a few hours' sleep while Max set up a workable Negotiation Center and also manned the phones.

The kidnappers had said they'd call again this morning. Some groups liked to jerk negotiators around and play mind games, but other kidnappers were punctual and didn't like wasting time. They all had their own agendas. Max wasn't sure what type this group fell into yet, but he suspected the latter. They wanted their money.

Max finished writing out the communication reminder notes the Crisis Negotiation Team used at every incident. Usually, the team brought them along but, since Max had been on vacation when he'd received the call, that had been impossible.

He'd hauled everything out of this old storeroom when he'd arrived that morning and piled it in the corner of the main office. It was a perfect space because it was close to the Legat's office and the investigation, but also self-contained.

He'd initially tried the door of one of the offices next to Brian Powell's room and had been met by an intensely territorial agent who'd told him in no uncertain terms that those rooms were strictly off-limits.

Whatever "Operation Soapbox" was, it was big, and they took secrecy very seriously.

Max dragged a table and three chairs inside the former storage space. He set up power strips and lamps, which he'd also borrowed off desks in the main office as there was no natural light in here. He'd beg forgiveness later.

He planned to set up a camp bed in case something happened where he or some other poor bastard needed to stay for long periods of time with little or nothing going on. He'd already sent in the purchase order request. May as well get a little rest, if possible. He looked around to see if he'd forgotten anything.

The visual reminders reinforced everything he'd learned in training and would help whoever was on duty when they were struggling with what to say.

Go back to basics.

Keep your ego out of the conversation.

Actively listen to what the other person was saying rather than simply waiting for your turn to speak.

Ask open-ended questions that encouraged the other side to divulge as much information as possible and use minimal encouragers to keep them talking.

Mirror the last thing the hostage taker said to you, or the most important three words of the sentence.

Paraphrase their wants and demands and complaints so they knew you understood them.

Label their emotions to create trust while not diminishing those feelings or views.

Get the hostage taker to feel safe by encouraging them to say *no*. *No* allowed people to protect their position. It provided a place from which they could move forward without worrying they'd given anything away.

Bend their reality regarding what was a fair ransom request.

Develop questions in advance so the kidnappers helped you solve problems.

"*How am I supposed to do that?*" was a way of asking for their help to figure out how to get what they wanted. CNU recommended using *what* and *how* questions that were open ended and always keeping the tone conciliatory. Questions that were answered with single words went nowhere and should be avoided at all costs, as should *why* questions that put people on the defensive.

Max had written out some questions for the negotiators to ask on any given day depending on what was happening and whether or not negotiations were stalled. First, they needed to know they were dealing with someone who had the power to make decisions about the girls' release and, most importantly, he needed proof of life without asking for it directly.

The nitty gritty of negotiations for money usually followed a fairly predictable pattern. Max took nothing for granted, but he was more confident with K&R cases than almost any other hostage situation. It was a business transaction, and kidnappers who killed their hostages rarely got paid.

Max was determined to get as much of this basic structure in place in case he was called away for another more urgent job. It was preferable to have someone who understood the nuances of the local dialect as the chief negotiator. He could and did work through interpreters, but that introduced another layer of possible miscommunication, and the delay factor wasn't ideal. Preferably negotiators were fluent in the language and also dedicated, trusted members of law enforcement or a capable family member. Adam Quinn was ideal and another Spanish-speaking negotiator he'd worked with in Washington State was joining them shortly.

The cell number the kidnappers were communicating with had been transferred to a phone here and all the ambassador's family's other cell numbers had been disconnected and changed. The calls were being recorded by communication experts at the FBI National Laboratory and, as per agreement, those recordings were being sent immediately from Quantico to federal police here in Argentina.

Max had also set up devices for real-time recording within the Negotiation Center. Multiple headsets were arranged on the table, but only one had a microphone attached so that only one negotiator could talk to the kidnappers at a given time. Other people could listen in to a call and pay attention to different aspects of the conversation.

Max looked around in satisfaction. This space allowed the negotiator some privacy to talk to the kidnappers without fear of interruption and the ability to replay phone calls on the spot and discuss the case in private. It also gave him a space to work without the Legat or the ambassador being able to walk in on him without warning.

And because it was the US Ambassador's daughter, Max had a sneaky feeling Catherine Dickerson would be unable to refrain from trying to interfere. He understood that. He was also sure he couldn't allow it.

Last night, after he'd said good night to Lucy, he'd gone

through Kristen's diaries. The name Miguel had turned up a few times in recent entries. Sounded like the boy she'd met online and had a crush on. Or like someone pretending to be a handsome boy named Miguel who liked a girl called KrisD. Max didn't trust online identities. Unless he knew better, he assumed everyone at the end of a social media account was a fat Russian dude in a tiny, airless Moscow apartment.

Was that unfair to fat Russians in tiny, airless Moscow apartments? Absolutely. Did he care? Only when he was wrong.

Max checked his watch. Buenos Aires was only an hour ahead of Virginia, so he decided to call his housemate and colleague back in Quantico.

Eban Winters answered with a disgruntled moan.

"Kidnappers haven't called back yet." Max told him.

"Not surprising, considering it's so early."

"Did the tech guys get anything from the kidnapper's call yesterday?" asked Max.

"Yeah. It came from a burner which was subsequently turned off. They got nothing except the call was made on the western edge of the city. We passed our data to the *Policia Federal de Argentina* who might be able to get more off it. Mike Tanner warned me that the PFA might stop the phone company from working with us directly though."

"Why would they do that?"

"Same reason we would if they were trying to solve a crime on our turf."

Max grunted. "Before I forget, I couriered Kristen Dickerson's laptop to Quantico overnight along with the ring I found at the site where the kidnappers changed cars. Should be arriving this morning. I had to hand in the cell that the kidnappers left behind to the local authorities along with the gun I took off that asshole who chased me through the streets of La Boca yesterday. The Legat insisted." Max had decided not to fight the guy on those issues. He liked to pick his battles. "He got a little pissed when I suggested we bypass the local authorities. Said he had to work with these guys after I left, and the locals wouldn't keep him in the loop if he didn't share what we found."

"*We?*" Eban snorted.

"My thoughts exactly," Max agreed. This was evidence Max found after the locals had missed it.

"I'll track the package and see if I can get a rush on processing. As you know though, most people are on vacation."

"Can you send me the results of the background checks on the ambassador's staff when you get them?"

"You have a suspect?"

"Not exactly." Lucy was a puzzle piece that didn't quite fit and, considering the circumstances, he needed more data. "And anything on the ambassador's husband."

"You know they've all been thoroughly screened?"

"Screenings can miss things. People can change. Someone mentioned he's a bit of a flirt. We need to make sure this kidnapping isn't revenge for some unknown offense he committed. Some jealous husband deciding to act up and make the guy pay."

Black swans. The totally unexpected factor that could sink a successful negotiation without trace.

"You've heard of Occam's razor, right? The simplest explanation is probably the correct one?"

And that explanation was usually cash, but Max decided to play devil's advocate. "If they wanted cash—ten million or ten thousand—it would have been easier to shake down a wealthy businessman who probably has K&R insurance, rather than bringing the weight of the US government to bear."

"Not everyone is smart enough to realize that."

"The abduction itself was professional as hell."

"I'm not saying they've never done this before. We both know kidnappings are rife throughout South America. But maybe they somehow focused on Kristen Dickerson as a potential victim and saw the dollar signs associated with a high value target rather than the big guns that might come looking for her."

Max put his feet on the desk. "That reminds me. According to Legat Powell, a Canadian diplomat might have been abducted and ransomed last year. He thinks the guy headed home immediately."

"That would definitely give them grounds to believe it might work. I'll dig into it."

"Thanks. Searching out the least guarded but most valuable target could have led them to the two Dickerson children. The Diplomatic Security Service don't believe anyone was surveilling the kids but then that could be their own asses they're protecting. We still need to figure out exactly how the kidnappers tracked Kristen on Christmas Eve. The kidnap was so well planned and executed that they definitely needed eyes on the victim."

"I agree."

They chatted some more and then Max said goodbye and glanced at the clock. He planned to go visit Irene's parents today and question DSS personnel and the drivers associated with the family. And then maybe call on the Canadian embassy in person.

Shit. That was a full day already.

First though, he decided to call the Legat and see if there was an update on forensics from the cell or gun Powell had forced him to hand over.

"Hey, Brian. Hate to bother you so early in the morning," said Max. "Did you receive the results back from the cell phone or gun yet?"

Brian moaned. Definitely in bed and, from the muffled conversation, not alone.

Was he married? Max didn't know.

Max squashed resentment that he seemed to be the only agent at work this morning—except the agent manning the Operation Soapbox offices. But everyone had worked through the previous night so maybe he wasn't being fair.

"I just woke up," Powell said. "Let me call you back." The guy hung up on him.

So much for that.

Max wandered over to the window in the main FBI office. It overlooked a walled-off parking area. Phillip Dickerson was getting into the passenger seat of a black SUV, Iain Bartlett got into the driver's side. The vehicle sped away, and Max wondered where they were going and if there had been any progress with the case.

The phone rang in the Negotiation Center, and he headed back inside. He turned on the recording equipment before answering the call.

"Hello, this is Max."

"I want to talk to the ambassador." Electronic disguise again. English. The voice distortion was apparently the sophisticated kind where the modulation was constantly shifting. Completely indecipherable and professional as hell.

"You're dealing with me. Who am I talking to?"

"Never mind who this is." The guy sounded pissed that he'd reached Max again, but he'd better get used to reaching him or one of his colleagues. "I want ten million dollars if you want to see the women alive."

Overnight, Max had saved the parents ten million dollars—but he was a long way from celebrating. That was fantasy money—a fantasy that certain government policies had helped drive.

"I wish I could simply say yes, no problem, let's meet up right now, and I'll exchange the cash for Kristen and Irene. Unfortunately, even if the family had that kind of money— which they don't—how are Catherine and Phillip Dickerson supposed to access it when the banks and stock exchanges are closed, and their money is tied up in foreign banks which take days to transfer those kinds of funds?"

He let the silence ring out and refrained from filling it.

"Someone can lend it to them." The man sounded less sure now.

"Do you know someone who can lend them that much money?" He kept his tone as someone appealing for help rather than sarcastic.

He received a grunt in reply.

"Do you have a name I can call you?" asked Max.

"Call me *el jefe*."

"Okay, el jefe." The boss. Max rolled his eyes, resisting the juvenile desire to call the guy *Jeff*. "Kristen's and Irene's parents obviously want their children back and are willing to pay what they can." Max kept emphasizing these hostages were youngsters every chance he got. "But how do I know they're all right?"

"Maybe you'll just have to trust me?" The voice sounded menacing. And who wouldn't trust a guy like that?

"I'd like to, el jefe, of course I would. But the family needs to know you can deliver the girls before they hand over any cash."

"What do you think, Max? Do you think I have the women?" The voice held an edge of anger which was not what Max was aiming for.

The guy wanted to get into a fight with him, and Max needed to defuse that tension. "I understand that you are angry, el jefe. You think we are doubting your word, and I can see how that would be upsetting for you. But do you think the families should pay the first person who calls and demands money?"

"Of course not." The tone turned affronted.

"So how do the families know that they are dealing with the person who is looking after their children? What if they pay someone who is taking advantage of the situation and then they have nothing left for you? Then someone has stolen your money, correct?"

Max held his tongue.

Finally, the kidnapper replied, "Perhaps Irene's parents will be more accommodating. I won't bother calling you again. I'll sell the ambassador's daughter to another group for the amount I want. Of course, they might not treat her so well."

"El jefe, we appreciate you treating the girls well while we figure out how to raise the money." Max needed to talk to the negotiator Irene's parents were working with ASAP. He couldn't risk them being at odds or worse, bidding against one another for their daughter's lives.

Max checked his board. Empathy. "I understand you are

in a difficult position, el jefe." *You fucking asshole.* "I know this can't be easy for you any more than it is for the parents who are worried about their kids. It must be incredibly stressful looking after those girls, keeping them safe from harm. Tell me what I can do to help resolve this situation as quickly and safely as possible, so no one gets hurt."

"Get me my money." Laughter crackled ominously down the line.

Max decided it was time to set another realistic anchor. "The Dickersons can raise $27,500 by the end of today. I can deliver it tonight and this nightmare is over for everyone."

The voice scoffed. "That is not enough."

"I'm sorry. We are trying to raise a sum of money that is acceptable to you. We are not sure how to raise more—"

"Perhaps if I send her daughter's fingers back to her one at a time the ambassador will find a way to come up with the rest of the cash."

The overt threat of violence was an escalation. This guy was playing hardball.

"I hope you will treat the girls with the same respect you would want your own children to be treated." The kidnapper was still on the line so, for all his threats, he wanted to make a deal. "We want to reimburse you for your time and effort. But how can we raise more money when all the banks are closed and the Dickersons' main asset is rented out on a year's lease and could take months to sell?" This was the truth which helped if the facts were researched by some erstwhile investigative reporter who then published it all over the damn news.

The key to asking "how" questions was to keep his tone calm and unaccusatory. "How" and to a lesser extent "what" questions made the kidnapper actively work with the negotiator to try and solve the problems of how to raise money. It made kidnappers consider the practical roadblocks in place to having their dreams of riches come true. It brought them back from fantasy land to the realms of reality.

"Tell them to sell off their diamonds and cars."

"They will sell any items of value that they possess. The cars here however belong to the State Department and not the Dickersons personally."

"Perhaps they should have bought kidnap insurance."

And perhaps guys like this should keep their damn hands off other people's kids.

"El jefe" hung up.

Max put down the phone and restrained from swearing until he'd turned off all the recording equipment.

He spent the next hour talking to the technicians unsuccessfully trying to unravel the real voice behind the distortion.

At least they seemed to be serious about the cash. The sooner they could get the ransom together the better. Assuming the State Department approved of the payment. That was above Max's pay grade.

Hanging up on the call, he checked his watch and called Quinn and asked the guy to come back in to monitor the phones. Max was about to call Powell again and demand he get his ass in here when the Legat finally called him back.

"The ambassador wants an update. I'll meet you upstairs in five."

CHAPTER THIRTEEN

L UCY HADN'T NEEDED to add false shadows under her eyes today. The bags were large enough to contain enough luggage for a two-week ski vacation.

Back to her usual anonymous self, she passed coffee around the room. Someone knocked on the door, and she went over to answer it.

Max Hawthorne stood there.

Her heart gave a little flutter.

"Good morning, Ms. Aston."

She stared idiotically because he looked even better this morning than he had in the bar last night. She gave him a smile in return, careful that the others didn't see it, and opened the door wide.

Max was a complication she didn't need but damn if she didn't like the guy. Even the fact he called her "Ms. Aston" rather than Lucy sent a happy thrill through her. It allowed them to maintain a more professional distance in front of the others.

Lucy fetched Max a coffee while the ambassador intro-duced him to *Comisario General* Benito Fuentes of the federal police and *Oficial Inspector* Hector Cabral, his chief of detectives.

Max paused for an extra-long handshake with Cabral.

Raised his brows. "You're the police officer who thwarted the series of kidnappings by the Brazilian street gang a couple of years ago?"

Cabral looked impressed by Max's knowledge and puffed out his chest.

Hector Cabral reminded Lucy of a cocky rooster. He was thick set and good-looking. Dark hair, olive complexion. His eyes didn't miss a trick. Lucy suspected that's what made him so good at his job. He was also sexist and an arrogant prick.

"The gang terrorized Argentina for six months. I was lucky enough that someone reached out to me via private means and we were able to create a small, covert, highly focused task-force that was airtight."

"Are leaks a common problem within the police service here, Inspector Cabral?" The lack of judgment in Max's tone allowed both Cabral and Fuentes to relax into the question. Lucy was impressed. These men were incredibly macho and didn't like their organization or their abilities questioned.

"No more than anywhere else," Fuentes shrugged and answered. "We've had our problems in the past, but we are weeding out corruption from the police force."

Which seemed to be the war cry of every political party that ran for election in this country. Lucy wasn't convinced they were any closer now than they had been twenty years ago. Then again, Argentina wasn't alone with problems of misfeasance.

"What updates do you have, Benito?" The ambassador's jaw was clenched but, aside from that, she looked coolly professional. The woman wore a green pant suit and enough makeup to hide any trace of her anguish.

Phillip had left earlier with Iain Bartlett. Another DS agent stood against the wall watching the police officers carefully. DSS weren't taking any chances with the ambassador's security. Neither police officer had been allowed to carry a weapon inside the embassy. Lucy bet that would piss off both men equally.

Benito Fuentes shifted, his starched uniform looking distinctly uncomfortable this morning. Or maybe it was the way he perched on the edge of the seat, sipping his coffee.

As Lucy handed Max his drink, their fingers accidentally brushed. His tightened on the cup to prevent the coffee going everywhere and their gazes collided.

"Sorry," she said quickly.

His gaze fell to her lips and, for a fraction of a second, Lucy felt that old shot of attraction burst through her like the flare of a match. She squashed it down.

She moved away once he had the espresso cup safely in hand.

The guy was gorgeous. Of course, she was attracted to him. She was allowed to give herself a moment to admire physical beauty if she wanted to. It would seem more weird if this current version of Lucy wasn't slightly discombobulated by the presence of such a charismatic, handsome man in her orbit.

"The lab worked all night on the cell phone left behind by the kidnappers in La Boca." No mention that Max Hawthorne had been the person to find it, Lucy noticed. "They are running tests for DNA and anything in the cell's memory, but it was a brand-new phone, likely bought for this purpose." Fuentes told Catherine Dickerson.

"What about my daughter's cell phone. You brought it as I requested?" The ambassador held out her palm.

It hadn't been a request. It had been a diplomatic order.

Fuentes hesitated, then dug into his side pocket. Pulled out a phone in a glittery silver case encased in a clear, plastic evidence bag. "Normally this would not be allowed, you understand."

"Normally my daughter would be home for Christmas and not at the mercy of a gang who kidnapped her in broad daylight in the heart of Buenos Aires. That phone belongs to the US Ambassador and diplomatic protocol demands you return it. I am assuming you checked it for prints and DNA?"

Fuentes nodded. "It had already been processed by the time we received your *request*. Tests are being run. We have the DNA and fingerprint samples that you provided for your daughter that we can eliminate."

The ambassador took the phone and closed her eyes for a moment before she handed it off to the DS agent who would check it for bugs and do a detailed examination of the content before returning it to her.

"Did you access the information on the phone?" Catherine asked.

Fuentes shook his head. "We hadn't got that far. We will be talking to the carrier for copies of her texts and messages."

"No." The ambassador's chin dipped. "That is not permissible. The FBI will go through the texts and messenger apps and share anything that might be pertinent. I will not have my family's private details up for public viewing."

A flush started to fill the *Comisario's* round cheeks. He didn't like being told what he could and couldn't do. He especially didn't like being told by a woman.

"You can access the phone number records but not any text or voice mail."

All the numbers for the family and embassy staff were being changed anyway.

Fuentes looked as if he was about to protest.

Max Hawthorne stepped in. "Did you have any luck tracking or backtracking the kidnappers' vehicles through the city?"

Fuentes looked at Cabral who shook his head. "Nothing yet. It is painstaking work that takes a lot of time and manpower." He shrugged. "And the kidnappers seem to have been incredibly sophisticated about this part of the plan. There were no cameras in the alley where they dumped the van, and there were an unusually high number of car thefts the previous day."

"You think they purposefully wanted to muddy the waters?"

"Yes." Cabral shrugged as if this were normal.

Max waited a beat. "Can you check to see if any older model orange or red VW Passats were reported stolen or found dumped yesterday?"

Deep furrows etched Cabral's brow. "Why?"

"I did pass that tip on to one of your people yesterday," Powell spoke up. "SSA Hawthorne found an eyewitness who says they saw the kidnappers get into a VW Passat after they dumped the van in La Boca."

"No one informed me of this development." The muscles in Cabral's jaw bunched. "I was not told of this." He fished in his pocket and handed out his cards to each of the men present. "That has my direct cell number on it. Call me in future. I don't want to miss a major lead. Who was this eyewitness?"

Max smiled. "They didn't give their name."

"They are probably lying." Cabral waved dismissively.

"They also gave us the cell that the kidnappers used to contact us."

Cabral tilted his head to one side as if Max had suddenly become more interesting. He said slowly, "And yet you didn't get a name."

"We didn't have time. They ran in the other direction when a group of thugs started to chase us through the streets." Max sounded convincing.

Lucy dropped her gaze to the floor. She didn't want anyone asking her questions and discovering she had a backbone when she refused to answer.

"I will check into any reports made on any VW Passats." Cabral's eyes glittered. He didn't like admitting there was something he didn't know regarding the investigation. "Have the kidnappers made contact again?"

"Earlier this morning." Max sipped his coffee, appearing relaxed even though all eyes were fixed on him. "It was probably the same kidnapper who called me yesterday, although they used an electronic voice disguiser again. He wanted to be addressed as 'el jefe.'"

Cabral stiffened.

"What is it?" the ambassador demanded.

"That's the name the Brazilian gang always insisted we use when negotiating with them," Cabral admitted.

"But they were all killed," Powell interjected.

Cabral smiled at him condescendingly. "Those at the house at the time of the tactical assault were killed, and any we could track down after that, but these animals are like cockroaches coming out of the cracks in the sidewalk when the sun goes down. They could be back. I will review the old files and talk to my people."

"May I be permitted to view the files?" asked Max.

Fuentes and Cabral exchanged a look.

Cabral opened his hands. "I don't see why not. Although my superior might want to have them redacted first." He looked at Fuentes.

Tit for tat for the ambassador pulling diplomatic status with her daughter's phone.

Fuentes seemed to realize this was an easy win for him. A show of cooperation and willingness that cost him nothing. "If Inspector Cabral has time out of his busy day…"

Cabral smiled. "Of course. Come down to *Jefatura* today and I will arrange it."

"Thank you." Max leaned forward to put his coffee cup on the table.

"The files are in Spanish." Cabral's expression looked slightly mean. "I don't think you speak the language, am I correct?"

"You are correct. Your English is perfect by the way. Where did you learn?" Max's smile hid all sorts of secrets. Lucy realized she wasn't the only one wearing a mask in this room.

Cabral shrugged. "I went to college in Florida for four years."

Max looked like he wanted to ask more questions, but Catherine Dickerson interrupted.

"What actual progress has been made in finding my daughter?" the ambassador demanded impatiently.

Fuentes leaned forward. "Ambassador, I assure you we are doing everything we can. We will find these people before any harm comes to your daughter."

"Do you have *any* suspects yet?" the ambassador pushed,

clearly unappeased.

Fuentes sat back and let Cabral take over. "The van was wiped clean with bleach, and the men wore gloves in addition to masks. We are investigating links to street gangs, organized crime, terrorists who hate the US."

Lucy saw Max's expression tighten a notch at that. Lucy did not want to consider what would happen to Kristen in the hands of Hezbollah or other terrorist cells, and there were definite links in the region.

"And we are making lists of other individuals who might have something to gain personally from taking the US Ambassador's daughter."

The air seemed to go out of the ambassador's chest, and she sank back against the cushions of the couch. "All the technology in the world, all the progress and surveillance and satellites, and we're no better off than we were half a century ago when trying to track down bad people doing bad things."

"We will find your daughter, I guarantee it," Fuentes said fervently. He and Cabral both stood. "We need to get back to work."

Cabral turned to Max. "Come down to the precinct if you want to get an update on the investigation, SSA Hawthorne. The coffee isn't as good." Cabral sent Lucy a look she couldn't interpret. "But we can fill you in on any progress and perhaps you can do the same for us."

"Of course. I'm here to assist. This is your investigation, Inspector Cabral."

Cabral nodded, apparently satisfied.

They made their way out of the door and the DS agent escorted them out.

When the doors closed, the ambassador shifted her gaze to

Max. "What aren't you telling me?"

"Nothing, ma'am. We're doing everything we can, but it's a process that will take time."

"Did the kidnappers let you talk to Kristen or Irene?"

Max shook his head. "No, ma'am. They demanded ten million dollars for the two girls' safe release."

Catherine's eyes widened frantically. "I don't have ten million dollars. If I did, I wouldn't be working for a living."

"Well, yesterday they wanted twenty million," Max said. "It's my job to get us to a realistic number."

"Phillip went to talk to a representative of our bank here in Buenos Aires. To see how quickly money can be transferred, but we don't have anything close to that amount." The color drained from Catherine's face.

"I know it isn't easy," Max said gently. "I'm confident I can bring the ransom down to an amount you can afford. I also need to talk to Irene's parents this morning. Given Irene's dad's position in his company, I suspect they have a K&R negotiator working with them. We need to be on the same page."

"Do you want me to talk to the British Ambassador again?"

"If you wish," Max said neutrally. "Like the Americans, the Brits won't negotiate with terrorists, and they will be happy to let us take the lead. They know that our usual position won't hold with the victim being your daughter, Ambassador. I'd like to try and meet up with their negotiator and see if we can collaborate. Make sure the kidnappers don't try to play us off one another. Especially as the kidnapper mentioned this morning ransoming Irene and selling Kristen off to a terrorist organization."

Catherine's hand went to her throat. "Just when I think it can't get any worse…" Her eyes reddened. "What do you think they are doing to her?"

Max pressed his lips together. "I don't know. No one can know until we get her back."

For a brief moment, the ambassador looked like a terrified mother rather than a powerful diplomat. Then she stiffened her spine and looked squarely at Max. "Do you have sufficient manpower?"

She'd placed the negotiator in an awkward position between her and the Legat.

Lucy watched Max calmly finish his coffee. "Considering the Argentines are in charge here and bearing in mind that the might of the Diplomatic Security Service and a team from SIOC are assisting us back in the States, then these extra agents who are arriving today should be enough to work any local leads. I will need a reliable and trusted interpreter if I'm to work closely with local police. Is there someone you can recommend at the embassy? Someone with some level of security clearance?"

"I'm willing to act in that capacity for you, Agent Hawthorne. Give Lucy time to catch up with the other things that need her attention." Miranda came into the room in time to answer Max's question.

Lucy was happy to see the slightly bemused look on Max's face. And as much as she hated the idea of Miranda being with Max all day, and perhaps sharing experiences like the ones they'd shared, she also knew it was for the best from both a personal and professional point of view. It prevented her spending more time with the guy and made it impossible for her to fulfill the Russian spymaster's request.

Win-win.

"No." Catherine Dickerson stood, a determined gleam in her eye. "I need you at my side, Miranda. Lucy is more than capable of assisting SSA Hawthorne with anything he requires."

Miranda blinked repeatedly, unable to hide her surprise.

Lucy stood there silently screaming "no."

Max shrugged like it was no big deal and devastation rolled over her. She did not want to be in a position of trust with Max Hawthorne. She didn't want to betray him.

IRENE WOKE TO bright sunshine and the sounds of birds chirping their accompaniment to the grinding pain in her joints from the hours spent on the hard floor. She caught her breath as a car drove up to the house, but from the unhurried closing of the door and amiable greetings, it wasn't a savior.

Male voices drifted up from the kitchen, but they were more hushed today, the excitement having worn off. Hopefully, they'd gone off the idea of doing terrible things to her. Hopefully, she'd convinced them she was more valuable as a hostage than a dead body.

Her tongue felt furry. Her brain cloudy from the aftereffects of the drugged water which she hated drinking. It wasn't like she had a choice. Don't drink it and die of dehydration? Drink it and pass out in a coma?

Catch-22 of survival dilemmas. The coma had won so far.

She frowned, vaguely remembering being woken in the night. Had Kristen really been here? That encounter felt like a dream.

Irene was pretty sure it had happened though because she remembered Kristen's feet had also been bare, and she wondered why they'd taken their shoes?

Had her friend gone back to her room like she'd promised, or had she run like Irene had urged? Probably the former. Kristen believed in fairy tales. Irene was more pragmatic.

She should have run.

If Kristen had escaped, assuming the cops didn't show up first, they'd either kill Irene and dump her body the way they'd originally discussed or take her to another location and continue to milk her parents for every penny they could squeeze out of their insurance company.

The sound of footsteps coming along the corridor drew her attention.

The kidnappers might not even know her friend was gone yet...

Who would it be? The older-sounding guy who seemed nicer, or the younger psycho who told her all the ways he wanted to defile her, believing that she didn't speak Spanish. Or maybe he knew and didn't care.

The door to her room opened.

"Ah, you're awake."

Irene knew it was dumb to be relieved it was the nicer guy rather than the nutcase, but here she was.

This man wasn't *nice*. But he treated her more kindly. She was pretty sure he was the leader, in the house at least, and therefore his authority had saved her from a worse fate—so far.

"I have your breakfast, which one of my colleagues pre-pared, and a small gift that I brought especially for you."

That made Irene sit up a little straighter. So he wasn't

aware of the fact Kristen had gotten out last night yet. Or this was a vicious trick.

The noise of what sounded like a breakfast tray rattling before being put down sounded close by. Also, the smell of some sort of fried food wafted in the air. Her mouth watered despite the chemicals they were feeding her. She was starved.

Something soft brushed the air in front of her, and she reached up, chains jingling. She discovered a large cushion that he let go of with an amused huff of air. No, not a cushion—it was a dog bed. The realization made it difficult to swallow. Because she was so damn grateful for this simple comfort.

She slipped it beneath her aching butt and thighs. It felt like Heaven. "Thank you."

Keys jangled. What she wouldn't give to get her hands on those keys.

He released her from the chain, and she staggered to her feet. He steadied her with an arm under her elbow.

"Careful now. You are weak and tired. Doing nothing is exhausting, no?"

Ha. Funny joke.

Being drugged and chained was exhausting. Terror and subjugation were exhausting. She forced a laugh. "I guess."

He led her to the bathroom door and let go of her. "Be quick. I will wait here."

Irene couldn't believe her luck but wasn't about to argue. She quickly used the bathroom and hurriedly washed her hands and dried them on her jeans, which now felt grimy. She thought there was a window in this room but did not dare risk pulling her hood up to see. What if he'd lied and was spying on her? She needed to show total compliance. Total obedience.

Her chance would come. Maybe tonight, if she could find a way out of these cuffs.

He led her back to the radiator, and she sat meekly on her dog bed. After he'd chained her up again, she wondered if she should have tried to run. Maybe she would have been able to knock this man over and get out of the front door before he'd known what was going on. And maybe one of the others would have caught her, or this man was armed and would have picked her off as easily as shooting ducks in a barrel.

"Here. Enjoy your food while it is still warm." He rested his hand on the top of her head like she was his favorite golden retriever. "Be a good girl, Irene, and maybe you'll get to go home to your parents, after all."

Then he left her.

She sat trembling with the tray of food touching her thigh. It was obvious that, for all his words, he was still contemplating killing her. It was only luck that she'd survived this long—luck and the promise of cash.

Even though she was no longer hungry, she forced herself to eat. She needed to keep her strength up. Anyway, if she or Kristen were caught trying to escape, this would be her last meal. She may as well enjoy it.

CHAPTER FOURTEEN

M AX WAS BUSY reading while Lucy drove.

The messages between Kristen and Miguel had been flirty, but not overtly sexual. Max felt like a voyeur on young love, but the really concerning thing was that this Miguel didn't seem to exist. The photo he used of himself didn't come up in any reverse image searches or in any databases the FBI could access, which was actually good news. But this kid wasn't registered at the school he claimed to go to, and he didn't appear to interact with anyone else on social media except for generic exchanges.

The IPS address of the computer Miguel had been using to talk to Kristen was cloaked with virtual private network, and the location wasn't immediately obvious. Some of the techs at Quantico thought they might be able to crack the location given time if this was made a priority. Unfortunately, the FBI had several high-profile cases all needing the lab techs' expertise. Did they prioritize the heavily-pregnant woman and toddler who were brutally abducted and murdered in Maryland, or the school shooting in Ohio? Or the serial killer operating in Alaska? Or the dark web puppeteer who was arranging online auctions where the bidders determined the fate of the victim?

The FBI was good at what it did but the amount of crime

that happened on a daily basis was staggering. Max believed in the basic human decency of most people, but those who weren't good or decent could wreak havoc on multitudes before they were captured. Max wished there was a better way than incarceration, but he'd faced down evil on multiple occasions, and there were some people who did things so depraved they should never be allowed out. Ever.

Was Miguel a computer nerd lying to impress a girl he wanted to woo? Or one of the kidnappers? Or the fat Russian sitting in his apartment in Moscow waiting for Kristen to break down and send him a naked selfie so the sextortion could begin?

Max didn't know. Not yet.

There were a lot of sick fucks out there, but also a lot of kids doing what was now considered normal.

Lucy pulled up outside an incredibly beautiful house; Spanish-style architecture covered in warm orange stucco with weathered, wooden shutters. They got out of her car, and the sound of raised voices could be heard from behind the nearby garden wall.

Max rang the Lomakins' doorbell as he and Lucy exchanged a glance. Whoever was arguing in the garden was getting louder. Max rang the bell again, longer and harder. The words cut off abruptly.

The Lomakins were both British nationals who lived in Palermo Soho, which was another nice neighborhood with expensive-looking houses and large, leafy parks.

A pale, tired-looking, brown-haired woman opened the door. The skin around her eyes was blotchy with tear stains. "Can I help you?"

Max held up his credentials, the gold shield gleaming in

the soft morning sunlight. "I'm Supervisory Special Agent Max Hawthorne. I'm a negotiator with the FBI. Is now a good time to talk?"

The woman's brow crinkled with concern as she looked from Max to the creds, which she examined intently before finally standing aside and letting them enter.

He waved Lucy ahead of him. She was wearing one of her ugly suits, but this one was in navy blue with a white blouse. Before getting in the Mini she'd scraped her hair back into a no-nonsense ponytail.

He knew she wasn't happy to be here, but it had taken all his acting skills not to high five the ambassador when she'd vetoed Miranda Foster's offer. For some reason, the idea of hanging out with the other woman all day didn't appeal—too high maintenance, too much presumed authority. Lucy was a far better result for him, but she didn't seem that keen.

He didn't know why he felt disappointed about that. Maybe because yesterday, they'd had a pretty good time despite the near-death experiences—or maybe because of them. And even their dinner had been enjoyable.

The woman closed the door, and they stood awkwardly in a large, circular foyer.

"We're here to see Mrs. Lomakin." Whom he strongly suspected he was talking to.

"That's me." Her lip wobbled in confirmation.

Max realized she thought he was here with bad news.

"I don't have any new information," he quickly reassured her. "I wanted to touch base with you and your husband regarding your daughter's abduction." Two girls peered over the bannister at the top of the stairs. He was guessing they were about ten and twelve. "Is there somewhere we can talk privately?"

The woman followed his gaze up the stairs. "Emily, Lisette, go play in your room until Mummy calls you, okay?"

The two girls nodded apprehensively and backed away, clearly upset.

An air of despair and uncertainty hung around the elegant house. Nerves were balanced on the razor's edge of fear.

Max and Lucy followed Mrs. Lomakin into a sitting room where a dismantled tree lay in pieces on the floor. Baubles were all neatly packed in their boxes on the coffee table. Christmas had been cancelled.

Max frowned. "Is your husband here? That way I can save time and brief you both at the same time."

Her mouth tightened. Was she one of the people who'd been arguing in the garden?

She walked to the hallway and shouted in the general direction of what was probably the kitchen. "Russell!"

"I'm busy," came a terse reply.

The woman shot Max and Lucy an apologetic look.

"It's important," Max insisted.

Mrs. Lomakin swallowed hard, then held up her hands in defeat. "This way, please."

They found Irene's father on the phone in the dining room. French doors opened onto a beautiful patio, and the breeze billowed filmy drapes that hung from a rod above the windows.

The man glanced at Max with worry straining every feature. Max flashed his badge.

"The FBI is here. I'm going to have to call you back." Russell Lomakin disconnected the call and strode over to shake Max's and Lucy's hands.

The couple obviously assumed Lucy was also with the FBI. Max didn't bother to correct them.

"Have you heard anything?" Mrs. Lomakin burst out. "Is Irene okay?"

"As far as I know, your daughter is still alive, but I have no direct proof."

The Lomakins' expressions flickered uncertainly.

"I've spoken to someone who claims to be one of the kidnappers. Did they contact you?"

Mrs. Lomakin's eyes shot to her husband. Her hands wrung one another, reflecting internal agony. "They told us not to say anything."

"Lori," her husband said sharply.

"What?" Lori Lomakin snapped. "Am I supposed to lie to the FBI now?"

"Yes, if it saves Irene's life. We're not even Americans." The man looked frantic. "If the kidnappers find out we are talking to the cops, they'll kill Irene. Isn't that incentive enough to keep your bloody mouth shut?"

Whoa.

Anxiety was ripping these people apart.

Max held up his hands, palms out. "I realize you are both under a tremendous amount of strain worrying about your daughter, but I think I can help. Is it possible to sit down for a few minutes and discuss this?"

Russell looked at his wife, his jaw locked, body tense—a man on the brink of self-destruction. Finally, he nodded.

"I'll make us some coffee." Lori Lomakin went to take a step toward the kitchen.

Lucy stood in her way. "Let me do that for you. You stay here and talk to SSA Hawthorne."

Lori Lomakin's expression crumbled.

Lucy was good with people. She was still a bit of an enigma to Max, but he got the feeling patience would work in his favor when trying to figure her out. As with lowering a kidnapper's expectations, eventually Lucy would realize she was stuck with him—at least temporarily—and adjust her reality. And then she might actually begin to enjoy herself again.

He hoped so, anyway.

He followed Russell and Lori outside. A stone patio led to three steps and a long green lawn. Potted plants filled every space in a cacophony of color. A small jacaranda tree in full bloom provided a dappled purple shade.

Max sat on an uncomfortable iron garden chair. Russell and Lori sat close together, but their body language screamed emotional distance.

"Forgive me for asking basic questions, but I'm trying to figure out exactly what I'm dealing with here. How long have you lived in Buenos Aires?"

Russell crossed his arms over his chest. "Four years now."

Lori Lomakin's lips pinched and she looked away.

"The girls all go to the International school?"

Again, the terse nod.

Sweat was beginning to form on Russell's brow. He wore a clean, pink shirt, no tie, and faded jeans. His hair went in every direction as if he'd been grabbing handfuls of it and twisting. Lori looked as if she hadn't slept or showered since Christmas Eve.

"Irene has been friends with Kristen Dickerson since Kristen arrived here, correct?"

Lori picked at the skin around her cuticles. Max noted she had raw patches around several nails. Even though it must sting, she worried the skin in a compulsive fashion.

"Yeah." Russell rubbed both hands over his face. "They're in a lot of the same classes. She and Kristen connected pretty quickly. There's a group of five girls who hang out together a lot."

"I assume the British Embassy's been in touch?"

Russell made a sound somewhere between a snort and a growl. "Some pompous ass came by and said they'd help any way they could, but that the British government does not, under any circumstances, negotiate with kidnappers. He also suggested this was our fault for letting our daughter out on her own and reminded us to be careful when talking to the media." Russell swallowed repeatedly. "He said the local police have a good record of dealing with these types of cases." Russell's voice rose. "But if that is true, why are there still so many fucking kidnappings in this country!"

"He also said we should get as much cash together as we can and pay the kidnappers." Lori's voice was level—not with calm but with numbness.

Russell dragged his hand through his hair.

Lucy arrived with coffee on a tray, and her eyes darted around the table with concern.

Max preferred Lucy outside the embassy because she allowed herself to show her emotions whereas, inside the embassy, she was as much an automaton as Lori Lomakin. He wasn't sure why but intended to figure it out.

He waited for Lucy to distribute the mugs and take a seat.

"What is your company doing about the situation?" Max asked.

Lori's face crumpled and Russell looked stricken.

"Not a lot." His voice was bitter.

"Not a lot?" Max mirrored. He waited silently even though he had fifteen thousand questions.

Russell swallowed audibly. "I fucked up." He laughed, but it sounded like heartbreak. Then the man started to cry, squeezing his eyes shut, silent sobs shaking his shoulders.

Rather than comforting her husband, Lori closed her own eyes and crossed her legs and looked away. Everything about her suggested she was on the verge of snapping.

Max exchanged a look with Lucy and saw the empathy he was feeling returned in her gaze. He didn't understand. Where was their company's K&R expert? Where was the negotiator?

It took the Lomakins a few minutes to get themselves back together and Max waited, giving them the space to grieve while he quietly sipped his coffee.

Finally, Russell wiped his eyes with a handkerchief he pulled out of his pocket. Lori took a deep breath and unwound her cramped limbs. She might not have been weeping on the outside, but the woman was wrung dry on the inside.

"Sorry," Russell said, taking a big swallow of coffee. "I haven't slept much since this happened."

"Don't apologize. I get how stressful this situation must be. What I'm trying to figure out is why isn't your company helping you deal with this?"

A pained expression moved over Russell's features. "Like I said, I fucked up. I accepted a new position this month, and my last day at the old job was on Christmas Eve. We hadn't told the girls yet because we didn't want to upset them over Christmas."

"We?" Lori's face distorted with rage. "You should never have accepted a new job without talking to me."

Ah, that would explain the animosity.

"But then when do you care about me and the girls when you're making career plans?"

Ouch.

"I work my ass off so you and the girls can have a good life."

Max was familiar with this marital dispute. His parents had divorced not long after their version of it.

Lori laughed harshly. "How's that working out for us now?"

Russell turned away, expression angry and mutinous.

"You do what you want and expect me and the girls to follow along like puppets."

The fissures in this marriage were becoming gaping cracks.

Max still didn't understand. "Are you saying that it's taking time for the companies to figure out which of them is responsible?"

"What he's saying," bitterness dripped from every syllable, "is that there is no insurance." Lori Lomakin's skin was so pale, Max worried she might faint. Only fear and resentment seemed to be keeping her upright. "The new job is in Brazil and doesn't start until February. The old job finished the moment Russell left the office for the last time on December 24th. We have no personal insurance that covers this kind of situation because Russ is too much of a cheapskate to buy it. Now look at us."

"It was six weeks," Russell said tightly. "We've lived here for four years and never had any trouble. How could I know that kidnappers would target one of Irene's friends and that Irene would be dumb enough to get involved." His voice rang off the stone walls that surrounded the garden.

It wasn't surprising that this was a serious issue between the two of them. Parents of abducted and murdered children often lost each other through the ordeal. Max didn't think these two would last the week.

But what did that mean for Irene?

"Irene knew you had kidnap insurance through your old company?"

Russell nodded miserably.

It seemed likely that Irene had told the kidnappers that her dad's company had insurance in an effort to increase her value to her captors. What happened when the kidnappers discovered Irene was mistaken?

They'd assume she was lying.

Would they kill her? Or punish her for what they would see as a betrayal? Max didn't like this situation at all.

Usually, he'd have had to walk away, but something about the ragged seams of this family bursting with grief, and the fact Irene had only been taken in an effort to rescue her friend, pulled his strings.

"How much money can you raise for the ransom without insurance?" Max tried to keep his voice calm and soothing.

Russell blew air up over his face. "We have stocks and shares we can liquidate to the tune of twenty thousand pounds in the next week or so. The girls all have college funds we can cash out—"

"And how are they going to afford to go to college?" Lori asked with anguish.

"What does it matter if Irene is dead?" Russell sliced back.

Max interceded before they tore each other apart. "I realize how awful this is, but you need to work together for the sake of your daughters, if not your marriage."

Russell looked at him with shock then, as if he'd never considered his marriage to be a potential casualty of this. Lori's mouth firmed. She knew. She was already halfway out the door.

"My dad has some money," she said suddenly. "He might lend us some."

"That miserly old bastard wouldn't piss on me if I was on fire."

Lori's eyes burned. "He's very fond of all the girls, especially Irene. Says she's spunky, like my mother was."

"How do you think Irene will be holding up?" Max asked carefully.

Russell scratched his nose. "She is spunky. If she wasn't, she'd have left Kristen Dickerson to her fate like the other girl did."

"It's always been one of her more endearing traits. She came out of the womb ready for anything." Lori smiled and finally seemed to let go a little of the overwhelming horror she must be experiencing. "She's strong and smart. As long as she doesn't argue with the men who've taken her…"

"She probably will though… She argues with me all the time." Russell slumped. He looked exhausted and on the verge of crying again. These people were way out of their depth.

"We have reason to believe Irene told the kidnappers that you have kidnap insurance through your work."

Lori went tense again. "What will they do when they find out it's not true?"

Max didn't answer her question. "You said they told you not to talk to the police?"

Russell nodded. "They called the landline early this morning. Told me they wanted ten million dollars." He dropped his face into his cupped hands. "We don't have ten million dollars."

These people needed professional help.

"Look, I will do my best to get both Kristen and Irene released by the kidnappers but, officially, I can only negotiate on behalf of any Americans present."

"You sound British," Lori argued.

Max inclined his head. "Born and raised, but I had to renounce my dual citizenship when I signed up for the FBI. I will treat the girls as a package deal but, if they release Kristen, then I'm officially done with the case." That bothered him. It would have bothered any member of the Crisis Negotiation Unit. "I do have a close friend who works in the K&R business."

"We can't afford to pay him if we need all our money to raise the ransom," Russell objected.

"He's a professional who will save you more than he costs in the long run, but your daughter would be his priority, and he knows how to work with me rather than against me so the kidnappers don't play us off one another. *If* he took this case, he would be doing it as a personal favor to me, but I know he's not going to want to work in a toxic environment." That sounded harsh, but his buddy wouldn't put up with childish fights between adults. "You'll have to work out your personal issues in private at a later date, when the kidnapping is resolved."

"We can do that," Russell stated confidently.

It was Lori who Max was looking at. Seeing her thoughts flicker over her features like words in a book. Anger, resentment, finally hope. "We'd be incredibly grateful to have someone helping us. Russell and I have a lot to deal with in our relationship. I called a marriage counselor last week in an—"

"I'm not talking to a marriage counselor," Russell muttered. "I don't need fucking therapy."

"Well, if you don't attend counseling, we won't have a marriage to save, but I can't make you do anything, obviously. It's going to be up to you." Lori smoothed her hands down her flower-print skirt. Her voice was quiet and resigned. She seemed to have come to a place of inner calm and understanding, about her marriage at least. "We would welcome this negotiator's help. Thank you for the offer to talk to him on our behalf. I will call my father and tell him what's happened. I won't ask for money because then he'd never offer it. But he might volunteer it once he knows how serious the situation is."

She held Max's gaze. "We will do whatever we need to do to bring our daughter home again, SSA Hawthorne. What else do you need to know?"

CHAPTER FIFTEEN

"THAT WAS INTENSE." Lucy slipped out of her suit jacket and hung it over the back of her headrest. She felt emotionally drained after that encounter, and she was only a bystander.

It had been bad enough to experience it with Catherine and Phillip Dickerson but at least they were able to get presidents on the phone at short notice. The Lomakins might be upper-middle class enjoying the good life, but without the financial cushion of the independently wealthy or the political connections of the Foreign Service, they were essentially powerless. And the kidnappers had made them too scared to even go to the police.

"Yeah." Max blew out a breath.

"Where to next?" They both climbed into the Mini and rolled down the windows to release the sweltering heat.

Happy Holidays.

"Argentine Federal Police headquarters at 1650 Moreno Street. I want to take a look at those files on the cases from the Brazilian street gang a couple of years ago." He gave her a searching look as if he wasn't sure how she might react to his request.

She resisted the urge to pat down her hair or otherwise fix her appearance.

"I need a trustworthy translator, but the information might include crime scene photographs and descriptions you might find disturbing. You don't have to do it. I can get someone else assigned."

Her heart gave a little tumble at the double hit. The fact he considered her trustworthy and the fact he didn't want to make her do anything she wasn't comfortable with made him the antithesis of everything else going on in her life right now.

She covered her fluster by adjusting her mirrors. "The ambassador wanted me to help you."

"I don't care about the ambassador, Lucy. If it adversely affects you then we're going to stop, and I'll figure out a better way."

Her pulse skipped along her veins like a lovesick fool. Which was dumb. This wasn't personal. He wasn't attracted to her. He was simply a super nice guy who happened to inhabit a red-hot body that had inadvertently reminded her she used to have a libido. Not his fault.

She cleared her throat. "It's fine. I have a strong constitution. If the photographs are too graphic, I simply won't look at them."

She reflexively gripped and released the leather-clad steering wheel. She'd have to figure out how to give the Russians information that was essentially worthless. She still hadn't figured out if they'd been the ones to take Kristen, in which case they would want to be kept informed so they could evade capture. It shouldn't be impossible to feed Felix and his cronies enough information to make it look like she was fully cooperating, but not enough so they could get away with anything.

Max smiled. "I appreciate your help. If you change your

mind or it becomes too much for you, let me know. We'll figure it out. Now if you don't mind, I need to make a call and beg a favor from a friend."

He pulled out his personal smartphone while she programmed her Sat Nav. She wasn't familiar with the federal police building. She thankfully hadn't had any reason to visit PFA's headquarters, until now.

She started driving. The streets were busy again with shoppers hunting for bargains.

"Hey, Andy? How you doing, mate?" As Max spoke to his friend, Lucy pretended not to listen. After a few minutes of catch up about mutual acquaintances, Max finally got to the point. "I need a favor."

He outlined the situation Irene Lomakin found herself in. Told this guy—Andy—that the parents had no insurance but could pay some money toward his salary. Max then offered to pay the difference in the shortfall, but he didn't want the parents to know.

Lucy glanced at Max in shock.

He met her gaze but didn't react.

"How soon can you get out here?" He looked at his watch. "That's great. Thanks, man. I'll email you the Lomakins' contact details. The FBI is taking the lead on the case, and I will try to get the girls released as a joint package, but I don't want things going sideways if Russell Lomakin starts negotiating on the side. He's a loose cannon I don't need."

After another few minutes of chat, Max hung up.

"You're paying his salary?" Lucy asked.

"Well, not really. I mean I offered, but I doubt he'll take me up on it. Plus, he won't be here more than a few weeks. His employer will undoubtedly require him somewhere else in the world in the not-too-distant future. He'll set everything up and find a local contact to run it through from abroad. It won't bankrupt me. He owes me a favor from way back."

"Where is he?"

"London. He can be on a flight in three hours. Has enough airmiles to fly business class for free."

"That's a heck of a favor. What did you do, save his life?"

Max's dark eyes met hers, but he didn't say anything.

He had saved his life.

"Don't tell me it's classified." Lucy laughed but suddenly it wasn't funny. She really didn't want to know anything classified.

"I think officially it didn't even happen, but Andy is a good friend." He paused and said slowly, "We'd have died for one another but, thankfully, we didn't have to."

Ice swept over Lucy's shoulders despite the heat. "He's lucky you had his back."

"I'm lucky he had mine."

It must be nice having that sort of support. Brothers-in-arms and all that.

She concentrated on the traffic, deftly weaving in and out of the other cars. Then she noticed Max watching her and realized her mistake. She purposefully cut someone off and received a blast of the horn. She waved an apology out of the window. "Sorry."

"No problem," Max said, but something about the way he said it suggested he wasn't fooled.

Shit.

They reached the city block that housed the *Departmento Central Policia Federal,* and Lucy drove around the beautiful yellow and white building with its baroque-style architecture.

Tall, electronic masts sprouted from the roof and the blue, white, and gold Argentine flag flew proudly above the main facade, held erect by two reclining, half-naked women. It was a beautiful building that seemed at odds with the mundane police work that must take place within.

Max peered up at the place. "Beats JEH hands down in the looks department."

Lucy smiled. "I've always rather liked FBI headquarters."

"You spent much time in DC?"

Lucy hesitated and knew she'd blown it. "Yeah. I used to work there."

"Where?" he asked curiously.

She sucked in a deep breath. "I worked for the Agency. Briefly." She didn't like admitting it, but it was part of her file. He'd find out if he bothered to look, and she was sure the Bureau was looking at all the embassy staff again. In excruciating detail. Lying about it at this point would look worse than admitting it.

He shifted in his seat to face her. "You worked for the CIA?"

Lucy swallowed. "Wild, huh?"

"It actually makes a lot of sense." Max's tone cooled, and his eyes turned more wary.

Lucy shot him a look. "What part of that makes sense?"

"The way you drive. The way you handled that guy in the alley yesterday. The way you avoid being the center of attention."

"I guess." She shrugged unhappily. "They taught me a few good things, but I'm not sure it was worth it."

"Why? What happened?"

"I don't like to talk about that time in my life." That was

the truth. She wasn't going to tell him the whole dirty truth. Couldn't. "I was only there for about a year. I didn't like how they did business, so I applied to the Foreign Service instead. It's a much better fit for me."

Max watched her carefully and Lucy was scared about what he might see. His earlier warmth had faded. That was a good thing. Right?

"I've never been a fan of spooks," he admitted finally.

"Me neither. What's your excuse?" She shot him an amused glance.

He shrugged, looking relaxed again, although Lucy knew she'd lost a few points in his eyes.

"MI6 keeps hounding me to work for them."

"They want you to spy against the US?" Lucy's voice rose. She didn't have to act like a rube most of the time. It came naturally.

"Of course not, at least not openly." He grinned. "They couch it as letting them know any information that might be useful to them, but I know where it's headed so I always say no. I'm not saying I don't exchange information with my contemporaries when necessary for a case. Everyone leans on contacts and it's a two-way street. But I detest spooks and make sure MI6 knows it."

She flinched.

"My contacts tend to be Department of Defense or people outside normal government channels like Andy." He shrugged. "I'm glad you're not in that world anymore. It would have chewed you up and spat you out."

"It already did."

Max's lips pinched sympathetically. "I'm sorry about that."

"Not your fault." It was her fault. She was the idiot who'd

fallen for a Russian operative.

Having driven around the entire police building, she spotted what looked like a visitor entrance where she pulled up.

She grabbed her jacket but hooked it over her arm. It was hot today and she didn't want to put it on. Lucy doubted anyone here would care about her appearance. Her hair was sweaty and pulled back in a pony, and her face was tired and bare of makeup. Buenos Aires was full of vibrant, beautiful women like the three from the bar last night. Lucy flew under the radar 99.9% of the time. Today would be no different.

She groped around for her smile even though she felt irritated for letting down her guard. Max came around the car. The way he moved was mesmerizing. The fluid grace of his muscles, the constant awareness of his surroundings. He reminded her of the DS agents when they were working close protection, except the sleeker, sexier version.

He paused in front of her, and she found herself staring up into those dark eyes.

"Don't forget to tell me if you find the files disturbing. I'll come back another time. I don't want to give you nightmares."

She already had nightmares.

Lucy shook her head. "I want to help Kristen any way I can. I want to help get both girls home."

He nodded and then took out his cell phone, pulled out a business card that was doubtless the one Hector Cabral had given him that morning, and called the guy while inspecting the imposing edifice.

Lucy took advantage of the moment to enjoy the architecture of the man's face. High cheekbones, soft lips, stubborn jaw. Eyes so deep and dark they pulled you in until you felt like you were drowning.

Perfect.

She was getting in way over her head with this guy. He kept getting better and better, and the fact he was this considerate of a woman who was definitely on the dowdy side made his behavior seem even more gallant.

Dammit.

She hated lying to him. If Max ever discovered the truth, he'd never trust her again. He'd despise her. She gave herself a few seconds of selfish enjoyment because it was all she'd ever have. Once he hung up, she snapped out of it and followed him to the side entrance where she spoke to the guard. Time to earn her keep while trying not to betray her country.

———————

LUCY WAS FORMER CIA?

Lucy?

What the actual fuck?

It made sense in a weird, twisted-logic sort of way. Who was the least likely person in the room he'd suspect to be working for the Agency? Definitely Lucy Aston. She didn't look anything like what he'd expect a spook to look like which made absolute sense. A trench coat and trilby would be a dead giveaway.

She was the gray man that the others didn't notice—but some of them must know she was former CIA. It must be in her background personnel file if she'd told him about it.

Did she wear baggy clothes and dye her hair brown to eschew her old Agency life, or was that what Langley had taught her to do—disguise herself so no one noticed her? Or was how she dressed a matter of preference? He still couldn't shake the suspicion that she was hiding in some effort at self-preservation. He'd suspected sexual assault in her past but now he wondered if it was simply a biproduct of being chewed up and spat out by the Agency.

Could be both.

Max glanced at Lucy again as they showed their IDs to the guard. What had she done for the CIA? Some sort of low-level analyst? A language specialist? Likely from what she'd told him earlier. She wasn't old enough to be too senior. It was a tough working environment, and he wasn't surprised Lucy hadn't stuck with it. Life in the grinder was no fun.

He intended to dig deeper. Call it professional curiosity. His innate mistrust of spooks came from working with intelligence officers in the field and being fed half-truths or downright lies in order for them to get what they wanted out of an operation. Spooks always believed the end justified the means, but that wasn't necessarily true—especially when he and his friends had been the ones to risk their lives.

Lucy spoke to the police guard to tell him they were here to see Hector Cabral. A quick phone call to confirm they were expected, and they were let through to a security desk where they checked in and had to leave all electronic devices in a small locker. As much as he hated parting with his phones, as much as he wasn't supposed to go anywhere without his work cell, if he wanted to see these files, he had to play by the host country's rules.

And damn sure CNU would be checking his phone when he got back to Quantico for any type of listening devices.

Spooks. Every country had them.

The inspector met them on the other side of the bullet- and blast-proof divider.

They shook hands, Cabral squeezing a little tighter than necessary and sweeping his gaze over Lucy's form in a way that made Max squeeze back just a little bit harder. Hard enough for Cabral's lips to thin.

Lucy's plain white blouse had gone limp in the humidity and clung to her curves revealing the outline of a lacy bra beneath. A blast of air conditioning had her nipples pebbling against the cotton.

And Cabral was enjoying getting an eyeful.

Max wanted to wrap her baggy jacket around her shoulders and protect her from leering male gazes that she didn't appear to notice. Her eyes were lowered the way she always did when around anyone else.

Was it an act? Or was the more laid-back way she behaved with him the act?

Although she'd mastered the art of staying in the background, when she did venture into the spotlight, men noticed. *Because most men were dogs.*

Max pulled his head out of his ass and got down to work. "Thanks for agreeing to let us examine your files. The FBI very much appreciates the PFA's cooperation in this matter."

Cabral's brown eyes were keenly intelligent. "We want to help in any way we can. Obviously, we expect to be informed of any leads the FBI comes up with in the spirit of cooperation so the PFA can act upon it."

Cabral was reminding him who was in charge. Max hadn't forgotten. This wasn't his jurisdiction. Max nodded. "Of course."

Cabral led them to a staircase, and they walked up to the third floor. In the center of the police station was the most magnificent courtyard Max had ever seen, surpassing the one at FBI headquarters by an ascetic factor of a gazillion.

Cabral indicated a door on the right. "That's my office. As always, I'll be working late tonight. Come find me there before you leave." He pointed out washrooms and a coffee room. "Help yourself to coffee or *maté*."

Maté was the caffeine-rich traditional beverage the locals drank.

Max checked his watch and realized they'd inadvertently skipped lunch.

Farther down the corridor, Cabral punched in a six-digit code to open a door. Max stepped inside to see two bankers' boxes on a small desk and another two larger boxes on the floor. The floor was polished hardwood, and there was a small, open window that let in the whisper of a breeze. Wooden shutters had been pulled closed to keep out the sun. Two plastic chairs that could have come out of any police station in the world sat side-by-side beneath the desk.

"I took the liberty of requesting the files out of storage after we spoke this morning. I had planned to examine them myself to refresh my memory but so far today, I've been too busy." He gave an eloquent shrug.

"I appreciate you doing this for us. If I see any similarities of note, I will inform you, although I'm sure you know both cases inside out."

"Never hurts to have a fresh pair of eyes." Cabral gave them the code to the door and then went back to his office, leaving Max and Lucy once again alone.

Max eyed the cameras in the room, which he was sure were live.

"Ready?" he asked Lucy quietly.

She nodded. "Where do we begin?"

Max looked at the dates on each box and picked up the oldest. "Let's start at the beginning."

CHAPTER SIXTEEN

F OUR COFFEES AND many hours later, he and Lucy had reviewed three of the four boxes.

The kidnap gang had been ruthless and had terrorized the hostage's families by torturing their captives, often while on the telephone as they demanded money from relatives. In one call, the spokesman of the group had described how the female hostage was being gang-raped by his fellow kidnappers and threatened that it would happen every day until the family paid the ransom.

The family paid up as soon as they were able to raise the money.

Max wasn't sorry the bastards were dead. They probably had sob stories and difficult childhoods, but it didn't excuse that sort of depravity. When someone treated their fellow human beings like property to barter and sell, they stopped deserving much consideration beyond how long they should spend in prison.

Not that the history books necessarily agreed.

He grabbed the fourth blue box off the floor and reached inside to dig out the final batch of files that dealt with the last known kidnapping and the eventual takedown of the group.

Lucy took a sip of her coffee, her arm brushing his. She'd rolled up her sleeves as the heat climbed throughout the afternoon. Max wondered if the local police had deliberately turned off the AC in this room to make them sweat, or if the old building's pipes simply didn't have sufficient power to reach this remote corner. He'd removed his suit jacket and tie, rolled up his sleeves, and was still feeling the heat.

Lucy put her cup down, and he noticed a series of six small moles that formed a perfect triangle on her forearm. Her skin was lightly tanned and covered in fine, golden, sun-bleached hairs. The contrast with his warm, brown skin was marked. She'd removed her glasses and set them on the end of the table.

He shifted, and their legs accidentally brushed. He moved his chair an inch to the right, but there was no avoiding physical contact in these close confines when the desk was so small and they both needed to look at the documents together. He tried to keep it professional, but he'd be lying if he said that over the last couple of hours, he hadn't started to see Lucy a little differently.

Was it the former CIA thing? As much as he hated spooks, there was no denying the concept was hot, even though she downplayed every asset she had.

Or perhaps that was the appeal, the fact he saw how pretty she was even when she tried so hard not to be. Did most people simply choose not to look that closely? Lucy Aston seemed like a mystery designed especially for him.

There were few things more compelling than an unanswered question, and Lucy was full of them.

Didn't really change anything.

He didn't mess around when he was working. And something about Lucy suggested she'd need an extra amount of care and attention when in a relationship. He shook his head at himself. He'd gone from being mildly attracted to Lucy to reminding himself he wanted to avoid long-term, long-distance relationships, all in the space of twenty seconds.

She might not even like men, but he'd be lying if he said he hadn't noticed those occasional flashes of heat that flared between them. Unexpected and clearly unwanted on both sides.

She picked up the top paper file and opened up the report. She translated the first page about the initial abduction of a woman called Camilla Marquez. Forty-three. The wife of a prominent banker in Buenos Aires. They'd snatched her from the parking lot of a mall the woman had been visiting. They'd used four men for the abduction, who all wore masks and had bundled the victim into a white, side-paneled van—just like Kristen Dickerson and Irene Lomakin.

One difference Max immediately noticed was these guys didn't ask for millions of US dollars. They demanded five million pesos which was about 65,000 US dollars. It wasn't chump change, but it was doable in a relatively short amount of time for many upper-middle-class families if they mortgaged the house and begged all their friends and family to lend them cash. According to the previous reports they'd read, the voice of the main negotiator was always electronically disguised—again, similar—but the screams and voices in the background apparently were not.

It could be the same gang but with someone more intelligent and less volatile in charge. Someone who didn't want to die in a blaze of bullets.

Max squeezed the bridge of his nose.

"Are you okay?" Lucy asked quietly. "Can I get you another coffee?"

He shook his head. "If I drink more coffee, I may never sleep again."

Lucy continued translating. "Camilla was kidnapped on a Tuesday, and the ransom demand came in the next day. Here it says that the police became aware of this kidnapping when the victim's sister heard about it from the victim's husband when he asked her for money. She secretly went to Cabral's house that night and told him everything. She was a friend of Cabral's ex-wife."

"Cabral was smart enough and had the right connections to swiftly instigate a covert reaction force," Max commented. "The sister showed a lot of balls approaching the cops. If news had leaked, Camilla would have been as dead as those earlier victims."

Lucy's lips were bloodless and tense. "It says the family paid the ransom as arranged. The police set up land, air, and drone support to follow the money."

Max took the photos out of the file and laid a couple on the table. They showed one of the kidnappers picking up the bag of cash after it had been thrown into a ditch north of the city.

Lucy read the report, moving her finger along the text to keep her place in case he interrupted with questions, which he frequently did.

"The cops followed the car of the guy who picked up the cash which was driven back into the city in a circuitous route designed to detect surveillance."

An SDR. Max assumed the CIA had trained Lucy in surveillance detection routes.

"Once satisfied he wasn't being followed, the kidnapper drove to a property south of the city, and the police waited for

Camilla Marquez to be released." Lucy hooked her hair behind her ear and leaned toward him.

He found himself watching her lips.

"It says here that the police tailed all the male occupants of that house for two days and eventually they were led to another more remote location in a poorer neighborhood south-west of the city. Camilla Marquez and some of the other victims described the place where they were held as rural and poor. Camilla had spied fields and someone else said they'd smelled goats." Lucy frowned. "I don't know what a goat smells like."

Max smiled in amusement.

"Once they were convinced they had the right place—as determined by the amount of booze and women seen arriving that Friday night, they waited for the women to leave and stormed the place in the early hours of Sunday morning."

Max took the other photographs out of the file, but he didn't show them to Lucy, and she didn't ask to see. The kidnappers had all been shot dead. Some had weapons in their hands, but many did not. And not all the women had vacated the premises. Had they been girlfriends of gang members or sex workers? They were possibly innocent victims of the police raid. No one had mentioned them as such.

Max had a feeling the cops were performing clean up and delivering a message to anyone who contemplated committing this sort of crime in the future. He found a photo of a thin pallet and a pair of manacles attached to a heavy radiator via a thick chain. A dirty dog's bowl sat beside the makeshift bed— apparently the hostages' water supply. A red plastic bucket was nearby that the hostages were expected to use as a toilet.

Camilla Marquez had been released, but the kidnappers

looked like they were all set for the next victim.

A lot of the money appeared to be spent partying on the weekend, although Max had no doubt a portion would have been funneled back to the gang's leaders.

He placed the photo of the radiator on the table and Lucy stared at it.

"It was a business for them." She sounded numb. "They didn't care about the victims at all."

"Nope, they didn't." Max put the photographs and files back into the box and placed the lids carefully on the top. These boxes told the story of untold damage and heartbreak— exactly the sort of things he tried to mitigate. The Argentine police had done a good job at shutting this kidnap ring down, but had someone survived and decided to revive what had been a profitable endeavor?

He checked his watch and pushed back his chair. "I've had enough of this for one day. How about we grab something to eat before we check back in with the troops?"

Lucy blew out a breath that caused the tendrils of hair around her face to flutter. "I wonder if there have been any updates?"

The good thing about not having access to his phones was the lack of interruptions. He could concentrate better.

"We'll check on the way out. But I need to eat."

Lucy nodded and hung her jacket over her arm.

"Let's go find Cabral."

When they reached Hector Cabral's office, the door was open, and he seemed to be holding some sort of meeting as ten to twenty people were crammed into the small space while he held court from behind the large desk.

Max knocked on the door, not wanting to interrupt but

also cognizant that the man had specifically asked to be informed when they were finished and ready to leave.

Cabral looked up and raised his hand to interrupt the person talking. "You are finished?" he asked.

"Yes. I appreciate you letting us examine the files."

"Did you see anything that led you to believe the ambassador's daughter's kidnapping was related?"

"It's a little early to say but, at this stage, I'd say it was unlikely."

Cabral's eyes widened a fraction. "Really?"

"There are similarities but also some stark differences."

The man smiled grimly. "Let us hope so."

Max returned the look. The last thing anyone wanted was the two girls being raped and tortured. "We'll get out of your hair. Thanks again for letting me examine the files."

"Keep us informed of your progress." Cabral barked, "*Agente* Ramon. Show the FBI the door."

A few barely concealed sniggers suggested Cabral was flexing his muscles in front of his subordinates, but Max was too old for pissing contests. The guy had done what Max wanted, and that's all that mattered to him. That was the art of negotiation. First, remove your ego from the situation. Then figure out what you wanted.

Agente Ramon came into the corridor and the male eyes inside followed her like iron filings to a magnet. She was short, probably only 5'2" with shiny black hair that hung all the way down to her waist. She wore skintight, black jeans, short-heeled boots, an electric blue blouse that was tight enough and unbuttoned enough to reveal the upper curves of her breasts. A deadly Glock-17 rode her hip.

Her eyes were tilted, darkened with kohl lines that curled

up at the outer edges. Her mouth wore a coat of cherry lipstick. The woman was a knockout.

"Follow me, please." Proving she also spoke perfect English.

Was that why Cabral had asked this woman to show them out when there was a roomful of men there?

She led the way with an exaggerated sway to her hips.

Or maybe that was why. Cabral was playing a game of temptation, hoping Max might spill a few secrets to the hot brunette.

Max glanced at Lucy, but her mouth was pinched, and her eyes were once again downcast. Impossible to read.

"Are you working the kidnapping case, Agente Ramon?"

She turned and waited for him and Lucy to catch up, but Lucy deliberately hung back.

"We were all called back in to work." Her voice was deep and throaty.

"That's too bad your vacation was put on hold."

"Actually, considering we're being paid overtime, no one minds too much. The criminals earn a lot more than we do." She shrugged like it was no big deal. Max had the feeling she knew exactly how incredible her body was and used it for best effect. Max wasn't immune to beauty, but he didn't like being manipulated. That was his job.

"Agente Ramon," he said. "The FBI appreciates all the help the PFA is giving us. We care very much about getting these girls safely home to their parents."

She gave an affirmative jerk of her head. "No one likes kidnappers. Hopefully, the ambassador pays the ransom as requested and the girls are released unharmed." Another shrug told of the fact she knew what happened when kidnappers didn't get their money.

"Hopefully, we can come to some sort of agreement with the kidnappers. There's no way the ambassador can afford millions of dollars."

She shot him a sharp look. "The American government won't pay? I thought that was just a public show of bravado."

Max held her gaze before they started down the stairs. "Would the Argentine government pay?"

Agente Ramon laughed, and the sound echoed off the walls. "That would depend on exactly who was taken and who was in power."

Max smirked. "Do the Argentines have any leads they haven't shared with us?"

Agente Ramon shook her head, and her ebony hair rippled in a wave around her shoulders. "I wish we did. Do the Americans?" she countered.

Or the Brits, for that matter, he thought.

"No."

She pulled a face that suggested she didn't believe him.

They reached the lockers, and he pulled out his phones and turned them on. His work cell started binging like a pinball machine.

One of the messages was from Eban. The lab had confirmed the presence of two DNA profiles on the ring Max had found in the alley yesterday afternoon. One belonged to Kristen Dickerson. The other was unknown.

"Hey, Ramon."

She paused on her way back up the stairs.

"We have a DNA sample from a possible suspect that we'd love to run against your databases. How's that for sharing?" He smiled, and she gave him a long, sultry look in return. Lucy stood beside him, pretending she didn't exist. It irritated him for no tangible reason.

"If you can talk to your evidence lab, I'll arrange for Quantico to forward the profile. With luck, you could have a hit to take back with you to the meeting."

Her eyes narrowed, clearly contemplating where this particular break might put her in the investigation.

"Fine. Come with me. We will talk to one of the DNA experts who is usually happy to do me a favor." She jerked her chin to indicate they follow her. Then she seemed to register Lucy for the first time, and her finely arched brows rose. "I don't know who dresses your friend, but my grandmother has some clothes she can borrow."

Lucy glanced at Ramon, eyes wide in surprise.

"My friend is standing right there listening to every word," Max bit out. "She dresses however the hell she wants."

Lucy looked back at the floor, and he watched the line of her throat ripple as she swallowed.

Had Ramon hurt her feelings? Lucy was such a mystery to him he couldn't tell. And he was skilled at reading people. It was what made him good at his job.

Agente Ramon shrugged like she didn't care how her words impacted Lucy. Then she led the way down the stairs to the lab.

Max stowed his anger. He'd thought something similar about how Lucy dressed yesterday morning. He was trying to pinpoint exactly when his opinion had changed and realized it was about the time he'd seen her pissed off at the Legat when wearing her workout gear which had hugged every inch of her body.

So maybe he wasn't quite as sanctimonious as he was trying to make out.

CHAPTER SEVENTEEN

"**Y**OU DIDN'T NEED to defend me back there, you know." Lucy took a quick drink of water to cool down. "With that police officer."

Max's lips kicked up in a grin. He grabbed his beer and raised it in salute. "Noted."

Dear god, he was gorgeous. And kind. She speared a lettuce leaf. She'd already polished off an enormous *Milanesa a caballo* as Max tried a selection of world famous barbecued Argentine *asado*.

The female agent's snide remarks about her clothing were actually a compliment to Lucy's skills at disguise. She'd met women like that before, plenty of them. The derogatory remarks in the past had carried a different type of barb. The favorite theme had been to mock her intelligence due to her "Barbie-doll" looks and long blonde hair. Certain men had treated her like an airhead for the same reason—the same guys who often hit on her for a date later. Forget her ability to speak six foreign languages or her accelerated Master's degree. They'd labeled her a bimbo and the most frustrating thing was, she'd gone and proven them right.

The Old Lucy had fought back and made a lot of enemies, which was not a good way to cultivate a career in an organization that relied heavily on contacts and cooperation. She'd learned all her lessons the hard way and was inordinately proud at how she hadn't responded to Agente Ramon, not even on the inside.

But Max hadn't known any of that. Physically, he saw what the detective saw, but he viewed Frumpy Lucy with a lot more compassion than anyone else had over the last year or so.

As a reward, she'd brought Max to one of her favorite restaurants on the outskirts of San Telmo. It would have been easier to grab a sandwich somewhere on the way back to the embassy, but they'd worked through lunch and would probably both be working long into the evening.

This area was the first to have been settled by Europeans and boasted cobbled streets and low-story colonials. It was in these narrow streets and shady squares where the world-famous tango had been born.

She took a large sip of Malbec and tried not to moon over her companion. She really should know better.

There were only a small number of tables in the restaurant and later they'd be cleared away for dancing. Christmas lights decorated the buildings and trees around the square. She'd almost forgotten it was Christmas. It seemed wrong somehow that everything looked so festive and happy when Kristen and Irene were probably locked up somewhere dark and frightening, worried about whether or not they were going to make it out alive.

Max's cell buzzed on the table, and he glanced at the screen.

"Word from the kidnappers?" She spoke quietly so as not to be overhead. A cool breeze lifted the tendrils of hair off her neck. She tied her hair back when she was alone with Max—she wasn't sure if it was some remnant of vanity, or simply the knowledge he'd already seen her this way and so it didn't matter as much. Probably a mixture of both. It was a relief to get the heavy mess out of her face on a hot day.

Max shook his head. "They haven't called back, and I don't expect them to yet. Adam Quinn has been manning the phones all day, and I was going to go in and spot him while he got some sleep, but he just texted to say the camp bed arrived, and he plans to sleep there tonight. He's a good guy, but we need more people. Another negotiator arrives tomorrow. That will give us the ability to train a couple of local agents while still tracking down as much info as possible." He carved off more of the perfectly grilled steak.

"Is it unusual for them not to call back?"

"Not at all. Especially at first. They will probably stay on the line longer when they become more confident we can't track them. My guess is they'll be chewing over what I told them this morning about the ambassador's cashflow issues. I'm hoping we can come to a more reasonable agreement in the next few days."

Lucy pressed her lips together as she remembered what she'd read in those police files today. Sadness overwhelmed her. "Do you think they're hurting the girls in the meantime?"

Max swallowed a mouthful of food and sat there quietly for a few moments. Then he met her gaze. "It depends one hundred percent on the moral code of these individuals and how much control the leader exerts." He frowned. "Just because they kidnapped the girls and are holding them for ransom doesn't mean they are necessarily going to assault them. But it also doesn't mean they won't. I can't say for sure." He blew out a breath. "I know that they are likely to kill the young women should the choice be between that or the kidnappers' freedom."

Lucy was sorry she'd asked. She'd destroyed the peace they'd been sharing.

"The idea that they're suffering breaks my heart and makes me feel useless." She laid down her fork. She was no longer hungry, but she'd almost finished everything anyway. Was Kristen getting any food? Was she still alive? "I guess I need to get better at compartmentalizing."

"No. You don't. Empathy isn't something to be ashamed of." Max shook his head and carried on eating. "I deal with these situations every day so it's not that I'm immune to suffering. I have to push it aside to deal with the problem in a way that is most likely to lead to the successful release of the hostages and less likely to lead to negotiator burnout." He wiped his mouth with a napkin. "I don't get the same frenzy-of-insanity vibe from the man I've been talking to on the phone that I got from reading the Brazilian gang's MO but..."

"What?"

She could see the reflection of fairy lights in the darkness of his eyes.

"Often the person making the phone calls is not the person directly taking care of the hostages."

The air huffed out of Lucy's lungs. She wanted to do something concrete. Track down the hostages and break the girls the hell out. She felt so helpless carrying on as if nothing had happened.

Except Max was correct. She couldn't function without food or sleep. And she couldn't do the job she was supposed to do until the ambassador released her from this temporary assignment. She may as well enjoy what she could.

What if the Russians were involved? She still needed to

send them some sort of update today. They'd expect it. Who knew what they'd do if she didn't jump when they barked jump? "Do you think this could be politically motivated?"

"If it was, I wouldn't expect the ransom demand to be for cash." He dragged the last piece of meat through the sauce on his plate and brought it to his lips.

"Some countries like to mess with our heads," she said carefully.

Max appeared to weigh her words as he chewed his food. "They do. And I'm not saying it's not possible but, if a foreign adversary started to change the rules of the game, then they put all their people working abroad at risk, and all those people's families. We do see people detained for bargaining purposes—China has been especially aggressive in this regard lately but snatching the relatives of embassy staff would produce a whole rash of blowback they probably don't want to deal with."

"What if they do it to stir up trouble and have no intention of getting caught in the act?" The Russians routinely denied everything, even when it was obvious to the rest of the world they were one hundred percent guilty.

Max watched her. Dark brown eyes taking in her features as if he were searching for a tell. "Do you know something you aren't telling me?"

"What?" Lucy blinked. "No! I just…" *Shit.* Except, maybe she had been trying to tell him something. "We were at Boris Yahontov's Christmas party when the ambassador received the news Kristen had been taken. I couldn't help thinking at the time that there couldn't have been a worse place for Catherine Dickerson to hear that information. Even though she didn't stick around or give an explanation as to what the crisis was."

She swallowed, remembering Yahontov's words to her and the way his eyes had filled with cool amusement when they'd had to leave. "It felt like the billionaire was enjoying her distress."

Max grunted. "That sounds like the Russians being very Russian. If we or counterintelligence uncover any hint of SVR or GRU involvement, then we'll dig further. If we find proof, then the shit will hit the fan."

The Russians would deny everything and probably accuse her. If they were involved, they were more than capable of making the girls disappear without a trace. And Lucy was expected to update them? How was she going to manage that without actually feeding them anything valuable?

How much would their other source be able to give them? Who was the other source?—that's what she really wanted to know.

She let Max finish his meal in peace. A man in the corner of the room began playing on the piano. It meant the dancing would begin soon. She wanted Max to see a professional couple perform this dance that was important enough to be considered a UNESCO treasure.

She let thoughts of the case go. It was impossible to worry 24/7. Her life was already a balancing act, and she didn't have the energy to add more anguish to her plate.

If she discovered the Russians had taken the girls, she would make sure the US acted on that information. Until then, she had to figure out what to feed them and what to hold back while still performing her primary duties.

A man with a bandoneon joined in with the music and a well-dressed couple came through from the back of the restaurant and struck a pose. Lucy sat up straight in anticipation. The man had slicked-back, dark hair and wore a black suit with a black shirt and black tie with silver threads that caught the light. The woman wore a skintight, strappy, burgundy top and a tight, purple-sequined skirt with a slit all the way up to her thigh. Her heels were three inches of lethal spikes. The couple stared intensely at one another as the dance began in front of the restaurant.

Lucy was glad she'd brought Max somewhere good, where he could get a feel for the true nature of Buenos Aires. The people here were warm and friendly. Like most big cities there was always some crime, but it still felt safe to walk most of the streets alone at night.

Max obviously worked hard, and she doubted he did much sightseeing on his travels to various kidnap hotspots around the world. She wanted to give him this.

The dancers began the intricate steps and movements that Lucy always found mesmerizing and sexy to watch.

Lucy found herself observing Max's face as he watched the dancers. His eyes were dark and intense, brooding almost.

Was he wishing he wasn't here with her, but rather with the pint-sized police officer with her imperious confidence and impressive rack? Or maybe he'd enjoy himself more if Lucy was her old perky, blonde self, the one Raminsky had all but destroyed? Bitterness rose through her mind at the memory of how hard she'd fallen for the man and how violently she'd crashed to earth. She wanted her old self back in the mirror, but she'd never be that naive again. Or that foolish.

And she didn't know how she'd ever find the courage to sleep with a man again. And maybe that's why she'd been so eager to adopt this new Lucy persona who hid in the shadows. So she could avoid men and their advances and not have to worry about her shattered heart getting obliterated.

She finished her wine and tried to banish Sergio from her mind, but that damned black and white photo told her exactly how much he'd cared about her. He'd cared enough to get a blowjob even though he knew their encounters were being filmed and would end up destroying her well-planned career.

A win-win from his point of view.

Misery welled up inside. She looked around in confusion when the man in the black suit took her hands gently in his and pulled her to the floor.

"What? No. I don't want to dance." She shook her head, but the guy was smiling and coaxing her. It was a thing they did with the tourists. The pity fuck in dance form.

A bitter laugh escaped her lips. She should be used to them by now.

The woman dancer had pulled a bald, chubby guy out of the audience.

Her wannabe partner put his arms around Lucy and began the steps as the musician started playing the music again. Out of the corner of her eye, she saw Max watching her with concern. Suddenly Lucy didn't want to be Frumpy Lucy Aston anymore—the wallflower, the ugly suit, the person who opened doors and made coffee.

The male dancer was patiently showing her the moves. He didn't need to. She'd been taking lessons once a week since she'd arrived in Argentina—as a workout, but also as a harmless act of rebellion against her need to be constantly in disguise.

"Stop. Wait a second." She took off her glasses and shook out her hair. Then she faced her dance partner with her head held high.

The male dancer held out his hands with a curious look.

Lucy nodded her acquiescence, then began following her partner's lead. Her instructor at her dance studio was demanding and always pushed for more and better.

She held this man's gaze as if he were the love of her damn life, and the steps came naturally, drilled into her after weeks and months of hard work in the dance studio. The dancer's palm felt hot through the cotton of her blouse. He twirled her and leaned her back over his arm, smoothing his hand sensuously down the front of her body and along her thigh and then pulling her upright again and sliding his hands down her back.

People were starting to clap when they realized she wasn't the total newb the man had presumed her to be and that she could hold her own on the dance floor.

It was nice to surprise people in a good way for a change. Apparently, the words of the gorgeous Agente Ramon had stoked some of the smoldering anger trapped inside her. Maybe Lucy didn't care what the woman said about her clothes because they were Lucy's disguise, but she did care that the woman had been staring at Max like she wanted to lick ice cream off his naked, flawless skin.

Which had nothing at all to do with Lucy.

A sudden change in tempo had her and her partner increasing the intensity of their footwork, pushing all thought aside as they did the high steps and entangled their feet around each other's legs as if they'd danced the tango together a thousand times. Lucy kept her expression serious but inside she was grinning, laughing even. They spun counterclockwise around the small plaza in a closed embrace. She wrapped her leg around his hip, and he pushed her away, only to snap her sharply back again.

It was sexy. It was electric.

Euphoria buzzed along her veins. Lucy felt exhilarated and alive for the first time in more than a year.

She dipped to the floor, looking up adoringly at this complete stranger. They ended with a dramatic pose, her knee between his legs, their lips almost touching. The music stopped, and the crowd went crazy.

She looked around, and Max was whistling between two fingers then clapping loudly. Warmth filled her, and she couldn't stop the grin that split her face. Then she caught sight of a familiar visage in the crowd. Tall, skinny. He had a sharp nose and wore a flat cap.

Lucy stumbled, and her partner caught her.

"*Perdoname.*" He made sure she was steady on her feet before taking her hands in his and kissing them. He slid a note into her palm, slick as a magician. She grasped it tightly, realizing that Felix had set up this whole scene, and she'd once again been stupid enough to let her guard down.

She fixed a frozen smile on her face and stumbled back to her seat.

"That was incredible." Max's smile was vibrant, and his eyes glinted with what could have been attraction in any other situation.

She nodded quickly and searched through her bag under the table, sneaking a quick glance at the note.

We are waiting.

She stuffed it deep into her purse and pulled out enough pesos to cover their meal even though Max objected.

"No," she said sharply. "This is my treat, remember."

And now, all that mattered was getting the hell out of there before humiliation swallowed her whole.

"LUCY," MAX SHOUTED. "Wait up." He had to jog to catch up she was walking so fast.

She slowed when he reached her.

"Where d'you learn to dance like that, or is that a dumb question?"

Flames flashed in her eyes. "The Agency did not teach me to dance."

He jolted because she'd gone from insanely sexy on the dance floor, to fiercely grim in the space of thirty seconds.

"I didn't mean the Agency. I meant Buenos Aires." But it was a pertinent reminder of who Lucy had been, or rather *what* she'd been, and how much he didn't trust spooks.

Her lips parted as her expression was filled with remorse. "I am so sorry. I didn't mean to snap at you. I needed to get out of there."

"It's not a problem." Max rested a hand on her shoulder, hoping to get her to relax again.

She reached up to touch his hand and then cast a glance over her shoulder and moved away from him. Was she looking for someone?

He looked down the street, but it was largely empty of anyone except tourists.

What had happened?

She'd relaxed around him earlier. Then, after that eye-popping dance, he'd expected the walls to be fully demolished, but she'd immediately resurrected them again. Why?

They began walking down a cobbled street to where she'd parked.

He let the silence rest for a minute then said, "That was

very cool. The tangoing. The look on the guy's face when he realized you were a pro."

She snorted. "I'm not a pro."

"You looked like a pro. I take it you had lessons?"

Lucy drew in a long breath and released it slowly. "Yeah, I had lessons. No one gets any good at the tango without a ton of lessons."

They were approaching her Mini.

She sighed softly. "I'm sorry I freaked out on you back there."

It was time to get back to work, but Max had questions. "Why did you? Freak out?"

She pinched her lips together and crossed her arms. "I really don't like being the center of attention."

Max watched the way her eyes flickered to him and away as if searching for his reaction. She wasn't telling him the whole truth.

The woman he'd watched dancing had been confident and sensual. She'd wanted to prove to the man who'd chosen her out of the dozens of people sitting near the café that he'd been wrong to assume she wouldn't know what she was doing. And she'd nailed every single sexy frickin' move. Then, at the end, something had made her regret her actions.

He opened his mouth to deliberately mislabel some emotion and prompt her to say more, but his work cell rang.

He answered and listened intently. "Be there in twenty minutes." He hung up.

"Did something happen?" Lucy asked, climbing behind the wheel of her car and removing the steering lock.

"The ambassador called a meeting. Diplomatic Security brought Kristen's belongings back to the embassy."

"They found something?"

Max nodded. "A tracking device in one of the packages."

Lucy started the engine, her lips compressed into a tight line. "That means these kidnappers are pretty sophisticated, right?"

Max nodded thoughtfully. "More sophisticated than most. It also means Kristen was absolutely the target of this abduction."

"I don't like this, Max."

It was the first time she'd called him by his first name, but he didn't have time to examine the feeling of warmth that invaded him as a result.

"I don't like it either."

CHAPTER EIGHTEEN

I RENE LEANED AGAINST the radiator, grateful the day hadn't been as scorching hot as the one before. She'd pushed the hood up onto her head so she could breathe more easily. The cushion she sat on made her situation much more comfortable despite the unrelenting cast iron at her back.

All day she'd drifted in and out of a medicated stupor, but something was bothering her. She was supposed to be doing something. She went to scratch her nose, and the heavy chains reminded her what it was.

Handcuffs.

She was supposed to be trying to figure out how to escape the handcuffs. She tried making her hand as small as possible and tugging and twisting the steel bracelet, but it jammed tight on her wrist bones. Her skin was sore and already showing signs of chafing. If she wasn't careful, the wounds could get infected.

Well, that would suck.

Dark humor almost made her smile.

Her breakfast tray sat nearby. They'd given her a plastic knife and fork. She sat up and tried the tine of the fork in the small hole in the cuffs, but it was too big and too brittle. She didn't want to risk it breaking in there and make them suspicious that she was trying to escape. She planned to be a perfect hostage, unless she had a real shot of getting out of here.

She sighed and leaned her head back and stared at the water-damaged ceiling. How the hell had her life become this awful battle for survival?

And how was she going to get out of these cuffs?

Her eyes caught on a nail in the shutter above her. She blinked and tried to stand, but her hands couldn't reach high enough to pull at that nail. She glanced around the floor. There was a wide skirting board. The joint where the wall recessed behind the radiator looked loose though. She reached around the side of the radiator and was able to grasp the edge of the wood. It was difficult to find purchase, but she dug her short nails in the gap and tried to work it free. She pulled until her fingers ached, unable to exact any real leverage. Her fingernail broke down to the quick and she swore and stuffed her sore finger into her mouth to soothe the sting.

She stared at the offending piece of wood. Then she tried again. She put all the force she could muster into another effort and shot backward, yanked up short by the chains when the board came free.

Ouch.

She winced at the noise and sat there panting for a few anxious breaths. Her hood had fallen off, and she grabbed it with her feet and hugged it close to her chest. Even though she despised the thing, it was also a refuge. Wearing it provided a form of safety. If she couldn't identify the men who'd taken her, then they didn't need to kill her. She couldn't afford to lose this stupid hood.

She placed it on top of the dog bed and went back to the piece of wood that had come loose. It was about twelve inches long, and there was one nail sticking out of the middle. Carefully, she pushed the nail out by pressing the strip against the floor. Then she placed the broken baseboard back against the wall, grateful when it stayed upright.

She arranged herself back on the padded cushion, spine against the unyielding cast iron. Then she pulled the hood onto her head like a hat that she could easily roll down if someone came in. Tiredness was dragging at her, and she didn't want to risk falling asleep without remembering to put the heavy cloth over her face.

She picked up the old-fashioned nail. Rolled it between her finger and thumb. It was rusty and left an orange stain.

She poked the nail awkwardly at the keyhole in the cuffs. She didn't have the first clue how to pop the lock, but she wriggled the metal in the tiny space for what seemed like hours.

Nothing happened. She needed a bobby-pin or a paperclip or a freaking miracle.

Suddenly, she heard someone down in the kitchen. The scrape of a chair. Proving, despite the silence, they'd been there all along. She looked down at her fingers, all brown with rust.

She quickly took the hood and slipped the nail into the opening for the drawstring. Then she washed her fingers with the little water that remained in her bottle, hiding the drips beneath her precious cushion. Her hands still smelled of iron, but it was diluted. She rubbed them quickly over her dirty jeans to get rid of the last of it.

Footsteps sounded on the stairs, and she pulled the hood over her head and lay down, pretending to be asleep.

Someone came into the room, but she didn't stir. She felt

them watching her and forced the breath slowly in and out of her lungs.

Finally, they picked up the wooden tray and retreated. She heard them head back down the stairs.

Had they given Kristen food? It sure hadn't sounded like it if she was being held on this floor. It was weird to treat them differently.

Irene wasn't convinced it was a good sign that they'd fed her a good breakfast.

She was too tired to try to figure it out. She let the drowsiness deepen into slumber. Let her worries dissolve for a brief window of peace. Tonight, Kristen would be getting out of here, but Irene knew she wasn't going anywhere. Not unless she could get out of these damn cuffs.

"WHERE HAVE YOU been all day, SSA Hawthorne?" The ambassador was seated behind her massive desk in her imposing office with her fingers steepled together. It was a power position. "We've been trying to reach you."

Her eyes held a dangerous combination of desperation and anger.

Max regarded her coolly. He was here at her pleasure, but she was not his boss. If she tried to take over the investigation, he'd report her to his acting Unit Chief at CNU. Having an ambassador who wanted to be closely involved in an investigation wasn't a unique situation, having one related to a victim was. Maybe he'd get replaced. Maybe she would. It was not an issue for him. Under the circumstances, she definitely had the most to lose.

Lucy closed the door behind them and went to stand over by the wall. She hadn't said much since they'd received the phone call telling them to get back here. Why did she distance herself that way? Miranda certainly didn't. She was standing at the ambassador's shoulder like a hungry pilot fish shadowing her favorite shark.

All the gang were here.

The Legat sat in one of the armchairs and Iain Bartlett from Diplomatic Security Service sat in another. Phillip sat on a couch off to one side. He looked like shit.

Max decided to stay standing. "What's happened?"

"We found this." Iain Bartlett held out a small electronic transmitter inside a clear plastic evidence bag.

Max picked it up and examined it. "Is it active?" Could they track it back to its owner by following the signal?

Iain shook his head.

"You're sure?" Max clarified.

"I had our chief technician look at it. He's an expert with this kind of technology. It's a common, low-cost, low-power transmitter that broadcasts a GPS coordinate every thirty seconds. He says the battery is already dead."

This was unusual for a kidnapper. Max wasn't sure if he'd ever heard of a tracker being planted on a potential victim prior to abduction before. He'd ask Eban to check further.

It was more like a high-stakes international espionage move than a street gang. Max thought about what Lucy had said at dinner when questioning if a foreign power might be involved.

"I would like to send it to the National Laboratory at Quantico to see if they can find any fingerprints or DNA or determine where it was manufactured and sold." The FBI had more resources than a lot of the other federal agencies. The tracking device might hold remnants of electronic data they could harvest too.

Iain Bartlett looked at the ambassador who nodded.

"I think you should also put this in some sort of shielded container, in case there's more to it than meets the eye."

"I'm all for extra precautions," Iain Bartlett agreed readily as he climbed to his feet. "I'll box it up and arrange the courier."

Max remembered the potential issues with his cell phones too. "Is your tech guy able to take a look at my cell phones? Lucy's too? We spent the afternoon at PFA headquarters and were forced to leave them in a locker." Max eyed the ambassador. "That's why you were unable to reach us earlier."

"Sure. Hand them over." Iain held out his palm, and Max passed over both his personal and work cells. He wrote the access codes on a piece of paper, and Lucy reluctantly did the same.

They all watched Iain leave the room then the ambassador asked, "Do you have reason to suspect the Argentines or anyone else, for that matter, would want to listen in on your devices?"

"No, ma'am. Not so far. I only know that it's a possibility I want to avoid."

She nodded abruptly. She knew the game, she wanted to know if the Argentines had started to become a problem because that was where she could make a difference.

Max didn't think they would. They wanted this solved as much as the Americans did. It was an embarrassing diplomatic incident that would put a black mark on the country's ability to keep foreigners safe. For an economy that depended extensively on tourism it was an issue they needed to fix.

"Have you made any progress at all, SSA Hawthorne?" The ambassador tried to keep her voice firm, but Max heard the underlying tremble.

"ALAT Quinn has spent the day manning the phones but the kidnappers haven't called back since I spoke with them this morning." Max slowly paced to the window. "Smart kidnappers keep the location of the calls and the location of the hostages strictly separate. They don't even take the cell phone they are using to make the negotiation calls with them to the site where the victims are being held. Agents at SIOC have not been able to trace the calls as they seem to have some sort of decoy system that is giving us a series of false readings. We have called in a security consultancy firm who is one of the best in the business when it comes to this sort of thing. Cramer, Parker & Gray."

Max knew Haley Cramer because of her relationship with his boss, and he had heard of Alex Parker by reputation. "If the decoy system can be cracked, these are the people to do it, but it will take time."

"Did Cabral give you anything new?"

Max could tell Catherine Dickerson was desperately clinging on to hope. He wished he had better news for her. "We spent the afternoon going through the cases related to the Brazilian street gang that operated a couple of years ago. There are minor similarities but whoever is running this show demonstrates a lot more restraint and less volatility so far."

Max helped himself to a coffee from the machine in the corner of the room. Lucy jolted as if thinking it was her job and that pissed him off. She was way smarter than a freaking coffee girl.

He told the ambassador about the predicament the Lomakins found themselves in *sans* insurance.

Catherine swore. "I spoke to the British Ambassador to Argentina. He didn't mention any of this." A frown furrowed her brow. "Now I think of it, the toad didn't say much of substance at all except to remind me that the British had a more delicate relationship with the Argentines than the US due to the Falkland Island conflict and to offer me any assistance he could."

Yeah, war would put the screws on a relationship.

"I put the Lomakins in touch with a contact of mine who will be here by tomorrow morning to run their end of the show."

"Is that wise?" Phillip said from the couch.

Max gave him a searching look. "Always better to deal with a professional than get into a bidding war with parents who are understandably emotional."

Phillip made a disgruntled face.

The last thing Max wanted was for the kidnappers to see the girls as separate entities. All they needed to do to bleed both families dry was declare that whoever handed over the least amount of cash would get their daughter back in a body bag.

"Anything else?" the ambassador demanded. She shot her husband a quelling glance.

"A local agent showed me some footage of the girls as they moved through the city on Christmas Eve." Agente Ramon had offered the material after the FBI had sent the DNA profile to be run through Argentine databases. Max didn't mention the DNA to anyone here yet. He didn't want to get the family's hopes up without a match. "I asked her to forward that footage to me so I can share it with you and your husband to watch and see if you recognize anyone in the background."

If nothing else, it would keep them occupied for a few hours.

"I'd like to know how and when the gang planted the tracker on Kristen, and you might be able to spot that on the footage."

"I think it was that day." The ambassador shook her head. "DSS check us all virtually every time we walk in the door. Plus, the bug was found inside one of her shopping bags."

Max nodded thoughtfully. "Agente Ramon suggested the most likely spot for someone to plant the transmitter might have been at the Christmas market and she said, unfortunately, that isn't covered by security cameras."

It was an interesting twist. These kidnappers seemed to have extensive knowledge of the city's surveillance system and used sophisticated methods. He hoped they weren't just starting their crime spree because they'd covered their bases well.

That reminded him. He was still waiting for a call back from the Canadians.

Phillip leaned forward and braced his elbows on his knees. "I'll examine the footage. See if I can spot anything unusual. It will give me something useful to do." The last came out with a twinge of despondency.

"How did they know she was going out that day?" The ambassador had reined in her anguish. "They obviously had this set up ahead of time. How did they know she planned to meet friends? Was someone watching the embassy?"

The tension in her jaw suggested DSS would be in deep shit if that was the case, but they didn't have enough personnel to prevent every conceivable threat.

Max sipped his coffee. "One of her friend group might have inadvertently told the wrong person. The PFA is investigating all members of each household. Also," Max hated giving away Kristen's secrets, but this was life and death. "Your daughter was secretly communicating with a young man over the internet."

"What?" Catherine looked at her husband, aghast. "Did you know about this?"

Phillip shook his head.

"Did you?" she shot the question at Lucy standing over by the wall.

"No, ma'am."

Max carried on. "Judging from the tone of the messages, it was a romantic relationship, but we don't believe they'd met up in person. It sounded like they were planning to though. She did mention she had plans to go shopping with her girlfriends on Christmas Eve about a week ago."

Catherine looked horrified. "How could she have been so foolish? Didn't she listen to anything we told her?"

"Kristen was very careful," Lucy insisted.

The ambassador was staring at her desk, every muscle clenched. "I checked her cell for any compromising images and there was nothing obvious, thank goodness. I didn't see any text messages."

"It was via a new social media platform. The FBI is trying to track down this individual. I will let you know if we succeed. Did *you* mention the fact Kristen planned to go out shopping to anyone? Maybe in passing?"

Catherine Dickerson's eyes flashed and narrowed as she thought back. Then she frowned. "Only that afternoon, Boris

Yahontov's wife asked me about the children. Phillip mentioned that Kristen had gone downtown shopping with her friends." Her focus sharpened. "You don't think the Russians are involved in this, do you?"

Brian Powell shifted in his seat.

"How would they have had time to organize the kidnapping on that timeline? That conversation was only a few minutes before she was snatched." Phillip scoffed. "It's impossible."

Not impossible but extremely unlikely.

"Do you have any reason to suspect that the Russians might be behind this?" Max shot a glance at Lucy. Did these people all know something they weren't sharing with him?

Lucy wouldn't meet his gaze.

"Brian?" the ambassador demanded.

The Legat cleared his throat. "I'm not at liberty to discuss it."

Which was a big fucking *yes*.

The ambassador seemed to inflate at his words. "If you have reason to suspect the Russians are involved in the kidnapping of my daughter I want to know." Her hand was already reaching toward her telephone.

"Ambassador. Don't. Please." Powell wiped his brow and shot a look around the room. "I'm not at liberty to discuss any of this in front of non-FBI personnel."

The ambassador's hand paused. What was she going to do? Call the Russian ambassador and demand they give her daughter back? She knew as well as the rest of them did the Russians would never admit culpability. Maybe she'd jump straight to calling US President Joshua Hague and let him exert the pressure in the form of sanctions.

"I want to know what you know." Her voice was flinty as ice chips as she stared at Powell.

Powell looked around the room and appeared to come to a decision. "Let's go to my office, and I'll brief you."

The ambassador climbed to her feet and headed for the door.

Phillip stood.

The Legat shook his head. "I'm sorry, Phillip. This is classified."

Outrage stretched Phillip's features wide as he looked in askance at his wife. Catherine said nothing. There was nothing she could do.

Miranda moved to follow her boss, and Powell held up his hand. "You too, Miranda. Sorry. This is strictly need to know."

"But the ambassador might need me." A line creased Miranda's delicate brow.

"This is non-negotiable. Nor will the ambassador be permitted to discuss what I tell her with anyone."

Miranda's mouth opened in shock, but there was no quarter given in Powell's tone.

Lucy hadn't moved nor had she blinked.

Max narrowed his gaze.

"Hawthorne," Powell paused on his way out the door. "You may as well attend. Everything we discuss will be classified and, if anyone leaks that information, I will lock them up. I don't care who it is."

Even the ambassador appeared a little taken aback by that declaration.

Max inclined his head and followed the agent out of the room. Whatever this was, it was big, and it probably involved Boris Yahontov, Russian billionaire and a close friend of the

Kremlin. Max hoped to hell it had nothing to do with the kidnapping, but he couldn't afford to ignore the possibility, not with two innocent lives on the line.

CHAPTER NINETEEN

A LL LUCY'S CONSIDERABLE acting skills were required to prevent her from pumping the air with joy when she was banned from whatever intrigue the Legat was sharing with Max and the ambassador. The note inside her pocket was burning a hole through her conscience. She didn't like deceiving Max, or the ambassador, for that matter, but she had no choice.

Max must think she was off her rocker anyway, the way she'd fled the restaurant. He was still being nice, polite, diffident, but there was a quizzical edge to his gaze now that hadn't been there before her ego had come roaring out in force, and she'd danced the goddamn tango.

Her trainer had warned her this could happen. Apparently, all it took was an attractive man and the desire to be wanted again. The need to connect with another human being.

Idiot.

As if the red-hot negotiator would want her, especially after the truth came out.

She slipped out of the embassy and walked three blocks to a small internet café. Despite the fact it was evening, perspiration slid down her spine. She was grateful for an excuse not to be carrying her phone. She wore sunglasses and had applied her lipstick in a way to deceive any facial recognition programs, not to mention potential suitors. No one wanted to date the Joker.

Inside the café, she paid cash and booked the computer under a false name. She avoided the surveillance camera at the back of the shop.

This was her life now.

Not what she'd originally envisioned.

She slid into an empty spot that wasn't directly next to the window but did look out onto the street. No one appeared to have followed her.

The possibility that the Russians might be involved in this kidnapping made the fact they were applying pressure to her make a lot more sense. How did she phrase the email without giving away the farm?

What did she know that they might not? What about the "little bird" who was also feeding Felix information? Who the hell was it? What might they reveal? She couldn't afford to be less than truthful.

The Russians must have tracked her today. How else had they known where she'd taken Max for dinner?

Had she failed to spot a tail driving through the busy streets of Buenos Aires? Possible, but she was normally good at surveillance detection. She needed to go over her car and make sure there wasn't a tracking beacon attached to it, or her. Although, if Felix was as cunning as she suspected he was, he'd have removed the tracker before he'd let her see his face in that crowd.

She bit her lip and began typing.

Spent the day at PFA HQ translating files from kidnappings that happened two years ago for the FBI as they are looking for similarities between the cases.

No way would she mention the potential DNA of the suspect that the PFA's lab was now running through their databases. Max hadn't even mentioned it to the ambassador yet, probably waiting for a positive result before getting hers and Phillip's hopes up.

Nor would Lucy reveal that the Lomakins did not have valid K&R insurance. She didn't want to give the Russians any potential leverage over a family in crisis—she knew what they did with leverage.

The plan tonight is to go through surveillance tapes of the ambassador's daughter downtown prior to the kidnapping.

Her words were truthful and accurate but revealed no real progress. Nor was she the one going through the tapes, but they didn't need to know that—unless their "little bird" mentioned it. She bit her lip. Only a small, select group had been present at the meeting so that in itself would be revealing.

That should keep them happy for now.

She pressed send, although she didn't sign it. The email was from an alias and not from any of her personal accounts. If the Russians were watching who came and went from the embassy, as she assumed they must be, then they'd figure out it was her making contact.

She headed back to the embassy. Her desk inbox was empty which was a relief. No new incriminating photographs today. And Miranda hadn't added anything to her usual never-ending to-do list. Perhaps her boss was handling everything herself after the ambassador had assigned Lucy to temporarily help Max.

Lucy wiped off the lipstick and tossed the tissue in the garbage. She knew better than to assume there wasn't more work for her to do. She didn't want to get called back to the embassy if there was something vital that had to be completed.

She knocked on the ambassador's office door and entered.

Miranda was on the couch next to Phillip as if she was comforting him. They quickly broke apart.

Lucy said brightly, "I wanted to make sure you didn't need anything else before I went home?"

Miranda climbed to her feet, cool and unruffled. Phillip covered his face with his hands, as if he'd been crying.

"Don't worry, I'll attend to anything else that Catherine needs today. I'm going to sleep here again tonight."

Lucy wasn't surprised. Miranda was devoted to Catherine and had been with her for nearly a decade.

"Check in with that FBI agent before you leave though and see if he needs you again tomorrow. He really should get his own assistant instead of poaching mine." Miranda began picking up the dirty coffee cups from around the room and putting them on a tray.

"Sure thing. I'll talk to SSA Hawthorne before I leave and text you his response." Lucy left with a spring in her step. She picked up her purse from her cubicle and then remembered she didn't have her phone. Dammit.

She headed to the offices used by the Diplomatic Security Service. She knocked and waited. Iain Bartlett opened the door and looked surprised to see her.

"Sorry, I need my phone." She'd hated handing it over, although there was nothing incriminating on that device.

"Wait there."

She blinked as he shut the door in her face. She didn't have a good read on Bartlett. He appeared to be a straight arrow with a decided lack of a sense of humor. Not that Lucy Argentina was a bundle of fun.

A few seconds later, she heard laughter from the other side of the door and overheard someone saying they'd have to pay him to fuck her.

Ice flooded her body and froze her to the spot. Although they didn't specify exactly who "her" was, she knew. Lucy knew.

Iain opened the door with a smirk. Lucy snatched her cell out of his hands.

He jerked back in surprise.

"You can tell whoever is in there that I'd pay him more not to touch me." She whirled and stomped away.

"Lucy," Bartlett called. "That wasn't what he…"

Lucy looked over her shoulder, and the guy trailed off with a grimace.

"Yeah, that's what I thought."

What an ass.

She wanted to go home and curl up on her couch and surf the TV, but she was duty-bound to check with Max, see if he needed her for anything else. She headed downstairs to the Legat's office. Knocked loudly on the outer door.

When there was no reply, she tried the doorknob, and the door swung open.

She stepped inside and frowned as she looked around. The room was more or less empty, but someone was hovering in the doorway of what yesterday had been a closet. It was the agent who was manning the phones with Max.

"Any progress?" she asked, walking toward him.

His eyes whipped over her, assessing. He relaxed when he recognized her. His eyes warmed. "Nothing."

"Any idea where SSA Hawthorne is?" Lucy asked.

"Lucy, isn't it?"

She nodded.

"He's in the conference room. I doubt he'll be long."

Even as he said it, people came streaming out of the short hallway that led to Powell's office. The doors off that corridor had always been shut whenever Lucy had cause to visit the Legat. Now she had to wonder what Top Secret investigation they were running from there—and what it had to do with the Russians.

She stood off to the side near the window. The man beside her rubbed the back of his neck as he stared out into the Buenos Aires night.

A lot more people came out of those offices than usual. Some were here to help with the kidnap case but also obviously with whatever was going on with this Russian investigation.

Damn.

How would this affect her job?

If the FBI arrested a Russian oligarch, the spymaster might put more pressure on Lucy, or he might burn her for spite when she didn't give him a heads up about an investigation and impending arrest.

It might scupper everything.

Max came out of the conference room, leaning down to converse with the ambassador who looked pale. Her jaw was firm as granite.

Lucy flashed back to the scene in the ambassador's office. Miranda and Phillip. Had she been hugging him or kissing him? Could they be having an affair? Lucy frowned, trying to think back on all of their interactions. Nothing stood out. It was far more likely the guy was in tears over the fact his daughter was being held for ransom by parties unknown.

Miranda had said earlier in the year she was seeing someone but hadn't mentioned anyone lately.

Max strode over to where Lucy and the other negotiator stood. The ambassador left with Brian Powell, his expression tense and unrelenting. Lucy couldn't read Max's face or guess as to what he might have been briefed on.

"You need something, Lucy?" Max asked with a grin.

She bit her lip, feeling foolish for being here—like she was stalking her high school crush even though she'd been ordered to seek Max out. "Miranda requested I make sure you didn't need me for anything else before I went home."

He shook his head. "Nope. I'm done for the day. I'm whacked." He grinned at her, obviously not feeling gauche or foolish the way she did. She hated that she'd lost all her self-confidence. That it had been obliterated by one man's actions.

"Although, if there's the chance of a ride back to the hotel I'd be grateful. I can grab a cab though if it's out of your way."

Lucy blinked repeatedly. Damn. She wasn't sure she should spend too much time with this guy. She already liked him way too much, and he was more observant than most people who worked in the embassy in seeing through her shields. "Of course, I can drop you off. Not a problem." She kept her voice bright and chipper. "What about tomorrow though? Miranda wants to know if you need me or not—"

"I do need your help tomorrow, *if* you can spare the time." Max folded his arms and dipped his chin. "I could try to find another interpreter, but this job requires security clearance, and I enjoy working with you."

A rush of warmth suffused Lucy's entire being. She bent over her phone to hide her reaction. "Let me text her quickly, and I'll—"

"You got your cell back?" he asked. "Can you show me where the DSS office is before we head out?"

"Of course." There went her plan to escape his company as quickly as possible.

"I need another five minutes here, if you don't mind?"

Lucy nodded and sat on one of the heavy, old-fashioned radiators on the edge of the room. Max shared a few words with Quinn and another man joined them who Lucy guessed was also part of the investigative team.

She looked around the office. Despite the late hour, a lot of the agents seemed to be settling down to work. Whatever was going on was huge.

What did it mean for her? She wasn't sure but suspected it wasn't good.

Max was finally ready to leave, and she was unnerved by the warmth in his gaze when it met hers. Like he saw behind the thick-framed glasses and out-of-control hair. He looked at her as if he liked the person he saw.

She needed to kill this thing that was growing between them before either of them got hurt.

———————

MAX SAT IN Lucy's Mini watching the bright lights of the Argentine capitol streaming over the gleaming metal of the hood. She'd been strangely quiet since they'd picked up his cell phones, and he'd been distracted for most of the drive, mulling over the information he'd been told about Operation Soapbox.

He glanced at her.

She looked bone tired. She'd drawn her hair back into a ponytail at the first opportunity after they'd left the embassy, and removed the glasses she wore around the office, revealing pretty eyes and the slightly scooped-out hollow beneath her cheekbones.

He probably shouldn't have begged a ride, but he was reluctant to say goodnight despite the fact they'd spent most of the day together. He kept remembering her dancing earlier. She'd been like a wild animal let out of her cage for a rare burst of freedom. And now she'd stuffed herself back inside and locked the damn door from the inside. He'd be lying if he said he wasn't more intrigued now than when he'd first seen her standing pressed tight to the ambassador's wall.

His mind went back to what Brian Powell had revealed to him and the ambassador.

The Bureau was running special investigations into three Russian oligarchs who'd apparently been committing large-scale fraud and laundering money via various illegal practices in the States. One of the three men resided primarily in Argentina, hence the FBI activity down here. His name was Boris Yahontov, and he'd been with the US ambassador when she'd received news that her daughter had been kidnapped.

Coincidence? Maybe.

It was a huge case. The sort that could affect international politics for years.

The Americans needed rock-solid evidence of his illegal activities in order to have him arrested by the Argentines and extradited to the US. It would require significant political pressure to force the issue and the Russians would be fighting it every inch of the way. The FBI had been about to request warrants for the man's arrest when the ambassador's kid had been snatched.

Didn't mean Operation Soapbox *was* connected to Max's kidnap case, but it was a hell of a fluke if it wasn't.

The investigation was tight. No leaks, which was essential if they hoped to catch Yahontov unaware. It was still possible that someone in the Argentine police force might tip the guy off after the warrant request was made, but the arrests needed to happen simultaneously here and in the US. There was a limit as to how long the agents in the US could delay, bearing in mind all these guys could jump on a private jet and speed back to Moscow at a moment's notice.

Yahontov might believe he was untouchable down here. He wasn't.

Or he might have arranged his own insurance policy in the shape of a seventeen-year-old girl. If that was the case, Max was even more worried about Irene Lomakin's fate. Kidnapping her did not serve that agenda.

Another daunting possibility was that, although the Russians might not have initially taken the girls, the kidnappers could sell the girls to the highest bidder—like they'd threatened to on the phone that morning. Russia would definitely be interested, more so if the Americans arrested Yahontov and the other two oligarchs.

It changed how Max needed to proceed with the negotiations. It turned a long game into a sprint race.

If the Russians got hold of Kristen Dickerson, the ambassador would be crippled. She'd need to be replaced at a time when the US would need an experienced diplomat at the helm to get Yahontov extradited to face charges in the US.

The Bureau was delaying for as long as they could before making the arrests in the US in the hopes Max could get the girls back. But if the oligarchs made moves to escape US soil, the Feds would move on both continents. It would be game over.

Everything so far pointed to this being a classic kidnap for ransom, but Max hated when counterintelligence operations became entangled in a case. It so often changed the focus from criminal investigation to information gathering. All Max cared about was getting the victims home safe.

Lucy pulled up at the hotel with a dramatic flourish.

Max levered open the car door. "Want to come in for a quick drink in the bar?"

He needed to unwind a little before he tried to sleep. It had been quite the day.

"I should get home."

"Someone waiting for you?" He wanted to bite his tongue, but he'd been wanting to know the answer to that question since last night, and it was the first time the opportunity had presented itself.

She shot him a look.

It really wasn't any of his business.

"No one is waiting for me. I'm tired is all." Her voice sounded bleak. "Watch out for beautiful Argentine women who try to throw themselves at you." She forced a quick grin and, even though it didn't last long, he caught a glimpse of the Lucy he knew was hiding beneath the surface. A woman who was smart and quick and fun to be with. And sexy. The way she'd tangoed with that guy earlier had been hot. That woman was someone he'd like to know better if circumstances were different.

So why smother her personality? He didn't get it.

He reached out and tucked a strand of hair behind her ear. "Why do you hide away in the background the way you do? You act differently when you're away from the embassy."

Her expression closed down.

"Is there an issue with someone at the embassy?" he pushed.

She shook her head, the muscles in her throat working overtime.

"You're like two different people."

Her eyes changed. Frosted over. "I'm a professional." The tone had bite. "My job is not about being in the limelight. It's about making sure the ambassador's needs are taken care of without getting in the way of her doing her job."

Shit. So much for his negotiation skills.

He must be more tired than he'd realized. Or maybe she was more prickly than he wanted to believe.

Fine. He gave a shrug and pushed open the door. He didn't have time for games. "My mistake. Good night, Lucy. Thanks for the ride."

He climbed out, and Lucy sped away the moment he closed the door. He stood there watching her taillights disappear. So much for him thinking that maybe they were developing some sort of... friendship. Ever since the restaurant she'd been on edge.

Right now, it didn't matter. He needed sleep but first he needed a quick drink. He headed inside and went straight to the Oak Bar. Grabbed a stool at the bar and ordered a whiskey. It was the same barman from last night but tonight the place was dead.

He sipped his drink and let the noise inside his brain settle. The single malt was smooth and warm as it slid over his tongue and seared his throat. It reminded him of home and probably cost the same as his monthly rent, so he wasn't rushing it.

The last thing he wanted was to hurry negotiations either and, yet, he might not have a choice. He glanced at the clock. Andy should arrive by morning and Max would breathe easier when that loose end was tied up. Andy would make Irene his top priority and make sure the Lomakins didn't do anything stupid.

FBI techs were investigating the Miguel connection. Max intended to see if he could interview Kristen's three other best friends tomorrow and ask if they knew anything about the guy.

Wheels were turning. Progress was being made. He had a good feeling about this DNA sample at least leading them to a suspect. With the ambassador's daughter's life on the line, he was hopeful the Argentines wouldn't react with force. There was a lot to be said for stealth and guile. As a former Special Forces soldier, he knew how he'd go about an op like this but, unfortunately, he wasn't in charge.

He blew out a big breath. Took another drink of whiskey and tried to put the worry out of his mind for a few hours.

A beautiful blonde wearing a figure-hugging red dress with a slit all the way up to her thigh strutted into the bar. She sat three stools down from him and ordered a martini.

She would certainly take a man's mind off his problems.

Her gaze caught his in the mirror behind the bar as she scanned the room. She gave him a wry smile.

Max didn't need her kind of trouble, no matter how stunning she was. Max raised his hand to the barkeep. "Can I get the bill?"

The woman sat up straighter and leaned toward him. "You're English."

He didn't bother to correct her as she moved a couple of stools closer.

"Where are you from?" he asked to be polite.

"Texas." She smiled and then swallowed noisily. "I live down here with my husband." She gave a bitter laugh. "My soon-to-be ex-husband."

"Soon-to-be ex-husband?"

"I caught the rat bastard cheating on me. Ten years of marriage and he's fucking his secretary. I should have known this would happen. He was married when he started dating me." She sipped her martini. "*I* didn't know he was married at the time, but I'm sure that didn't matter much to his first wife either."

"I doubt it did," Max agreed.

Her bare arm brushed against his. Max knew it wasn't accidental.

"So what do you do?"

He took another sip of whiskey. He'd been hoping for some peace and quiet which maybe said how dull and mundane his life had become. He didn't do anything outside work except keep up with family and friends, and even that was becoming more and more infrequent. "This and that."

"Hmm. My name is Teresa. What's your name?"

Max smiled. He wasn't interested. It wasn't just because of his professionalism either. Another woman who was frustrating and difficult kept hijacking his thoughts. She might not be stunningly beautiful but there was something fundamental about Lucy Aston that tugged at him.

"Now you're playing hard to get." The blonde swiveled in her stool and leaned back against the bar, hair falling in thick waves behind her. The thin straps and plunging neckline revealed a knockout body. "I like hard to get."

She touched her finger on the back of his hand where it rested on his thigh. "You know, I came down here hoping to find someone to help me avenge the fact that I've been wronged."

Max shouldn't ask but, first and foremost, he was law enforcement. "Avenge?"

She leaned closer and whispered, "In the bedroom. Naked. Limbs entangled."

She looked over his shoulder and Max saw her eyes widen. Max turned, half expecting to see the cheating husband. Instead, Lucy stood there with a stricken expression on her face.

He smiled in welcome, but her eyes darted to the blonde at his side, and she whirled around and strode out the door.

"Lucy." He stood.

The blonde moved closer and put one palm against his heart and the other slid lower. "Don't worry about that little mouse. I can show you a much better time."

Max removed the woman's hands. He put a note on the bar to cover the check. "Thanks for the offer, Teresa from Texas, but I'm not interested." Then he took off after Lucy.

CHAPTER TWENTY

LUCY'S LUNGS BURNED as if she'd inhaled fire. Mortification scorched her cheeks.

She couldn't believe she'd come back to apologize to Max and had humiliated herself this way. At least she wasn't performing sex acts in front of strangers, but would she never learn?

After driving away angrily, she'd felt obliged to return and smooth things over. She'd told herself she'd apologize and basically bore him with as much tedious introspection as she could dredge up about her life. She couldn't afford for him to suspect anything was off with her.

The real problem was she wanted him to like her. She wanted him to be attracted to her despite the shapeless clothes and messy hair and unflattering makeup. Or rather, because of it. She wanted Max Hawthorne to be the sort of guy to appreciate someone for their brain and not their looks.

Considering she was disguising her looks and personality and coming across as a temperamental moron, that was a reach. Not to mention she was a lying hypocrite because she thought he was the handsomest guy she'd encountered since—

She cut off her thoughts.

Max Hawthorne was a weakness she couldn't afford but here she was, moth to a flamethrower.

And for all Max's talk about not hooking up during a case, he'd looked more than a little interested in the stunning blonde in the red cocktail dress who was draped all over him—and who wouldn't be? The woman was a knockout.

Lucy's throat tightened. Once upon a time, she'd been a woman who men had drooled over when she walked into a room. And here came her ego roaring back again, trying to destroy the tiny remnants of her soul that weren't already dead.

She ran up the carpeted steps but, in the dim light of the hotel, she missed a step and stumbled.

Strong arms caught her from behind.

"Lucy, are you all right?" Max's hands braced her hips as she steadied herself.

Desire coiled low and velvety in her abdomen and rushed through her body for the first time in fifteen months. Her mouth went dry, and she pushed out of his grip.

She wasn't supposed to feel this way ever again. It was dangerous. It led to destruction. Max let her go, a frown creasing his brow.

Lucy was messing everything up again with her seesaw emotions. She wasn't supposed to run on emotion now. She was supposed to be a machine. Apparently, she needed a lobotomy to achieve that zone again whereas just a few short days ago she'd been so damn good at it.

"Max." She forced his name over her lips. "I am so sorry. I should never have come back—"

"I invited you for a drink." He put his hands in his pockets, deceptively casual.

"*Ha.*" Could she be any more of a rube? "That was before you met Ms. Sexy-Red-Dress back there."

A small smile touched one side of his mouth, and a line cut into his cheek. "She's a bored spouse who wants a revenge fuck because her husband cheated on her. I was the first man to cross her path. No more or less involved than that." He tilted his head to one side. "I told you, I don't get involved when I'm on a case."

"Oh…" She swallowed uneasily. She seemed to be endlessly making a fool of herself in this man's presence, and he showed infinite patience by bothering to explain himself when he didn't have to. But his kindness wouldn't survive the truth. He'd already made that clear.

She had the feeling Max Hawthorne was honest to a fault. He wasn't a professional liar the way she was. Sure, he used words and mind games to get what he wanted when working with kidnappers and killers, but that was different.

She gripped her hands, massaging her fingers together. "I actually came back to apologize about earlier. You were right. I do stay in the background at work and try to make sure no one notices me."

His dark eyes watched her intently. Was he suspicious of her?

"Ironically, most people *don't* notice that about me but, apparently, you do." She quirked a brow, hoping to make him smile and release her from the intensity of his gaze.

He didn't. "Why?"

She shook her head and took another step toward the entrance. She didn't want to lie but couldn't tell the truth. "I don't like to talk about it."

Well, *that* was certainly true.

"Why join the Foreign Service, why learn to tango, for that matter, if you don't want anyone to notice you exist?"

She stopped moving. His words ensnared her. His dark eyes held her in place.

She opened her mouth but couldn't utter an answer that wouldn't be a complete lie. Her ego had made her eager to show herself in a good light...after all the training she'd done. All the warnings she'd received. Now he needed an answer or else his suspicions might rise even further.

She hugged herself and gave him some of the truth. "I was involved with a man who turned out to be not very nice. It affected me badly."

Max's expression slowly morphed from probing inquisition to subdued rage.

She opened her mouth, releasing an unexpected sound of anguish. She couldn't hold his gaze and looked down at the thick carpet, noticing a swirl of gold amongst the red. She wished she could disappear into that carpet like a ghost— which was exactly what she'd been trying to do since she'd arrived in Argentina in May. "He didn't hit me or anything like that." Her voice shook. "But he damaged me emotionally. He damaged me a lot."

Sergio Raminsky had unmade the Lucy she'd been.

"So I'm sorry if my actions don't always seem to make sense." She swallowed noisily. "All I can say is I'm doing the best I can."

When she looked up, Max's expression had turned into regret. He opened his arms wide, and she stepped into his embrace without even thinking. She rested her forehead against the warm cotton of his shirt. The heat of his body immediately began melting the ice that encased her heart and fresh pain throbbed along her veins.

He hugged her closer and she found her arms unlocking

from her sides and going around his back, gripping him hard, this almost-stranger who'd managed to destroy all her defenses with his observant nature and compassionate manner.

She inhaled him. The remnants of some sort of citrusy cologne and healthy male pheromones. He felt even better than he looked, the sculpted muscles of his back rock hard beneath her fingers.

She swallowed to loosen the stone wedged in her throat. She needed to let go. They were in a public place. An elegant lobby where anyone could be watching them. Anyone could be recording this interaction to use against one of them in the future. Even so her fingers clenched tighter and she couldn't let him go.

"Lucy," he whispered into her hair. He squeezed her and rocked her gently. "I'm sorry."

She was sorry too. So damn sorry.

Lucy would not see Max hurt. She could not sacrifice someone with such bone-deep integrity. She would not. She pulled back and caught sight of the woman in the red dress walking arm-in-arm with a bald man toward the elevators.

Lucy froze as she stared after them.

Max twisted to follow her gaze. Amusement curved his beautiful lips. "See? I told you she was searching for a good time. Unless that's the rat-bastard husband."

There was something nigglingly familiar about the man. As he and the woman in the red dress turned toward the elevator, Lucy caught a glance of the man's profile. The breath was sucked right out of her chest.

Holy shit. It was the Russian. Felix.

If she confessed that she recognized the man as Russian

intelligence, all Max's red flags would go up. She was a nobody in the Foreign Service. She wasn't supposed to know the identity of a spymaster, but she had to do something.

"Max," she said urgently. "Please don't turn around or react." She placed her hand on his shoulder and pulled him down so she could whisper in his ear. She couldn't risk anyone overhearing this conversation. "Any chance she could have been a plant?"

"What do you mean?"

"Like a honeytrap?"

He pulled away and rubbed the back of his neck in a way that allowed him to glance at the woman as she and Felix climbed into the elevator.

Lucy stood on tiptoe so she could reach his ear. "That man…he looks vaguely familiar. I think I saw him at the Russian embassy when I visited with the ambassador in the summer." It wasn't true, but it was a definite possibility, and Lucy was not letting Max stroll unaware into a cage of bears.

His expression went from easy-going to scary in a heart-beat. He gave a small laugh. "Holy shit. Her accent was flawless…"

Was the woman in the red dress a setup or a potential victim? Was the woman's life in danger? Were the Russians planning to kill her and pin it on Max? Felix was on the hotel cameras with her…unless he somehow controlled hotel security.

Max appeared to be grinding his teeth.

"Maybe it's coincidence," Lucy suggested lamely. "Or my old Agency training kicking into high gear." *Fifteen months too late.*

"I don't believe in coincidences." His expression narrowed.

Lucy shivered. "You better check your room for bugs."

"The fuckers might have been through my room already." Thoughts were running through his eyes. Violent thoughts. "They wouldn't have found anything useful, but even so…"

"You can't stay here." What if he was in danger for some reason? Felix seemed particularly eager to know what the FBI were working on. "You should get your stuff and check out."

It was almost midnight and they both had to get to work early tomorrow.

Max rolled his shoulders. "I can take care of myself."

Bile rose in her throat at the thought of him doing something reckless. "That's your Y-Chromosome talking."

His eyes narrowed. "Did he see you spot him?"

Lucy shook her head and glanced around, although no one appeared to be watching them. "He's bound to know who we both are though."

Max was obviously running various scenarios through his head. "I don't want them to know we suspect they're spying on me. If I check out of here, they'll know they're busted. Maybe one of the techs at Quantico can trace where any surveillance feed is going to. Get some proof of what the fuckers are up to and maybe we can use it against them." The muscles in his jaw clenched. "But the idea of sleeping in a room where someone is spying on me makes my skin crawl."

Lucy shuddered in reaction.

"Do you have a couch?" he asked.

Duh. "Of course, I have a couch."

"Can I sleep on it?"

She frowned. "How would that be any different than you checking out? What possible reason would you have for coming home with me?"

Max took a step toward her and cupped the back of her head with one hand.

What was he doing?

His other arm caught her around the waist, pulling her tight against him even as he eased her backwards, off balance—like they were dance partners and he was doing a low dip.

Then he was leaning toward her, slowly, staring at her lips as if he were going to kiss her—which was ridiculous. She blinked up at him in bemusement until his lips actually touched hers, softly, gently. Her mouth parted on a gasp as her body went lax with sensual overload.

It felt so good.

He felt so good.

He kissed her, closed mouthed, with a slow determination that made something inside her unfurl, like a tightly bound rosebud finally flaring open. Like Sleeping Beauty waking after a hundred years. The slight scent of whiskey on his breath was earthy and hot, like flames on a log fire. The urge to sample more of him ripped through her. She opened her mouth and touched the tip of her tongue to the seam of his lips. Felt him groan in reaction.

Her fingers clenched desperate handfuls of his suit jacket. His heat seared her body like the energy of a solar flare. She felt his lungs expand as he inhaled. Then he pulled slowly away and smiled down at her.

"Because of this." Warm eyes met her befuddled brain. "Because lonely Supervisory Special Agent Max Hawthorne is infatuated with Lucy Aston and plans to have his wicked way with her."

He pulled her upright as her body rejoiced "*Yes*" then sent her crashing back down to earth when he added, "Of course, I'll sleep on the couch."

"I have a spare room with an en suite. You'll be completely separate from me. I won't intrude on your privacy at all." It came out in a rush, as though reassuring him he'd be safe. From her.

But she also knew if she didn't stay far away from the temptation of this man, she was going to wander naked into his room and accidentally stumble into his bed.

Lucy Argentina was desperate, after all.

One side of his lips curled up and Lucy couldn't stop thinking about his lips smiling against her skin.

Her pulse skittered. Dear God. Fifteen months ago, her libido had been obliterated. Even the thought of intimacy had repelled her. Max Hawthorne had walked into her orbit and everything had started to realign.

It was dangerous. It was delusional. And even though she was doing everything she could think of to keep him safe and not to compromise him the way Raminsky had compromised her, it could still happen if she wasn't careful.

Associating with her was a risk. Kissing her in public was skydiving from the edge of the atmosphere. She couldn't let it happen again, but she also couldn't let him be in danger when the Russians were more than willing to hurt people to get what they wanted.

"Let's hurry."

CHAPTER TWENTY-ONE

K RISTEN DIDN'T KNOW what time it was or how much time had passed since her abductors had last visited. It had been hours since she'd heard any noise in the house, although the thick wood of the wardrobe tended to muffle sound. Which was probably why they'd stuffed her in here. At least it hadn't been so suffocatingly hot today, although she definitely stank of sweat.

They'd let her out briefly that morning for her ablutions and had given her more water and an apple to eat. The scent of fried food had wafted up the stairs at some point, sending her stomach into lustful spasms, but they hadn't given her any.

Deliberate torture or callous disregard?

What did it matter?

Her food from last night was long gone, and she was so desperately in need of the toilet, she was doing everything she could not to think about it.

She had been tempted to sneak out and use the bathroom, but she had to hold it. Based on the pattern so far, she expected someone to turn up and let her out soon.

What if they didn't? How did she even know if it was night or day? How would she know when the best time to escape would be?

But if she timed it right, the kidnappers might not know

she and Irene were missing for hours. And, depending on where they were, they might need that time to find help. If she timed it wrong, she risked walking straight into one of her captors as they came into her room, along with all the unintended consequences that would bring.

Finally, the bedroom door banged open and she jolted.

As the catch rattled, she made sure the hood was pulled down low over her face.

"¡Levántate!"

Ugh. She braced herself. It was the nasty guy. Even though the older guy scared the shit out of her with his knife and gruff demeanor, she preferred dealing with him. This guy was unstable. She was pretty sure he was on drugs. Hopefully, he'd be more interested in his next fix than doing anything bad to her.

She climbed to her feet and immediately fell against the doorframe because her limbs were so weak. She was shaking from lack of food.

He grabbed her arm, pinching the skin hard enough that she cried out.

"¡Rápido!"

Was she keeping him from a previous engagement? *So sorry to inconvenience you, motherfucker.*

"Sorry." Of course, she was sorry. She was scared out of her freaking wits because these people were assholes.

He dragged her to the bathroom and then yelled at her to pee.

Fresh fear stole over her in a wave. She knew she needed to be very careful not to provoke him in any way.

It was dark outside. She pulled down her jeans, trying to cover herself with her shirt at the same time.

She could hear him scratching around in the other room and reveled in the knowledge he wasn't watching her. She finished up and took time washing her hands. The rope swelled when it was wet, but it was worth that added discomfort to have clean fingers for even a short time.

She felt her way to the door and stood uncertainly on the threshold.

He grabbed her arm, and she tripped as he pulled her along. *Jesus.*

She got to the wardrobe almost out of breath when he shoved her inside. She sank to the floor and he tossed a water bottle into her lap along with another apple. Then he closed the door with a vicious bang.

Kristen lay there in stunned silence.

Obviously, he was pissed about something.

She gathered up the water bottle and apple and placed them neatly beside her. She couldn't wait to get out of this place, but what if Irene couldn't get out of the cuffs?

Kristen didn't want to·leave her friend but maybe the best solution was her escaping out the window and leading the cops back here. She swallowed. Did that make her a coward? She didn't know.

She was terrified so she probably was a coward.

She ate her apple slowly. Savoring the sweet flesh. When she got out of here, she might never eat another apple again. She wiped her sticky mouth on the damp rope, then reached for the ledge where she'd hidden the knife.

And found nothing.

She sat up on her knees and ran her hands frantically along the ledge. Had it fallen off? She searched every inch of the entire wardrobe. After five minutes of frantic activity, she sagged against the unyielding wood. That bastard had found her plastic knife. He'd taken it. And with it he'd taken her only hope of escaping and of rescuing her friend.

MAX WALKED INTO Lucy's modern apartment and looked around with interest. It was almost blindingly white with framed black and white Ansel Adams prints hanging on the walls.

He'd collected an overnight bag from his room and made sure everything left behind was impersonal and unimportant. He hoped the Russians hadn't read Kristen's diaries which had been in his safe, but if they were watching him then the chances were, they had. He'd called Brian Powell on the drive over to Lucy's, but the guy hadn't picked up. Max had contacted Eban instead, and the other agent was going to confer with counterintelligence agents in DC. Eban promised to send Lucy some photographs in the morning to see if she could identify the man she thought she'd seen with Teresa from Texas. Max hadn't seen his face.

Lucy had nodded listlessly when he'd passed that on, but she hadn't complained. She looked utterly exhausted and her features were drawn tight.

Max couldn't believe he'd kissed her. At the time it had seemed like the most perfect ruse, but the kiss had blown his mind. That one slight touch of her tongue had shot his blood temperature to boiling and it had taken every degree of self-control that he possessed not to push it further.

She had a sweet mouth and a passionate heart, and he hated that someone had hurt her. He couldn't afford to kiss her again or risk anything else happening between them. The idea of taking Lucy to bed was beginning to invade his thoughts. He found her crazy-attractive with her messy hair and baggy clothes.

He had the impression she wasn't that experienced with men. He did not want to hurt her when he left, and he couldn't afford to be distracted from the case when the situation here was ramping up.

He needed sleep so that tomorrow he could persuade the kidnappers they'd reached the families' limits in terms of cash. Maybe they could throw in some jewelry or a stereo system to really drive the message home. If the kidnappers proved intractable when it came to the money, then maybe they were working for Russian intelligence. Maybe there never had been any hope of getting Irene or Kristen released.

He'd ask Andy if he had any connections he could tap into when the guy arrived in the morning.

"Do you want anything to eat or drink before you go to bed?" Lucy stood in her kitchen looking nervous. He paused. He had forcefully kissed her and then invited himself over to spend the night seconds after she'd confessed to him that she'd been badly hurt by some asshole.

Was she scared of him?

He hated that idea.

He dumped his bag by the doorway.

"I'll take some water, please."

She poured two glasses from a filter jug in her fridge. She handed him one and then sipped her own. Her eyes were wide behind the glasses she wore. She seemed to have no idea how pretty she was.

He looked around. Tried to put her at ease. "Nice place."

She produced a tired huff of breath. "It's okay. I have a great view and it's a safe area."

The apartment building had good security with gated underground parking and a security guard in the garage and another in the front lobby. She also had an interior alarm system. She obviously took safety seriously, and he was relieved about that. He'd seen enough bad shit happen to people when he'd been a street agent and a soldier to last him a lifetime.

He drank thirstily and went to the tap for a refill. Lucy stood awkwardly to one side. She gave a sudden frown and removed her glasses, massaging her forehead.

"You okay?"

"Headache. I'll grab a tablet after I get you settled."

"Just point me in the direction of a place to sleep, and I'll get out of your way." His plan was to search every inch of his belongings for any hidden listening devices. After that, he would pass out into a coma for a few hours.

The way she was watching him with those hazel eyes made him think about things he shouldn't be thinking about. She pushed off from the counter. "You're down here."

He grabbed his stuff and followed her along a short, tiled corridor then came to a door at the end. She let him go ahead. It was a plain, white-painted room with a double bed made up of white sheets and duvet cover.

"There are fresh towels in the vanity in the bathroom. Help yourself." She worried her bottom lip with her teeth.

"Lucy."

Her eyes snapped to his.

"I've got this. Get some rest. I'll see you in the morning."

She nodded, her shoulders relaxing as if she were relieved.

He felt a whisper of regret that he wasn't going to get a repeat of that kiss any time soon. And it wasn't like he spent a lot of time kissing women, certainly not as much time as he'd like, come to think about it. His life didn't have much opportunity for softness or sweetness. There were sporadic hookups. The very occasional girlfriend who generally lasted for the duration of his temporary posting. But no real comfort. No connection.

He hadn't realized how lonely that was until he'd met Lucy. Her life seemed to reflect the same emptiness as his. It wasn't a reassuring realization.

"Goodnight, Max," she said softly as she turned to leave.

"Night, Lucy. Sleep well."

SLEEP WELL. IF only.

Lucy lay in bed that night watching the shadows creep across her ceiling while trying not to relive that kiss over and over again. The feel of his arms around her. His body pressed against hers. The strength of him holding her off-balance as he took what he wanted from her mouth.

She'd been dumbfounded by lust.

The fact Max was only a few feet away on the other side of her apartment ramped up the ache she was feeling. The tingle, low in her abdomen, the growing need for satisfaction that kept intensifying even though she'd thought it was dead.

Not dead. Dormant.

And the kiss would never happen again. It could never happen again.

After hours of fantasizing about his hands and lips on her body, about how he might slide his fingers over her until she was begging, about how his cock might feel beneath her fingers, how it might fill her…she finally gave in to the need to touch herself.

It was the first time she'd allowed herself sexual pleasure since she'd discovered Sergio Raminsky's betrayal, and tears streamed down her face as she slowly pushed herself to that edge.

Her release, when it came, ripped through her body in great waves of pleasure that lashed through her and made her buck on the bed. And still she felt empty and dissatisfied when she lay there lax in the aftermath.

Hours later, just before dawn, the text message she'd been expecting finally arrived. She got up. Dressed in running gear. Tucked a keycard in the invisible pocket in her running pants and slipped quietly out of the apartment door.

CHAPTER TWENTY-TWO

M AX WOKE WITH a throbbing hard-on that wouldn't quit even after he climbed out of bed. His entire being felt aroused, and he knew it had as much to do with the erotic dreams about a certain assistant PA as it did with testosterone.

He headed to the shower but, rather than help cool him off, his imagination conjured up images of Lucy naked and wet. He soaped himself all over but then gripped himself in one hand and squeezed his eyes shut as he leaned his arm against the cool tiles. Defeated, he jacked himself until the pressure in his balls released all over his hands. His body bucked, and he held himself still for a few deep breaths to try and get himself back under control.

Obviously, it had been longer than he'd realized since he'd last had sex. When this case was over, he intended to get well and truly laid. He had some ex-girlfriends who might be interested in rekindling something brief and hot. The thought failed to excite him. An image of Lucy biting her lip while wearing her black-framed glasses flashed through his mind.

He groaned again. He obviously had a previously un-known, totally unexplored Personal Assistant fetish.

He cleaned up, toweled off, and dressed in jeans and a clean chambray shirt—hopefully, the suitcase Eban was sending finally arrived today as laundry was low on the priority list but becoming increasingly necessary. He straightened the bedsheets before leaving his bags packed and ready to go on the middle of the bed.

The smell of coffee drew him into the kitchen and there stood Lucy, freshly showered, dressed in a cream linen suit that hung loosely off her hips. Maybe she'd lost a lot of weight but hadn't treated herself to new clothes. Maybe that was why nothing she wore fit except her yoga pants. She'd applied some makeup today—apparently in an effort to cover up the bruise-like shadows beneath her eyes.

It wasn't working.

She held out a mug of coffee made exactly the way he preferred it.

He took the mug, avoiding touching her fingers because he was trying to clear his brain regarding this woman and didn't want that weird electrical pulse that seemed to flow when they connected scrambling his thought process.

"Sleep well?" she asked.

With a burst of surprise, Max realized he'd slept like the dead. "I did. Thanks."

And now they were back to an awkward silence where he tried to forget he'd spent most of the night dreaming about fucking her every which way and had then masturbated in her shower while thinking about her wet and naked.

He shook his head at himself and sipped his coffee. Lucy would be horrified if she knew. Not that she ever would. *Shit.* He cleared his throat. "You?"

"Like a log." She smiled, but it didn't reach her eyes. She still looked tired. "Want some breakfast?"

Max shook his head. "We can grab something on the way in if that's okay. I want to get to the Negotiation Center early."

Kidnappers often stuck to a schedule, possibly because of family or work constraints. Even hostage-takers had lives.

Lucy took a quick chug of coffee.

"Did Kristen ever mention this boyfriend of hers to you?" he asked.

Lucy shook her head and washed up her cup, placing it on the draining board. "She didn't but, although we're friendly, she didn't confide in me that much. She knows I work for her mom and would be obliged to tell the ambassador anything relevant. Have you found him?"

"Not yet," he admitted.

Lucy's eyes widened. He probably shouldn't have even said that much. The FBI couldn't track down a teenage boy? Why the hell not?

How about because he didn't exist?

Max's work cell dinged. He read the message out to Lucy. "The FBI Tactical Operations guys are going to access my hotel room today and search for bugs and plant cameras of their own so they can keep an eye on anyone entering when they shouldn't." He grimaced. "It's supposed to look like I'm using the room, but they say it's cool if I don't want to sleep there. Ha. No kidding."

He'd worry about finding a new hotel later. Maybe where all the other new agents were staying to deter SVR operatives hanging out in the bar.

Eban also sent him a slate of photos to show Lucy.

"Recognize any of these guys?" He passed her the phone while he washed up his mug, then stood behind her as she scrolled through the images. Her hair smelled of jasmine. She stopped scrolling when she reached a gaunt-looking, bald bloke.

"Him. Or someone that looks a lot like him." A frown pinched her eyes as she looked up at him over her shoulder.

He ignored the fact her gaze rested on his lips.

Max nodded. It certainly could be the man from the elevator last night.

He messaged Eban with Lucy's answer and went to grab his bags.

His cell rang as he strode back to meet Lucy by the front door. He dropped his bags.

Eban didn't bother with any niceties. "Holy shit. She identified Anotoly Agapov, former KGB, who is now high up in the SVR."

Ice slid down his spine. "That doesn't sound good."

Lucy was watching him with big eyes.

He headed into her kitchen out of earshot. It wasn't that he didn't trust her, but he also didn't want her to pass any of this onto the ambassador. Lucy was already privy to classified aspects of the case because of his need for an interpreter, but he needed to remember, no matter her clearance level, that she didn't work for the Bureau.

"Don't mention this to anyone. Not even the woman you're working with. We need to figure out what it means. Counterintelligence will lead on this aspect of the investigation not the Legat," Eban warned. "I sent Lucy Aston's more detailed background files to your email, but she's squeaky clean. Short stint at the Agency. No details about what she did there, but that's the CIA for you."

Max wondered if the man who'd hurt her was involved in her decision to leave the CIA. It made him angry, but he didn't have time to get distracted from a case that was becoming increasingly complex.

"TacOps also planned to tap into the surveillance videos from the hotel after they went through your room. I'll suggest they make that a priority so we can confirm his identity. If Agapov tried to set you up with a Russian agent, then this thing is starting to stink of some sort of espionage rather than a straight-up kidnapping."

"Or they're trying to get the girls for themselves to use as leverage and perhaps hoped to use me to facilitate that," Max murmured. "I need to go."

"I'll call you later. Hey," Eban said. "Watch your back."

SOMETHING WAS GOING on.

It was morning. Kristen sat up. She'd started to recognize the subtle change in the quality of the darkness and gauge the slowly rising temperature by the stickiness of her shirt.

She could hear the shuffling of footsteps and the chink of chains. More than one person was in her room, talking in guttural tones outside her wooden prison.

Had they discovered her abortive plot to escape and decided to lock her to a radiator the way Irene was chained up in the other room? Perhaps they'd decided to let them stay together? Another thought shot through her brain. Were they moving them?

Or...hope carved its way craftily past her guard, maybe her parents had paid the ransom, and she and Irene were about to be released?

She pulled her matted hair back from her face and knotted it into a bun. Then she pulled the hood over her face.

Whatever happened she wouldn't react. She wouldn't give

them the satisfaction of seeing how terrified she was. Or how disappointed if they weren't being released. If only she could stop her teeth from chattering as if she were in a freezer rather than a stuffy wardrobe, then maybe they'd believe her.

The voices moved out into the hallway, too far away to make out the words, but not far enough to suggest they'd left.

Her heart raced, but there was no escape and no answers. The desire to cry rose up, and she pushed the tears away. She thought about her mother and her mother's fierce spirit. Kristen tried to channel that. She straightened her shoulders and listened attentively in an attempt to hear what the hell was going on over the frantic rush of blood through her ears.

CHAPTER TWENTY-THREE

L UCY STOPPED AT a local café and ran in to grab them some breakfast. Max wasn't hungry, but he forced himself to eat. Who knew when he'd get the chance again? His cell buzzed. Miranda Foster. The ambassador wanted an update.

With Russian Intelligence officers crawling out of the woodwork, Max needed to proceed carefully. Counterintelligence agents were in communication with the lead case agent for Operation Soapbox. This whole thing was becoming a giant house of cards that the slightest breeze could bring tumbling down. The main casualties if everything went wrong were the lives of two innocent girls.

Max texted Miranda back to say he'd be there in two hours. He needed time with the team first.

Miranda replied with a single digit. 1.

Max's mouth tightened.

Lucy's cell buzzed in her purse as she got back in the car. He'd bet money that was Miranda ordering Lucy to make sure Max was there within the hour. Lucy passed him a large paper bag filled with warm pastries. Neither spoke as they ate. They'd shifted into an easy kind of silence.

A few minutes later, she drove through the gate into the embassy grounds. They both showed their passes while security checked the car for possible explosives. Lucy parked.

Max went to grab his bags out of the trunk.

"Leave them there if you want." She tossed him a key. "My spare. No one's going to touch your stuff here and, if you need anything, you can come back and grab it." She shrugged like it was no big deal.

He grinned. "I could get used to this Personal Assistant schtick. Thanks."

"Ha." She knew he was teasing her. He liked that.

They headed up to the Legat's office, and the place was buzzing with FBI agents. Most were working on Operation Soapbox. However, some were helping track down vehicles used in the kidnap and searching for this mystery guy, Miguel. Others were coordinating with the experts at the National Lab, tracking down the bug planted on Kristen.

The Legat was officially coordinating both the kidnap investigation and the Argentine arm of Soapbox. He was leaving most of the running of the kidnap case to Max. Max was fine with that, but it didn't leave much time for him to man the phones or brief superiors.

He walked into the Negotiation Center. Quinn had dragged his laptop in here and was working away.

"Anything from the kidnappers?" Although Max would receive an automatic text if that number was called. He glanced at the clock. 7:46 AM.

"Nothing." The ALAT tried to cover a yawn. "Sorry. I slept on the cot. It was as comfortable as it looks."

Max nodded. Rate things were going, he might be sleeping on it tonight. No way did he fancy getting into bed with his coworkers watching from SIOC. Or the fucking Russians for that matter.

He'd rather stay with Lucy but was wise enough not to

mention that to her. He enjoyed her company.

Sure, buddy.

It had nothing to do with hours of burning fantasies and an unsuccessful cold shower. But he didn't want to hurt her, and something about Lucy struck him as incredibly fragile and that was taking into consideration the dropkick she'd pulled on that knife-wielding asshole the other day.

"We have another negotiator arriving today," Max told Quinn. Hopefully with a suitcase full of clothes for him and more cash for the ransom. "I'll come back and take over for a few hours after I've spoken to the ambassador. Let you grab a shower."

Thoughts of his own X-rated shower had him glancing at Lucy again. What would she think if he confessed he'd begun thinking about her as more than a colleague? He had no idea and wouldn't risk it during a case.

When *would* he risk it? When he was back in DC or on another flight to another country with a K&R problem?

Max opened his mouth to say something further to Quinn, but the phone started ringing.

Showtime.

He urged Lucy all the way inside the former closet and closed the door. In the meantime, Quinn had turned on the recording equipment and pulled on a listening headset. Max handed one to Lucy and then answered the call.

"Good morning, this is Max."

"Ah, *Max.*" The kidnapper sounded buoyant even with voice distortion. "This is el jefe, you remember me?"

"Of course, el jefe." In reality he was another asshole kidnapper in a long list of asshole kidnappers.

"Do you have my money, Max?"

"I have some of the cash. I would be happy to drop it off for you today in exchange for the two girls."

"How much?"

Max did a rapid calculation in his head as to what the Feds had provided plus what the Dickersons and Lomakins could put together in a pinch. "The two families together can raise two hundred fifty-seven thousand US dollars by the end of the day."

Usually, he'd avoid naming a number first, but this wasn't a normal kidnapping. Not anymore. Other factors were at play, and he needed to get ahead of the potential for the Russians to interfere.

The hostage taker was quiet so long, Max thought he had him on the hook, considering the offer. "Assuming you have the girls."

"Ah. You want proof of life?" There was the sound of shuffling and footsteps. The creak of a hinge.

Suddenly a scream pierced Max's ear. *Shit.*

"Say your name." The electronic-disguised voice sounded like evil personified. "Say anything I don't want you to say, and I will cut off your lips."

The distortion was turned off for a second.

"K-Kristen." The voice trembled in fear.

Max glanced at Lucy for confirmation that this was indeed the ambassador's daughter.

Lucy nodded. Her eyes were wide. Mouth pressed into an anxious line.

The voice distortion returned. The guy was a total pro. "And how much do you think your life is worth, Kristen?"

"A lot. It's worth a lot."

"Not to this man. This man, Max is his name. Do you

know Max?"

Presumably Kristen answered with a shake of her head.

"This man, Max, who probably works for the US government, thinks you're worth virtually nothing. How much do you think he thinks your friend is worth?"

"I don't know." The girl's voice was shaky and slightly muffled.

"More or less than you?"

"M-more?"

"Good answer." He laughed. "According to your friend's daddy, he can raise two hundred fifty thousand by the end of today, which means Max here thinks you are worth precisely seven thousand dollars."

Fuck.

There was the sound of a fist hitting flesh and a girl's piercing cry which turned into muffled sobs. A few seconds later, a full-blown scream of agony sounded down the line.

Shit. Fuck. Bollocks.

This was bad.

Lucy looked as if she was going to puke.

Max desperately tried to deescalate the situation. "El jefe, talk to me. Is it fair to punish the girl for my mistake?"

He checked his watch. Andy should be at the Lomakins' house by now but, obviously, the kidnappers had already gotten hold of Russell. Irene's father must have promised to scrape together every penny he could beg, borrow, or steal to save his baby girl.

This was why Max needed Andy in place ASAP. No father should have to bear this torment.

The sobs were growing quieter in the background.

"There! I have your seven thousand dollars' worth of the

ambassador's daughter. The pinkie of her right hand—her wedding rings will still look pretty. I will mail it to the ambassador so that she takes me more seriously."

"Is that how much it would take? Two hundred fifty thousand for each girl?" Max strove to keep the judgment out of his tone, even though he wanted to rip this man's head from his shoulders.

In the K&R world, violence was punished by crisis negotiators cutting off communications and lowering the amount of ransom payouts. Anything else rewarded the terrorization of victims. But when governments were involved, when the daughter of a United States' ambassador was on the chopping block, certain rules went out of the window—such as UN resolutions not to fund terrorists. Unfortunately, some of the kidnappers knew this too.

If possible, he wanted all these bastards locked up so they didn't continue their evil trade, but his priority was always the safety of the hostage.

"Hmm. Now that I think about it, that is still not enough money after all the efforts I have made. Not when I've had several offers for much more."

Max swore silently.

"I don't think the other buyers will care she isn't as perfect as she used to be, you know? And perhaps I'll no longer be able to control the behavior of my men. It is a shame, but we are growing bored, Max. Bored and tired of being treated like fools. Have seven hundred forty-three thousand dollars ready by tonight to add to the Lomakins' two-fifty-seven or the girls will both be sold to someone who appreciates their value. Any tricks like GPS trackers or explosive dye, and the girls disappear forever. Any drones or aircraft trying to follow the money and both girls die. Do you understand?"

"I do. You'll release them both when you get the money?" An even million bucks.

"I will release them after I have counted the money to make sure it is all there. You have my word."

The word of a man who liked to torture human beings for cash. Great.

"I'll call tomorrow with instructions."

The man hung up, and Max wanted to smash the headset into the wall. Instead, he placed it carefully on the table. "Sonofabitch."

Before Quinn or Lucy could speak, he dialed Russell Lomakin's phone number.

His friend Andy answered.

"Thank god you're there." Max explained what had just gone down with the kidnappers. "Russell should have called me after he spoke to them," Max said between gritted teeth.

"The guy is fried. I don't think he's slept in days, and the wife is no better off. Don't worry. I'm here now. I've got all their phones and instructed them not to leave the house for the foreseeable future. I think they already hate me so that's nice."

"Shit. I'm sorry, buddy."

"Don't be. This is what we do. Right now, they hate me. If we get their kid home, they'll send us Christmas cards for the rest of our natural-born. If we don't, well, then I guess I can live with the hate."

"Does he have that amount of cash on hand?"

Andy laughed. "Hell no. He's a bullshitter and he's desperate. What I don't get is, why are you moving so fast?"

Max wished he could come clean with his friend, but he

couldn't. "There are complications," he said carefully. He wasn't about to mention Kristen's possibly severed finger or the Russian interference.

"Do I need to know?"

Max was silent for a long pause that should tell Andy as much as his words did. "You might try reaching out to any contacts you have at the Foreign Office. See if there are any…rumors floating around the place."

Andy swore. Max agreed.

"Make sure Russell finds a way to have two hundred fifty-seven thousand used US dollars in cash by the end of today. The kidnapper said he would give us details for the exchange tomorrow. Do not let Russell anywhere near the bag drop. If they call you again, let me know straight away."

"I've got this. I won't let you down."

A stab of emotion hit him in the throat. He missed these men, these comrades in arms he'd shed blood with and whom he trusted with his entire being. "Thanks, mate. I owe you one."

"No worries. Hey, I spoke to Noah and Logan who are still in Montevideo. If this does wrap up sooner rather than later, I'm going to spend a few days with them there. Maybe you can join us?"

He hoped so. "We'll see. Let's get these girls home first."

Max hung up. A few seconds later, his cell rang. He was expecting Eban to be calling with an assessment of the latest kidnapper call, which had gone to shit. Instead, it was Agente Ramon.

"We found a match to the DNA on the ring you found." Her gravelly voice purred over the line. "Cabral was pissed I ran the tests without his permission. In fact, he threatened to demote me." She didn't sound too worried.

"Who was the match to?"

"I can't tell you that." The sultry voice became firm.

He rolled his eyes. "What do you think I'm going to do, tip off the suspect?"

"I hope not because then I'd have to arrest you." She made it sound flirty and suggestive.

Max grimaced. "What happens the next time I have information to share or evidence that might lead us to a suspect? The *Comisario General* assured the ambassador that we'd collaborate on this case with PFA taking the lead on the investigation, but now you're closing us out from evidence we provided." He let the silence ride for a full ten seconds before adding, "Should I go through Interpol next time?" And all the red tape that involved.

"Fine. His name is Alberto Nuñez. He's a taxicab driver who's had a few run-ins with the law—mainly drugs, although he's never been convicted. The PFA will stake out his house and follow him. With luck, he'll lead us straight to the girls."

"Does he have known associates?" Max wrote down the name so he could pass it on to his people.

"We are investigating but need to be careful. We don't want him to know we're onto him."

Duh.

Could it be this straightforward? Were the Russians simply nosing around because they suspected the FBI was building a case that might entangle one of their people? Was the kidnap a simple K&R that just happened to have occurred at the same time?

"Will you call me if the PFA makes a move to arrest him?"

Ramon snorted. "Cabral might fire my ass for telling you

this much, SSA Hawthorne. He is not a patient man, but this came from a piece of evidence you provided. You deserved to know it paid off."

"I appreciate you getting back to me despite possible repercussions. The FBI will be happy to cooperate in any way necessary."

He heard Ramon hum wistfully into the phone, and she made her voice deeper and more provocative when she said, "And I will be happy to reciprocate, Max. In fact, I'm looking forward to it."

He frowned as he hung up. What was with all these beautiful women giving him green lights when the only person who interested him was the woman beside him who didn't seem particularly interested?

"We have a match from the DNA on the ring we found in the alley. Let me shoot a message to my colleagues at CNU, and then we'll go update the ambassador. Don't discuss this outside of this office."

There was a knock on the door, and Max leapt to his feet to answer it before Lucy could do so. He wouldn't turn her into his general dogsbody.

Catherine Dickerson stood there, eyes narrowed. Miranda and Iain Bartlett stood behind each shoulder. "It seems the only way to get an update from you, SSA Hawthorne is to physically track you down."

He was not looking forward to telling her about this morning's call with the kidnappers. "Good morning, Ambassador. Let's find Brian Powell, and I'll bring you both up to speed."

CHAPTER TWENTY-FOUR

L UCY SAT ON the radiator as she waited in the Legat's main office. Powell had decided that the briefing be conducted behind closed doors, which meant she and Miranda were left twiddling their thumbs until they were finished.

Adam Quinn was once again monitoring the phones, and another FBI agent sat at her desk typing something up with a look of intense concentration on her face. Everyone else was in the briefing.

Were they about to start making indictments or arrests? Lucy frowned. If that involved taking Yahontov or some other powerful Russian into custody, then her career was screwed. Felix would burn her the moment he realized her intel had proven useless.

As much as Lucy had a job to do, as much as she did not want those photographs to be seen by anyone else, she would not help people who hurt innocents. The memories of those screams over the telephone this morning would haunt her nightmares.

She'd made contact with the Russians before Max had woken up. She demanded an answer as to why Felix was in Max's hotel last night.

She'd received an immediate but cryptic reply. "To make sure you are doing what we told you to do."

Which was what?

Keeping them informed of the FBI investigation? Or seducing Max?

She'd sent them an update yesterday. It was a risk to contact them again so soon. Why were they so damn squirrelly about knowing what was going on? What were they really up to?

They'd obviously deployed their backup weapon in the red dress in case Lucy hadn't "used her charms" on Max. Her mouth went dry. The idea of seducing Max the way Sergio had seduced her made her ill. Not because she wasn't attracted to him—she definitely was. But more than that. She liked him. She really liked him.

She would destroy herself before she hurt Max Hawthorne.

Miranda came over to stand beside Lucy, a look of sadness washing over her features as she stared out the window.

"The last few days seem to have lasted years." Miranda turned to lean against the nearby wall.

Lucy nodded in agreement.

Miranda's lips formed an unamused smile. "I haven't seen my apartment in forever. Good thing I don't own a cat."

"Didn't you have plans to go away after Christmas?" Lucy had planned to cover Miranda's absence.

Miranda nodded. Tired lines formed around her eyes. "I was supposed to head to the beach tomorrow, but I can hardly leave Catherine and Phillip now. They need me."

"Sorry. I know you were looking forward to it."

"It doesn't matter. I'll go when this situation is over." Miranda waved away Lucy's concern. Her lips widened into a smile, and she lowered her voice. "I notice you and the negotiator seem to be getting on well."

Lucy felt her face grow warm as she remembered the kiss they'd shared and the fantasies she'd woven around it in bed last night. She forced a nonchalant shrug. "It's just work."

"Pity." Miranda stretched out her neck.

It was a pity. The longing that had been growing inside Lucy since Max Hawthorne had walked into the room seemed to constantly expand. Too bad it was doomed from the start.

"How are Catherine and Phillip really holding up?" Lucy changed the subject.

Miranda's eyes widened and then she grimaced, looking pensive. "About as well as you'd expect. Neither of them is sleeping. Phillip spent most of last night crying while he went over footage of the girls shopping on Christmas Eve."

The image of Miranda and Phillip sitting close together on the couch last night flashed into Lucy's brain.

"Is he okay?" asked Lucy.

"Not really. He blames himself for not taking better precautions. I suppose we all do." Miranda stared down at her pretty shoes.

The FBI agent who'd been typing stood and strode quickly through the door, as if she had something important to share with the Legat.

Miranda brushed imaginary lint off her jacket. "Catherine worked until one AM and then finally allowed me to give her a sleeping pill. I woke her at seven."

"How's Kevin handling things?" asked Lucy.

Miranda's shoulder twitched. "He's in his room playing video games most of the time."

Emotion balled in Lucy's throat. She should have visited him. She texted him quickly, to remind him she was there for him if he needed anything. But he was a fifteen-year-old boy. He wasn't likely to cry on her shoulder.

"You could pop up and see him if you want," Miranda offered. "I'll text you once they come out of the meeting."

Lucy was torn. "SSA Hawthorne specifically asked me to stick around until he was done."

Miranda tilted her head. "Do they have any leads on the kidnappers yet?"

Max had told Lucy not to tell anyone anything, but her boss would find out about the ransom soon enough anyway.

"There might be a ransom delivery tomorrow." The ambassador would ask Miranda to help gather all the necessary cash together, so Lucy wasn't spilling secrets. She wouldn't tell the Russians about the drop. She would inform them that additional agents had been assigned to assist with the kidnap investigation. They'd likely already noted the increased number of Feds working at the embassy. It might throw them off the scent as to whatever else was happening in the Legat's office.

Miranda's face lit up. "Kristen might be home soon? That is definitely good news. I hope they didn't hurt her."

Lucy looked away.

Miranda started wandering around the desks. "I wonder if I should organize a short break somewhere when she does get home. Where the family can relax in peace but have all the things they might need?" She frowned as she pondered.

Lucy remained quiet. She didn't know what would be best. It depended on what kind of shape Kristen was in.

Agents suddenly came pouring out of the inner sanctum. The ambassador's expression was grim as she walked through the room. Miranda immediately went to her side, vying with

Iain Bartlett for space.

Max headed toward Lucy deep in thought. His phone rang, and he stopped to answer it, staring out of the window. He hung up.

"Change of plan," he told her. He opened the door into what he rather grandly called the Negotiation Center. "Take a break," he told Quinn quietly. "I'm going to have CNU transfer the calls from the kidnappers to my cell for the next few hours. A negotiator called Jennifer McCreedy out of San Fran will be here in about three hours. I'll be back by the end of the day to confer on any strategy for the drop tomorrow, assuming we have an exchange. In the meantime, the ambassador will obtain as much of the money as she can put her hands on. Get some rest while you can."

"Where are we going?" Lucy asked Max as he started striding away.

He turned and waited for her to catch up. "You ever been on a stakeout?"

Lucy laughed. "A stakeout? Don't be ridiculous. What are you talking about?"

ANGER WAS THE only thing keeping Irene from sinking into madness.

She'd passed out when they'd cut through the bone. A blessing in this ongoing nightmare. The bastards had carried her back to her room and chained her to the radiator again. Pain radiated along every nerve fiber as the numbness faded. Tears flooded her eyes, but she refused to let them fall.

Why had they cut off her finger when Kristen was the one

they were threatening on the phone? It sounded like Irene's dad had done everything in his power to cooperate with these bastards, and the Americans were lagging behind.

None of this made sense.

Irene wanted to lash out and smash something.

They'd taken her down to the other room before they'd even begun talking to the negotiator on the phone. They'd planned this little demonstration of sadistic power no matter what the other man said to them.

Irene had thought maybe the kidnappers were going to hold them in the same place. The large wooden wardrobe sat in the middle of the room—exactly as Kristen had described it.

Confusion had sprouted when one of their captors had sat on the floor with Irene cradled in front of him. He'd held her tightly and slipped his hand over her mouth as the older guy, the man she'd thought was kinder than the others, had spoken on the phone.

She'd listened to the call with interest. Why bring them together? Was it some sort of proof of life test? She'd relaxed at that thought. That had made sense. No one was going to hand over that amount of cash unless they knew for sure they had her and Kristen.

But they hadn't asked her to speak. Instead, they'd used her screams of terror and pain as a substitute for Kristen's.

Three kidnappers had been in the room, each one wearing a mask. They'd lifted her hood so she could see the large garden snips they'd brought along to do the job. She'd panicked and fought when they'd grabbed her shackled hands. The man holding her had hooked his hands into the crook of her elbows and left her bound hands trapped and immobile. She'd screamed when she'd felt the cold bite of steel pressing into her skin. The agony when they'd kept asserting pressure against her unprotected flesh.

Who wouldn't scream in that situation? Inside, she was still screaming.

Bile formed in her mouth as she thought of them doing the same thing again to extract more money from hers and Kristen's parents. She wanted to hurt them back. To cut off their fingers like it was no worse than snapping a twig.

The shock was slow to wear off.

Irene pushed the hood up enough so she could exam her butchered hand while she lay curled up on her side. The kidnappers had wrapped a bandage around the wound, but it had bled through.

They were arguing again downstairs. Someone was saying one of them was an idiot who needed to fix his mess.

Was that her? Was she the mess?

She sat up and fought the woozy feeling. She wasn't going to lose all her fingers so they could get more money. She'd kill herself first.

Last night, she'd waited and waited for Kristen to come to her. Irene had intended to tell her to leave and find help for them both. There was no way Irene was getting out of these handcuffs anytime soon. But Kristen hadn't come.

Something must have happened. Maybe she'd been knocked out with a sedative. Perhaps she'd been unable to jimmy the lock on the wardrobe, or maybe she'd been caught making the attempt?

Irene didn't know what had happened but today she'd heard the terror in her friend's voice. Absolute horror and terminal regret. This wasn't Kristen's fault. This was all on the heads of their kidnappers.

Irene refused to let in the sliver of hope that the ransom would be paid tomorrow, and they would both be released. Hope hurt more than cynicism and despair, and Irene was already hurting too damned much.

CHAPTER TWENTY-FIVE

L UCY FOLLOWED MAX down the stairs and out of the front doors of the embassy. Onto the street.

"Where are we going?" She didn't have time to go on a wild goose chase.

Max looked both ways then grabbed her hand, leading her across the road, through the park and down another street. She was out of breath, they were walking so fast.

A battered old van pulled up to the curb, and the door opened. Lucy froze to the spot.

Did he know something?

Was this some sort of black-ops rendition led by Max, and she'd been completely clueless?

Please, no.

He let go of her hand, climbed into the van. After swallowing the large lump in her throat, Lucy followed. It was that or run, and she was pretty sure it would be pointless trying to outrun Max Hawthorne. Time to face the music.

The door was pulled quickly shut behind her.

Inside were three men all dressed in jeans and t-shirts. One was tall and lean and had light brown hair starting to gray at the temples. He had piercing blue eyes and tanned skin.

"Unit Chief Jon Regan." He shook hands first with Max then with Lucy. "Excuse me while I run a wand over you both."

His grip was firm, and he didn't let her go.

Lucy felt nervous. Those eyes of his didn't appear to miss much. Seemingly satisfied they had nothing on their persons, he opened a small box. "Cell phones."

"I need the work one in case the kidnappers call."

Regan nodded, held out his hand for the phone, and tossed it to a second agent who grabbed a laptop and attached Max's phone while sliding the phone itself into some sort of shielded case. He tapped quickly and then set the laptop into a tray to check the phone for spyware.

Max placed his personal cell in the container, and Lucy dug hers out of her small purse and placed it in the box which was then snapped shut. Jon Regan held out his hand for her purse, which he examined thoroughly again with his bug detector.

When he was finally done, and they'd been cleared of electronic listening devices, he said, "Meet Isaac Navarro and Dexter Kim."

The first man was behind the wheel and looked to be in his early thirties. He wore a bored expression and had soulful dark eyes that were almost a match for the beauty of Max's— and the guy knew it. The second man who'd set up the laptop was slightly older and had a grin that lit up the whole interior of the van. He slid into the passenger seat and turned to watch them as Navarro pulled into traffic.

Lucy stumbled when the van jerked forward.

"Better grab a seat," Regan told them.

She did as suggested, sitting on the bench that ran down the center of the cargo hold. On one side was an array of screens. The other side was stacked with equipment cases.

"This is Lucy Aston. My...interpreter." Max offered with a smile.

"I know who she is."

Lucy froze.

Jon Regan's eyes gleamed as he hit a key on a laptop. A picture of Max bending her over his arm and kissing the heck out of her filled one of the screens. She was clutching at his jacket like she never wanted to let go. Unlike other images she'd viewed recently, it was one of the most beautiful things she'd ever seen.

A line of humor creased Max's cheek. "Emergency tactics for convincing the possible bad guys I'd had a better offer regarding where I slept last night."

"Well, you convinced me," Regan said with a sly grin. He pressed another button, and the image of the man who'd called himself Felix came up on screen. He was sharing a drink with the woman in the red dress. "Anotoly Agapov. Russian Intelligence. He came in via the back entrance after you ran after Miss Lucy." Cynicism rang through Regan's tone, as if he'd seen it all and believed none of it.

The idea of deceiving this man was daunting.

"I believe 'Teresa from Texas' sent him a text after you left." Regan pulled a face. "Unfortunately, I haven't been able to hack their system yet to see what it said."

"She have a room at the hotel?"

Regan nodded. "They had an adjoining suite. Something tells me if you'd gone back to her room, you'd have been starring on the adult movie channel before midnight."

Lucy felt like she'd been gutted with a knife.

"Assuming they didn't kill him first," Navarro said darkly from the front seat.

Max shot the guy a look. "What about my room?"

"Bugged." Regan looked almost bored. "Dex dressed up as a housemaid this morning and found several. They didn't even try that hard to conceal them. We didn't remove them. I want you to go back there later today. Maybe settle in for an hour before you get a phone call from your lovely interpreter temptress suggesting you are about to get lucky again." Regan wiggled his eyebrows at Lucy.

She told herself to smile back at him, but her face refused. The muscles weren't working.

"There's some sort of beacon coming from Lucy's car that we suspect they're tracking," Regan said.

She jolted.

"How'd the Russians know I was traveling with Lucy?" asked Max.

"Russians like to know everything." Regan shrugged but really it was the million-dollar question. "No doubt they are watching the embassy, unless they have sources inside."

"A spy?" asked Max sharply.

"More likely an asset. Witting or unwitting." Regan held her gaze as he said it. Lucy willed her expression to remain blank.

Navarro blasted the horn and yelled at someone in Spanish for cutting him off. Regan looked out the front windscreen.

Released from Jon Regan's penetrating gaze, Lucy stared down at the floor of the van. What did he know? What did he suspect?

How? Why?

"That was why I had you run across the park and meet us without telling anyone where you were going. Unless Argentine police are in cahoots with the Russian Foreign

Service—which has been known to happen if you remember that drug bust a few years back in the Russian embassy no less—they won't be able to track us."

Lucy cleared her throat and tried not to shiver. "What should I do about the bug on my car?" She'd suspected they'd put a transponder on her Mini, but her superficial search that morning had failed to turn up anything.

"We can go over it for you later if you want. Then leave it in place until you really don't want them to know where you're going."

Lucy nodded.

Max crossed his arms. "What's the plan now? Why'd you call this meet?"

Regan coughed into his fist. "Well. I had a little time on my hands while Navarro was hacking the hotel's security system and Dex here was busy straightening the sheets and changing the towels in your hotel room. I was on the phone updating the guy at CNU—"

"Eban?"

"Yeah, Winters. And he told me you had the name of a possible suspect in your kidnapping case. Alberto Núñez." The lines around Regan's eyes did not detract from his good looks. "And I decided to see if I could track the guy down."

Max tensed beside her. "Did you?"

The smile that crossed Regan's features was sly and self-satisfied. "Damn right I did." He brought up a photograph of a hunch-shouldered scrawny guy with a pointy chin and shifty eyes. "Meet Alberto. You can call him Al."

"How do you know he's the right guy?" Lucy frowned.

Regan tapped his nose. "Trust me. And I also somehow managed to find out his cell number and," he pressed another button and another screen lit up with a red dot overlaid on a map of the city. "His cell phone just happens to be in Buenos Aires at this exact moment. What are the chances?"

The chances were pretty good, considering.

"You're positive this is the right guy?" asked Max.

"I'd bet my balls on it." Regan nodded.

"Won't the Argentine police have all this information too?" asked Lucy.

Regan leaned forward to smile at her around Max. It didn't quite reach his eyes. "Yes, eventually, but they have to go through all the proper channels. We don't. You know why that is, Ms. Lucy Aston?"

She shook her head.

"Because we don't exist."

———

THE TACOPS GUYS parked the van on a busy street in the Boedo barrio, a working-class neighborhood west of La Boca. The vehicle's windows were tinted to prevent anyone looking inside and spotting the equipment.

"Are you familiar at all with this area?" Max asked Lucy.

She shook her head. She looked uneasy. He supposed Jon Regan with his steely gaze seemed pretty intimidating, but these guys were the best of the best at covert surveillance techniques. However, they were doing something that wasn't a hundred percent legal.

She had nothing to worry about professionally. He'd dragged her along with him. And from a safety point of view, she was surrounded by American law enforcement, three of whom were armed.

Cafés lined the streets and Max watched a man push a stroller down the sidewalk while local moms wrangled children as they tried to enjoy coffee outside with friends.

"According to the phone signal, he's in one of those apartments." Regan pointed to a building above a bodega with an ornate-looking, carved-stone balcony.

"Do you think the girls are being held there?" Lucy asked him.

"I don't know." Max caught Regan's gaze. "Any chance of getting some ears inside?"

"Dex, Navarro," Regan ordered.

Both men climbed out of the van and slammed the doors shut. Max heard the rear doors open and realized there was a false back to the van. Ninety seconds later, he heard them pulling a ladder off the roof and, when they walked past, they wore white overalls and were carrying drop cloths under their arms, the ladder stretched between them. They moved unhurriedly through a small unimposing doorway that led to the apartments above, and no one tried to stop them. No security. Not even a locked front door.

"What are they going to do?" asked Lucy.

"Nothing I can say out loud," Regan replied.

The guy was careful in case he was being recorded. Max appreciated that. His phone buzzed. That it had again been cleared of any potential spyware was reassuring.

"Brian Powell is looking for me." Max texted him to say he was in a meeting and would call him back later.

They all watched the front of the building. Dex came out and rummaged in the back of the van again. He left carrying a large pot of paint, some green tape, and rollers.

"Will they actually paint the place?" Max asked.

Regan shrugged. "If they have to." Then he held out his cell to show him a text from Navarro. It showed an electrical socket with the front plate removed.

"What happens if the local cops turn up?"

Regan checked his watch. "Won't take that long."

Lucy grabbed Max's bicep. "I see him."

Sure enough, there was Alberto Núñez coming out of the front door of the apartment building with a ball cap pulled low over his eyes. He wore shades and scanned the area as if looking for cops.

Definitely squirrelly.

Regan's cell buzzed with another text. Navarro warning him that Alberto was heading their way.

"Does he know he's blown?" Max asked.

"I doubt it, but he sure as hell looks nervous." Regan didn't even look at the guy directly.

"Should I call the cops? Before he gets away?" Max itched to jump out and arrest the guy but, not only did he not have jurisdiction, that wouldn't tell them where the girls were being held if they weren't in this apartment. And who knew how el jefe—assuming Alberto himself wasn't the boss—would react to having one of his men lifted. The guy might assume Alberto would roll on him and kill the girls before making a run for it.

Regan shook his head. "We can't afford to have the cops know we're in town. If we're caught, a whole bunch of shit hits the fan. They'll catch up eventually and we'll see if we pick up anything off the bugs we plant in the meantime."

Max shoved his cell into his pocket. "I'm going to follow him."

"Don't get made," cautioned Regan.

Max opened the door just as Dexter and Navarro strolled

unhurriedly out of the apartment carrying their ladder.

Lucy followed. "I'm coming too. You don't speak the language."

Good point.

Alberto was rapidly disappearing down the street.

"Can you track us?" he asked Regan.

"Sure."

"Let's see if this guy leads us to the girls."

Max grabbed Lucy's hand as they set off down the street at a fast walk. Alberto was thirty yards in front of them and obviously in a hurry to get somewhere. Was he late for his shift guarding the hostages or had someone tipped him off that the cops were looking for him?

Alberto ducked into a convenience store on a corner.

Max put his arm around Lucy's shoulders and hugged her close as they hurried to catch up. They passed the shop entrance, and Lucy stared up adoringly at his face. "I see him walking down this side street."

Max nodded, and they crossed the street before turning right and following along on the opposite side.

"There's a subway station up ahead," Lucy warned him. She kept her expression and body language loose. Max smiled down at her. She was a natural.

Alberto crossed to their side of the street and shot them a glance, but they were busy being absorbed by one another. Max figured they looked like a guy meeting his girl for lunch. He enjoyed the feel of Lucy against him. He hoped she was good with it, although she was the one who pressed closer and laughed as if he'd said something witty.

Alberto was only ten feet in front of them when they got to the head of the stairs for the *Subte*. He raced down into the tube station. Max let Lucy go first, tamping down on his inclination to simply grab the guy. Lucy skipped down the stairs, and he followed, staring at her, pretending to be infatuated.

Lucy walked up to the ticket machine and paid for a card for him. Thank god she was here else he'd have been screwed.

She whirled and grabbed his hand and tugged him to follow her. He grinned. He wasn't sure where Alberto was but, most likely, he'd gone ahead of them.

They reached the platform. No sign of Alberto.

"Shit," Max said.

Lucy turned to him and grabbed the front of his t-shirt and went on tiptoes to press a kiss to his lips. "He's sitting on the bench behind the woman with the stroller."

Max hugged her to him and let his hands rest on her hips as he looked over her head. He spotted Alberto. Did the guy know they were following him?

Max pulled his cell out of his pocket and called Regan. "We're in the Boedo subway station."

"Which direction is he going?"

"Toward the city, I think. That's the next train anyway." He could hear Regan and Dexter plotting their route.

The noise of an approaching train had Lucy stepping away from him. He gripped her hand. Then kissed her knuckles. Lucy blinked at him from behind her glasses.

Had he gone too far? It had felt completely natural to kiss her after she'd kissed him, but it didn't mean it was right. "Sorry."

The edge of her lips curled. She squeezed his fingers back.

Then the train was there, and Alberto was first in line to get on, cutting in front of the woman with a stroller and young child in tow. Max and Lucy took their time getting onboard. They got on one carriage down. It was crowded and Max glanced anxiously through the window. The beeps started, warning that the doors were about to close.

"I've got a bad feeling about this," he said.

Sure enough, Alberto jumped off just before the doors closed. Another train approached the opposite platform. He dashed onboard while Max swore into the phone at Regan. "The guy bailed at the last minute. Jumped on the train heading out of the city. Can you head to the next station?"

"We'll never make it in this traffic." Regan's voice was calm. "Something spooked him. He's in the wind now."

"Did he take his cell with him?" Maybe they could track him and maybe he'd lead them to the girls.

"Negative. It's still sending a signal from the apartment."

"Did he make us?"

"I don't know, did he?"

Max didn't think so, unless he was a RADA-trained actor. The guy was making sure he wasn't followed, which didn't exactly scream innocence.

"Get off at the next stop, and we'll pick you up," Regan told him.

Max hung up, and it took him a second to realize he was still holding Lucy's hand.

"Sorry." He let her go, wishing unaccountably he didn't have to.

CHAPTER TWENTY-SIX

L UCY COULDN'T BELIEVE they'd lost their only suspect. *Dammit.*

She climbed into the van and sat dejectedly at the end of the bench.

"You two sure you didn't tip him off?" Regan asked.

Lucy pondered how the guy had acted when they'd followed him. He'd been hyper-vigilant and on edge before he'd headed into the subway. He hadn't noticed them except for that brief glance. She shook her head. "He was spooked before he even saw us."

"Maybe he's always twitchy." Max commented.

"He has a drug problem. I was getting meth-head vibes from him when he walked past us in the hallway," Dexter said.

The thought of Kristen and Irene being at the mercy of a guy like that made Lucy's stomach twist. "Did you hear anything from inside the apartment?"

Regan shook his head.

"How long before the locals get there?" Could Irene and Kristen be inside right now? Could they need medical attention?

Regan shrugged, seemingly unconcerned. "Apartment is rented out to a guy name of Manuel Gonzalez. Dexter is running a background check on him looking for any links to

Alberto. There's a chance Manuel is another of the kidnappers, but he might simply be a friend letting Alberto stay. Or Manuel might be fictitious, and the place is being used to hold the girls, but I'm not buying it."

"Why leave his cell phone behind now? Was he tipped off the cops are looking for him?" asked Max.

"That would be my guess," said Regan.

Lucy was inclined to agree. "With all the surveillance cameras and the facial recognition in the city, why get on the subway if he thought the cops were after him?"

"That's why he wore the ball cap and glasses," Regan told her. "My bet is he got off at the next stop and has a vehicle parked there or someone is picking him up. Call your contact at PFA. Remind them to track Alberto's cell in case they are only staking out his home. We want them to find that apartment."

Max did just that. He spoke to Agente Ramon, and it sounded like she was giving him shit about knowing how to run an investigation.

Lucy wasn't impressed. For all the woman's tight clothes and confident swagger, Ramon hadn't been the one finding the physical evidence or following Alberto into the subway—no, that had been the FBI and Lucy. She wished they hadn't lost him. Dammit.

Max caught her gaze for a second before he looked away. Lucy figured Ramon was flirting with him again and didn't like how that made her feel. Slightly ill. Definitely jealous.

Dangerous emotions designed to get her into trouble.

Max hung up. Rubbed the back of his neck. "They have eyes on his place of work and also on the family home where he lives with his mother. Ramon says they're waiting on the warrant for the cell phone number and records."

"We could go back to the apartment," Lucy looked up. "One of us could deliver a parcel or something. See if anyone answers the door."

"I like how you think, lady." Jon Regan held her gaze. "But I'm serious about the fact we can't risk getting caught down here. Our TacOps careers would be over. And *that* would be a massive loss for our country."

"Amen," Navarro muttered.

"What if the girls are in there?" Lucy demanded. "What if Kristen needs medical attention?"

"I know it's difficult to not jump on every lead, but you need to keep your eye on the endgame." Regan's expression was not unkind. "We'll pick up any noise or movement inside that apartment and have a camera on the door to monitor if anyone enters or leaves. Argentine police aren't far behind."

"If the kidnappers are there, we run the risk of instigating an armed standoff if we corner them, which is never good for hostages," Max added.

"We'll drop you back at the embassy and then go monitor the apartment from a safe distance until the locals arrive." Regan checked his watch which looked like a real-deal Rolex and then glanced at Max. "I want you to go back to your hotel room around five tonight. Valet park the Mini and one of us will go over it to find the tracker and put it in the glovebox so you can ditch it when the time comes. Order room service and maybe snuggle for an hour—nothing X-rated." He was teasing, but it made her blush. "I'll give you a call and you can devise some sort of emergency and rush out of there. Head back to Lucy's place—"

Max stiffened beside her. "I was going to check into another hotel."

Regan rolled his eyes. "And give us another place to monitor? *Fuuuck*."

"It's fine," Lucy said. It seemed almost inevitable. "You can sleep in the spare room again."

"Bad luck, buddy." Regan grinned.

"Don't be an asshole," Lucy snapped.

"It's my natural state of being." Rather than looking shocked by her words, Jon Regan looked satisfied. "Figured you weren't as submissive as you liked to pretend."

Shoot. Lucy looked away. So much for training. Regan knew exactly which buttons to press.

Navarro pulled the van to a stop in the same place they'd picked them up. Max jumped out and held out his hand to help Lucy.

"Thanks." The door slammed shut and the van sped away. Lucy stared after them. "Interesting friends you have."

One side of Max's lips quirked up in a smoking-hot smile. She put her head down and started to march across the grass toward the embassy. She had a job to do.

Max fell into step beside her. He was quiet, and she had to clamp down on the desire to fill the silence.

They headed straight up to the ambassador's office. Stacks of money were piled on the coffee table and couch.

"Where have you been?" Catherine Dickerson snapped when they walked through the door. Everyone looked up with wide eyes. Kevin sat next to his dad, counting bills.

"If you're talking to me, ma'am, I was following a lead." Max took the ambassador's anger on himself.

Lucy didn't miss the fact he angled himself slightly in front of her. She didn't think she'd ever met a better human being.

"What lead?" the ambassador asked.

"I'm not at liberty to say," said Max.

"Lucy?" Miranda pressed.

Lucy's mouth dropped open in surprise.

"She's not at liberty to say either," Max said firmly. "What's the problem?"

Catherine wiped her hand tiredly over her face. "We don't have enough money for the ransom. Phillip was able to mortgage the property in the States and had a banker's draft arranged through a friend of his at the bank." When she looked up, she appeared to be fighting tears. "We only have six hundred eighty-three thousand here. That's sixty thousand short."

"I have six thousand I can add. Sorry it's not more," offered Miranda.

Lucy was taken aback at her generosity. It wasn't as if their pay was spectacular.

Iain Bartlett added, "I can add a thousand."

"Me too," Lucy added. She kept cash in her apartment for emergencies.

"I have permission to add fifty thousand to the pot," Max told them calmly.

"Is it tagged in some way?" Catherine's lips pinched, caught between hope and disapproval.

"We won't risk our child's safety for the sake of a few thousand dollars," Phillip added sharply.

Except they wouldn't have enough money without those "few thousand dollars," Lucy thought with irritation.

"There are transponders located in the bags, but they will never find them. And better to have some idea where the money is in the event they don't release the girls as promised,"

Max admitted.

"No dye packs or traceable bills?" Phillip asked.

Max shook his head. "Only the transponders that look like wires in the structure of the bag. Even if the kidnappers find them, they won't know what they are."

Catherine blew out a long breath. "I hope to god you're right."

"That still leaves us two thousand short," said Phillip.

"I have that in my savings, Mom, right?" Kevin asked.

All eyes shifted to him. Kristen's brother looked uncomfortable but determined. "Can someone take me to the bank to withdraw it?"

Lucy fought the urge to cry.

Phillip's eyes glistened. "I'll do it, son." He ruffled the kid's hair and broke the spell.

"Do the Lomakins have the money they need?" Catherine asked.

Max crossed his arms, which inadvertently showed off the muscles in his forearms. Lucy tried not to notice. "I plan to call the negotiator working with them and check on their progress shortly."

Catherine rested her hands on her waist and surveyed the room with forced positivity. "Okay. If everyone can retrieve the cash they offered, Phillip and I will be eternally grateful. And we will pay you back when we are able."

Phillip nodded and he, Kevin, Miranda and Iain Bartlett left the room. That left the ambassador, another DS agent, Lucy and Max in the room. Catherine started placing stacks of bills into batches.

"I'll run back to my apartment and grab my cash," Lucy offered.

"Help me out for a few minutes first," Catherine said over her shoulder. Lucy immediately obeyed. Max looked more hesitant.

"I need to get back to the Negotiation Center. A new negotiator arrived earlier along with that money from DOJ—"

Catherine turned to the DS agent who stood against the wall. "Give us the room."

He left, reluctantly.

Lucy went to follow.

"You may as well stay, Lucy. You already know more than I do."

She hesitated. "Yes, ma'am."

Once the DS agent closed the door, Catherine bit out, "Did they cut off my daughter's finger today?"

Lucy watched Max exhale slowly. Then he went over to move some bills into what Lucy figured out were thousand-dollar piles. "That's what they wanted us to believe, yes."

Catherine's chin rose and she looked away. "Do you really think they'll release Kristen and Irene tomorrow?"

"In my experience, when a kidnapper agrees to a price and that cash is delivered as per their instructions, they will release the hostages, but it might take a few hours."

"What about…" Catherine's eyes shifted to Lucy again. Lucy pretended to be engrossed in creating neat stacks. "The other possible players."

She meant the Russians. Lucy wasn't supposed to know, and the FBI obviously hadn't updated the ambassador on the latest developments with Max and the honeytrap the Russians had tried to spring on him.

"The FBI is working on it, ma'am. Currently, I'm waiting to hear if the Argentine Federal Police has tracked down a possible suspect—"

"What?"

"They didn't tell you?"

Catherine's nostrils flared with anger. "They did not."

Max straightened. He'd done that on purpose, Lucy realized. Deflected the ambassador away from grilling him.

"I really need to get back to the Negotiation Center. I need to collect that money from the Legat's safe, talk to the Lomakins' negotiator to make sure they are on track, and update my people."

Catherine's gaze sharpened. Then she laughed. "You distracted me."

Max smiled. "I gave you information. I would love some answers myself. Especially when the *Comisario General* promised to keep you up to date, did he not?"

Catherine inclined her head and went to sit behind her desk. "He did. And I intend to see that he keeps his promises. I'll call you if he tells me anything useful. In the meantime, please bring that money here ASAP." She looked around at the piles of money. "I have never been more grateful for, nor more resentful of, inanimate objects."

"I'm sorry you're going through this, ma'am," Max said quietly.

The ambassador nodded sharply. "Let me deal with *Comisario General* Fuentes. I will pass on any progress he's made to you." Both Lucy and Max started heading to the door. "SSA Hawthorne."

He stopped. Turned. "Yes, ma'am?"

"Don't mess this up. I want my daughter back alive."

———

MAX'S PHONE RANG.

"I found Miguel," Eban said.

"What? How?" Max was striding back to the Negotiation Center with Lucy at his side.

"Haley Cramer's firm managed to identify a smartphone that was likely being used to message Kristen and post on social media. Phone was registered to someone who is deceased using a false address. It was turned off the day Kristen was kidnapped and hasn't been turned back on since."

"That's not suspicious at all."

"Yeah, really."

"Can you send me a list of locations where it was used?"

"Sure. What's happening down there?"

"I'll tell you later." When he couldn't be overheard. "Do me a favor and transfer the kidnappers' number back to the Negotiation Center will you?"

"Sure thing. I'll call you back. Quentin says 'Hi' by the way."

"You spoke to him? I take it he's having fun?"

"Seems to be living the high life."

"Good for him." Max grinned. "Did you speak to Darby?"

"Briefly." Eban closed up again.

"Right on." Max gave the guy a break. "I need to do something. Call you back in a few."

Lucy's stomach rumbled loudly. She wore a worried frown. She flicked a glance at him and then smiled in confusion when she caught him staring at her.

"What is it?" she asked nervously.

"We skipped lunch again."

"It's becoming a habit." She sounded sad, and it had nothing to do with food. Trying to get these girls home safely was becoming a race against time. Stopping for lunch seemed wrong and yet that was exactly how burnout started—by not taking the time to deal with the basics. There was always a crisis in his world. Someone always needed saving. But today he'd rather go hungry.

He reached the Legat's office. The large office area was empty except for one lone agent.

Max strode to the Negotiation Center and gave a perfunctory knock on the door before walking in.

"Jen!" He hugged the woman who was based in San Fran. He'd helped train her a few years ago at CNU. She was one of the best negotiators he'd ever encountered.

"Max! I have a suitcase for you. I left it with security because I'm too lazy to carry it up all those stairs."

"I'd kiss your feet, but I don't want to get weird."

"Too late for that." They grinned at each other. Jen looked behind him to Lucy and held out her hand. "I'm SSA Jennifer McCreedy. Most people call me Jen."

"Lucy Aston. I'm one of the ambassador's assistants but was reassigned to help Max navigate the city and the language barrier."

"Nice to meet you, Lucy."

"You have the rest of the money?" Max asked.

Jen kicked a big black bag on the floor. "We arrived together via an official diplomatic transport plane. I felt pretty special even without the black passport."

"Let me grab the rest of the cash and take it up to the ambassador's suite and have her sign for it. That way I don't need to worry about being responsible if it disappears."

"Things are happening fast," Jen commented.

"You have no idea."

"I'm going to run back to my apartment to pick up that extra cash," Lucy told him. "I'll meet you back here in half an hour."

"Be careful." He didn't like the idea the Russians were tracking her vehicle.

Max headed off to deliver the Fed's money to the ambassador and her security team, making sure she signed the official forms some bureaucrat at headquarters had forwarded him.

He called Andy on the walk back down to the Legat's office. The Lomakins had the cash, and Andy had them creating thousand-dollar bundles to keep them busy.

"I don't usually do drop offs but this time I might have to," Andy muttered quietly.

"No way. I'll arrange a diplomatic car to pick up the cash as soon as it's ready. We'll hand over both sets of money together."

"That would be great. I'm not comfortable with this amount of cash in this house. Also, it's a good excuse to punt the kidnappers to talk solely to you while I carry out babysitting duty."

Max's thoughts exactly. "Can it be ready in an hour?"

"I'll have it ready. Then I'll shoot these two full of single malt and Benadryl and see if I can get them to sleep for a few hours."

"Don't let them out of your sight. And maybe hide the kitchen knives." Max was only half joking.

They hung up and he called Iain Bartlett to arrange the diplomatic vehicle and security for the cash. By the time he finally got back to the Legat's office, Jen and Lucy were chatting again like old friends.

Afternoon rays of sunlight shone on Lucy's skin and made her complexion glow. She'd pushed her hair back behind her ears. Her suit was wrinkled. Hair was a mess. But she was pretty.

He looked around, but the other agents who now filled the office seemed immune to her allure.

"Hawthorne!" Brian Powell strode out of his office with his phone pressed to his ear.

Max shut the door behind him. "What is it?"

Powell said something into his cell and then muted the microphone. "Care to tell me how you know a woman name of Abigail Blanco in La Boca?"

Shit. He exchanged a look with Lucy. Obviously, someone had made the connection. But Max had made a promise to the woman, so he played dumb. "No idea who you're talking about."

Anger twisted Powell's features. "Then you might want to get down there and explain why your business card was found stuffed between a dead woman's teeth."

No. Max closed his eyes and inhaled. That poor old woman.

Lucy had covered her mouth with her hand, eyes huge.

"She's the person who gave me the cell phone and told me about the orange VW Passat." Max raised his face to the ornate ceiling. "Fuck!"

"Cabral wants you down there pronto."

Max's eyes narrowed. "Cabral doesn't give me orders."

Powell thrust out his chin. "They are the legal authority in this country."

"I'm not the one who failed to interview potential witnesses or missed collecting physical evidence in a public space, evidence which led to the one real suspect we now have in this case. That's all on the locals." Max was aware of other agents coming into the room. Shit. He knew better than to get into a public pissing match like this. He didn't want to get sent home when they were close to a potential resolution. Where was his empathy? Where was his finesse? But the image of that old woman, the knowledge someone had killed her because he'd barged into her home was like a jagged wound across his chest. It had momentarily knocked him sideways.

It wasn't Powell's fault.

"Sorry, Brian. I know you're only trying to do your job." He took a deep breath. "I can't believe someone killed her for talking to us."

Powell's anger dissolved. "Looks like someone somewhere is sending a message that no one talks to the cops and gets away with it."

Max pressed his lips together. "I'll go speak to Cabral."

Powell glanced at Lucy. "Aston too. He wants both of you." He checked his watch. "And I think he meant right now."

Powell started talking on the phone in Spanish as he headed back to his office. Max glanced at Lucy. Her eyes were wide with horror.

He walked over to her. "You don't have to come."

She crossed her arms. "It's easier if I get it over with. Men like Hector Cabral like to assert their power over people. If I don't turn up, he'll take it to the ambassador, and she won't be happy."

"I'm not about to let anyone blame you. You drove me to the scene as instructed. I'm the one who knocked on that woman's door. You wanted me to leave her alone."

Lucy shrugged, still hugging herself. "Cabral can't hurt me, Max. But knowing our actions put that woman in mortal danger—that hurts me."

And that was all his fault. They both knew it.

CHAPTER TWENTY-SEVEN

L UCY DIDN'T BOTHER parking near the harbor this time. She used her Sat Nav to guide them through the narrow streets of La Boca to the area where the van had been dumped.

It was easy to find because of the multitudes of police vehicles blocking the road. Lucy parked a few streets away. She and Max got out and walked back to the police line where a crowd had gathered.

Lucy had used the few minutes alone when rushing back to her apartment to grab the money for Kristen's ransom to send a message to the Russians. She'd mentioned the arrival of more agents to help with the case—hopefully allaying any suspicions they might have about the extra personnel—and she'd also told them she was working on the negotiator. That was what they wanted to hear so she gave them it, even though it was a lie.

In all her dealings with the SVR, she'd been careful never to even hint at a witness in La Boca, but what if she'd inadvertently given it away? The knowledge Abigail Blanco was dead because she'd spoken to them severed Lucy's heart in two.

A cop checked Max's credentials, then Lucy's ID. He spoke into his radio, warning of their arrival, and then lifted the tape for them to duck beneath as the crowd murmured around them.

"Something tells me Cabral wants me publicly castigated." Max's tone was level, but Lucy knew he wasn't unaffected.

They turned down the narrow alleyway and her footsteps faltered when she saw the open doors of a Medical Examiner's vehicle parked a little beyond Abigail Blanco's gate. The vehicle was empty. The body must still be inside the apartment.

A policeman waved them impatiently along as if they were late for an appointment. Emotion began to swell in her throat.

"You don't need to do this, Lucy," Max said quietly. "This is not in your job description."

"You have no idea what's in my job description." She felt numb except for the growing sense of failure. If she'd done her job better, faster, if she'd kept a closer eye on Kristen. If she'd refused to translate between Max and this woman, maybe Abigail Blanco wouldn't be dead.

At the bottom of the stairs, an officer handed them paper booties and latex gloves which they both slipped on. Max squeezed her arm in silent support.

She found herself following him up the stairs the way she had a couple of days ago except this time the eyes on them were openly hostile.

"Watch that step," Max warned her as he climbed over a broken plank.

"That wasn't broken when we were last here," Lucy observed.

Max nodded.

As they walked toward the front door, Cabral stepped out.

Lucy was once again reminded of a rooster as he puffed out his chest. He took a step back then raised his hand to indicate they should step inside.

"I assume you know this woman, Hawthorne?"

Max tried to block Lucy's view, but she needed to see. Actions had consequences. Sometimes she felt like she was part of some intricate game of cat and mouse where nothing really mattered, but actions had real life and death consequences and she needed this visceral reminder.

Her damaged pride did not compare to this brutal murder.

Abigail Blanco lay on her back on her living room floor. Her right arm was bent at an unnatural angle. There was blood spatter on the coffee table and her nose had been broken, face battered. Blood pooled around her body, suggesting the old woman had lingered for some time before she'd succumbed to her injuries.

Cabral held up an evidence bag with a piece of white card inside. "This is yours?"

Max nodded.

Cabral turned it around. There was another number handwritten on the back in blue ink. "And this?"

"My personal cell. Do you know what time she was murdered?"

Cabral tilted his head. "Maybe you can tell me?"

Max stiffened. "Are you suggesting I had something to do with this woman's death?"

Cabral's smile didn't come close to his eyes. "As far as we know, you and Ms. Aston were the last people to see her alive."

"Except for her killer," Max said evenly.

The creases at the sides of Cabral's eyes formed deep crow's-feet. "We're supposed to be working together, Supervisory Special Agent Hawthorne."

"Did you find Alberto yet?" asked Max. A not-so subtle

reminder that Max had given the PFA the evidence he'd picked up in the street below.

Cabral's expression flattened. "I'm asking the questions here. Why was your card in this victim's mouth?"

"I gave it to her after we spoke on Christmas Day." Max seemed to realize it was too late to protect her now. "She's the person who gave me the kidnapper's cell."

Cabral shook his fist angrily. "Why did you not tell me her identity? I might have been able to protect her."

"She said no police." Lucy dragged her eyes away from the woman's corpse. She hadn't died easy. She hadn't died quick. Some sadistic bastard had enjoyed beating her. "She didn't trust your organization."

Cabral's eyes widened. Because she was talking back to him or because of her words? He hid his reaction with a sneer. "Instead, she trusted two foreigners and look where it got her."

Max bared his teeth. "We never mentioned her identity to anyone."

"Which is why you're on the suspect list." Cabral was enjoying this.

"*Inspector* Cabral, I understand that you must be as saddened and frustrated by this brutal killing as I am, but I would be the stupidest murderer in history if I left my own business card on the victim. While I might not be a genius." Max's self-deprecating humor was designed to establish rapport. Lucy understood this but she resented it all the same. "I'm not an idiot. This is a message directed at other witnesses warning them not to talk to the police, don't you agree?"

Cabral looked irritated. He wasn't getting the reaction he'd expected from either of them and, despite his words, he wasn't about to have them arrested. The political fallout could backfire violently enough to cost him his job. The man was too sharp to fall into that trap.

"Did you find DNA on the cell phone I gave you that the kidnappers left behind?" Max asked. "Chances are one of the kidnappers heard about the two tourists nosing around here on Christmas Day and being chased through the streets and came back and tortured her to find out what she told us."

"A gang came upon us when we were just outside her gate," Lucy said woodenly. Despite her and Max's promises they should have gone to the cops and offered Abigail protection. The result would not have been any worse.

The Medical Examiner zipped up the body bag and two assistants placed the woman's body on the stretcher. She was so light it looked as if it took no effort at all to lift her.

Moisture gathered in Lucy's eyes, and she couldn't swallow.

With grim deference, the men carried Abigail Blanco out of the apartment and awkwardly down the stairs on her final journey.

"That outside step wasn't broken on Christmas Day," Max addressed the evidence technicians in the room. "You might get lucky and find fibers or DNA if the killer's foot went through it."

The techs looked at Cabral who nodded reluctantly. "What else did she tell you?"

"She only said that she saw the men get out of the van and into an orange Volkswagen. They left all the van doors open, and she found the phone on the ground, so she took it and put it in her freezer."

Cabral's mouth curled. "Did she give you a description of any of the suspects?"

Max shook his head. "She didn't see anything. Or was too scared to say."

Cabral grunted, apparently unimpressed.

"What's the time of death?" asked Max.

Cabral let out a long-suffering sigh. "The ME was not that forthcoming, but he said no longer than a few hours."

"Did you search the apartment?" Max asked. He was still thinking about the case. Lucy was remembering the look of trust on Abigail's face when they'd left her on Christmas Day.

And at the end, when that sweet old woman had faced the man who'd beaten her to death, she must have believed Lucy and Max had lied. That Lucy had betrayed her trust despite all her promises. She wanted to bend over in pain.

God. She couldn't breathe. She moved away to the balcony and looked out through the thick vines. A woman stared back from another apartment twenty feet away. Her eyes were wide with fear. She shook her head and quickly went inside her home and closed the door.

"Did you question the neighbors?" asked Max.

Cabral took a step closer to the negotiator but was at an immediate height disadvantage. He whirled away. "Do not tell me how to do my job, Max Hawthorne, FBI." He said the last loudly enough that it rang out around the neighborhood. He waved Max's business card at him, making a show of his anger and revealing Max's name for anyone within hearing distance.

Max's jaw flexed with tension. "If your men had done their jobs properly in the first place then I wouldn't have found two pieces of vital evidence after they'd left." Max wasn't shouting but he definitely wasn't using his late-night DJ voice.

"They have been reprimanded." Cabral seemed to grow bored of the whole thing, probably because neither Lucy nor

Max were cowed or begging for his forgiveness. The other man didn't seem to care about the woman who'd died. She was nothing to him. A weapon to use against an opponent. And that's how Cabral viewed Max, Lucy realized with sudden clarity. Cabral was battling with Max as to who was going to solve this case and get the glory. And the Argentine police officer did not like to lose.

———————

KRISTEN HAD WEPT until there were no tears left after witnessing the men snip off Irene's little finger. It had been hours ago now. They hadn't fed her today, and she wasn't sure she could have eaten anyway. She had one bottle of drugged water that she was sipping slowly in the hopes it might be less debilitating consumed that way, but she could barely lift the bottle to her lips.

Images from earlier flashed through her mind in an endless reel. They'd yanked up her hood so she could talk into the phone—and then they'd forced her to watch as they'd mutilated Irene, pretending it was Kristen so her parents could also suffer.

Why not cut off Kristen's finger? Why switch Irene's screams for her own? The only good reason Kristen could think of was they didn't want to risk her health. And the only reason to be concerned about her health was if they didn't plan to release her anytime soon. They wanted her in good health—like a piece of livestock.

Who did they plan to sell her to? According to her mother, Hezbollah were active in the region. Kristen shuddered at the thought of being held by that group or any terrorist organization. These men were bad enough.

Three of the four men who'd originally snatched them off the streets had been in the room earlier today. They'd worn their masks and Kristen had to wonder if they always wore them but kept her and Irene cowed and subdued by scaring them too much to even take off their damn hoods.

The leader had held Kristen tight, clamping her jaw closed so tightly she had bruises, then holding up the phone with his other hand, while the other two had inflicted violence on Irene.

Kristen tiredly wiped sweat from her forehead with her bound arms. The ropes were starting to rub her skin raw in places. She wanted to sob with rage and frustration, but it wouldn't help her or Irene.

Was she alone here? Was it night or day? She blinked at the faint sliver of light that snuck inside her prison. Still daylight then.

Her stomach growled despite the nausea that seemed to be a constant companion nowadays, probably from the drugs in the water or the images that whirled through her brain.

She wanted to scream and yell for help, but the threat to cut out her tongue was still paramount in her mind, now more than ever after seeing how easily they had maimed Irene.

Sitting here like a turkey waiting for Thanksgiving seemed dumb but she had to plan carefully. Would they come and let her out to use the bathroom later? Maybe give her some food? They usually did, so she'd wait until afterward and then she'd do everything possible to get out of this fucking wooden prison.

She put the water away from her even though her throat was gritty and dry. She knew that if she didn't escape, she would be handed over to another group and they might make this wardrobe look like a palace. She'd rather risk an escape attempt than walk meekly to her fate.

Even the thought of death had her shuddering. She wasn't ready yet. She didn't want her life to end here. She wanted to live a long life. Fall in love. Travel. She wasn't ready to give up. And she wasn't ready to give up on Irene either. Her friend needed her now more than ever.

———————————

MAX TOOK THE car keys out of Lucy's fingers. "I'll drive."

He was worried about her. She had barely spoken since they'd arrived at the crime scene, and viewing dead bodies shouldn't be forced on a Foreign Service employee simply because members of local law enforcement were feeling vindictive.

She slid into the passenger seat without argument while he took the wheel of her beloved Mini. She took off her glasses and closed her eyes, massaging the bridge of her nose before leaning back against the headrest.

He programmed the Sat Nav to map the route to his hotel as it was almost five o'clock. He glanced at her again and didn't like the paleness of her skin, or the fragility of her delicate features.

"I'm sorry, Lucy. I should have handled Cabral. You shouldn't have had to see that."

"I'm responsible too." She looked almost physically ill.

Her vulnerability struck him deeply.

"None of this was your fault. I made you keep pushing when we were outside Abigail's door. I never imagined they'd send someone to kill her. It's their fault, not yours."

"It's done now." Her voice was rough with emotion.

Max needed to catch these bastards. It had to be the kidnappers. Who else had so much to lose that they'd beat a woman in her eighties to death for talking to law enforcement? Especially as the gang who'd chased them hadn't known they were law enforcement...

"Why kill her now?" he asked more to himself than Lucy.

"What do you mean?"

"I can see the gang who chased us swinging back to her place on Christmas Day and reading her the riot act or even smacking her around a little for talking to us, whatever." He followed the directions on the map and wound his way through the narrow streets. "But why wait until now to kill her? It doesn't make sense."

Lucy frowned and sat up. "Maybe the killer only recently learned she spoke to the police?"

He huffed out an unamused laugh. "Funny how that happened *after* I gave the PFA a DNA profile to run through their system which gave us our first real suspect."

Lucy blinked at him. "You think someone in the local federal police force is feeding information to the kidnappers?"

He didn't want to think that. "It seems quite the coincidence that the day we actually get a suspect name, our only witness to the vehicle exchange is found murdered. And who was Abigail scared of?"

"Do you think Alberto did it? Someone tipped him off and he went and killed Abigail?" Lucy's eyes grew huge. "Maybe that's where he went after we lost him today?"

That was exactly what he was thinking. "He was determined to lose any surveillance. How hard would it have been for him to make his way to La Boca from that apartment we tracked him to in Boedo?"

"It's only a few miles. He could have walked or jumped in a cab."

"Yeah," Max added. "Killed Abigail and then disappeared back to wherever the girls are being held, waiting for his cut of the ransom money."

"That's despicable." Lucy drew her knees up to her chest.

Max took a left, loving the car even though his heart was heavy with regret.

"Where are we going?" She registered their surroundings for the first time.

"It's almost five." He glanced over at her. "Regan wanted me to spend some time in my room while he checked your Mini for tracking devices, remember?"

"It slipped my mind." A shudder ran over her hunched shoulders.

"You could go get a meal in the restaurant. You don't have to be in my room."

Something flickered through her eyes. "No. If it helps to pretend we're in a relationship, I'm happy to do it. I don't want the Russians getting suspicious, especially if they are involved in the kidnapping."

Because then they'd probably be responsible for Abigail Blanco's death, and they'd almost certainly have informants in the local federal police force.

"I'll order room service and we can eat something for a change."

"I'm not hungry." Lucy's stomach made a noise of protest. Then her expression changed, and he knew she was thinking about the crime scene again.

"Don't," he said quietly, taking her hand in his and squeezing her fingers. "Let's concentrate on taking care of the basics, doing our jobs and catching these bastards."

She nodded but it was clear she wasn't even close to being over this.

He valet parked, hoping that Regan and his team knew what they were doing. He wrapped a protective arm around her shoulders and walked her to the elevator. When they entered his room, he turned her around to face him and placed a tender kiss on her forehead. That was for the cameras.

It felt wrong to enjoy the contact, but he did anyway.

She closed her eyes. Clutched the front of his shirt.

He was aware of unseen eyes cataloguing his movements. His skin crawled at the idea of spending any time in this luxurious space.

His cell rang. Making Lucy step away from him.

Regan. "It's done."

"But I just got here," Max complained loudly for show.

"If I were you, I'd go catch a few hours' sleep while I could. Looks like it's gonna be a long night."

"Fine. I'll call you when I'm done there."

"Don't bother. I'm planning on getting some sleep myself." Regan hung up.

Max brushed Lucy's hair off her forehead. "Sorry. I have to run out and grab something."

She caught his fingers. "Stay with me again tonight."

Her eyes held his and seemed to promise more than the spare room. But he was being fanciful. And hopeful. She was good at this.

He nodded, strangely unable to speak. They got out of there, slamming the door on the way out.

CHAPTER TWENTY-EIGHT

D ESPITE HER RESISTANCE, Max picked them up a burger and fries from a fast-food restaurant on the way back to her apartment. Once they got there, she opened a bottle of merlot and poured them each a large glass as they stood in her kitchen and picked at their food.

Lucy tried to swallow a fry, but it got stuck in her throat. She washed it away with a gulp of wine. She coughed.

Max rubbed his hand down her back. "Are you all right?"

Suddenly tears flooded her eyes, and she pulled her glasses off and tossed them on the counter. She covered her face with her hands. He drew her to him, his palm cradling the back of her head.

Maybe it was the lack of sleep over the last few days. Or the stress. Or the horror of seeing Abigail Blanco's beaten body, but Lucy's system had hit overload and she couldn't hold it together any longer.

The desire to confide everything to this man almost overcame her. But then he wouldn't be holding her this way. Then he wouldn't be comforting her. Instead, he'd be pushing her away and questioning her and it was so long since anyone had held her. Fifteen months, one week, two days, to be exact.

He lifted her in his arms and carried her towards her bedroom. Placed her carefully on the bed. He kissed her forehead again and she wanted more.

"Sleep," he said.

When he went to withdraw, she caught his hand. "Stay."

He pressed his lips together in a line of reluctance. Then he nodded and climbed into the bed. He sat against the headboard and pulled her to his chest as she tried to dry her damp eyes on his shirt.

His hands soothed her arm and her back. The heat of him warmed her through to her bones.

Shadows danced against the white walls as she listened to his heart beating solidly in his chest. The shades were still drawn, a consequence of rising before the sun that morning.

The distant sound of rush-hour traffic lulled her.

She found herself drifting off to sleep but, the moment she closed her eyes, the image of Abigail's face flashed into her mind. She jerked and Max's hands tightened on her arms.

"What is it?" he asked softly.

"I see her whenever I close my eyes."

He snuggled Lucy closer. She looked up and met his dark gaze. She felt herself free falling. Then his eyes dropped to her lips and her breath hitched.

He wasn't supposed to see her in this way. His pupils weren't supposed to dilate as if they liked what they saw when they looked at disheveled Lucy. His nose wasn't supposed to flare slightly as though the scent of her called to him the way his did to her.

He stared into her eyes, and her heart hammered. Her nipples tightened. Desire coiled inside her low and tight. She thought he was going to kiss her. Instead, he said quietly, "I should leave you alone."

"Why?" Her voice squeaked.

"I don't want to take advantage of you."

She played with his shirt buttons as she remembered how he'd told her he often mirrored words to build rapport. "Advantage of me?"

He swallowed audibly. "You're upset."

"Upset?" She shifted as she said the last, straddling his hips and pressing herself against him.

He groaned. "Lucy."

She pressed a kiss to the side of his mouth. "What?"

His hands sat on her hips, unmoving. "We can't. You're distressed," he repeated.

"I'm trying to take my mind off being distressed."

He groaned again. "That's my point exactly. You're not thinking straight. I don't want to hurt you."

She drew the pad of her finger down the side of his beautiful face. "You won't hurt me." She would happily swap even physical pain for the grief and guilt currently shredding her insides.

His hands unconsciously moved her against him even as he tried to talk himself out of this. But she wanted him. She wanted this.

"I'd love to forget some of the nightmare the last few days have been by having sex against every surface in this room. It doesn't have to mean more than that." Her voice caught, and he pulled her closer against him, one hand sinking into her hair and the other anchoring her against his hips.

He kissed her quickly, hungrily, then pulled back. "I want to, shit, Lucy, I've been thinking about this ever since we were sitting in that room together reading those police reports yesterday."

She laughed. "Seriously?"

"Wrong of me, I know."

It was perfect. She stretched against him and nipped his chin. She could feel his resolve evaporating. "Show me what you've been thinking about."

He hesitated, staring deep into her eyes as if he could see into her soul.

She thought he'd back away then. Run from what he saw.

Instead, he began undoing the buttons of her blouse. She started to shrug out of her jacket, but he used the material to trap her and draw her closer. He nuzzled her neck, the sensitive skin where her pulse throbbed. Then lower, over her collar bone and the soft flesh of her breast. He licked her through the lace, the friction of his tongue, the roughness of the material against her nipple making her toes curl. She moaned as she raised her face to the ceiling.

"I wasn't the only one noticing you either," he whispered.

"You don't have to lie to me." She laughed shakily because of the riot of sensations he was creating. "I was there."

"And yet," he murmured, "you are blind to those around you."

That was crazy. Old Lucy had observed men noticing her. New Lucy had spent a lot of time perfecting her disguise. "No one notices me when the likes of Agente Ramon are around." She was proud of the fact she could hold a conversation when her world revolved around what his lips were doing to her body.

"They don't notice you the same way I notice you, but they are aware." He turned his attention to her other breast and the throbbing between her legs intensified.

Why did Max see her when others didn't? Was this real...? How could she ever trust in *real* again, especially when she was the one deceiving others?

He twisted until she was lying on the bed, still trapped by her ugly clothes, him lying alongside her. Max slid her skirt up to reveal a lace thong and he held her still while he looked his fill. He cupped his hand over her sex, and she pressed up against his palm, desperate to relieve the ache.

"No offense to your suit, but your underwear kicks some serious ass."

Her lingerie was a weakness, a means of clinging to some part of her old life in a way that she'd assumed no one would ever discover.

She pressed against him again, and he dipped a finger beneath the lace, brushing her clit and tracing her opening and making her gasp. He did it again. And again. She lay there trapped and quivering and feeling as if she could come from the slight brush of skin against skin.

But it still wasn't enough. Not now. The floodgates of desire had opened and only having him inside her would be enough to satisfy her now.

She wriggled and he released her with a reluctant smile. She shrugged out of the confining shirt and jacket while he found the waistband of her skirt and undid the button. Lucy slipped the skirt off and tossed it away. She was in her underwear and he was fully clothed, but instead of making her feel vulnerable, she finally felt his equal.

She dragged his shirt out of his pants and quickly helped him undo the buttons. He climbed out of bed and hung his clothes over her vanity chair, proving his brain was still functioning while hers seemed to have been turned to mush.

This was just sex for him. A quickie.

For her it felt as if she'd escaped a dark prison that had

held her captive for far too long. It felt like a revolution. It felt like a coup.

His body was unbelievable. All carved muscle with a sprinkling of black hair over his excellent pecs that arrowed down into his boxers. But it wasn't his abs that had finally drawn her back into the light. It was the way he saw her, the way he treated her, as if she mattered, as if he really cared. She didn't kid herself he felt more for her than that. He was a good person. A beautiful soul, inside and out. Right now, she was appreciating the out.

He climbed on to the bed and sat against the headboard. "Come here, Lucy."

She straddled his legs. Touched him through his shorts, hot and hard. She wanted him inside her. She wanted to experience that feeling of fullness, of completion.

He kissed her again then pulled his head back slightly, a grin on those full lips. "I dreamt about you last night."

"Me?" She blinked in surprise. "What did you dream about?"

"About this. About you. Doing things to you that were not entirely appropriate given we work together." His eyes were intense. He was trying to figure out whether that turned her on or repulsed her.

She leaned closer to his ear. "I couldn't sleep for thinking about what this might be like between us. I touched myself thinking about you being so close."

The muscles in his jaw flexed. "I guess I can feel a little less guilty about what happened in the shower this morning then."

"What happened in the shower?" she asked with a grin.

"I'll show you later."

That sounded delightful.

She went back to touching his body. Running her hands over his collar bone and across his deltoids. The pulse in his neck throbbed, and she leaned down and kissed the tender skin and watched his heart speed up.

He skimmed his finger across the top of her breasts, and a wave of gooseflesh formed in the wake.

He frowned. "You are so beautiful."

"I'm not."

He was going to ask her questions about her appearance again, and she didn't want to answer them. Not now. Not later. Not ever.

Did he deserve to know the truth? Under normal circumstances, he deserved nothing but pure honesty. But this was a matter of national security and, if anyone had been taught the potential dangers of pillow talk, it would be her.

She kissed him instead. Took those lips of his on a test-drive. It didn't take much coaxing on her part before he'd forgotten the questions that must be in his mind. Like how did a wallflower morph so quickly into a sex kitten?

It wasn't much of a secret. Most wallflowers were sex kittens in disguise.

Her fingers traced the taut muscles across his stomach. "You keep in good shape for a negotiator, Supervisory Special Agent Hawthorne."

His hands curved around her waist and lifted her off him, then dragged her down the bed until they were lying side by side.

He kissed her fingers one by one. "I never know when I might have to go hand-to-hand with a member of the Foreign Service." He leaned over. "Or mouth to mouth. Or mouth to neck..." He kissed his way down her body and, by the time he was finished, he'd named and kissed every part of her anatomy.

She was quivering with sensation. And the horribly tender sense that Max was possibly the best person she'd ever met. With Sergio, she'd believed he was too good to be true and had been proven correct. With Max, she knew he was a wonderful and kind human being. She hated that what had happened with Raminksy was now tainting everything else in her life, including this interlude with Max. She didn't want him to hate her when the truth came out. But he might.

He rolled up and off the bed and, for a frantic moment, she thought he was done with her. He left the room and she raised herself up on her elbows. She heard rustling.

Then he came back with a smile on his face and a strip of condoms in his hand which he tossed on the bedside table.

She raised a brow and he grinned back.

"As I've said on several occasions, I don't generally hook up when I'm working. However, as a former SOF soldier I always carry condoms as part of a survival pack."

She laughed. "Nice save."

"It's true." He came down beside her, his grin igniting a feeling inside her that felt almost out of control. It wasn't lust. It was something she'd rather not examine but thought she might hoard as a memory until she was old and gray.

"Then again, I am good at talking my way out of difficult situations, or so I've been told."

"You should turn it into a career."

"I'll look into that." His hand rested on the curve of her waist. His skin was dark beside hers, making her look washed-out and pale. He kissed her again. "This is one situation I don't want to talk my way out of."

The shadows were deepening as dusk fell. It made it easier to pretend that they might have a chance at more than this. Maybe a proper fling. She knew it wouldn't happen. They might have an hour or a night or a couple of days but, as soon as Kristen's kidnapping was resolved, he'd be gone.

She cupped Max's jaw and pressed her thumb to his lips before leaning leisurely forward for another taste. Then he took control of the kiss, rolling her onto her back and settling between her thighs.

He kissed her and stroked her skin, learning every sensitive inch, unclipping her bra and tossing it aside. Cupping her breasts and suckling until her eyes closed in pleasure. She tried to touch him, to speed it up when she couldn't stand it anymore, but he grabbed her hands and pinned them above her head with one of his while he continued to drive her crazy.

"Max." Her voice was pleading.

His other hand slipped lower and he touched her sensitive flesh, slipping one finger, then two inside her. She pressed her feet into the mattress and bucked against him.

"I don't think I can wait any longer." His voice was deep and gravelly.

"Then don't."

He chuckled as he released her and reached for a condom, quickly rolling it on while she kicked off her panties.

Then he was back, and she opened for him, welcoming him inside her, needing this. As he pushed deeper, she held his gaze, drowning in the liquid depths of his eyes, letting him see who she really was even if she couldn't tell him. That he was a man she could give her heart to. He was a man she could love if she'd had the chance.

She tilted her hips and took him deeper as he found the

rhythm that made them both gasp and groan and cling. Again and again, over and over. She did not want this to end. She would live in this instant for an eternity if she had the choice, poised on the edge, waiting for the crash that they both knew was coming. Her release made her cry out in pleasure as Max pushed deeper and harder and did the same.

Their heartbeats pounded against each other's chests, and he drew her against him and carefully rolled them so she was sprawled on top of him.

"That was amazing," he said quietly.

She nodded, not daring to raise her gaze to his in case he saw the tears of regret that started to form. Regret that she hadn't been completely truthful with him. Regret that he'd leave soon. Regret that she might be labeled a traitor before this was all over. Max might hate her, and she wouldn't blame him one bit.

MAX GOT RID of the condom while Lucy dozed. Then he climbed back into bed and drew her against him, pulling the sheet over them both. He should probably get some sleep too, but damn if he wasn't hard again.

It had been a while since he'd been involved with anyone but, even so, he wasn't some randy teenager driven by lustful hormones looking for any chance to have sex. He was a grown-ass man.

He tried to count sheep, but his mind kept wandering back to the fact that Lucy was naked in his arms and his dick just wanted to know when they could do it all again. What was it about this woman that gave him such a buzz?

Her hand curled around him even though he thought she was asleep. "Hello."

He groaned.

"Ready for round two, I see?"

She leaned up and kissed him and then she shuffled lower in the bed, straddling his body as she worked her way lower.

Every drop of blood in his body headed south and it was just as well he was lying down. Her lips kissed along the rigid length of him. Then her tongue came out to play.

The image of Lucy doing this to him, with her big eyes and innocent face staring up at him to see if he liked what she was doing, sent a shot of something strange and unfamiliar through him. A weird mix of lust and tenderness.

He sank his fingers into her hair when she took him in her mouth. It was so good he might explode before he was ready. His grip tightened on her hair. He wanted to let go and fuck her mouth the way he wanted, but he'd been raised with manners.

"Come here." He pulled her off him and tugged her until she had moved all the way up his body.

"Hold on," he warned her, and she gripped the headboard in surprise as he shuffled lower and settled her onto his mouth. He lapped and played until she was panting. He touched her clit, and she cried out as she came.

Then he grabbed a condom and put it on, moving behind her as she knelt facing the headboard. She was so wet he slipped easily inside. And then she was once again sliding over him, gripping him, driving him crazy. He bent her forward and wrapped himself around her, then clamped two fingers tight around one nipple while his other palm pressed against her clit, and she came again with a sharp cry. Her muscles spasmed around him, squeezing him, milking him until he couldn't hold back any longer. He came with an explosive blast that ricocheted from his head to his balls igniting every nerve in between.

Then they both crashed, finally falling into a dreamless sleep.

CHAPTER TWENTY-NINE

S OMETHING WOKE IRENE. The stealthy pressure of a heavy foot on a creaky floorboard. The whisper of air moving outside her door.

A shiver ran over her spine.

Why was someone creeping around in the dark? Was it Kristen?

It didn't sound like Kristen—it felt like menace rather than hope.

Could it be rescuers?

She sat up cautiously.

Her mind throbbed as much with sorrow as pain. She kept flexing her sore hand, expecting the missing finger to curl. It didn't. It was nothing but a painful stump now.

She stuffed the trauma and worry of her situation down to the pit of her stomach and swallowed hard to keep it there.

Another creak.

Was it the wind on the old house?

Another groan of wood straining under the weight of a human being. Someone was definitely moving around. The hair on her nape slowly rose in awareness and trepidation.

The door to her room was pushed open, and the hinge ground out a protest.

She couldn't see with the hood over her face, but she felt a male presence watching her.

The footsteps came closer, and someone knelt beside her.

They didn't speak, and that was when she knew with certainty that this was not a rescue mission. A hand tried to push her down onto the floor, but she resisted.

"Acuéstese y no se mueva," he demanded. *Lie down and don't move.*

Her mouth went dry with fear. It was the demented kidnapper. He'd brought her food a couple of hours ago. This was the first time he'd ever returned before dawn.

Why the hell would he want her to lie down? She pressed back into the solidness of the radiator and refused to budge.

"¿Quieres que suelte las cadenas?"

Did she want to get out of these chains? "Si."

And now he knew she spoke Spanish, but he hadn't been trying to trick her. Alcohol was ripe on his breath. He was drunk.

Then she heard another set of footsteps come into the room, and her heart pounded and sweat bloomed. The second person closed the door, and the snick of the catch felt like a stab to the heart. She knew exactly what these two wanted.

"What do you want? Go away." She curled into a tight ball. When she sensed one of them close to her, she kicked out at them, barefoot.

He yelped and scuttled away.

She could feel them both assessing her. Predators eyeing the caribou calf. Looking for an opening.

Why were they being so stealthy? Because they didn't want someone else in the house to hear?

"Help!" she screamed. "Help me!"

The men swore and one of them threw himself on top of

her but hit his head on the radiator and rolled to the side, groaning with pain.

Irene screamed when her assailant landed on her maimed hand. She twisted away from him but was brought up short by her restraints.

Then she felt fingers on her throat, squeezing, telling her to shut the fuck up or he was going to kill her.

One of them lifted her chains and unlocked the padlock that connected her handcuffs to the heavy links.

"Don't worry, little one. We won't hurt you."

They dragged her to her feet and, for a second, she thought she'd been mistaken about their intentions, but then the other one nudged her across the room. He pushed her again and, this time, she hit the edge of the old musty mattress.

He shoved her and she landed on her front, dust from the bed rising in a cloud that choked her even with the hood over her face. She rolled onto her back as adrenaline flooded her. She cycled her feet to kick anyone coming close, but they split up, one of the men going to the other side of the bed and grabbing her cuffed hands. She cried out when he squeezed her wounded hand.

Bastard.

The other man used her distraction to climb on top of her and pin her with his weight.

Irene couldn't believe this. Like they hadn't already destroyed her life, butchered her body. How was that not enough for them?

"You are animals," she screamed at them. "You are pigs."

They spoke in Spanish, but she understood every word. "Shut her up in case the boss comes back and hears."

She screamed louder until the guy above her head knelt on

the mattress and planted his other hand over her mouth. The canvas of the hood made it impossible to breathe. She turned her head to the side, desperate to find enough air not to suffocate.

He opened her shirt. No. No. No.

They made comments of appreciation about her body, and she wanted to shrivel with humiliation. They were both laughing as one guy began undoing her jeans. She still fought him, but she heard something else in the background. She heard footsteps.

Kristen. Please god if it was her friend then *run*. Don't try to save her. The odds were impossible. Run, and they might somehow both survive this nightmare.

The footsteps were coming toward her room.

Neither man heard as they prepared themselves to rape her. They struggled to get her jeans off her hips because the denim was so tight, and she wasn't helping them.

They both froze when the door opened.

"El jefe, she tried to escape. We were—"

The sound of a silenced bullet cut her attacker off, and she felt him slump over her lower legs. *Oh my god.*

"That's for being sloppy." Another bullet, and she felt her attacker jerk again. "That's for being a filthy pig."

The other man was begging for forgiveness. She heard the scramble of feet and the sound of more shots. Somehow, the second guy was able to get to the bathroom and slam the door shut.

She lay there frozen as she listened to the guy with the gun, the boss, fire several shots into the lock on the door.

Irene could picture the scene as the dead man slid off her legs onto the floor. She heard the man with the gun kick in the bathroom door and then she heard what sounded like a scuffle.

Irene leapt off the bed and pushed the hood up enough to see. Then she ran. Fuck it. She didn't stop to rescue Kristen. Remorse gutted her, but she knew she'd have one chance and one chance only.

Her jeans were thankfully so tight they didn't fall down. She ran so fast she was already down the first flight before the lead kidnapper appeared to realize she'd made a break for it.

She heard him running after her but didn't let it distract her. Get to the door. Get outside. Hide.

She slipped, and a bullet glanced off the wall ahead of her. She flung herself around the corner at the bottom of the stairs and headed toward the kitchen underneath her chamber, betting that the backdoor of the house was the most likely one to be unlocked.

She had no doubt he'd kill her if he caught her.

She hit the kitchen at full sprint, eternally grateful it was empty of people, and pivoted right. The doorway was in front of her.

She grabbed the handle and panicked when it didn't open, but the key was in the lock.

She twisted it even as she heard her captor draw closer.

The key turned, lock clicked, and Irene threw herself out into the darkness.

———————————

LUCY AWOKE TO the sound of the shower running. *Max.* She blinked at her alarm clock. One A.M.

Her stomach growled. She was starving. She needed to eat.

She also needed to clean up.

She climbed out of bed and pushed open the bathroom door, walking into hot steam. Max was faintly visible behind the fogged-up glass, and her heart gave a little sigh.

Gorgeous.

The door opened, and his arm snaked out and pulled her under the stream of water with him.

She gave a little squeal, feeling young and foolish in a way she'd forgotten. He pushed her against the wall and planted an elbow either side of her head.

"I hope you wanted a shower." His eyes were amused.

She ran her arms up his sculpted chest. "Funnily enough I did."

She raised up on tiptoes and kissed him deeply. Then he lifted her off the floor, and she wrapped her legs around him and, once again, she was on fire.

The length of him rubbed along her clit as he leaned down to kiss her neck, her breasts. Driving her crazy. Driving her wild. If he didn't get inside her in the next sixty seconds, she was going to implode.

"Wait," Max ordered and slipped out of the shower. Then he was back with a condom.

Her nails dug into his back as he lifted her again. "Hurry."

He positioned himself at her slick entrance and pushed inside, and it felt so good, so right, she bit her lip to hold back a moan.

She tipped her head back as Max filled her perfectly. She saw the pulse in his neck kick up a notch and then he began pounding into her, all raw power and honed male beauty. They were both wet and slippery, and his grip on her bit into her muscles with a delicious sharpness. It was incredible. It was amazing. Once again, she never wanted it to end.

He changed the angle, so he was rubbing her clit every time he pushed inside and then he braced her against the wall as he let go with one hand and pinched one of her nipples. Tight.

Her body electrified, and she spasmed and came in a rush of white light and pleasure that hit her like a tsunami.

He followed with a tortured groan and, when he was finished, stood there with his chest heaving. When they were both destroyed and barely able to stand, he let her feet slide slowly back down to the floor.

Then he pulled away, got rid of the condom, and grabbed shampoo, squirting some into her hair and lathering up a foam. He drew her more fully under the spray and rinsed the shampoo and applied conditioner, smoothing it gently over her scalp and to the ends of her hair. He took the shower gel and soaped himself and then her before rinsing her hair and their bodies. The gentleness was killing her.

Finally clean, both of them sated, he turned off the water and Lucy stood there staring at him.

He cupped her face. Kissed her. "You're beautiful."

She blinked stupidly.

Tiny droplets of water clung to his lashes. He looked magnificent and she couldn't believe she was with him even for a short time. She did not deserve him.

She kissed his palms. "So are you."

He reached outside for towels and wrapped one around her, and then tucked one around his hips. He stepped out and offered his hand to her, like she was getting out of a carriage. She laughed. His fingers tightened.

Her stomach growled again and this time he laughed.

"Time to refuel."

Lucy nodded. "I have frozen pizza. Or we can reheat the burgers."

"Anything sounds good. Then we can maybe catch a few hours' sleep before—" The sound of a cell phone ringing cut off his words. He grimaced. "Or maybe not."

CHAPTER THIRTY

MAX STRODE INTO the Legat's office and was taken aback by the number of people working at two in the morning.

"Are you guys here because the kidnappers called or is something else about to go down?" he asked an agent standing nearby.

"I can't say," she replied which was all the answer he needed.

He nodded a thanks and headed over to the Negotiation Center.

He tapped on the door before he entered.

Adam Quinn had been manning the phones on the graveyard shift when the kidnapper had called.

Jennifer McCreedy had already made it in from wherever she was staying. Max realized with a start he hadn't even asked her what hotel she was in. Was that because he'd been hoping what had occurred between him and Lucy would happen? That for all his "I don't hook up on a job" spiel, he'd been subconsciously hoping to change that with Lucy this whole time?

He didn't regret them having sex. He wanted more. Shit, he was already wondering how they'd be able to see one another again when this was all over.

Lucy followed behind him, and he held the door so she could come inside. She wore black jeans and t-shirt and a dark red hoodie. Her hair was still damp from their joint shower and pulled into a tight ponytail that exposed her fine bone structure. Her glasses once again camouflaged her eyes.

She looked gorgeous. How did people not notice?

He spotted the ambassador and her husband, followed by Miranda and Iain Bartlett coming in the door to the Legat's office. They all looked like they'd rolled out of bed and appeared as startled as he was by the feverish activity in the Legat's office.

He pinched his lips together. He didn't stand a pup's chance in hell of keeping these people out of this stage of the kidnapping so instead he'd try to corral them and keep them busy. He ushered them all into his closet and closed the door, blocking out the distraction of what looked like another major operation about to go down.

"Catherine, Phillip, please take a seat over there." He pointed the parents to the camp bed. It might not be particularly swanky, but they'd have less distance to hit the floor should the worst happen. He wished he'd had the chance to review the tapes privately before they'd turned up. He turned back to Quinn and ignored the others even though he was intensely aware of every breath Lucy took.

"What do we have?"

Quinn looked at his notes. "They called twenty-four minutes ago with details of where to drop the money. They want one person to deliver the funds. They said they'd call back in thirty minutes with directions. They said no cops. No drones. No trackers in the money else the girls die."

"What are the chances this is a trick? That they'll take the money and not release the girls?" Phillip asked.

Max stared at the man. "Successful kidnappers have their own reputations to think about. I'm hopeful that the fact we came up with what they asked for will mean they will keep up their end of the bargain, but there are no guarantees."

"Does the person delivering the money wait around for the kidnappers to hand over the hostages to them?" Miranda asked with her arms crossed tightly over her chest.

Max shook his head. "It's not like the movies. We hand over the cash and then we hope and pray they release the girls."

"What's stopping them keeping the cash and the girls?" Catherine demanded.

"Not a damned thing, Ambassador. Except their desire to be paid should they ever pull this sort of job again in the future. If they kill the hostages no one will trust their word." That reminded him that the Canadians still hadn't called him back. Too late to follow up now.

"What's to stop them taking our money and then selling the girls to someone else as threatened?"

Max shook his head. "Again, nothing, but we are out of choices and out of time." He indicated the Legat's room with a thumb over this shoulder. He couldn't speak freely as not everyone here had been read in on the case, but Catherine Dickerson and Iain Bartlett understood the urgency. If the Legat was about to request arrest warrants be served for certain Russian oligarchs, it must mean they were doing the same in the States. Operation Soapbox was about to launch criminal indictments and the shit was about to hit the fan.

The Russians would certainly increase their efforts to find and buy the ambassador's daughter, even if purely for spite. It was a now or never time for this ransom payment.

"Where is the money now?" Max asked.

"In the Diplomatic Security Service offices," Iain Bartlett said.

"I suggest for Irene's and Kristen's sake you do not place any additional trackers on that money. I realize how tempting it is."

Iain nodded, although Max could tell he was reluctant in his agreement.

He was about to ask Quinn to play the tape when the phone rang. He, Quinn, and Jennifer picked up headsets.

"Quiet everyone. Not a word." Max answered the call. "Hi. This is Max."

The electronic voice sounded more menacing than usual. "You have thirty minutes to get to the corner of *Charcas* and *Laprida*. One lone female in the car. One million dollars in unmarked bills. Take this phone and wait for the next set of instructions."

"We need a little more time."

"Time has run out, Max. Do it or both girls die." El jefe hung up.

"I'll deliver the money," Jennifer said easily.

Max shook his head reluctantly. "You don't know the area."

"I'll do it," Miranda said quietly.

Everyone looked surprised.

She looked around. "I speak the language. I know my way around the city. It doesn't sound like a difficult or dangerous job, providing I do what I'm told, correct?"

Max would be lying if he wasn't relived when the ambassador didn't veto that plan. He didn't want them sending Lucy out there because they considered her more expendable. He certainly did not.

"They'll probably send you on a wild goose chase around the city to make sure you're alone and not being followed. All you have to do is follow their instructions and drop the money where they tell you. Then come straight back here immediately afterward."

Miranda pressed her clenched fists together in front of her. "I can do that."

Max stood. "Bartlett, get your people to bring all the cash down to the parking lot, ASAP."

Jennifer already had a cell phone ready, programmed with the kidnapper's number.

She handed it to Max who handed it to Miranda. "Remember. The kidnappers might plant spies along the route to report in on your activity. Don't fuck it up. Let's go. The clock is ticking."

They hurried out of the room and all raced down to the parking lot.

They reached Miranda's BMW. She climbed in and one of the DS agents jogged toward them and put the bags on the passenger seat.

Max checked his watch. Miranda turned the key, and everyone's heart caught when the engine didn't turn over.

Miranda tried again. "What…?"

"Take my car," Lucy offered.

Miranda looked startled. "Your car?" She blinked, but Lucy was already in the driver's seat of her Mini which was parked next to Miranda's. The engine purred to life.

Lucy got out and Miranda climbed in. The bags were transferred. Max checked his watch again.

A cry of frustration came from inside the vehicle. "It's a stick shift. I can't drive a manual," Miranda exclaimed.

Max breathed out impatiently.

Miranda climbed out, looking around for another car.

"We're running out of time," said Max, mentally running through options.

"I'll do it." Lucy climbed into the passenger seat and started programming her Sat Nav.

"But—" Phillip started, clearly unconvinced by Lucy's competence.

"No time for buts." Lucy stated. "I need to go. Now."

She was right. Even though Max hated this, they had no choice. He nodded to Miranda. "Give Lucy the phone."

Miranda thrust the cell at Lucy and stepped back to the ambassador's side. Max tapped on the glass of the passenger window, and Lucy rolled it down.

"Do as they tell you but don't enter into any situation that looks dangerous. Don't let anyone else get in the car and don't get out unless you are obviously alone. The last thing we need is them taking another hostage. They probably won't have eyes on you the entire time, but they might not be the only interested party you need to worry about." He leaned inside and opened the glove compartment, surreptitiously palming the small tracker TacOps had found on the car earlier that evening. It felt like a million years ago. He didn't want the Russians able to track Lucy or the money while she was driving alone around the city streets at night.

He was being cryptic. The Russian involvement in this case and the bug in Lucy's Mini was now a separate counterintelligence investigation, and Max had been told not to inform anyone of its existence.

The FBI could track her via the cell phone and the money bags. It would have to be enough.

Lucy held his gaze. "I've got this, Max. See you in a few hours."

He nodded and stepped back, all sorts of emotions battling inside him. He wanted to hug her and kiss her. Wanted to tell her to be careful, that he'd drive the car, but rationally he knew this was normally a low-risk part of the operation. The danger generally associated with the money drop was the bagman running off with or skimming a cut of the cash. Lucy wouldn't do that. He'd trust her with his life, let alone a million dollars.

She put her car in reverse and pulled out of the space and then sped away.

Phillip put his arm around his wife's shoulders. "What do we do now?"

Max looked from one person to the next. "Now we wait."

CHAPTER THIRTY-ONE

MAX WENT BACK to the FBI offices on the second floor. When the others tried to follow, he insisted they head back to the ambassador's office or the Dickersons' apartment and that he would inform them immediately there was any news. There simply wasn't enough space for seven tense adults to occupy the former broom closet. The negotiators needed a distraction-free workspace.

The Legat's office was still buzzing, and he tried to ignore the frenzy of activity going on. He spoke to Brian Powell about what was happening in what was technically his case. The man looked fraught, so Max told him he'd keep him updated and left the guy to it.

Powell's career would either soar or crash-and-burn tonight. Max didn't envy him.

Max checked his watch. Lucy had less than five minutes to get to the first rendezvous. He stepped into the Negotiation Center. Agents at the Strategic Information and Operation Center at headquarters would be tracking the calls and the money bags.

Quinn and Jennifer looked at him. The atmosphere was strained. Nothing unusual about that. K&R was a fine line between success and failure, and this was one of the most dangerous periods.

"Any updates?" he asked.

They both shook their heads.

"Let me know when they make the next call."

He stepped out of the room, leaving the door ajar, and called Andy. Despite the hour, the guy picked up on the first ring.

"Money's on its way," Max told him.

"Shit."

That wasn't the expected response. "What's up?"

"I reached out to some old friends of mine like you suggested and, a few minutes ago, I got a call back from a guy who works in Vauxhall Cross." Britain's Secret Intelligence Service. "He says there's growing evidence of a Russian asset working in the US embassy in Buenos Aires which muddies the waters a little."

"What the *fuck*?" When Max had suggested Andy reach out to his sources, he'd expected rumors of Yahontov's imminent arrest to reach his ears, not a spy scandal.

"Yeah. Pretty intense."

"What makes them think that?" Max was very aware of all the other people around him. This might be why the counter-intelligence division had jumped all over the Russians trying to set him up in a honeytrap. They already suspected a problem.

"Earlier this year, an encrypted message was captured coming out of the Russian embassy, and the Brits happened to have a cypher for that stretch of time. The message referenced plans for a dam in Africa. The Brits warned Langley. Later that same month, the Americans thwarted a terror attack on the facility. Guess who designed that dam?"

"No clue."

"Phillip Dickerson."

Shit.

"He couldn't have been the only one with access to the plans?"

"No, I doubt it, but I don't have any more details."

"Do the Brits have someone inside the Russian embassy?"

Andy laughed. "That's well above my buddy's pay grade and mine, for that matter."

"Do the Americans know about this?" It was one thing to warn a foreign country about a possible impending threat. Another entirely to compromise sources.

"I'm not sure, but other sensitive intel has surfaced around the world that could be linked back to either the Dickersons or someone at the embassy in Buenos Aires."

So, the US intelligence services must be aware of the potential leak from someone at this embassy. "Do they have any ideas as to the identity of the spy?"

"Nothing confirmed, but my buddy sent me a photograph snapped a couple of days ago of someone from the embassy taking a meet with a major league SVR player. I'm going to text it to you even though I shouldn't."

The image loaded slowly. It was grainy and dark, but Max recognized the sharp profile of the Russian Lucy had pointed out to him at the hotel. And he was intimately familiar with the curve of the woman's cheek. The shell of her ear.

Lucy Aston kissing Anotoly Agapov in the middle of the night. Cold and cruel, the image drilled into his temples. His lungs seized. His vision tunneled.

The image gutted him.

He reached out a hand to steady himself against the wall. No wonder she recognized the guy.

"When was this taken?" He sounded as if he'd inhaled a

demon.

"Christmas night. About eleven PM local time."

After she'd left him in the bar.

After she'd left him in the bar—Lucy had changed and rendezvoused with a Russian spymaster.

Ice flooded his system. What the ever-loving fuck?

"Recognize her?"

"No." Max had no idea why he lied. Maybe so Andy didn't freak out and alert the Lomakins. Maybe because he wasn't ready to admit what a damn fool he'd been. Or maybe because his heart wasn't ready to believe it yet.

It wasn't because of any desire to protect a traitor.

He felt as if he'd been pummeled by a heavyweight boxer.

The phone inside the Negotiation Center rang.

"I have to go, Andy. I'll keep you updated." Max stepped back inside and closed the door.

It was the same electronic voice from before. The voice told Lucy to go to the next location.

"Okay," Lucy replied. Her voice was steady, betraying no hint of nerves. Betraying no hint of duplicity.

Could she be a traitor? Would she betray the girls?

"Who is this?" the kidnapper asked sharply.

"My name is Lucy. Lucy Aston."

There was a long pause. "Don't be late, Lucy Aston."

The kidnapper hung up. Quinn marked the new location on a paper map pinned to the wall. So far, Lucy was following instructions to the letter.

A buzzing sound started inside Max's head. Anger or hurt? Or trepidation? He wasn't sure. How could he have been so foolish? She'd raised his internal alarm bells the moment he'd met her. He'd known something about her wasn't right, and he'd ignored his instincts.

Fool.

He tried to figure out what this all meant for the hostages. He didn't know. A short while ago, he'd have bet his life Lucy was straight up and honest. Now his belief in her and in himself had been shattered.

Anger started to seep through and outcompete the softer emotions like hurt and betrayal. Anger that she'd used him.

Was she the ultimate honeytrap? Did she think he'd forgive this kind of treachery, or did she never intend to see him again?

That was a distinct possibility.

He stepped out of the room and called Jon Regan from TacOps. "Did you remove all the bugs you found on Lucy's car?"

"Yup."

Max swore.

"Why?"

Max had no idea who he was allowed to reveal this information to. If Lucy worked for the Russians, she'd have already warned them that the FBI were about to move on their warrant requests and Yahontov would likely be in the wind. The ransom money at this point would be a bonus.

Judging from the relative quiet in the office now, Operation Soapbox had launched. It was out of his hands now.

His hands shook at the fact he'd let the hostages down. These two girls would pay the price for his ineptitude, but he wasn't willing to give up on them yet.

When the money wasn't delivered, the kidnappers might kill the hostages...or maybe Lucy would make them a better offer to turn the victims over to the Russians.

He didn't want to believe it, but how could he ignore the evidence he'd seen with his own eyes?

"Lucy just left on a money drop. I took the tracker out of her car because I didn't want the Russians following her."

Why would they put a tracker on her car if she worked for them?

Maybe they didn't trust her either?

"You can track her phone, right?" Regan sounded as if he were getting up and dressed.

"Sure, but the kidnappers might tell her to dump that cell and leave another for her to use somewhere." Or the Russians might.

"What about the wires in the bags?"

It made sense that Regan knew about them. Hell, his team had probably made them. But Lucy knew about the trackers too and, if she planned to double-cross them, then she'd dump the bags first chance she got.

The silence on the end of the line sounded deafening.

"What aren't you telling me?" Regan snapped.

The guy was perceptive as hell even when he wasn't in the same room. Time to fess up. "A few minutes ago, I was sent an image of Lucy secretly meeting with Anotoly Agapov on Christmas night. And there's a rumor there's a spy working at the embassy."

Regan swore. "And Lucy's the one doing the drop? How the hell did that happen?"

Max explained about Miranda's car not working.

"She disabled the PA's car?"

Max pulled a face. "When? She hasn't been out of my sight except when she went to grab the ransom money last evening."

"I guess you didn't use the spare room then." Regan

sounded commiserating rather than accusing. Max felt like shit regardless. "We're on our way. We'll park in the usual place. I have a couple of ideas we might be able to use to track her."

"Thanks. I'll be there as soon as I can." Max hung up and scraped his fingers over his scalp. Lucy's grief over the old woman's death—was that an act? The way she'd made love to him...

Fuck. Fuck. Fuck.

He needed to get ahead of this mess. He needed to talk to his colleagues at CNU and, unfortunately, he needed to inform the ambassador because, one way or another, Lucy had met up with a Russian spymaster the day after the top diplomat's daughter had been kidnapped. And, considering Operation Soapbox had just launched, this could not be good.

THE KIDNAPPERS STILL hadn't fed her today, and she figured they weren't planning to. Kristen had heard some kind of scuffle about an hour ago, but since then it had gone silent. She sat inside the wardrobe. She felt stronger for not having drunk the water but was so parched, her tongue had welded itself to the roof of her mouth.

She kicked out at the wardrobe but froze at the noise it made. It was solid wood, but her legs were strong. She kicked again, and the sound seemed to resonate around her wooden box. She hesitated.

What if she was about to make a massive mistake?

On the call this morning, the lead kidnapper had said he'd wanted the ransom money ready for tonight. Did that mean they could right now be picking up the cash? Maybe counting it?

Had they released Irene? Was that what the commotion had been about earlier?

Or were they patiently waiting for the money. Was the suggestion they had found another buyer for her simply a bluff? They might have mutilated Irene to avoid the full-blown wrath of the United States.

She didn't know.

A shiver radiated from her chest. What if she was sitting here like a lamb to the slaughter, simply waiting her turn?

She kicked again but stopped when she heard the heavy tread of footsteps coming into the room. She held her breath, panicked when she realized she didn't have her hood on. She scrambled around and found it. Her heart hammering as she dragged it over her matted hair, her breath loud and hoarse.

"Have you forgotten the rules, *mi hija*?"

Don't make a sound else I will cut out your tongue.

Fear pounded like a living thing inside her. She'd already seen them inflict that sort of damage to Irene. He wasn't bluffing.

"No, sir."

"Good. Keep quiet, and it will all be over soon. Your parents have sent the money. In a few short hours, you'll be released."

A wave of relief swept over her, so strong she sagged against the floor.

"But if you make a noise or try to escape, I will be forced to punish you and I might change my mind about releasing you."

The words hung heavy in the air like the threat they were.

"Be a good girl and keep quiet." The footsteps moved

farther away as Kristen lay terrified in her prison.

MAX STRODE TO Ambassador Dickerson's office. Knocked on the door and Phillip opened it.

"Any news?"

Phillip meant about the ransom payment and the release of the hostages, but it was too early. Frankly, if what Andy had told him about Lucy was true, this man might never see his daughter again.

"Let the man in, Phillip." The ambassador sounded agitated.

Max slipped inside. She sat with her arm around her son, both of them on the couch. It was only the family members for a change.

"The kidnappers are still directing Lucy around the city." He cleared his throat. "I need a word in private if I may, ma'am."

Catherine's brows drew together, and she shifted away from her son before standing up.

He'd spoken to Eban. General consensus was, this ransom drop was likely fucked. The constant churning in his gut made him feel as if he might be sick. "Alone, if possible."

Her eyes widened in alarm.

Phillip threw up his hands in exasperation. "Fine. Kevin and I will go play some video games." He pointed a finger at Max. "I want to know when the money is dropped off."

The feeling in the pit of Max's stomach reeked of failure, but he didn't let it show. He nodded, and the man and his son closed the door into their apartment.

"What is it, Max?"

Max pulled out his phone to show Catherine the evidence of her assistant betraying them all when Brian Powell burst into the room. "We have a big problem, Ambassador."

Catherine frowned. "SSA Hawthorne was about to explain."

"Was he now?" The tone was derisive.

What the fuck did that mean?

Brian Powell opened a tablet and turned on the screen. "You might want to sit down for this, Catherine."

"Get on with it, Brian," she snapped.

Powell opened a photograph of a blonde bombshell, her face upturned in ecstasy as she rode some guy into oblivion in a fancy hotel suite.

Catherine squinted at the screen. "I recognize the guy. That's the Russian, Sergio Raminsky—"

"The man who shot the Russian Ambassador to the United States last year?" asked Max.

Powell nodded.

Max frowned. He didn't get it. Then, slowly, the identity of the blonde clicked into place.

"Is that Lucy?" The ambassador's voice rose in horror.

Max felt as if he'd been poleaxed. It was all true. Lucy was in league with the Russians. His heart hardened to stone and seemed to rattle in his chest.

"Yep." Brian glanced at Max with an expression that told Max everything he needed to know. Next shot was going to show him fucking Lucy in bed last night. It had all been a choreographed act. She'd set him up and sold him out.

Powell swiped his screen, and there was a camera still from the hotel security video with him dipping Lucy over his arm and kissing the hell out of her for show.

Max frowned, even as the other two looked scandalized. That was all they'd got? "Who sent you these?"

"They arrived anonymously," said Powell.

Max shook his head. "This doesn't make any sense."

If Lucy was working for the Russians, they'd have much more damaging material than that.

"What doesn't make any sense is that you are involved with someone who is obviously working for Russian intelligence and that same person just left the embassy with a million dollars in ransom money," Powell stated sternly.

Catherine inhaled sharply.

"You're off the case, Hawthorne," Powell stated firmly.

Max's head shot up. "What? That is not your decision to make, Powell."

"No," the ambassador's voice crackled with rage. "It's mine. You fell for the oldest trick in the book, and my daughter might now pay the ultimate price." She whirled and walked over to a side table. She picked up the phone. "I want a full sweep of the embassy for electronic surveillance devices. Yes, now."

She slammed down the receiver.

"I'll go back to the Negotiation Center—"

"Oh, no, SSA Hawthorne. You are done here." Catherine Dickerson's face was effervescent with rage.

Sweat formed on his brow. He'd never been kicked off a case before. They needed him. This was his expertise. He opened his mouth to explain the kiss, to show them the photograph he'd been sent from British Intelligence. But it would only make things look even worse, he realized.

"Collect your things and head back to DC. I never want to see your face again."

CHAPTER THIRTY-TWO

L UCY PROGRAMMED HER Sat Nav to an address in Tribunales. Driving around the streets of Buenos Aires in the middle of the night at the whims of these unknown kidnappers should have been scary, and yet she felt exhilarated.

Perhaps that was the effects of last night still buzzing through her system. In her mind she'd been constantly comparing Max to Sergio, which wasn't even remotely fair. Max dedicated his life to rescuing hostages with as little violence as possible. Sergio had used his good looks and charm to target and destroy as many people as the Russian Federation directed. The only thing the two men had even remotely in common was the fact the external packaging was flawlessly beautiful.

A terrible realization hit her. She took a corner at speed and had to work to correct the fishtail. She'd fallen for the guy in a way that made her feelings for Raminsky look like a teenage crush. Max Hawthorne was the real deal.

Not that it mattered.

She swerved around another corner, applying the handbrake enough to keep the car in the center of the road.

There wasn't any hope for a relationship. He'd still despise her when he discovered the truth, and she wouldn't try to stop him. He was better off without her.

If she delivered the ransom and the girls were released, she could go back to doing what she was supposed to be doing for as long as possible. It might be hours or days, but she might get lucky. Her cover was probably about to get blown if the FBI were moving on Yahontov. Seeing him arrested would be worth the release of those awful images. It was the price she'd always known she'd have to pay eventually.

Or the Russians might hold onto their evidence and try to squeeze more out of her before burning her. Their "little bird" might require assistance in escaping, in which case Lucy would be more than happy to help. More than happy.

Her priority right now was rescuing Kristen and Irene. The sooner she got this money into the kidnappers' hands, the sooner she'd relax. A little, anyway. Her part in this kidnap saga would be over and hopefully the girls would be safely back with their parents by morning.

Her personal phone rang, and it jarred her out of her thoughts. Not the cell given to her by the negotiators, but her personal cell which wasn't "personal" at all. She didn't usually carry it but, following orders, she'd taken it from the safe in her apartment yesterday along with the cash she'd donated to the ransom. She'd given up any concept of having a private life when she'd signed up for this gig. She ignored the call. Whatever they had to say, she had more pressing issues to deal with right now.

She thought back on what she and Max had done last night—that had been very personal. Secret and private—not out of shame. It was simply too special to spoil by sharing it with anyone else.

The cell rang again, and she swore. It had to be important

if they called twice. She dug into her purse for the device.

"Aston, you need to get out." It was her CIA handler. "You've been burned."

She frowned even as she raced to the next rendezvous point. "*What*. How?"

"Russians sent the FBI Legat photos of you with Raminsky. Also, a photo of you kissing the CNU negotiator."

"What photo?"

"Don't worry." Her handler laughed. "You have your clothes on this time."

Bastard. Like he held any moral superiority. She wracked her brain. The hotel. The only time she'd kissed Max with her clothes on had been at the hotel for the sake of the cameras.

Shit.

Her mouth went dry. "I'm literally in the middle of a ransom drop."

"What?" His voice rose.

"The kidnappers wanted a female." She hefted out a long sigh. "It's a long story."

"Get your ass the hell out of there."

"I can't abandon this job and let the US ambassador's daughter face the consequences." She didn't like the silence that followed her declaration.

Eventually he spoke. "I can't tell you what to do, Lucy— oh, wrong, I'm your fucking boss. I can tell you exactly what to do. Get the hell to the safe house now, without anyone following you."

"And what do you suggest I do with the million dollars in small bills?"

"I don't give a shit."

"You're not seriously telling me to dump the money and

let the girls die?"

"That's exactly what I'm telling you. This mission is blown. I want you out of the country before the Argentines or the Russians realize who you really work for. Got it?"

Hell no. She couldn't do it. If she told him she couldn't do it, he'd probably deny she even existed or tell the Agency she'd gone rogue. He'd hang her out to dry and let her rot in federal jail.

"Got it." She hung up. Shit.

Her work cell rang. She ignored it. It was probably the people at the embassy panicking she was about to run off with the cash because they bought into the notion she was a traitor.

What about Max? What did he think?

Emotion rushed her. She didn't want to know what he thought of her. Not after what they'd shared. If he turned on her, she didn't think she'd ever recover.

She ignored the incessant ringing because she was only seconds from the next pitstop. When she got there, she sat for a few moments waiting for new instructions. She turned the ringer off on her work cell.

After ten, fifteen seconds, the kidnapper's cell rang again. As she answered it, she knew the FBI agents would be listening in the Negotiation Center. Max would be listening with a growing sense of horror.

"I want you to get out of the car and walk over to the fountain in the middle of the square. Take *all* your cell phones with you. Even the ones you think we don't know about." The mechanical voice sent shivers through her.

Dammit. Lucy hesitated and scanned the small square she found herself in. No one was around. She didn't really have anything to lose.

She got out. Locked the car and walked over to the fountain still holding the cell to her ear.

"Look at the base. There's a brown paper bag. Looks like a piece of garbage."

She saw it and squatted down. Inside was another shiny black cell.

"Slip the new cell into your pocket." She did so.

"Now listen to me very carefully. I want you to throw the other cell phones you are carrying into the water."

Lucy hesitated. If she did that, she'd be completely on her own. No connection to her CIA handler, no connection to the negotiation team or Max—who probably hated her right now.

"Do it. I have eyes watching you."

Lucy glanced around. Was he bluffing? Something skittered down her spine. She didn't think he was bluffing. And what difference did it matter? The CIA had told her to abandon the mission and get to the safe house. This would allow her some plausible deniability about not answering the phone while covering her ass. Her handler knew all about covering his ass.

Chances were the FBI would be tracking her right now, worried she would skip off into the sunset with a million bucks, abandoning the girls to their fate. She would never do that. They didn't know that.

She pulled out both phones, work and personal, and dropped them one after the other into the bottom of the fountain.

"Now this one." The voice in her ear commanded.

With a heavy sigh she did what he demanded.

Then she hurried back to the car. Quickly transferred the cash out of the bags that Max had given to the ambassador and tossed them out of the window. She wouldn't risk the FBI deciding she was dirty and trying to arrest her and messing up the ransom drop. The only way to prove she was trustworthy was for her to deliver the cash and maybe figure out where the kidnappers were holding Kristen and Irene.

Her pocket buzzed. She answered the new phone.

"I want you to head south until I call again. If you contact anyone, I'll know, and I'll kill both girls."

Lucy hung up and headed south, avoiding all of the surveillance cameras she knew about, going down back alleyways and keeping under the speed limit so as to not attract the attention of the cops.

She'd failed in so much. She would not fail in this.

CHAPTER THIRTY-THREE

MAX WAS ESCORTED to the parking lot like a common criminal.

"Do you need a ride to the hotel?" Powell asked condescendingly.

Max narrowed his gaze. "I think I've got it."

He wasn't going to the hotel. Most of his belongings were still in the back of Lucy's Mini except for what was in the Negotiation Center. He trusted Jennifer McCreedy to take care of his laptop and all the negotiation equipment until this shitshow was sorted out.

Powell shut the door, and Max stood there stupidly for a second. Then he headed for the gate, passing the two empty spots where Miranda's and Lucy's cars had been.

He paused.

Miranda must have gotten her car started or had it towed.

Max frowned. When had Lucy interfered with Miranda's car?

He called Iain Bartlett. "Did Miranda use her car after five o'clock last night?"

"I'm not supposed to be talking to you."

"Did she?"

"Miranda hasn't left the embassy grounds since this whole mess began. She's been sleeping here."

"Thanks." He hung up. It was possible that Lucy had popped the hood yesterday when she'd nipped out for that one half-hour period. Bold to do that when a security team and cameras were monitoring the place. He called Bartlett again. "Check the security footage of Miranda's car over the last twenty-four hours, will you?"

"I'm a little busy searching the embassy for bugs," Bartlett said testily. "Why?"

"I want to know if Lucy tampered with Miranda's car or not. And I'd like to see the proof if she did."

"Fine. I'll let you know as soon as I get a chance."

"Thanks." Max hung up and headed through the darkness toward where Regan said he'd be waiting. As promised, the green van sat idling on the side of the road.

Max climbed inside, nodded to Regan, Dexter, and Navarro.

He pointed out something else that was bothering him. "How did Lucy know that Miranda would volunteer to be the bagman?"

"Miranda volunteered, not Lucy?" Regan said.

"Yep. Then Miranda's car wouldn't start, and Lucy offered her the use of the Mini but when Miranda got inside, it turned out she couldn't drive stick shift, so Lucy went instead."

Regan's brows rose, and he pulled a face. "The kidnappers specified a woman?"

"They did. Another negotiator volunteered first, but she doesn't know the area. Miranda volunteered next."

Regan nodded thoughtfully. "Seems like a pretty random way to guarantee being the person to leave the embassy with the cash."

"Unless Lucy disabled Miranda's car and knew in advance

she couldn't drive a standard," Navarro said.

"Pretty sophisticated," Dexter said from the front seat with what sounded like admiration.

Things weren't fitting together the way they should. This was why Max hated counterintelligence. There were always layers and layers to wade through, and you never really knew when you'd reached the truth.

"A few minutes ago, she dumped all her phones and the wired bags according to our sensors," added Regan.

"Dammit." Max glanced at the screens and the unmoving red dots. He couldn't think of a single reason she'd do that unless she was planning to ditch them and disappear with the cash.

He ground his teeth in frustration. He was desperate to move. Navarro pulled out onto the city roads.

"I take it the only reason Lucy is suspected of being a spy is the photo British Intelligence sent you via a friend?" Regan said, watching him. The man seemed full of secrets. Maybe they'd been tasked with figuring out if Max was a co-conspirator or simply a patsy. He hated that he was the latter.

Max opened the image and passed his phone to Regan who showed it to the others and then sent it to himself.

"She must have met Anotoly shortly after she left the bar at the hotel after eating dinner with me. She never mentioned she had another date." Max tried hard to control the resentment in his voice. "The Legat was also sent a photograph of Lucy with some Russian agent, Raminsky." That photo was seared into Max's brain.

"Raminsky?" All three men said as one.

"Yeah, why? You know him?"

The other men shared a look. Regan finally spoke. "He was

a high-level operative. One of his specialties was seducing vulnerable women and blackmailing them."

Max frowned. "Know anyone in the CIA we can ask?"

"Why?" Regan asked, gaze narrowed in suspicion.

"Lucy used to work for the Agency."

"Now that is interesting." Regan's expression suggested there were a million thoughts running through his brain. "I think there's a lot more to Lucy Aston than meets the eye. I haven't read her file yet. I was busy setting some other things up." Regan's brows crunched. "Why'd she leave Langley?"

"Something happened with a guy. She was vague about the details. I'm guessing now it had to do with Raminsky," said Max.

"It doesn't add up. The Foreign Service wouldn't have hired her if they'd known about Raminsky, and I can't see the CIA keeping schtum on her reference letters. Secondly, if the Russians had any sort of leverage over her, they'd want her to stay in the CIA regardless of what she wanted. Much more useful to them there than in the Foreign Service."

They were driving through the city streets. Max didn't know if they were simply hoping to see Lucy speeding around in her Mini or if they were trying to get as far away from the embassy as possible. Both worked for him.

"Russian Intelligence was pretty messed up after what went down on Christmas Day last year. Maybe they didn't have time to contact her and exert the right amount of pressure before she quit," Dexter suggested.

"The Russians rarely waste *kompromat*," argued Regan.

"They were pretty shook," Navarro agreed with Dexter. "I can see it happening. Maybe she quit before the CIA found out about the relationship with Raminsky and then she joined the

Foreign Service. The Russians let it ride because she was still useful."

"Why burn her now?" asked Regan.

"My contact said that there was some sort of material intercepted coming out of the Russian embassy in the spring." Max frowned. "Let me text him and see if he knows exactly when."

Max needed to call Andy and prepare him for the goat fuck that was surely coming. Prepare the Lomakins for the worst. Instead, he texted him the question while Regan speed-read Lucy's record on the screen.

"The Russians also sent the Legat a still from the camera showing me kissing Lucy in the hotel." Felt like a million years ago. "What I don't get is why they didn't send something much more compromising from last night?"

He stared down at the floor of the van and no one said anything. He couldn't believe he'd been this idiotic.

Max's phone dinged. Andy had written back. *February.*

Max looked at Lucy's file. "The intercept from the Russian embassy happened in February. That's several months before Lucy arrived here in early May." He frowned.

"What if…" Dexter began.

"Lucy Aston…" Navarro added, checking an intersection before turning right.

"Secretly never stopped working for…" Regan grinned.

"The Agency…" Max finished. His head was spinning. "Wouldn't someone in the embassy know Lucy was sent to spy on them?"

Regan's eyes scanned the details in Lucy's file. "Not if Langley didn't know who to trust. She could be part of the Special Activities Center and acting in a deep undercover role.

Maybe she was in it for the long game."

"Maybe she allowed herself to be compromised in the first place," Navarro suggested. "So the Russians thought they had leverage."

"Pretty hard ass," Dexter added.

That idea filled Max with rage, which didn't make sense. Why was it worse to see Lucy as the manipulator rather than the victim?

He didn't know why.

"Or Raminsky did what he usually did and stomped all over a young woman's reputation without giving a shit how much damage he left in his wake, and the CIA decided to use the situation for their benefit."

"Use her as bait, you mean?" Max said.

"Yep. For whoever the actual spy in the embassy is, to lay a trap that somehow compromises them," said Regan.

What Max was really wondering was what had last night meant to her. That's what was driving him fucking crazy about this situation. And the fact he didn't know if he'd ever be able to trust a word she said to him again in the future...assuming he ever saw her again.

"Doesn't the ambassador usually know about any CIA intelligence officers inserted into the embassy?"

"Not if she or her family are potential suspects," said Regan. "CIA can't specifically investigate US citizens unless the person in question works for the CIA themselves—always possible at an embassy. But if the Agency sent a deep plant because they knew a traitor was operating somewhere in the embassy? They wouldn't necessarily tell anyone. Lucy would simply have to turn over any evidence she uncovered against an American to the FBI for further investigation."

"You think Catherine or Phillip Dickerson could be spying for the Russians?" The idea left a metallic taste in Max's mouth.

Regan shrugged. "Nothing could surprise me, SSA Hawthorne. Not anymore."

Max desperately wanted to believe Lucy wasn't a traitor but what if he was kidding himself? "But if Lucy is actually a triple agent, why'd she ditch her phones and the wired bags? Why now?"

"You said the Russians sent those pictures to the Legat?" said Regan.

"Yup."

"So, she's blown. Her handler would have told her to get the hell out of there. The CIA won't confirm she works for them unless they've uncovered their spy. They'd rather let her take the fall for stealing the kidnap money."

"Or she's dirty and laying down her exit strategy," said Navarro.

"And what about the girls?" Max braced as they went around a corner. Navarro sped up again.

"The girls would be your problem, not the CIA's."

Which was why he hated spooks.

"Was the kidnapping a coincidence?" asked Max. "It seems like a hell of a stretch."

Regan shrugged. "I don't know. I doubt it. The timing stinks. Where is she?"

"Heading west out of town," Dexter answered.

"Who? *Lucy*? How do you know?" Max leaned forward.

Dexter turned in his seat and raised a tablet. "We tapped into the signals from her Sat Nav system and her Fitbit. Assuming she's hasn't reprogrammed the system to send out fake coordinates—"

"Which usually takes more time to set up, especially if you're driving," Navarro chimed in.

"She's about ten minutes in front of us but can probably go faster than we can."

"Let me call CNU and ask if they've traced where the kidnappers are calling from." As Max made the call, he stared in hope at the moving dot that Regan had now put on the screen in front of them.

Following Lucy right now had more to do with making sure she didn't run off with the ransom and doom the girls to a grisly fate than their personal relationship but, even so, he desperately wanted to talk to her.

What happened if she was working for the CIA rather than being a spy for the Russians? He was supposed to detain her until they could figure it out. Could he do it? And what did it mean for them? Was there even a chance of a "them"? Certainly not if she worked for the Russians, but if she was a patriot? He didn't know how he'd feel about her being an intelligence officer. Not anymore.

Then he realized none of that mattered. Right now, the only thing that mattered was paying the ransom and getting the girls to safety.

Whatever had bloomed between himself and Lucy, oh, so briefly, probably wasn't real. Not on her part anyway. She was just a spook doing spook things.

And, while it sucked, it wasn't important right now. *Mind on the job, Hawthorne.*

Lucy was driving on a highway on the way out of town. She'd been in the car for over ninety minutes, and adrenaline was starting to crash when she needed it to keep her wits sharp. She opened the window to blast in some fresh air. Checked her Sat Nav. She was only thirty minutes outside the city limits. There was a junction up ahead.

The phone rang. She answered.

"Take the next exit. Head west." They clicked off, likely worried the FBI were somehow tracing the call.

She drove another six miles down a rural road with farmland on either side. The few houses she spotted were dark.

The phone rang again. "Half a mile you'll get to a crossroads. Pull up twenty yards before you get there and place the money securely into two garbage bags that have been placed under a rock. Take the bags you brought with you and put them back in your vehicle. Then leave. If we see you again, we will kill the hostages."

Lucy scanned the ditch along the side of the road as she drove. Sure enough, her headlights picked up two large, black sacks pinned beneath a large rock.

She slammed on the brakes and then backed up a few yards. She checked the area but didn't see anyone around. She jumped out and strode to the bags, carefully easing the rock off of them and grabbing them before the wind could snatch them.

She ran back to the Mini and scooped piles of cash into the black plastic. She tied and dragged the first bag down into the ditch and repeated the process with the second bag. She scoured the Mini, checking under the seat to make sure she wasn't missing any money.

She got back into her car. Quickly did a three-point turn

and headed in the direction she'd come from. Out of sight of the crossroads, she flipped off her lights and slowed to a crawl. She reached a small vineyard and turned into the driveway.

She needed to swap vehicles. The Mini was too recognizable. She hoped she'd be able to come back and collect her beloved car later and make recompense for the crime she was about to commit. She grabbed her Glock from under the seat and stuffed it in the back waistband of her jeans. She rolled silently up beside an old shed. Quietly got out. She was worried about dogs or the owners waking up, but nothing moved, and the silence seemed to hum over the landscape.

She'd spotted a truck on the way past but, beside it, tucked inside an open garage, was a small motorbike. Even better.

She made a call on the latest cell phone the kidnappers had given her.

"Trace this call," she whispered to the person on the other end of the line. Then she pocketed the cell without hanging up.

She grabbed the helmet from the handlebars and pulled it on, adjusting the fit. It took a moment to bypass the lock and get the engine started and, the moment she did, she was off, speeding down the road without any lights, hoping she hadn't already missed the kidnappers picking up the ransom, but also praying she didn't catch them in the act.

She approached the junction and, sure enough, the bags were gone. Headlights heading off to her left were her best bet as nothing else moved in the Stygian night.

CHAPTER THIRTY-FOUR

"**L**UCY TOLD ME to trace this call." Max put his work cell on mute then handed it to Regan who started typing numbers into a program the likes of which Max had never seen before.

"Got it and relayed the call to agents at SIOC who are also recording and tracing. Gives us plausible deniability," Regan explained. Then he overlaid the coordinates over the Sat Nav signal, but the Mini wasn't going anywhere. It had stopped briefly near a crossroads and then turned around and started heading back toward them. Then it had stopped again.

"Either she disabled the Sat Nav or she's changed vehicles," Max noted.

A few minutes later, they reached a small vineyard.

Navarro pulled in and, sure enough, there was Lucy's beloved car.

A light went on in the farmhouse.

"Okay, let's get out of here before they call the cops. We cannot be found operating in Argentina." Regan repeated what seemed to be a mantra for him.

"Wait." Max opened the door and ran over and opened the trunk of the Mini, inordinately glad to see his bags in there. He grabbed them and ran back to the van.

"I hope it was worth it," Regan muttered as Max climbed

back in before Navarro quickly reversed.

Max dug out the weapon he'd picked up in Colombia and checked the chamber, shoved an extra magazine into his pants pocket. "Sure was."

Max fished his personal cell out of his pocket. Called Eban who was at SIOC liaising with the negotiators back at the embassy. No one was going to tell the Legat or the ambassador where the negotiators were getting their intel from. Let them assume it was some high-level drone or something. "Eban. Are you tracking the call on my work cell?"

"We are. And triangulating where the call is originating from, presumably Lucy Aston?"

"Yeah," said Max.

"Legat in Buenos Aires is worried she's working for the Russians?" Eban probed.

"He is," said Max. "I'm not so sure."

"Asshole will be hearing from me when this is all over. Expelling you from the embassy." Eban grunted.

"Doesn't matter," Max assured him. All that mattered was finding the girls, and Lucy.

"I'm searching for as much information as possible. I have Alex Parker helping me out, even though it's the middle of the night."

"Thank him for me."

Lucy hadn't been forced to make contact with Max, but she hadn't wasted time explaining her actions either. He still didn't know what was going on, but he wanted to trust her. "She switched vehicles. We're following her again thanks to the cell phone signal."

Regan leaned between the gap in the front seats to say something to his colleagues.

"Have the negotiators at the embassy received any word about the girls being released yet?" Max held onto the edge of the bench as Navarro put his foot down.

"Negative, but I'm assuming the kidnappers haven't counted their cash yet," Eban replied.

"True."

"We did finally track down Miguel."

"And?"

"Just a dirt-poor kid with a knack for hacking. He fell for Kristen but didn't think he was good enough for her so invented a background he thought she'd like. Then he got trapped in the lies when they got to know one another better. Knew he was going to be a suspect when the young woman was kidnapped and didn't want to get into trouble, so he disappeared. No evidence he's involved in the abduction. I'm pretty sure Alex Parker is going to put him through school."

Max huffed out a laugh. "Hope he deserves it."

"Everyone deserves a chance."

"You're right. I hope Kristen forgives him for deceiving her." Max was aware of Jon Regan watching him with a knowing gaze.

"Max," Eban said.

"What?"

"Be careful."

"I'm not planning any heroics." The handgun was a precautionary measure that Eban didn't even know about, but he knew Max.

"Yeah, well, plans can go to hell in the real world."

Max looked around at his newfound colleagues. "We're simply following what we hope is the money."

Eban grunted and Max hung up before he could say anything else.

"Where is Lucy now?" asked Max.

"A couple of miles ahead so I'm going to try to catch up some." Not easy in an old van although she might be driving something of a similar vintage.

"Let's hope we don't lose this cell signal. Otherwise, we're sunk."

Max frowned. "Any chance of getting satellite images of the area that I can start examining?"

"Use the computer on the end," Regan told him.

Max did as he was told. The area was sparsely populated. The perfect place to hold hostages.

He hoped Lucy's phone call to him proved she was on the same team as he was, rather than her attempting to lull them all into a false sense of security while she executed her escape.

The thing was, he wanted to believe in her. She was the first person he'd wanted to believe in in years.

———————————

IRENE WATCHED THE house. Her skin itched, especially where her finger used to be. The bandage was dirty. Infection could be a problem and yet still she sat here, watching her prison from the outside.

When she'd run into the night, the man had chased her at first, even shooting at her a few times, but she'd managed to dodge and weave and get out of the gate and hide in the trees. Evade him. He hadn't pursued her for long. She was pretty sure he'd gone back inside to finish off the other kidnapper before he could also escape. Or perhaps he knew she couldn't get far.

Later she'd snuck back, crawled behind some pieces of old rotten wood that were leaning against the crumbling stone wall near the garage. It was probably full of spiders and vermin, but they were preferable to the other monsters.

Her teeth chattered, and she hugged herself hard.

Was Kristen still inside?

It was concern for her friend that had made her stop and turn around. In the darkness, it had been hard to tell where she was. It was more remote than she'd anticipated. There were bushes and walls that formed a maze around the property. She couldn't see any lights from other houses and couldn't hear any cars. It felt as if she were in the middle of nowhere, but she knew she'd heard traffic during the day, so there must be a highway not too far away. Right now, the area was quiet as a crypt.

A man moved in front of the kitchen window. Pacing and checking his watch. Seeing his face made her very afraid. If he knew she was watching him from the darkness, he'd never stop chasing her.

The room above the kitchen where she'd been held was dark. Were the bodies of the other kidnappers still there?

Probably.

His car was parked beside the house. She'd been tempted to steal it. But she wouldn't risk it without her friend, and she couldn't risk going back inside until he was gone.

Kristen's words about the tree beside a window at the front of the house flittered into her mind. The man was on the phone now and seemed to be busy doing something, but she couldn't see what. She edged out of her hiding spot and moved furtively along the wall of the garage. She kept an eye on where she put her feet as she crept behind his car and then dashed along the driveway to the front of the house. She worked her way around to the overgrown lawn. Remnants of an old path were visible in the darkness.

She ran past the massive, boarded up, front door and windows, farther around until she was at the far side of the house.

The sound of a car engine had her diving for cover, her heart pumping madly. A shudder ran over her flesh. What if they'd come to find her? To track her down? What if they brought blood hounds?

There was the tree Kristen had mentioned. It was gnarly and twisted. The last place they'd think to look for her would be back in this derelict, old house.

Irene eyed the tree. The bark was coarse. The branches bent rather than straight but tightly packed together. She touched one. It seemed solid. It should hold her weight.

She hesitated. She'd always loved climbing trees, but she was handcuffed, and her right hand throbbed with pain. Even if they did have tracking dogs, it would be easier for her to run and never look back.

Kristen might already be dead.

What if trying to rescue her was a waste of time?

And what if it wasn't?

She stood looking up into the dark foliage not knowing what to do. To be brave, which had gotten her into this predicament in the first place, or to run and to trust luck that she could escape and find someone trustworthy to ask for help?

Even as she weighed her options, she knew she couldn't leave her friend. Not now. Irene reached up for a branch above her head and started to climb.

CHAPTER THIRTY-FIVE

L UCY FOLLOWED THE vehicle at a distance, terrified of getting too close and equally terrified of losing them, which she could easily do if they turned off their headlights.

She shadowed them for twenty minutes, the person ahead going through several rudimentary surveillance detection routines but nothing Lucy couldn't handle. She was grateful the roads were virtually empty of traffic in this quiet part of the country. She hoped to hell the cell phone call was still connected. It was her one link to backup. Assuming Max trusted her enough to listen.

Which he probably didn't, but the FBI would want to know what she might be up to. Even if they thought she was a bad guy, and in the wind, they'd track the signal. Even if they thought it was a wild goose chase, surely, they'd track her.

And, in doing so, hopefully they'd be able to get a location on the girls...assuming the person who picked up the ransom was going to where the girls were being held.

She frowned. After reading the reports regarding the other hostage incidents, she realized that might not be the case, but this would hopefully give the FBI some sort of starting point should the hostage takers renege on their promise to release the girls.

Up ahead, the vehicle turned into a driveway. Lucy pulled

up on the side of the road. A stand of trees stood between her and wherever the car was going. It had to be a house. Lucy rode bumpily into the woods as far as she could go, parked the bike, and got off the machine. She took off the helmet and checked the cell in her pocket. The call was still connected.

"I followed the car that I am hoping picked up the ransom"—otherwise she'd feel like an utter fool and look like a rank amateur—"to a rundown villa where I am right now." She looked around and hoped Max was still listening. "Actually, I don't even know where I am."

"Lucy." Max used that deep mellow tone that wanted to stroke all her senses and make her purr.

"Sorry, Max. I'll explain later." She cut him off, hardening her heart against anything he might say. She knew he'd be mad and trying to work his negotiator magic on her, but she needed to focus. "I'm going to explore the property. I'll make sure they don't see me. I am not planning to make a move. I simply want to see if this is the right place before we waste more time."

She debated what to do with the cell and ended up leaving the line open but putting the ringer and notifications on silent. Then she stuffed it back in her hoodie pocket. Maybe it would serve as some kind of witness if the kidnappers caught her. Some sort of evidence in her defense.

She crept forward, aware that dawn wasn't that far away and preferring the dark for her scouting activities. She hurried through the trees, careful of her footing on the old, gnarled roots.

Up ahead, surrounded by brambles and overgrown brush, was a tall house enclosed by a walled garden.

A light was shining on the ground floor.

She crept forward, skirting the briars and reaching a twelve-foot wall. She found a place where she could climb the crumbling stone and took in the scene. There were two cars in the driveway.

She needed to get closer, much closer. She decided to stay on this side of the wall and use it for cover. See if she could figure out if this was where the kidnappers were hiding or simply an old farmhouse someone was in the process of renovating.

If she'd lost the money, her efforts might all be for nothing, or perhaps the girls had already been released while she was playing covert-op games. She didn't mind looking like an idiot, she was used to it. But until she knew for sure she wouldn't give up on the opportunity to help Irene and Kristen get out of this nightmare alive.

KRISTEN HAD DRIFTED off in an exhausted slumber when the scent of something noxious hit her nose.

She struggled into a sitting position.

What was that?

Nail polish?

No. Not nail polish. Her heart gave a terrified squeeze and then raced so fast she worried she might have a cardiac arrest. Gasoline. It was gasoline.

The man had told her he was going to let her go but, instead, he planned to burn her alive. And she'd trusted him. She'd trusted that he was telling the truth and had simply sat here like a fool.

The idea of burning to death scared every other thought

out of her head. She'd rather be shot and die than be con-sumed by flames. She'd rather have her tongue cut out.

She was done being a whipped dog. She lay on her back and shuffled closer to the one end. Then she kicked the wood with all her might and, even though it didn't budge to start with, she did it again and again. Because she would break it. She would get out of this fucking box. She would escape.

———————

"ANY PROBLEMS?" SHE grinned at him as she came in the door.

"Nothing I couldn't handle." He pulled her to him and kissed her hard. "You have the money?"

"In the car. Give me your keys, and I'll transfer it. I'll pour gas on my car after you've set this place alight. Hopefully, it will slow them down until we cross the border. You have the passports?"

He nodded and pressed the keys into her palm. "In the glovebox."

Her eyes danced. She was his equal in every way, and he was looking forward to starting a fresh life with her some-where else. A million dollars was a nice nest egg.

"Come on. We need to get moving," she urged.

He hesitated.

"What is it?" She'd always been good at reading him. The kidnappings had been her idea. They'd practiced on a young diplomat from Canada to check their operating technique. It had worked flawlessly.

But this time was different. Originally, they'd planned to sell the ambassador's daughter off to the highest bidder using the black market in *Ciudad del Este*, but things had changed.

When the police had identified Alberto, it had been time to settle for less money, sooner, with fewer chances of being identified or getting caught. That meant they weren't letting the hostages go. It didn't sit well.

"We could release them… We could be over the border in a few hours—"

"You mean you haven't done it yet?" She spoke sharply.

He shook his head.

"Either of them?"

He shook his head again.

"But the others?"

She meant the men he'd persuaded to help him with this scheme. He nodded. They'd all been easy to kill. They'd been scum.

The girls though…

She stroked his jaw then rose on her tiptoes to kiss him. "We've been over this. We can't afford any witnesses."

"They never saw our faces."

She drew in an annoyed breath. "How can you be sure?" She held out her hand for the matches. "Do you want me to do it?"

He frowned. "No. I wouldn't make you do something I couldn't do."

She kissed him again, and desire sparked along his nerves. She was the fire in his blood. His reason for living. He wanted to give her the kind of life she deserved.

"Go do it. I'll put gasoline on my car. As soon as you're finished, we can get out of here."

The sound of banging started upstairs.

Her eyes flared and then narrowed in annoyance.

He pulled out his gun. "Don't worry. I'll take care of it."

He didn't tell her about the one that had gotten away. He should have. The police might already be on their way, but he doubted it. The girl would be scared and lost. There weren't many houses around here, and she'd be worried about who to trust. It would take time for her to find her way to a town or a police station. She was too smart to flag down the first available car. It could be one of the kidnappers. He liked her. She had loyalty and spunk, and that was more than could be said for most people. She reminded him of himself at that age before bitterness had corroded his worldview.

More banging.

"I'm going," he said before the woman he loved could say anything.

"Hurry, or else I'll leave without you."

He grunted. He'd half expected her to run with the money and show him up for a total fool. The fact she hadn't, warmed him—not that she'd have gotten far alone.

The banging turned to a loud crack as he started up the stairs. Sounded like Kristen Dickerson had finally found her backbone. Pity she had to die now.

CHAPTER THIRTY-SIX

R EGAN HAD HOOKED up the cell Lucy was using to a speaker so everyone could catch what she said.

"What's going on, Luce? Talk to me."

No response.

They almost missed the turn. As soon as Navarro realized, he pulled to the side of the road. Max checked the satellite images with Regan peering over his shoulder. "I'm guessing this is the place." He pointed to a building about half a mile down a nearby driveway. There were a couple of outbuildings. "Got any NVGs?"

"Sure." Regan looked torn. "We can't be caught here."

"So you've said."

Regan handed Max a pair of night vision goggles then grabbed a pair for himself. "First sign of the cops I want you two gone," he told Navarro and Dexter.

"Yes, boss."

Dexter climbed in the back.

Regan shook his head. "I'm serious. One of us we can pass off as a buddy of Max's helping out. More than one and it will be obvious we're using official resources in a very unofficial manner."

"We'll be heroes if we find those girls."

"And we'll all be reassigned, if not fired, if this goes to

hell."

"So why are you risking the job you love, boss?" Dexter grinned at the man.

Regan pulled a face as he grabbed a weapon and handed Max a ballistics vest. Then he handed Max a personal radio so they could all communicate with each other without juggling cell phones. "You guys have got years ahead of you. I can retire any time I want."

Max's cell buzzed with a message from Iain Bartlett. The call to Lucy was still live, and he figured whatever the man had to say could wait.

"Call CNU. Tell Eban what's happening," Max said urgently. "Find out everything you can about this place."

"Wilco."

"Let's go." Max got out of the van and the first thing he noticed was the silence. Regan hopped out beside him and they both started toward the driveway.

"We need to observe," Max warned. "They might decide to release the girls as planned."

"They might," Regan agreed. The murmur of his voice rang clearly in Max's ear.

They started moving faster. Not a jog but a slow and careful run. Everything about this felt wrong but maybe he was being paranoid because of the Russian involvement. Maybe this was just a normal kidnap and ransom.

The house came into view.

Where the hell was Lucy? Was she armed? Max hoped she was armed. "Let's split up. I'll take the front, you take the back."

Regan nodded. "Watch your back."

He and Max melted into the night.

IRENE MADE MORE noise than she wanted climbing the tree. It must have grown since the place had been abandoned—one of the branches penetrated the ground floor window like a sword. Higher up, the limbs were thinner but held her weight—just.

Irene managed to sit on one branch and scoot her way along to get closer to the window. She'd done a lot of gymnastics in the past, but this was the hardest thing she'd ever attempted with no safety mat. She leaned forward and grabbed the bottom sash window, easing it upward.

It made a racket that seemed to reverberate through the night and around the nearby woods.

She didn't wait to see if anyone heard. If they caught her in the tree, she was dead anyway. Waiting wouldn't change a thing.

The window jammed about twelve inches up and wouldn't go any farther. She eyed the gap. She was pretty sure she could fit through it but, if she didn't, she'd either be stuck half in and out, or she'd fall to the ground.

She looked down. It wouldn't be pretty. She swallowed. Her throat was dry, and she hadn't had anything to drink in hours. Still, at least her thought processes were clearer now even though she worried she might be getting a fever.

The tree limb started to bend in an unnerving fashion. She launched herself through the opening of the window. Her shoulders caught, but she was able to grab onto the radiator—of all things—gripping tightly with her remaining fingers, ignoring the way the cuffs pressed into her raw skin and the way the sill cut painfully into her hips. She scrambled with her feet then found purchase on the rough masonry. She pulled herself into the room even though the edge of the frame seemed to scrape every inch of skin off her back.

Then she lay there on the floor, eyes watering, and chest panting, trying to catch her breath and listen at the same time.

Her nose wrinkled. She could smell gasoline. Crap. They were going to torch the place. Maybe they'd already taken Kristen somewhere else? Maybe they'd stuffed her in the trunk of the car when Irene had been climbing the tree?

Shit, shit, shit.

Irene didn't want to be burnt alive while rescuing someone who wasn't even here.

Then the sound of banging registered. *Oh my god.* It had to be Kristen trying to get out of the wardrobe. Irene turned back to the window and levered it all the way open. It was their escape route, and she wouldn't have time to fix it later if someone was chasing her with a gun. She crept over the old wooden floorboards, not for the first time wishing she had shoes.

Had they set the place alight yet? She sniffed. She didn't smell smoke, but this old house would go up like a tinderbox the second they struck a match.

She eased the door open a millimeter and froze. She saw the kidnapper's back as he entered Kristen's room. He was carrying a gun.

Irene shook with fear. Then a voice from downstairs made the man pause, and Irene eased the door fully closed before he turned around and saw her. She held onto the handle and prayed he didn't come in her direction.

CHAPTER THIRTY-SEVEN

L UCY SLIPPED SILENTLY into the kitchen and took a few cautious steps forward. She raised her Glock and aimed it at the woman who stood with her hands on her hips just inside the hallway.

Lucy frowned. She recognized that form, that hair, even if she was dressed in casual clothes. "Miranda?"

The woman whirled and put her hand on her heart. "Lucy!" Her voice dropped to a loud whisper. "You scared me. We have to go quickly. I caught a glimpse of a man going upstairs with a gun. I think he has Kristen."

Everything came sharply into focus.

"Why are you here?" asked Lucy.

"I received a tipoff from a friend of mine and decided to check it out."

"Alone?"

Miranda looked surprised for a second. Lucy never questioned her boss. "I didn't want to disappoint the ambassador if I was wrong."

"And you intended to rescue the girls? How exactly?"

Miranda shrugged and looking suddenly unsure. "I guess I was hoping it would come to me."

I bet you did.

"How long have you owned a gun?" Miranda frowned.

"Do you even have permission to carry that thing?"

"Since I arrived in Buenos Aires. And, no, officially I don't." Lucy stretched her neck to the right. "Blame it on leftover paranoia from when I worked at the Agency."

Miranda pushed her red hair off her brow and laughed. "Oh, come on. You were a two-bit analyst who only lasted six months."

Lucy allowed a small smile to curve her lips. "That's right."

Because the truth was classified.

"Well, now you're here we can go rescue the girls. Or we can wait outside and call the cops." Miranda tried to sidle past her.

Lucy backed up a step. "I think we should both go rescue them." Lucy indicated the other woman move ahead of her using the barrel of her gun.

"Why are you pointing your weapon at me?" Miranda's voice rose high in fear. She was talking way too loud for anyone scared of being overheard by violent kidnappers. "Unless you're somehow involved with taking the hostages."

Always accuse your enemies of the things you are guilty of. Classic Russian disinformation tactics.

"Move it."

Miranda hesitated. "You can't seriously suspect me? I thought we were friends?"

Lucy held her gaze. Pressed her lips together. "I thought so too."

Miranda's eyes went huge as she realized Lucy wasn't buying her denial. "Please…"

"This was all your idea. You orchestrated the kidnapping." All the things snapped into place. "That's where you were at lunchtime on Christmas Eve when you disappeared. You were making sure everything was ready. Did you plant the bug on Kristen?"

"You're insane."

"You told them she planned to visit the Christmas market. That's how they knew where she'd be."

The sound of movement came from upstairs, and both of them glanced that way. Were all the kidnappers upstairs? How many? Were they planning to set fire to the place and kill Kristen and Irene? Or release them and burn the house where they'd held them in order to destroy evidence? Had Lucy messed everything up by trying to be the hero?

Lucy wanted to rush past Miranda and run up the stairs. But if she turned her back on this cobra, they'd all be dead. The smell of gasoline was thick in the air. One spark, and the whole place could ignite.

"Don't be ridiculous. I would never hurt Kristen." Miranda sounded a little desperate. "Put the gun down, Lucy. You've gone mad."

Lucy smiled. "I hate to break it to you, but I don't take orders from you anymore. Actually, I never did. I was sent to unearth a suspected Russian spy operating out of the Argentine embassy, and I guess we could say I finally completed the mission."

The Dickersons had been suspects as had Miranda and all the DSS agents, but so had every other person employed at the embassy. Lucy had been embedded in the hopes the Russian spy would make contact with her or slip up, but they never had. Until now.

Miranda's expression morphed from feigned confusion to unfeigned anger. "There's no way you're some covert operative. I don't even know how you got a job in the Foreign

Service. There are pencils with more intelligence and motivation than you have. I'm going to make sure Catherine hears about this."

"I am sure Catherine can't wait to talk to you." Lucy didn't take her eyes off the woman, but she moved so she could also see the staircase as she heard furtive footsteps above. "Why did you do it? Spy for the Russians, I mean. It's obvious the kidnap was for the cash."

Miranda sneered. "Oh, please, you think you're going to get me to confess to some trumped up charge."

"I don't need you to. Your involvement in this will be reason enough for the FBI to interrogate you. I'm curious about your car though. Did you disable it so I'd have to do the drop?"

Miranda huffed out a frustrated breath. "I didn't orchestrate anything. My battery was dead. The dealership told me it might need replacing last time it was serviced." Miranda's mouth twisted. "I guess I should have started it up a few times, but I forgot with all the excitement."

"That must have made you furious." Sudden insight popped into Lucy's head. "The Russians are the reason you didn't leave the embassy. It wasn't concern for Catherine or Phillip. It was fear for your own skin. What did they want?"

Miranda pressed her lips firmly together and didn't say a word.

"Don't tell me. It was information about the investigation the Legat was running, wasn't it? And then when you couldn't get past Powell's security measures, they started to threaten you, didn't they?" Lucy knew she was right. It was exactly what they'd done to her. "Do the Russians know you planned this?" Lucy didn't think they did, else there would be better security at this property, assuming the hostages were here. "Oh, man, they are gonna be so pissed when they find out.

"Is that why you were in such a rush to get your hands on the ransom money? Because it was obvious arrests were about to be made, and you knew the Russians would never forgive you if their precious oligarch was detained?"

Miranda's eyes widened enough for Lucy to know the truth had struck home.

"Actually," Miranda finally snapped. "It was your fault we had to speed things up. You and that negotiator. Once you identified one of the kidnappers, we knew we had to move fast."

Miranda was no longer pretending not to be involved. That was progress. Lucy hoped Max was getting all this.

"And the fact the Legat launched his indictments tonight was a coincidence?" Lucy pressed. "I find that hard to believe."

Miranda raised her chin. "I might have warned my contact that I feared the FBI were about to act and that I believed Boris Yahontov was the primary target of their investigation."

"You used the FBI operation as a distraction for both sides."

"I had to escape." Miranda finally acknowledged the truth. "I'm dead if the Russians find out about any of this."

Suddenly a figure appeared on the darkened stairway. Two figures. Lucy kept her gun trained on Miranda.

It took her a moment to recognize the man hiding behind Kristen Dickerson. The one holding a gun to her head. Lucy didn't acknowledge the anguish on Kristen's face. She couldn't allow herself to be distracted.

"My my. The federal police must not pay well," Lucy said dryly.

Hector Cabral had a feral expression on his face. "What is she doing here?" he asked Miranda.

"She must have put some sort of transmitter in the money."

"You were supposed to check it." His voice sounded implacable, but Miranda tried anyway.

"I *did* check it. They must have lied about what they were doing."

Lucy let them argue, let the uncertainty remain, let the divisions widen. Then she wedged them further apart.

"I don't have any beef with you, Cabral. I want Miranda here for selling America out to the Russians. Let Kristen go, and I'll give you a head start before I call the cops."

"The Russians?" Hector's brows rose.

"She's lying. It was nothing. I had a few conversations with them and, the next thing I know, there's money in my bank account."

Lucy smirked. "There's a word for that."

Miranda shot her a glare and directed her words toward Hector. "They kept pressing me for more information, even though I said no. They threatened to hurt and expose me if I refused."

Cabral's mouth twisted. "That's why you persuaded me to help you pull this off?"

"No." Sweat formed on Miranda's forehead. "I want to be with you. I love you. But the Russians would never have let us alone. We could never have been together without changing our identities and for that we needed the cash."

Hector nodded but didn't look pleased.

"Unfortunately, those excuses won't fly with Langley, Miranda," Lucy said dryly. "The security services don't tolerate people selling information to foreign adversaries for any reason." The stench was starting to give Lucy a headache. Were the cops on their way? She needed to keep stalling. Where was Irene? Was she still alive? "Not to mention how the DOJ will feel about you kidnapping the ambassador's daughter."

"I'm not planning to discuss it with the DOJ," Miranda gritted out.

Hector nudged Kristen down a step. "What exactly are you planning to do with the gun, *chica*? You want to kill the girl?"

Miranda ran past Lucy, but she stuck out her foot, and the woman crashed to the floor.

Lucy didn't dare take her eyes off Cabral. She moved toward him, gun pointed, but he still had Kristen in a tight grip, and Lucy knew he would kill her if she got too close. They did a little dance around one another. And she let him circle toward the exit.

Miranda crawled into the kitchen.

"If you so much as think about squeezing that trigger, I will take you out, Cabral. You will be dead." These weren't Max's negotiation tactics, but she was a simple intelligence officer trying to save the girl and salvage her pride.

"So will Kristen," he replied, unfazed.

"Leave her unharmed, and I'll let you and your little paramour jump in the car and head off into the sunset." Technically her mission was uncovering the identity of the spy, plus she wanted the girls more. Hopefully someone somewhere would be close behind Bonnie and Clyde.

Cabral eased backward through the kitchen doorway.

Lucy aimed at his head. She wasn't about to let them leave with Kristen in tow.

He seemed to realize she wasn't bluffing. He shoved Kristen hard into Lucy's line of fire and jerked to the side when Miranda threw a lit piece of paper into the hallway.

Lucy grabbed Kristen, and they both stumbled away from the kitchen. Lucy covered Kristen with her body as the initial *whoosh* of flame ignited around them.

In seconds, fire blocked the exit to the kitchen. Cabral raised his weapon and Lucy pressed Kristen tight into the corner wall as he started shooting. They were just out of his line of fire, but they couldn't stay here for long. The fire was already getting too hot.

She waited for another second and risked a quick peek around the corner. Cabral was gone.

"Let's go!" Lucy yelled.

"Where to?" Kristen asked desperately.

"We need to find another way out of the house."

Kristen grabbed Lucy's hand with her bound ones and ran back toward the stairs. It was hot, and they needed to get as far away from the blaze as possible.

They reached the next floor, but the flames had traveled ahead of them. They went up another level, and Lucy worried they were going to get trapped.

Irene threw a door wide. "This way, quickly!"

Lucy was thrilled to see the other girl alive. Irene led them to an open window which was a good escape route, but the gush of fresh air was also fanning the flames in their wake. Flames rushed up the stairway now and along the walls. Lucy slammed the door shut, trying to slow the conflagration.

She pulled a knife from her boot and cut the rope that bound Kristen's wrists. Kristen shook out her hands to get the blood flowing again.

Lucy stuck her head out the window. Saw the tree. "Kristen, get your ass into that tree and work your way to the bottom."

"Have they gone?" Kristen asked nervously.

"I'm not sure, but we can't stay here. Go!"

Lucy looked at Irene's handcuffs. At the dirty bandage wrapped around her hand. *Damn.* She met the girl's determined gaze. "I don't have any cuff keys on me." And didn't have time to pop the lock.

She held the girl's gaze even as smoke rose up around them. She coughed. Smoke was starting to get thick.

Irene surprised her with a grin. "I climbed up wearing these. I think I can make it back down."

This young woman was unbelievable. "Go."

CHAPTER THIRTY-EIGHT

MAX CROUCHED NEAR the front of the house on the east side. He spotted Miranda Foster and Hector Cabral running out of the house toward a vehicle parked there. Max was confused for a fraction of a second and then he was pissed.

Cabral threw a match into a second car and it whooshed into flame.

Shit.

"I already checked both cars for the girls. They were empty." Regan's voice came over the comms system. "Want me to take those two out? Disable the vehicle?"

Max was relieved about the girls not being in the cars but that meant they were probably still in the house. His priority was to get them to safety and find Lucy.

"Negative. We know who they are now. They won't get far." He crouched, immobile in the shadows of some shrubs as they drove away.

"Local cops have been dispatched." Dexter spoke into his ear.

"Inspector Hector Cabral is in the driver's seat. Locals might not be willing to arrest another police officer."

"Let's worry about that later," Regan said sharply. "The house is on fire."

Max stood up and, sure enough, the flicker of orange

glowed through some of the old, shuttered windows. Cabral had set fire to the house probably to destroy evidence. Question was whether or not the girls were still inside, and whether or not they were alive.

Max ran around to the front of the building looking for a way in. The main door was nailed shut.

He kept going. Where the hell would they be? The place was enormous, and he didn't have time to search every room.

And where was Lucy? Worry for her ate at him.

And then he saw movement and hesitated. Someone was climbing out of a window on his left. It looked like the Dickerson girl but hard to tell even with NVGs. She flung herself into a tree. Branches bounced. Leaves rustled. She almost fell but managed to cling on to the trunk.

"I see one of the girls climbing down a tree around the west side. I'm going to help," Max told the others.

"On my way," Regan said. "Dex, Navarro, follow the getaway car at a discreet distance until we know which way they're headed. Come back if I call you."

Max began climbing the tree to help Kristen.

She spotted him and froze for an instant, eyes massive and scared.

"It's okay, Kristen. I'm an FBI agent. You're safe."

She swallowed. "Okay." She twisted around and looked up. "I'm fine. Please help Irene. She's still wearing handcuffs."

"Did you see Lucy Aston anywhere?" But Kristen was concentrating on climbing down the tree and didn't answer him.

Dammit. Max hated the fear that was clawing at his insides. Was she okay? Or was she trapped in the inferno?

He wanted to check his cell, but he had to get these girls

out first. Do his job—although his job usually meant being stuck on the end of a phone line. Not this time.

He quickly scaled the tree and saw Irene trying to maneuver out the window with cuffed hands.

She saw him, hesitated for a split second, and then kept coming. "I've got you." He grabbed her and pulled her over his shoulders in a fireman's lift.

He glanced up and met Lucy's gaze for a fraction of a second. Everything he felt exploded inside his mind. Fear. Anger. Pride. Relief. Mainly relief.

"Get the hell out of there," he yelled.

Hardly the most romantic greeting.

She smiled, and his heart gave a little kick.

He quickly made his way back down the tree, and Jon Regan grabbed Irene off his shoulders. Max went straight back up for Lucy.

She had a leg over the sill and had grabbed onto the nearest branch. He heard the crack as she swung onto it, and the branch snapped. She lurched for the trunk but couldn't make it. She was falling. He lunged for her, but she had too much momentum for him to hold onto the trunk, but he sure as hell could hold onto Lucy.

She caught at branches to slow their descent and he got under her, determined to break her fall. He landed hard enough to knock the wind out of his chest. She landed on top of him.

They both lay there, stunned.

The scent of smoke surrounded him, but he couldn't breathe. He stared up into the darkness watching the sparks flying up into the night, worried he'd broken his back. Slowly his muscles started working again, his lungs started pulling in air.

Lucy groaned and climbed to her knees, hovering over him. "Max, are you all right?"

He stirred.

"Please. Don't move. I'll call an ambulance. I don't think I can stand it if you're hurt because I'm an idiot."

He slowly levered himself up onto his elbows and shoved the goggles off his face. "Jesus, Lucy. Stop putting yourself down like that."

Jon Regan corralled the girls near the corner of the house. He had his weapon out and was in full protective mode.

Somehow, unimaginably, they'd made it out of the inferno alive.

"I'm sorry for not being completely honest with you before," Lucy said so only he could hear—except he was plugged into the other guys via the earpiece.

He started to laugh but winced as the muscles in his back complained.

"Are you okay?" she asked.

"Was it real?" he asked, wanting to know. Needing to know. She'd lost the glasses and pulled her hair away from her face. She smelled of gasoline and smoke. A black smudge streaked her cheek. She had never looked more beautiful.

"You and me." He pushed. "Was that real?"

She bit her lip, and his heart clenched. He didn't even care about the humiliation factor. His heart was too busy breaking.

She kissed him long and slow, then pulled back. "It was real, but you might not appreciate my whole sordid life story."

"You aren't a traitor." It was a statement of fact. Not a question.

Her eyes met his. Her gaze open and honest. "I can't tell

you much, Max, but I can tell you I'm not a traitor."

He dragged her down for another kiss. "That's all I need to know."

He felt her melt. Relief and hope rushed through him. Lucy wasn't who he'd thought she was. He had the feeling she was even better. And maybe now, after completely rebuilding his life after leaving Special Forces, maybe he could allow himself to open up to the idea of a relationship—of at least trying. He knew there were no guarantees and Lucy might not be interested, but he was interested. He was definitely interested in finding out who Lucy Aston really was.

He climbed to his feet and pulled her with him. They had to move, but they still needed to be careful. With such a high-level cop being corrupt, who knew who else was involved in this scheme.

Regan led the way, and they wove through the trees toward the road where they planned to rendezvous with Dexter and Navarro. Then they'd get everyone the help they needed while Argentine and US law enforcement searched for the fugitives.

"Regan and Hawthorne rescued the girls and found Lucy," said Dexter.

"I am also wearing an earpiece, bruh."

Dexter grinned. Navarro was surly. It was his way of showing affection.

"I knew Lucy was legit." Dexter adjusted the air vents.

"You didn't know shit," Navarro grumbled.

They both heard the sound of a car engine approaching.

"Did so." Dexter knocked Navarro's elbow, and the other man glared at him.

They were well hidden behind thick bushes. They waited a few seconds, letting the car that flew past get a short lead. Then they pulled out.

They both wore NVGs and had all the lights off in the van. Dex was filming the events to record any clues that might help capture the fugitives in the future.

They drove for about ten minutes, maxing out the van's speed as the fugitives were not hanging around. They went around a gentle curve in the road and through another sparsely wooded area.

Two hundred yards ahead of them the car they were following lost control and careened off the road. The tires looked shredded.

Navarro slammed on the brakes before he also ran over the spike strip.

Dexter froze as four figures rushed out of the shadows, two on either side of the fugitives' car.

He and Navarro both had their weapons drawn, but they'd barely comprehended the scene in front of them when the men fired through the windows and shot both occupants repeatedly.

"Regan. Anotoly Agapov and three of his associates murdered the two kidnappers right in front of us." Dexter watched as one man leaned inside the driver's side and popped the lock. "And now they are making off with the ransom money." Or maybe they were looking for the hostages?

"Get the hell out of there."

Navarro was already backing up, but the Russians seemed to be uninterested in them. Dexter had no doubt they wouldn't hesitate to kill them if it suited their purpose. Navarro did a quick U-turn, then sped away from the murder scene.

"What the fuck just happened?" Dexter asked in a daze.

"You don't betray Russian Intelligence and live to tell the tale," Navarro said darkly.

"What about Lucy?" Dexter asked with concern. Was there another hit squad on their way to the house? Were Regan and Hawthorne and the girls in danger?

"Lucy was always one of ours," Regan murmured in his ear. "I'm not saying they'll be sending her flowers unless they're laced with Novichok, but they understand the game. Lucy played it better than them this time, and they know it."

"Even so, let's get everyone to safety ASAP. And maybe get Lucy back to the embassy in case the Russians change their minds," Dexter said nervously.

"What about the money?" Navarro sounded pissed.

"We have the girls, and the kidnappers are dead," Max said. "I don't care enough about the money to start a gunfight with a bunch of desperate ex-KGB operatives."

"Do not engage with those motherfuckers unless they come for you first, in which case you can blast them to kingdom come," Regan ordered sharply.

Dexter smiled at his colleague. "I love my job."

Navarro grunted, but Dexter swore he saw the faintest of smiles curve his lips. He loved his job too.

CHAPTER THIRTY-NINE

K RISTEN REACHED OUT to hug Irene. They sat on the floor in the back of the van in a journey strangely reminiscent of their abduction a few days ago.

They both stank, and Kristen didn't even care.

"I'm so sorry." She squeezed Irene, barely able to believe they'd made it out alive. "Sorry for everything. I tried to get out of the wardrobe like I promised the other night but that one guy, the one who was skanky, he found the plastic knife I'd hidden and nothing else I tried worked on the catch. I should have gone that night like you told me to."

Irene leaned against her. "It wasn't your fault. You were brave waiting for me. I'm grateful but next time listen to me, will ya?"

Tears welled up. "But it's my fault they cut off your finger. If I'd escaped maybe they wouldn't have done that."

"They would have done worse." Irene shivered.

"It should have been me. I don't know why it wasn't me."

One of the guys who'd rescued them, the cute one with the muscles and eyes that barely left Lucy, spoke. "There are a thousand possible scenarios as to what might have happened if any of the circumstances changed, but the bottom line is kidnappers often like to play mind games and I suspect they considered Irene more disposable than the US Ambassador's daughter."

Kristen flinched. "You're not. You're worth ten of me."

Irene wiped her eyes. "Don't be nuts." She held out her bandaged hand, the handcuffs now thankfully removed. "I don't care about losing my finger so much as I care about living. But fuck those bastards for doing that to me. Fuck them."

The hot guy shifted to the end of the bench closer to them. Lucy sat to the side on top of some cases.

He held out his hand to shake hers. "I'm Max, by the way."

"The negotiator?"

"That's right." He smiled at her then turned to Irene. "Can I take a look at that wound and put some antibiotic cream on it and a fresh bandage?"

Irene nodded and hesitantly held out her hand.

Max carefully unwrapped the soiled dressing without saying a word.

Kristen didn't want to look but forced herself to. The wound was raw and ugly. She winced. "No one will notice, Irene."

Irene flexed her hand and winced. "It looks ugly. I don't even care. People can look all they want and then they can fuck off."

"I like this girl," the older guy near the front said. He pulled out the first aid kit and handed it to Lucy who opened it and found the things Max needed.

"It looks a little infected. We have doctors waiting at the embassy."

"Did you call my parents?" Irene asked anxiously.

Max nodded. "I spoke to a friend who is working with them. He's taking them to the embassy to meet you. They've been very worried."

Irene's eyes were huge as she nodded. "I've been worried about them too. I bet they freaked."

No one said anything which meant they had really freaked. Kristen could imagine how her own mother had reacted.

The older guy gave them a bottle of water and a bag of chips each. It all tasted like heaven.

Irene frowned and wiped her mouth. "Why are you here, Lucy?"

Lucy leaned forward. "I'm going to let you in on a little secret."

Lucy glanced at Max. Kristen could feel the electric buzz between them. It almost made her smile despite everything.

"I have been working undercover for the CIA since I arrived. Searching for someone selling secrets to the Russians."

Kristen's brows rose. She'd heard the conversation earlier, but she hadn't been paying attention. She'd been too scared of the kidnapper putting a bullet in her brain. It sounded like something out of a spy novel.

"I found that person tonight. It was Miranda. Your mother's PA."

Irene's mouth opened in shock. "What the hell? And she arranged for Kristen to be kidnapped?"

It made Kristen's stomach churn.

Lucy's expression softened. "I'm sorry. I know you've known her forever."

Kristen grimaced. "I never really liked her though. Kevin despises her."

"You and your brother have excellent taste." Lucy's smile faded. "What I'm guessing is Miranda was looking for a way out. It's not a great place to be, caught between taking risks to betray your country or being exposed as a traitor."

Lucy shot another look at Max.

Kristen wanted to fan herself at the heat that arced between them.

"She and the main kidnapper, who was a policeman, were probably behind the kidnapping."

The blood drained from Kristen's head, and she had to lean against the back of the van. Her hair was greasy and gross. She pulled it back from her face and sat there with her hands wrapped around her skull.

"I don't know why he did what he did. Maybe they were in love, but it seems like a shitty excuse to hurt people." Lucy flashed Max a look that he didn't catch. Kristen did though.

"He probably resented the fact criminals got rich while the public servants didn't," Max interjected.

"I don't think he was entirely bad," said Irene.

"How can you say that after what he did to you?" asked Kristen.

"He shot at least two of the other kidnappers," Irene spoke as Max carefully wrapped a new bandage around the now cleaned wound. "They were going to rape me."

Kristen tightened her grip around her friend's shoulders. "You are so brave."

"Not really. Anyway, the older guy, he came in before they could do it and killed them both. That's when I managed to run into the garden. I think he let me go in the end."

"The bastard had them cut off your finger…"

Irene pulled her hand back and cradled it against her chest. "I know." She shrugged. "But he wasn't all evil. It's hard to explain."

"You're both really brave," Lucy said.

"So are you," Kristen stated firmly. "You saved me from that horrible man. And when Miranda lit the gasoline, you didn't panic the way I did."

"It's training."

"I want that sort of training," Kristen said firmly.

"Better sign up for the FBI then, ladies," one of the guys at the front called.

Lucy guffawed. "I'm pretty sure it was the Agency who trained me. Not the feebs." Then she winked at Kristen.

Kristen could not believe this woman, who'd seemed like such a quiet and downtrodden human being, had all the time been hiding this badass persona. Kevin was going to freak.

Maybe it meant Kristen didn't have to be scared her whole life. Maybe she could learn to be a badass too.

"Thank you. All of you." Kristen fought tears because she didn't want to cry. She wanted to be stronger than that. "You saved me. Irene had already saved herself, but you saved me."

The atmosphere charged and changed. They knew. Everyone in the van knew they'd helped save their lives tonight. They knew they'd made a difference. And Kristen realized she wanted to do something similar with her life. Fight the bad guys. Come out swinging.

CHAPTER FORTY

T HEY ARRIVED AT the embassy in the TacOps van. Isaac Navarro drove straight up to the front gate and demanded entry by laying on the horn. The fact they'd called Iain Bartlett to meet them would hopefully help get them inside pronto.

Lucy wasn't sure what kind of reception she was going to get. She sat in the back with her arms around the two young women. Everything had been worth it to get these two out alive. Her bosses—*all* her bosses—were going to be pissed with her, but she didn't care.

Max kept shooting her looks, and she didn't know how to interpret them. Yes, he'd wanted to know if what they'd shared was real, but it didn't mean he cared for her. He'd already told her how he felt about spooks.

Maybe it was a matter of pride, wanting to know he hadn't been duped the way she'd been duped. She understood that. If she could have confronted Sergio after she'd found out he was a Russian Intelligence Officer sent to compromise her, she would have done so.

Although Sergio would have no doubt lied.

He'd been a lot better at the game than she was.

Suddenly, they were inside the embassy gates, and the door was flung open, and they all spilled out.

She let the girls go ahead because she knew their parents would be frantic. She followed slowly, reluctant to confront anyone.

Max waited at the door and held out his hand for her. He let go as her feet touched the ground. She curled her fingers to try to retain the sensation of his touch. Regan was arguing with security who was going over the van with an explosive detector. They wanted to look inside, and he refused.

Navarro and Dexter had both pulled ball caps low over their brows and sidled out of the limelight.

One by one they entered the building after DSS searched them. Iain Bartlett pursed his lips as he checked her out. When he was done, he shook his head slightly. "You had me fooled."

She fought the urge to say sorry. She wasn't sorry. She'd been doing her job same as he did his job every day. Lucy pulled the kidnappers' cell phone out of her pocket. Max had cut the call earlier in the van. "Do you have an evidence bag?"

Bartlett held one open and she dropped it inside. "The kidnappers left that at the fountain location where I was instructed to dump my phones into the water."

"We found your other devices. I suppose they told you to ditch the bags too?"

"Yes." She wasn't about to admit that her CIA handler had told her to abandon the money and the girls to protect the Agency's ass. And maybe that was Lucy's way of protecting the Agency, though she had to wonder if it deserved the lengths she'd gone to.

She caught up with the others inside and there were the Dickersons hugging Kristen, all of them sobbing. And Irene's family was there too. Her father had broken down to the point he was sitting on the floor rocking Irene in his arms.

Lucy watched as Mrs. Lomakin knelt down and put her arms around both of them.

Maybe they'd get through it.

Maybe they wouldn't.

Max was across the room talking to Brian Powell and the other negotiators. Probably explaining what had gone down tonight and what boiled down to a massive security breach. Shit was going to hit the fan with the news Miranda Foster was a Russian agent and had been murdered by them while trying to flee.

A man approached her with a frown on his face.

"Aren't you the chick who was caught on camera with Anotoly Agapov?"

Lucy looked him in the eye. "If by chick you mean Intelligence Officer then yes, I am. Andy, isn't it?"

"Ah. That's going to make my contact at the British embassy piss his pants."

"Happy to help."

He smiled.

Max came over and clapped his buddy on the back. "Lucy, you met Andy? Andy meet Lucy."

"We've been introduced." Andy looked amused. "And now my job here is done, I'm off to Montevideo for some sunshine and surf. Coming, Max?"

Max looked at Lucy, but she couldn't read his expression.

"I'm going to be tied up here for a little while. I might be able to make it for a few days after I talk to my boss." He thanked his friend who'd traveled thousands of miles to help him. That was friendship. That was commitment.

Andy gave her a nod and walked over to Irene's family.

"The Argentine police picked up Boris Yahontov on his

way to a private airfield. He was minutes from escaping," said Max. "He'll be extradited to the US to face money laundering charges."

She nodded curtly. *Good.* Didn't matter how rich someone was. They needed to answer for their crimes. "Miranda warned him to create a distraction to help her escape. She wasn't even certain he was the target."

"The Russians are all panicking apparently, which probably explains why Agapov eliminated Miranda before she could be interviewed by the CIA." Max shifted his feet. "They don't know we have her on record admitting her actions. That was good work."

The Americans also had her murder on film. Hard to deny that sort of evidence.

"They must have followed her when she left the embassy." Whether they'd killed her because she'd tried to escape their grasp or because the Russians didn't want her telling the Americans exactly what she'd given to them over the years, Lucy wasn't sure. They'd probably never find out without a sit down face-to-face with Agapov.

She shrugged. "Even though it is likely she was the only spy, everyone who works here will need to be polygraphed and interviewed regarding what they knew." She grimaced. It was sucky to work under the shadow of suspicion.

She could feel Max staring at her.

"What?" She felt itchy and confused. The job here was over, and she didn't know what she was going to do next.

"Do you want to talk about it?"

She finally met his gaze. "Do I have to?"

"No." He shook his head. "I saw one of the photos."

She pressed her hand to her stomach. She didn't have to

ask which photos he meant.

"I'm sorry," he told her.

Emotion made it hard to speak. "About what?"

He stood a little closer. "Because I suspect you had to make some tough choices. And I also suspect what I said about spooks made you think you couldn't confide in me."

"I'm not allowed to confide in you regardless." She crossed her arms over her chest. She didn't know how she felt or what she wanted. Or why she was so angry with Max.

"I realize you don't really care what I think."

Her eyes shot to his. "That's not true. I do care. I… I don't know what I want. I don't know what I want to do with my life now this op is over. Ever since I discovered Sergio Raminsky was Russian intelligence, and that I compromised my integrity, the only thing that mattered to me was proving to Langley that I was worthy."

He closed his eyes, and she could see she'd upset him.

He opened them again. "You are worthy."

"I didn't feel worthy."

"What about now?" he asked softly.

She just looked at him, unable to speak.

"Listen. We both have many hours of debriefing in front of us, and," he took her hand in his, "I don't know, maybe you have to go off on some other mission." He took out his business card, and Lucy tried not to think about poor Abigail Blanco who'd died because of their investigation.

Lucy felt utterly exhausted and weary of her life.

"I know you have my cell numbers, but that's also my home address. You may not know what you want, but I'd like to see you again. I don't want you to disappear from my life. What we have is special. I'd like the chance to explore it more.

We might not get too many more chances." He pressed the card into her hand and walked away.

She stared after him, feeling as if she were being torn in two. Worse than finding out about Sergio. Worse than the humiliation of having to tell her boss about her mistake. Those feelings were about shame and personal failure. This was about something completely different.

"I would never betray my country, Max," she called after him.

"I know that, Lucy," he called back. He walked away with her staring longingly at his back. She'd told herself never to build fantasies around a man again, but god, she wanted to. She looked down at the card he'd put in her hand. And the small, blocked letters written there. "TRUST ME. TRUST US."

The gaping hole started growing inside her again. She almost panicked and ran after him. Threw herself at him. Begged him to love her.

He'd already forgiven her, she realized. He already thought she was worthy of starting a relationship with. Old Lucy would have been all over the offer...

She realized, despite all her bluster, all her self-talk, she was still Old Lucy inside, but she was an amalgam now. Stronger, fiercer, wiser. She hadn't done anything wrong with Sergio. She wasn't depraved or deviant. They'd had sex. It was the Russians who'd perverted that encounter. Degraded her.

She'd only been doing her job, and she'd castigated herself for her mistakes, allowed herself to be exploited because of her humiliation and hurt. She had to figure out how to stop punishing herself.

Max knew how to compartmentalize, separate his emotions from the job. The way he'd been regretful over Abigail

Blanco's death, but it hadn't crushed him. The way he could function as a human being even when people depending on him were suffering. It wasn't easy, but it had to be easier than what she put herself through.

She hadn't betrayed anyone. She had never deserved the censure of the Agency or from herself. She'd made an error in judgment and had paid for that error in spades.

She was good at her job. She had to learn to let go of the setbacks. She'd helped save Kristen and Irene and had identified the Russian spy. That was enough reparation.

She was done now.

The realization had the weight falling from her shoulders like chains. She was free and could do whatever she wanted with her life. She looked at the card again.

TRUST ME. TRUST US.

The question was, what did she really want?

The ambassador looked up and caught Lucy's gaze. Kristen ran over to grab her hand and tugged her across the room.

"Lucy saved me. Miranda and the man who held me planned to kill me. She risked her life, shielded me from bullets and fire and then helped me and Irene escape down a tree. She almost died falling out of the tree."

"Not my finest moment." Lucy admitted. She knew Kristen was trying to help make her look good. Catherine Dickerson would undoubtedly be furious that the Agency had sent someone undercover to her embassy, especially as everyone based there had been on the suspect list, including the ambassador herself.

Catherine gathered her daughter close again as Phillip and Kevin joined them.

"Thank you, Lucy. Thank you for saving our daughter."

Catherine held out her hand.

A lump formed in Lucy's throat as she took it. "I'm glad I could help."

"Is it true Miranda was a Russian spy?" Kevin asked excitedly. His eyes were red, and he'd obviously shed a few tears. Now he was looking for a distraction.

Lucy straightened her spine and leveled her fiercest CIA officer look at the young man she really liked. "Russian *Agent*, not spy."

Kevin grinned. "I always knew you were a badass." He took his sister's hand in his, held on tight. "And I never liked Miranda."

Lucy laughed. "You obviously have great instincts. You could probably work for the Agency."

Phillip put his hands over his son's ears. "Nope. Never gonna happen."

Everyone laughed. Catherine turned serious. "I never suspected her." She swallowed tightly. "I considered her a friend." She slanted Lucy a look. "I suppose I now have to train two new assistants."

Lucy pulled a face. "Sorry, ma'am."

Catherine kissed Kristen's temple. "Doesn't matter. Nothing else matters. Just Kristen and Irene being home safe. Miranda being exposed."

"And us kicking some Russian ass," Kevin put in with a fist pump.

"Kevin," Catherine's eyes were huge with shock as she tugged her daughter toward the inner door. "Come, let's get cleaned up and get Irene's hand examined by a doctor."

Lucy tried to remain behind, maybe disappear out the back door. Kevin reached out and snagged her hand and pulled her along with the rest of the family.

"I want to know more about working for the CIA," said Kevin loudly.

Lucy laughed and then stage-whispered, "First rule of working for the CIA is you don't talk about the CIA."

"Like fight club but cooler?"

Lucy let herself be carried along. Maybe she could spare an hour to make sure the families were okay. Make sure Irene was okay. After that, she needed to leave. Disappear. Vamoose.

But she was already burned, and she was burned out. There was no going back to what she'd been. She had to figure out what she wanted next. And whether or not that future included taking a chance on a certain good-looking FBI negotiator with an accent to die for.

CHAPTER FORTY-ONE

M AX LAY ON a sun lounger in Montevideo with his eyes closed.

All he'd wanted for months was to hang out with his buddies, but now he was here the only thing he could think about was Lucy.

She'd disappeared on him a few days ago. By the time he'd got out of interviews with the Diplomatic Security Service, the Legat, and the ambassador, Lucy had slipped away from the embassy. He'd dropped by her place, but no one had answered the door. DSS swore they didn't know where she was. The resident spook had claimed ignorance.

The Russians had tempered their response to the arrests of three of their nationals when US officials had shown them the video of Agapov's assassination of Miranda Foster and Hector Cabral. The Russians then claimed Agapov had gone rogue and had even made reparations for the ransom money that had been stolen. Agapov had disappeared. Chances were, he was already back in Russia, although Max figured the guy better avoid any windows for the next decade.

Max rolled over and checked his cell for the thousandth time that day. It was New Year's Eve, and everything felt wrong.

Logan Masters eyed him knowingly.

Max ignored him.

"Who wants another game of water polo?" Noah Zacharius asked.

They'd spent most of the morning in the pool, then they'd crashed here for a few hours as they'd spent most of last night at a casino and were planning to do the same again tonight. Max was trying to have a good time. He hated being so 'not in the moment' when these men meant everything to him.

Inside he ached to get on a plane and find Lucy even though he didn't have a clue where to start. Were her parents really doctors on the west coast? Did they live on an estate? He didn't know. Wasn't sure how he'd find her if she didn't want to be found. Realistically, he knew he should wait for her to come to him, but what if she didn't believe he was serious about her? What if she didn't trust that the connection that had bloomed between them might be the real deal?

Max closed his eyes.

Logan's phone dinged with a text. "Hmm."

They all waited for Logan to add to his comment.

Noah cracked first. "Hmm, what? Did he find her?"

Max slid open an eyelid.

"He sure did," Logan's smile was self-satisfied and all-knowing.

Max took the bait. "Who?"

Noah sat up and wrapped a towel around his neck, showing off his tattoos that the local women seemed to appreciate. "The woman you've been moping over since you got here."

Max groaned. He was a terrible friend. "I've been shit company. Sorry, guys." His pulse picked up. "But what exactly do you mean by he found her?"

Logan grinned. "Did we mention that a good friend of

ours runs the Farm?"

"The Farm?" Max mirrored although he knew what the goddamn Farm was. The CIA's training facility.

Andy came over and sat beside him on the lounger. Taz stretched his arms over his head.

"And?" asked Max.

Logan glanced at Andy. "Killion said he has her home address. Ugh, but…"

"But what?" Max spoke between gritted teeth.

Logan made another noncommittal sound.

Max prayed for the patience not to kill one of his best friends.

"She didn't return to the States yet."

Max whipped off his sunglasses. "Then where the hell is she?"

Andy sent him a worried look. "You don't think the Russians went after her, do you?"

Max covered his face with both hands. The idea of anyone hurting Lucy while he sat around here like a spare part had his blood pressure spiking.

"I have to go back. Track her down."

"I don't think that's a good idea." Andy shook his head.

"What the hell else should I do? How would you feel—"

"I think," Andy interrupted him. "That you should look a little closer to home before you start chasing your tail all over South America."

Max shook his head. "I can't sit around here doing nothing. I'll track those bank notes. Find Agapov and get the Russians to swap Lucy for him. Can you lend any equipment? Maybe a pilot?"

His friends all looked at one another and smiled. They

weren't taking him seriously.

Frustration started to build.

Andy put a hand on his shoulder. "Before you start planning your own black-ops mission that might start World War III, maybe you should check out that blonde over there on the lounger who can't take her eyes off you."

There were thousands of beautiful women in this city. "I'm not interested in other women…" Max glanced over at the female in question even as he dismissed her. Then he looked back, and his eyes widened. "Fuck."

"She is hot," Logan agreed.

"I'd do her." Noah smiled his approval.

"Lucy," said Max.

Noah winced. "I meant it as a compliment."

Max wasn't listening. Noah wasn't an asshole. He worshipped women. But he wasn't getting near this one.

Max strode around the pool deck. And although her eyes were covered with oversized sunglasses and her hair was short and spiky and dyed bright blonde, Max recognized her.

She watched him come to her. She wore a red bikini that showed off her lush curves. Max loved how confident she looked, but he'd loved her just as much in her ugly suit.

The "L" word struck him like a two-by-four in the forehead. This had to be love. Why else had he been feeling so damn wretched and now felt like a bottle of champagne ready to pop?

He sat on the lounger next to hers, facing her.

She swung her legs around and sat up. "Max."

He reached out and removed her sunglasses. Stared into her pretty hazel eyes. Then he smiled and cupped her face with his palm. Everything felt brighter again. Everything felt right.

"Lucy."

She grabbed his wrist and squeezed. "I figured it out."

"Aha." Small words of encouragement to keep the other party talking.

"What I wanted."

"Hmm."

"It's not a life in the Agency. I mean, it was fun before the Raminsky debacle, but it never felt like something I'd do forever."

"Okay." Keep her talking. Wear down her expectations.

"And," three lines appeared between her eyebrows, "well, it's not that exciting…"

"Exciting is overrated."

"The State Department offered me a job in DC. Working in their translation office."

"That's fantastic, providing that's what you want to do." DC was close enough to Quantico they could see a whole lot more of one another. He kissed the palm of her hand and took hold of her other hand too.

She smiled, and he was captivated by the spark there, a spark she didn't try to douse or hide. "I also figured out I wanted to see where you and I went. To trust the feeling even though I've never felt anything like this before."

Max let his smile run free. "I'd like that too."

He kissed the inside of her wrist. Heard her ragged inhale.

"How about we start with a date?" he said carefully.

She laughed. "How about you start by introducing me to your friends. Then I'll get out of your hair. I just wanted to talk to you before I started the drive home. I couldn't concentrate thinking about how I didn't tell you that before I left."

"Wait. What?"

She laughed. "Which bit?"

Max scrubbed his head. "All of it. Also how did you find me?"

"Ah. Well. A senior intelligence officer reached out to me via certain channels and told me that a certain FBI agent was trying to track me down. I gave him permission to share my address if he told me where you were."

Max grinned. "And you came to find me."

A slight blush touched her cheek bones. "But I know this is a vacation with your friends. I don't want to get in the way of that."

He loved his friends, but he wanted her here too. They wouldn't mind Lucy joining them, especially as he hadn't been much fun without her. "You're planning to drive home?"

"Only to Cartagena. Then I'm putting the Mini on a boat back to Miami."

She was only driving through South America alone.

He pursed his lips. He didn't know if this was a test or not, and he didn't want to mess it up. "Are you in a rush to get back?"

She shook her head.

He breathed out slowly. "How would you feel about staying here with me for a few days and then me joining you on the drive back?"

Lucy shook her head. "I really don't want to get in the way of your—" She yelped as he swept her into his arms.

"Is that your bag?" He nodded to a tote.

"Yes."

He dipped her so she could grab her bag and coverup off the side table. Then he strode over to where his mates all sat with ridiculous grins spread across their ugly faces.

"Noah, Logan, Taz. You've met Andy." Max gripped her tight. "Say hello to Lucy."

"Hello, Lucy," they said in unison.

"Lucy and I are going to catch a few hours' sleep before we meet you for dinner later. Okay?"

Noah threw him his shirt which Lucy caught. Then Max turned and carried her into the hotel, across the lobby, and into the elevator.

"In terms of keeping a low profile, I'd say you score a zero, Supervisory Special Agent Hawthorne."

He laughed and raised her in his arms so he could kiss her on the lips. "Let them look. I have the most beautiful woman in the world in my arms."

She shook her head. "What if I decide to wear ugly suits and glasses I don't need?"

Max shrugged. His fingers tightened on her flesh. "I don't care what you wear or what you think you look like. I think you're beautiful."

She reached up and touched his face. "Max?"

"What?"

"I think I'm falling in love with you." Her voice was small. "If that scares you, we should probably walk away from each other sooner rather than later. I don't want my heart broken again."

He felt a twist of something in his chest and then a flare of heat. "I have no intention of going anywhere, Lucy. I have no intention of breaking your heart."

The smile that lit up her face filled the gap inside him and made him feel whole for the first time in years.

He walked into his hotel room and laid her on the bed and stretched over her, closing his eyes and savoring the sensation of her skin against his. She wrapped her legs around him, and he breathed out a sigh of relief. Finally, finally everything felt right in his world again.

He leaned up so he could look down at her. "How about we practice the tango?"

She rolled him so she was on top, gripping his fingers, staring into his eyes like he was the only man she'd ever see. "I don't know. It's a very intense dance. Takes a lot of time to perfect."

He shook his head. "I am more than willing to put in the work."

One corner of her mouth twitched. She leaned down and kissed him, long and slow. "It's very sexy too."

"Very sexy," he agreed.

And then he rolled her again, and she laughed, and it was the first time he'd really heard her laugh. He wanted to hear that sound every day. He wanted to make her happy.

He swept her hair back and stared into her green-brown eyes. "Let me know if I get it wrong."

She stared back, and they weren't talking about the tango anymore. They weren't even talking about sex. It was them. Their relationship. Their journey.

She touched the side of his face. "Same. Let me know if I mess up or go in the wrong direction."

He nodded and then he tickled her, and they figured out the tango together.

USEFUL ACRONYM DEFINITIONS FOR TONI'S BOOKS

AG: Attorney General

ASAC: Assistant Special-Agent-in-Charge

ATF: Alcohol, Tobacco, and Firearms

BAU: Behavioral Analysis Unit

BOLO: Be on the Lookout

BUCAR: Bureau Car.

CBT: Cognitive Behavioral Therapy

CIRG: Critical Incident Response Group

CMU: Crisis Management Unit

CN: Crisis Negotiator

CNU: Crisis Negotiation Unit

CO: Commanding Officer

CODIS: Combined DNA Index System

CP: Command Post

DA: District Attorney

DEA: Drug Enforcement Administration

DOB: Date of Birth

DOD: Department of Defense

DOJ: Department of Justice

DS: Diplomatic Security

DSS: US Diplomatic Security Service

EMDR: Eye Movement Desensitization & Reprocessing

EMT: Emergency Medical Technician

ERT: Evidence Response Team

FOA: First-Office Assignment

FBI: Federal Bureau of Investigation

FO: Field Office

FWO: Federal Wildlife Officer

IC: Incident Commander

HRT: Hostage Rescue Team

HT: Hostage-Taker

JEH: J. Edgar Hoover Building (FBI Headquarters)

K&R: Kidnap and Ransom

LAPD: Los Angeles Police Department

LEO: Law Enforcement Officer

ME: Medical Examiner

MO: Modus Operandi

NAT: New Agent Trainee

NCAVC: National Center for Analysis of Violent Crime

NCIC: National Crime Information Center

NYFO: New York Field Office

OC: Organized Crime

OCU: Organized Crime Unit

OPR: Office of Professional Responsibility

POTUS: President of the United States

PTSD: Post-Traumatic Stress Disorder

RA: Resident Agency

RCMP: Royal Canadian Mounted Police

RSO: Senior Regional Security Officer from the US Diplomatic Service

SA: Special Agent

SAC: Special Agent-in-Charge

SANE: Sexual Assault Nurse Examiners

SAS: Special Air Squadron (British Special Forces unit)

SD: Secure Digital

SIOC: Strategic Information & Operations

SSA: Supervisory Special Agent

SWAT: Special Weapons and Tactics

TC: Tactical Commander

TDY: Temporary Duty Yonder

TOD: Time of Death

UAF: University of Alaska, Fairbanks

UNSUB: Unknown Subject

ViCAP: Violent Criminal Apprehension Program

WFO: Washington Field Office

COLD JUSTICE WORLD OVERVIEW

COLD JUSTICE SERIES
A Cold Dark Place (Book #1)
Cold Pursuit (Book #2)
Cold Light of Day (Book #3)
Cold Fear (Book #4)
Cold in The Shadows (Book #5)
Cold Hearted (Book #6)
Cold Secrets (Book #7)
Cold Malice (Book #8)
A Cold Dark Promise (Book #9~A Wedding Novella)
Cold Blooded (Book #10)

COLD JUSTICE – THE NEGOTIATORS
Cold & Deadly (Book #1)
Colder Than Sin (Book #2)
Cold Wicked Lies (Book #3)
Cold Cruel Kiss (Book #4)
Cold as Ice (Book #5)

COMING SOON…
Cold Silence

The *Cold Justice Series* books are also available as **audiobooks** narrated by Eric Dove, and in various box set compilations.

Check out all Toni's books on her website
(www.toniandersonauthor.com/books-2)

ACKNOWLEDGMENTS

Writing is always difficult but writing in the midst of a global pandemic is especially hard. My heart aches for the millions of people affected by COVID-19. Please continue to protect yourself from this virus and I hope 2021 brings an end to the devastating ravages of this virus.

In regard to this book, my thanks go to Kathy Altman who really is a gem of a critique partner, and to Rachel Grant who always makes me work harder to get the details correct.

Biggest appreciation this year goes to my assistant, Jill Glass. Without her help, I may never have written a single word! Thanks also to my amazing cover designer, Regina Wamba, for her gorgeous artwork, and to my formatter, Paul Salvette, for his dedication to doing a good job. Also, to Jessica at Inkslingers PR for her support. Credit to my editors, Deb Nemeth, Joan Turner at JRT Editing, and proofreader, Alicia Dean. I appreciate the role you all play in making my books shine.

More than ever, thanks to my family. I couldn't have done it without you!

ABOUT THE AUTHOR

Toni Anderson writes gritty, sexy, FBI Romantic Thrillers, and is a *New York Times* and a *USA Today* bestselling author. Her books have won the Daphne du Maurier Award for Excellence in Mystery and Suspense, Readers' Choice, Aspen Gold, Book Buyers' Best, Golden Quill, National Excellence in Story Telling (NEST) Contest, and National Excellence in Romance Fiction awards. She's been a finalist in both the Vivian Contest and the RITA Award from the Romance Writers of America. More than two million copies of her books have been downloaded.

Best known for her "COLD" books perhaps it's not surprising to discover Toni lives in one of the most extreme climates on earth—Manitoba, Canada. Formerly a Marine Biologist, Toni still misses the ocean, but is lucky enough to travel for research purposes. In January 2016, she visited FBI Headquarters in Washington DC, including a tour of the Strategic Information and Operations Center. She hopes not to get arrested for her Google searches.

Sign up for Toni Anderson's newsletter:
www.toniandersonauthor.com/newsletter-signup

Like Toni Anderson on Facebook:
facebook.com/toniannanderson

See Toni Anderson's current book list:
www.toniandersonauthor.com/books-2

Follow Toni Anderson on Instagram:
instagram.com/toni_anderson_author

Printed in the USA
CPSIA information can be obtained
at www.ICGtesting.com
LVHW040710080124
768390LV00030B/152